Michael Carson was born in Merseyside just
after the Second World War. Educated at
Catholic schools, he then became a novice in a
religious order. After leaving university, he
took up a career as a teacher of English as a
foreign language and has worked in various
countries, including Saudi Arabia, Brunei and
Iran. He has written four previous novels,
Sucking Sherbet Lemons, *Friends and Infidels*,
Coming Up Roses and *Stripping Penguins Bare*
(also available in Black Swan).

Author photograph by Pinsharp

Also by Michael Carson

SUCKING SHERBET LEMONS
FRIENDS AND INFIDELS
COMING UP ROSES
STRIPPING PENGUINS BARE

and published by Black Swan

YANKING UP
THE YO-YO

Michael Carson

BLACK SWAN

YANKING UP THE YO-YO
A BLACK SWAN BOOK 0 552 99524 X

Originally published in Great Britain by
Victor Gollancz Ltd

PRINTING HISTORY
Gollancz edition published 1992
Black Swan edition published 1993

Set in 11pt Linotype Melior by
County Typesetters, Margate, Kent

Black Swan Books are published by Transworld Publishers Ltd,
61–63 Uxbridge Road, Ealing, London W5 5SA, in Australia
by Transworld Publishers (Australia) Pty Ltd, 15–23 Helles Avenue,
Moorebank, NSW 2170, and in New Zealand by Transworld
Publishers (NZ) Ltd, 3 William Pickering Drive, Albany, Auckland.

Made and printed in Great Britain by
Cox & Wyman Ltd, Reading, Berks.

For Martin Drury and John Edgar

Now finale to the shore,
Now land and life finale and farewell,
Now Voyagers depart, (much, much for thee is yet in store,)
Often enough hast thou adventur'd o'er the seas,
Cautiously cruising, studying the charts,
Duly again to port and hawser's tie returning;
But now obey thy cherish'd secret wish,
Embrace thy friends, leave all in order,
To port and hawser's tie no more returning,
Depart upon thy endless cruise young sailors.

Walt Whitman

1

GULF STREAM

'Tis the gift to be simple. 'Tis the gift to be free,
'Tis the gift to come down where we ought to be . . .

Shaker song

'That looks heavy,' said the assistant in the sweet shop.

Benson told the woman that it was very heavy indeed. 'Maybe too heavy. You see, I'm only allowed forty-four pounds on the plane . . .'

'A *plane*! Where are you going?' asked the woman, clearly in awe of aeroplanes and their passengers.

An old lady came in at just that moment, so he was able to share his achievement with her too. 'America . . . er . . . the United States. I'm going there for nearly three months. I'm a university student, you see. It's a working holiday. They've got a scheme . . .'

'Fancy!' said the woman behind the counter.

'Serve this lady first,' said Benson magnanimously. He had ages before the Aer Lingus bus took him to the airport.

The old lady asked for a quarter of liquorice torpedoes and got a smile from Benson as a reward for her excellent taste. As the assistant was clattering out the rainbow of sweets on to the scales, she discussed his impending journey with the old lady.

'You wouldn't get me up in one of them things!' said the old lady.

'Me neither, dear, but there's no stopping these youngsters.'

'I'm a bit worried about my weight . . . I mean the weight of my suitcase. If you're over the limit they charge you an arm and a leg,' confided Benson.

'That'll be ninepence, unless there's anything else.'

With a shaking hand the old lady offered a shilling. Benson considered the hand. There it was twelve inches away from him. But in a day's time it would be thousands of miles away. The hand took its change and waved to him. Benson smiled back and the old lady walked out of his life. *Good-bye, my Fancy!* It was unlikely that they would ever meet again. The thought made him momentarily merrily melancholy.

'Now what can I do you for?' asked the woman.

'Er . . . Yes. I'd like a *Private Eye,* a *Guardian* and some lighter fluid. Two sachets . . .'

'Here's the lighter fluid. The papers are over there.'

'Yes.' He darted over to the newspaper stand and picked up his purchases, holding them up for the woman. 'And a box of fruit pastilles.'

'There you are. They'll probably give you a barley sugar before you take off – that'll be 8/3d – but you'd have to give me a lot more than a barley sugar to get me up in one.'

Benson paid. 'I know. I'm a bit scared too. Of course, it might be just excitement. It's hard to tell where one ends and the other begins.'

'Is it?' asked the woman, giving him a look which said the border was very clearly marked on the map of *her* life.

Benson accepted the change but made no move to leave the shop. After all, he was not going to have another friendly chat in an English sweet shop for almost a quarter of a year.

Put like that it seemed a terribly long time to be away. His fear – or was it excitement? – grew as he explained to the woman the ins and outs of managing a trip to North America at the tender age of twenty-one while still maintained on a government grant, a government grant to which this shopkeeper was contributing her widow's mite. 'I've got this special visa in my passport and I'm allowed to work as a camp counsellor. Lots of children go away to summer camp and they can't get enough Americans to look after them so they get British students. With the money I earn I'll be able to travel around America. Of course I had to save up for my charter flight. It's sixty pounds return. Well, it hasn't been easy. I've had to work in the holidays to get the money together. Still, I think it'll be worth it. I've never been abroad.'

'You young people,' said the woman.

* * *

Benson in his window seat over the wing of the Aer Lingus 707 was thinking about the woman in the sweet shop as the plane began its mad dash along the runway towards take-off or doom. And thinking of the woman made Benson think of tomorrow's headlines in the newspapers on her stack, announcing the tragic crash at London Airport the previous evening.

This time yesterday he was standing there, right where you are now. A lovely young man from up north. Perfect manners. And a very tasteful Antler suitcase. He said he wasn't sure about the difference between fear and excitement. Well, the poor little bleeder certainly found out last night.

Benson's copy of *Ireland of the Welcomes* slipped off his lap and slithered down in front of his duty-free bag at his feet. He looked at it momentarily but did not even think to retrieve it. He was too busy steering the plane by hanging on to armrests, watching the back of the seat in front of him shuddering, the wing outside the window wobbling as it whizzed past the blur of green, the hangars, the red-and-white painted huts.

He wished he had been able to hold on to *Ireland of the Welcomes*, for inside there had been a copy of the Aer Lingus prayer and, though he had let out a worldly smirk as he read through it during the endless wait before take-off, now he was prepared to recite its

11

sentiments about being supported by The Lord as they flew through His heavens with a great deal of sincerity. Surely it ought to have left the ground by now! We must be half way back to London. All this shuddering can't happen every time it takes off. *O my God, because Thou art so good, I am very sorry that I have sinned against Thee and by the help of Thy Grace . . .*

But before Benson could finish the prayer the plane had left the ground and he was forced back in his seat *. . . I will not sin again . . .* He found himself repeating the last sentence automatically as he watched the semi-detached suburbs of London passing beneath him. He thought how the least crisis sent him running back, craven, to his old ways and was disgusted with himself for about thirty seconds. Then a small white cloud appeared below him and he looked down at the miracle of Benson seeing his first cloud from the top. Of course, it looked more or less as it looked from the bottom. No angels sat on them playing their harps. Mum must be farther away. Still, it was another first on this day of firsts.

The *No Smoking* sign went off and he could hear the long cabin relax. Benson went so far as to pick up his fallen *Ireland of the Welcomes*, turning to the pages of special offers. He frowned when he saw that he could have saved five shillings if he had waited to buy his Benson and Hedges Special Filters instead of pouncing on them in the cornucopia of the airport duty-free shop. Then he saw the advertisement for an Aer Lingus flight-bag. Yes, he thought. I'll have one of those.

'Your first time?' asked the man next to him, who had not returned Benson's smile when they first got on the plane.

'Yes. Isn't it yours?'

The man laughed out smoke from his cigarette. Benson, reminded, reached into the pocket of his

Crimplene jacket and lit his second to last No. 6. He badly wanted to open his carton of duty-frees but had been informed by severe red writing on the bag that they had to be exported intact, so didn't dare.

'This is my third trip to New York.'

Benson was impressed. 'Is it?'

The man nodded.

'Take-off's a bit scary,' observed Benson. He stiffened. 'What's that?'

'The wheels going up. Don't worry. You're safe as houses.'

'Yes. What are you going to do in America? I'm going to be a camp counsellor.'

'I did that the first time I was Stateside. Last year I worked at a restaurant. The pay's better and you don't have the hassles. This year I'm going to get straight on a Greyhound and head west. It's easy to pick up jobs on the way, I reckon.'

'Is it? I thought the visa was only good for being a camp counsellor.'

The man flicked his cigarette ash into the little ashtray in a worldly manner. 'That's what they say, but once you're in the States no-one gives a damn.' The man's voice had taken on an American twang.

'I've been a bit worried about being a camp counsellor,' Benson said. 'I'm at Camp Manley. You weren't there, were you?'

'Never heard of it. Still, almost everyone on this plane's going to a summer camp. There are thousands of them.'

Benson nodded. The man opened his copy of *Playboy*, shutting Benson out. Benson consoled himself by smiling his best smiles at the passing stewardesses, delighted that they kept smiling back. Then he gazed out of the window at the wing, wondering how planes worked, willing this one to go on doing it.

Two days later, Benson came up from the Times Square subway station for the first time, saw steam rising from a manhole in the middle of Broadway and wondered if he should tell a policeman. An acrid smell of burning pretzels from a sidewalk stall assaulted his nose. He stood jittering at the top of the steps which led back underground and smelt another strange smell rising up behind him, a smell that had winded him when the doors of the subway opened. It wasn't nasty exactly, but neither was it nice. A bit like the subway ride in from Jackson Heights.

Still, there would be plenty of time to decipher the components of the subway smell and list its ingredients in a perfumed postcard to Meryl back home. Sweating, he looked around him at the tall buildings and the news of race riots in Buffalo going round in lights on the New York Times Building, the spectacular advertisement for Coppertone, showing a little girl having her swimming trunks yanked off by a puppy below the slogan, 'Don't be a paleface!'

He waited for the DON'T WALK sign to change, frowning at a fat woman with swollen ankles who, despite clear instructions to the contrary, was bent on crossing and was being given hornblasts and abuse for her pains. She's jay-walking, he thought. Funny term for it. Still, if Broderick Crawford were here she'd get a good hiding. A man smoking a large cigar was standing next to him. Benson tried to give the man a smile but got a blank look back. The woman had made it to the other side. The traffic whizzed past. I am in Manhattan, he thought. WALK came up as soon as he had mentally commanded it to, and he followed the cigar man's fumes across the road, smiling at the winking green miracle. Then he stared into Florsheim's windows.

There did not seem to be many bargains to be had in the shoe department, he thought, busily changing dollars into pounds as he went. His eyes lit on a rather nice pair of powder-blue suede shoes, but they wanted $19.95 for them. Thieves! He would just have to make do with his sandals and the pair of almost new desert boots he had brought with him.

Manhattan was an expensive place. Walt Whitman hadn't warned him about that. He left Florsheim's and walked round the corner into Broadway. He browsed in front of a shop selling Chinese imports. There were some nice Chinese characters done in brass. They were $2.49 plus tax. He could afford a few of them but now was not the time to be thinking of buying presents. He had ten weeks and six days to go before he saw Home again. He would be practical and save shopping until September. Between now and then there was work to do, experiences to open his mouth to and swallow whole, people to meet, addresses to swap, tears to shed, Dearest Him to find.

He turned away from the shop window and looked back up at the buildings. He reached into his Aer Lingus flight-bag to find the street map Lee-Chun had given him back at the apartment. To get to see the Empire State Building he would have to walk east along 42nd and turn south on Fifth Avenue. Yes, that was as easy as anything. New York was almost as logical as he was.

Then he heard, coming from a loudspeaker set up outside a record shop a couple of doors up, Lulu singing 'To Sir With Love'. He postponed the Empire State Building for a moment and followed Lulu's siren call.

The record shop was pretty pathetic, much smaller than Evered Davies in Aberystwyth. He gazed at the record sleeves in the window. Many were like the ones he had lusted after at home but they were made of a thick cardboard. *Pet Sounds,* his favourite Beach Boys', for instance, was just the same as his copy, but the photograph of the Beach Boys feeding the goat was, he felt, definitely not as well reproduced.

Then Benson noticed that a man was looking at him from inside the record shop. Did the man think that he had been looking at the thing in the window too long? All the way over on the subway Benson had been smarting rather from what the man in the bookshop in Jackson Heights had said to him as Benson browsed through American paperback editions of novels, thinking them on the whole not half as tastefully done as English ones. 'This isn't a library, bud,' he had said. Just like that. Meekly Benson had held out a copy of *The Confessions of Nat Turner* and bought it without a word. The man had not said anything to him as he took the money and handed him his purchase. He had left the shop, feeling appropriately alienated. Shortly after, passing a bank with a sign in the window which announced, 'Courtesy Spoken Here', he thought that it might be a good idea if they taught the bookshop owner that language. On the shrieking subway Benson had been able to come up with witty ripostes that left the bookshop owner begging for mercy. But by then, of course, it had been too late.

Benson jiggled about. Was he going to go in because he wanted the record or because he felt ashamed to walk away? It was, he decided, a bit of both. In his two days in America he had discovered that it could be a most intimidating place. The first person he had spoken to in Queens, a girl wearing shorts, he had asked the way to the subway station. She had backed away from him and, when at a safe distance, screamed raucously, 'I know what you want!' He hadn't been able to think of an answer to that either, though he had thought of plenty since. Then there was the weeping

Negro lady on the seat across the track from him on the subway station. She might have had the courtesy to say something when he had taken his courage in both hands to shout across the track, asking her what the matter was. But no, she had just continued crying, looking straight through him from where she sat under the picture of the happy Chinese girl eating a sandwich next to the legend, 'You don't have to be Jewish to enjoy Levi's bread'.

Benson found himself walking into the record shop. 'Er, wasn't that Lulu singing the theme song from *To Sir With Love*?' he asked the man.

'Ninety-nine cents plus tax,' said the man. He was smoking a cigar too, still looking out through the window at the news going round in lights. Benson mentally kicked himself. He wasn't looking at me at all.

'Er ... what's on side B?' he asked, as the man produced the record from under the counter, wondering whether he was being wise to lash out on a record.

'Uh?'

'The other side. The opposite one to "To Sir With Love"?'

The man pulled the record out of its sleeve. As he did so he put his thumb on the playing surface and Benson frowned at him severely. One would think, he thought, that a person who makes his living from selling recorded sound would know how to handle his merchandise. If I, once having made my purchase, decide to put finger-marks all over the grooves, then it's my prerogative. It's the man's duty to see that his goods leave the shop in mint condition, isn't it? But he did not communicate any of this to the salesman. He knew he would buy the record even if side B was really sloppy. For a start he already saw himself being able to use 'To Sir With Love' to help Jung-Ja with her English.

And the cover, when the man turned it over, showed a picture of Sidney Poitier in front of a class. That alone was worth the ninety-nine cents plus tax, finger-mark or no finger-mark.

'You mean the flip side?' asked the man.

'Yes.'

'"The Boat that I Row".'

'Hmmm, I've not heard that. Is it good?'

The man looked at Benson hard, and not particularly warmly. He sighed a long sigh and placed the record on his turntable. Benson went to the door, where Lulu was belting out a quite jolly song about her boat not being able to cross no ocean but being big enough for two. He listened to the first verse and chorus as it wafted out over Times Square, noting with some satisfaction that a Negro had stopped and was listening to the song, stepping rhythmically up to the window. Benson moved his head from side to side to show the man that he too was under the spell of the song and was not totally lacking in rhythm and soul. He thought that the man smiled at him and he smiled back. He returned his head to the inside of the shop. Then he thought, too late, that he could have told the Negro that Lulu was English – well, almost – just like Benson. That might have broken the ice. The trouble was that everything in the New World happened so fast. He was too slow on the draw. Social intercourse shot him down and left him writhing on the sidewalk, speechless.

'I'll take it.'

'Dollar four,' said the man, ripping the pick-up off the record disrespectfully.

That must mean that the tax was five cents. He would have to watch the tax like a hawk. Benson searched for money, being careful to check that he was not handing the man any of his English change. The man took the money, put the record in a rather nice bag that Benson thought he would keep carefully – attaching it to his wall at Pantychelyn hostel in Aberystwyth with little loops of sellotape, a Benson invention – and handed it across the counter to him without a word.

'Thank you,' said Benson, checking his twenty-one cents change.

The man nodded, looking out of the window again.

Benson left the shop. The Negro had disappeared. That was a pity. It was lovely being abroad and everything, but it was a bit lonely too. He crossed Broadway, stared into a shop with a big sign for Te Adoro Cigars above it. An advert for Kools caught his attention. 'May I have one of your cigarettes, Steve? Mine taste so dull.' And Steve replied, 'Sure. Kools are what you're looking for. Bet you stay with them.' I'll have time to see if Steve's right. Once my duty-frees have gone I'll try Kools. Then he realized that he had walked west instead of east.

He turned on to Fifth Avenue and started to walk downtown. Loneliness was forgotten when he saw the Empire State Building ahead of him and the realization came that he was actually looking at the building he had looked at so often on the cover of his Golden Guinea record of the 'New World' Symphony. There it was. In front of him. Here and now. In the year of our Lord 1967 . . .

America was true after all.

Dr Griffiths out of sight of America, in the year of our Lord one before last, had put forward the proposition that America, viewed from the perspective of Aberystwyth at any rate, was a matter of faith. The evidence that America existed might be strong – somewhat stronger than was altogether wholesome. Sometimes, Dr Griffiths asserted, the aroma of America positively appalled him. Still, its existence as an entity remained a matter of conjecture. Nobody had believed Christopher Columbus, after all. Perhaps he had just come to the edge of the world, stared over the brink into the blackness and rowed like mad back to Spain, concocting whoppers on the way. There was room for doubt. All the evidence might be a tissue of lies. The episodes of *Cheyenne, I love Lucy, Gun Smoke* . . . the chewing gum found on cinema seats while watching the rubbish that purported to come from a continent thousands of miles to the west, might not, in fact, come from that continent at all but from somewhere else. Perhaps Benson's packets of Kent had really been manufactured in Nottingham and only pretended to come from America. In short, maybe America was a big, brash fiction.

Benson, along with the other first-year philosophy students, had been quick to argue that common sense dictated that America – or something rather like it – *must* exist. If America wasn't credible then what *was* credible? This had not fazed Dr Griffiths in the least. He had closed his eyes on his students and informed them that they had ceased to exist. Dr Griffiths' non-existent students looked at one another. Owen Powell had put his index finger to his head and twisted it, crossing his eyes as he did so, only to be confronted by Dr Griffiths' beady glance.

'I know you think this discussion is, to say the least, implausible,' he had said, 'but, believe me, it is central to our discussion of appearance and reality. Mr Benson, what do you think about the existence of America?'

Benson, for the sake of peace and quiet, had replied: 'I would say that all the evidence points one towards the conclusion that it exists. Of course I cannot prove it.'

'Good, that's a reasonable point of view. But until you have stood on it, verified it with your senses, it is not a one hundred per cent proven proposition.'

Dr Griffiths had then gone on to discuss Bishop Berkeley, leaving Benson at any rate a little dubious about a continent.

Anyway, he thought as he looked at the building rising up to greet him, I have proved the existence of America to my satisfaction. Of course, I won't be able to prove it when I get home, but most reasonable people will believe me. Then the thought struck him that it was now home whose existence felt open to argument. Perhaps I've just dreamed my life up to now! I cannot prove England's existence. It's a matter of faith. This thought sobered him.

He entered the cool ground floor of the Empire State Building, was further sobered by having to part with a dollar, and followed the signs to the lift. His ears popped as the lift whooshed him heavenward. He pinched his nose, blowing to make his ears pop back. Life would never be the same again. I, Martin Benson, am ascending the world's tallest building! There are probably people reading the *Guinness Book of Records* entry *as I speak* and wishing themselves in my shoes . . . well, my sandals. He looked down at his sandals, a summer gift from Alice, his stepmother. He had had to trail over to Liverpool with her like some child to get them while Carole, his baby half-sister, behaved in a Carole-like fashion, pointing to the obvious from her stroller and burbling incoherently, then looking up, as proud as Archimedes fresh out of the bath, to receive Alice's congratulations, while Benson pulled faces at her. Pulling faces was all he could ever think to do with Carole. Sometimes he held her hand or bounced her on his knee too, singing 'Dom Dom Diddle Diddle' but it was all a bit lame. Quite often he wished that Carole would just disappear for a few years, coming back only when she had something useful to contribute.

Alice had been bossy about the sandals. It was her opinion that Benson would buy something impractical and unsuitably up-to-the-minute. The ones he favoured, that would have done him well if ever he were called upon to play Jesus in the Oberammergau *Passion Play*, had received the thumbs-down and he had ended up with a pair that Alice liked, thinking them practical for walking while keeping him cool.

'You'll be able to polish them,' she had said, though this did not seem like much of a recommendation. Benson saw people in mythical America laughing at his sandals and his only possible defence of them being that he could polish them. Anyway, you couldn't polish them. At least, not easily. The polish would get stuck in the petal-shaped holes and have to be picked out with a pin. They were not very different from the tiny pair that Carole sported. Still, after an initial protest, he had not voiced any further complaints about Alice's choice of sandal. She held the purse-strings. She had bought him and Carole an ice-cream on the way home. A bonus for being a twenty-one-year-old good boy.

No, you couldn't polish them. The Negroes in the subway station, standing next to lines of thrones on which cigar-chewing men sat while their shoes were cleaned, had been about to ask him if he wanted a shine, but then, looking at his sandals, had stopped, regarding them with their mouths open. Benson was a bit stuck when confronted by the shoe-shine men. One side of him felt that he ought to contribute to them, help them get their share of the American Dream. But he hated the thought of himself on one of those thrones with a Negro at his feet. It was just not seemly.

The group of sightseers had to change lifts on the

eightieth floor. A further ascent to the eighty-sixth at a speed that put Owen-Owen's lift to shame. Then the doors opened. Benson passed a souvenir kiosk and suddenly was gazing at the whole of midtown Manhattan with the East River behind that and the endless blue blur of Queens, in the middle of which was Jackson Heights and the apartment he was staying in with Lee-Chun, Sung-Il and Jung-Ja.

He walked around the viewing balcony, seeing Manhattan from every aspect. He rummaged for his Kodak Colorsnap 35, a loan from Dad, and snapped away, only realizing after taking half a dozen slides that there was still another vertical journey to be undertaken before he could say he had reached the very top. He had taken two of the view of the Chrysler Building, a skyscraper he was very taken with. Meryl had told him to give the Chrysler Building her love, as it was her favourite and represented the highpoint both literally and metaphorically of the Art Deco style. He remembered Meryl showing him a photograph of it. A woman was lying out flat on one of the decorative cornices at the top of the building taking a photograph at what looked to Benson like a very odd angle. She was risking her life for the shot but hadn't made sure that the sun was behind her. But it stood to reason that the sun must be behind the man who was taking the photograph of the woman taking the photograph because his had come out just right. He thought how disappointed the woman must have been to have risked life and limb only to get home to find everything fuzzy.

He joined the queue for the next lift. Again he had to put two fingers over his nose and blow to equalize the pressure. It was a bit like what he had to do when he went down into the fifteen-foot end at New Brighton baths. He wondered why when going up in the lift he

23

did not have to blow every fifteen feet. There must be an answer to that but, if there was he didn't know it. He was Arts. C. P. Snow would disapprove of him greatly because Benson had only a tenuous grasp of one of the two cultures which C. P. Snow went on about.

The wind was blowing hard at the top. He walked around the gallery, trying to find a place away from the other sightseers. When he did finally, he looked over at the great pinnacles jutting up like paschal candles from the end of the island. He could see what he thought might be the Brooklyn Bridge. He consulted his map, being careful not to let the wind blow it out of his hands. Yes, it was the Brooklyn Bridge. He had imagined many times what he would do when he actually got to the top of the Empire State Building, since first reading Walt Whitman, in fact. He looked to left and right, opened his mouth and spoke to the view:

'Ah, what can ever be more stately and admirable
    to me than mast-hemm'd Manhattan?
River and sunset and scallop-edg'd waves of
    flood-tide?
Er . . . de dum de dum de dum . . .
What gods can exceed these that clasp me by the
    hand, and with voices that I love call me
    promptly and loudly by my nighest name as I
    approach?'

Benson stopped his recitation, though he could have gone on, wanted to go on, felt his heart rising higher and higher than the Empire State Building, pulsing stronger than the city at his feet. But some people had come to share his windy outlook and he cut short his rendition. There was plenty of time. Some day soon, and he would know when, he would deliver the omnibus edition.

The thought struck him – where had it come from? – that if he dropped a ham sandwich off the Empire State Building and it hit some poor passer-by on the street below, it would kill him just as surely as if he had dropped a brick on him. It felt like a piece of information he might have read in a comic, not like sound science. Probably wouldn't make C. P. Snow smile upon him. For a start, the sandwich would disintegrate on the way down. The tomato would fly one way, the ham the other. Even if the sandwich were wrapped in a piece of greaseproof paper, it would still hit the person as something intrinsically softer than a rock, wouldn't it? He had also heard that if you jumped off the top of the Empire State Building you'd be dead before you got to the ground. Well, that would be a relief. Still, there was no chance that he could jump off. The criss-cross wire was so close together that you could hardly insert the lens of a Kodak Colorsnap 35, let alone a ham sandwich, still less a broad-shouldered Englishman of 12st 5½lb who wanted to be 11st 7lb. Mind you, the railings were a recent addition. Benson had seen in the film of *On The Town* how the sailors had almost fallen off the top at one point. Probably it was after that the owners of the building had put up additional barriers. People might try to imitate the sailors. Then of course there were people in the world who were actually wicked enough to push you off. He looked around anxiously.

Benson's eyes were watering from the wind. He went inside and bought himself a root-beer in a paper cup. He had never tasted root-beer, had chosen it from the selection on offer because it sounded like it might be something that Walt Whitman would have drunk, but realized even before tasting it that he had made the wrong choice. It was as if someone had dissolved a generous extrusion of Macleans toothpaste into soda water and then offered it for sale. He tasted it and pulled a face. He looked around at the woman who had sold it to him. She just looked back blankly at him. Probably after selling root-beer to thousands of appalled visitors year after year the joke had begun to pall. He drank it down, not wanting to waste it but neither wanting to taste it. A notice said that the volume of the Empire State Building was 37,000,000 cubic feet. There were 60 miles of water pipes, 6,500 windows to wash, 60,000 tons of steel – enough to build a double-track railroad from New York to Baltimore – Fancy! Then he placed the paper cup back on the counter. The woman told him to put it in the trash. It seemed odd that she did not want to take it back and give it a wash. It would do for at least a couple more poison chalices. And it wasn't as if she was rushed off her feet.

I should write a card to Meryl now, he thought. He bought one from the kiosk. It showed both the Empire State Building and the Chrysler Building at night. He wrote:

Wish you were here! I am at the end of the arrow. I have a spiffing view of your favourite building. It's a lovely day, but a bit windy. Apart from Lee-Chun and a Korean couple staying with us in the apartment I haven't met anyone yet. I leave for my camp counsellor job after the weekend. People are a bit brusque, but I'm excited all the time. Hope you are well. Give Hugo a hug from me. The subway smells of bodies, cigarettes, scent, newsprint, petrol and the earth exhaling.

Uncle Martin xx

He addressed it to Meryl's parents' address and put the postcard back into his Aer Lingus flight-bag.

Then he returned to the wind and the view. He gazed over the West Side. Tony and Maria had lived there. *Te adoro, Anton! Te adoro, Maria!* He stared up to no-go Harlem. *Sometimes I feel like a motherless child . . .* He wished he had someone to talk to. Then he pulled himself together, took the lifts down to ground level – teaching a child beside him how to blow to equalize the pressure – and went off in search of the Brooklyn Bridge.

*   *   *

Though Benson might have had the occasional doubt about the existence of America in the past year or two, he had only recently come to believe that he would ever travel there to prove its existence once and for all.

America was dubious in all sorts of ways. Meryl, his best friend in Aberystwyth, had opined that to visit such a place while it was doing the most dreadful things in Vietnam was unseemly. Benson, after a night of agonizing, had returned with the swiftly banged-together opinion that the Aberystwyth soil on which they were standing was not free of blood. There was no innocence anywhere. The recent Six Day War had bled out the very British Balfour Declaration. In fact, he had gone on, if one were looking for innocent bits on the planet one would be hard-pressed to find one. Meryl had walked straight into his trap and suggested Iceland. Benson delivered the swift *coup de grâce* by replying 'Fish,' which had shut Meryl up.

Lee-Chun had suggested the possibility of a trip to Benson towards the end of his first year at Aberystwyth university. Initially, the idea had only lodged for about the same amount of time as most ideas entered his bed-and-breakfast head. Not for long at all. Ideas came for the night, were kept up long after their

27

bedtime and left exhausted, saying to the next guest, *Rather you than me, mate!* But Lee-Chun had kept returning to the subject. He was going off to New York when he finished his year at Aberystwyth. His friend had a business importing hair-pieces from South Korea and had offered him a job.

Benson, head-over-heels on the wilder shores of platonic love with Lee-Chun, had leapt at the chance of following him – a year later – to the New World, though he was not quite sure whether helping a friend in the hair-piece business was quite what Lee-Chun ought to be doing. He had a Masters Degree from the University of Seoul and a Diploma in International Relations from Aberystwyth, after all. Yet here he was actually contemplating going into *trade*.

Lee-Chun had hardly figured in Benson's life during his first term at Aberystwyth. He had had other things on his mind. The post of vice-president of Aberystwyth University Overseas Students' Society had kept him busy, along with many other things over which, looking back, he would have liked to draw a veil. That term had finished with the humiliation of the overseas students' dinner-dance. Enoch Mohammed had failed to book it. Not only that, but he had run away from Aberystwyth with the proceeds. Added to this was Meryl's pregnancy and her sudden conversion to Catholicism. It was really not surprising that Benson had had little time to consider the appealing qualities of Lee-Chun.

But in the second term he had had more time on his hands and was looking around to widen his circle. His attempts at making Omar, a Sudanese student of animal-husbandry, his Dearest Him, had quickly run into the sand. Benson had visited Omar at his bed-sit in Merthyr Terrace several times, convinced that Omar had to be, if not a fully fledged homo, at least a chap

28

who would have a go. After all, he had had Omar home for Christmas and Omar had spent two evenings with Andy, hadn't he? But when Benson went round to follow up on his knowledge, dropping the broadest hints imaginable about *not really feeling one way or the other about girls, wondering if he were really all there, feeling great emotion towards friends*, all Omar did was nod his head sagely and proceed to other matters.

He had stayed on good terms with Meryl as her tummy had slowly but surely rounded and the looks the two of them got as they walked through the town became curiouser and curiouser. Benson knew what the people who looked at Meryl were thinking and often stared them right back until they dropped their eyes self-consciously. That fixed them. But Meryl was not in the least concerned.

Benson had also learnt during that second term of his first year that he would have to work harder if he hoped to get through the all-important first year examinations. This necessitated great swathes of time spent studying at his desk in Pantychelyn hostel. This study led to a lack of physical activity which, in turn, led to a filling of his fat cells, cells he knew were there, waiting behind his fly-buttons – along with the usual thing – to swell up and humiliate him.

One day at dinner Lee-Chun had suggested that he and Benson play a game of squash together. Benson said he didn't have a racket, but was told that they could be hired. Not having any other excuse, he walked indifferently up the hill to the sports centre, where Lee-Chun had reserved a court.

He had not enjoyed his first game of squash. The ball went everywhere but the places Benson managed to stagger to. Lee-Chun on the other hand caught the ball with panache wherever Benson's racket managed to push it, and neatly insinuated it into corners, lobbed it so that it bounded a foot in front of the wall or skimmed off three walls in quick succession, before landing at an angle impossible for a shoe horn to get any leverage. Benson had never sweated so much in his whole life. He was lost in admiration for Lee-Chun's prowess, and for his thick, hugely muscled, hairless legs which were attractively bowed in shape. He lost every game, and on their subsequent matches kept losing every game. At first he did not mind. It seemed quite natural that he should lose all the time. Lee-Chun was a foreign guest, after all. It would not be seemly for him to be defeated by native Benson. Sometimes he got so tired that he would try to make Lee-Chun call off the rest of the match, but Lee-Chun kept asserting that they had hired the court for half an hour and half an hour they would play.

Then, during their fifth session, Benson felt the still-born seed of competition arising from sources he did not know he had. He was suddenly very bored with losing. He tried his best to win a game. It did not happen that day, though it almost did. The next match, how-ever, it did. Lee-Chun congratulated him, putting his arm round Benson's waist. Benson, pleased as anything to get an affectionate hug, while worried that Lee-Chun might have discovered the least spare sections of his spare tyre, wondered what new byway was opening up, and whether the time might not have come round again to start walking mournfully over Constitution Hill in the drizzle, reading *The Shropshire Lad* to an imaginary camera team sent along by *Late Night Line Up* to do a feature on 'The Other Face of Love'.

Lee-Chun was six years older than Benson and had done all sorts of things that Benson hadn't. He had been in the Korean army for three years, had made parachute jumps and fired guns and bayoneted targets.

He was fiercely anti-communist and rather favoured the American involvement in Vietnam. Benson, who had not been able to find a good word to say about that dubious country's foreign policy, suddenly began to see the other side too. For, Lee-Chun asserted, if the Americans didn't stop Communism in Vietnam it would knock all the other countries over like a line of dominoes. It wouldn't stop with Vietnam. Cambodia would be next; Laos and Thailand would follow them. Perhaps Malaysia and Indonesia.

These countries were far from being abstractions to Benson. His work for the Overseas Students' Society had given him tongue-tying names, heart-stopping faces, to make living flags of them. He hated to think of Porn-Chai, his Thai friend, running away with his family from communist bombs and bullets, all their possessions roped to the back of a Honda 50, as was the case in Vietnam whenever he turned on the television. Porn-Chai was, like Simeon his Ghanaian friend, studying plant-breeding. He wore a silver object with a glass front around his neck. Inside was a tiny statue of the Buddha. Benson wanted one badly, even suggesting at the end of the first year that Porn-Chai might bring him one back from Thailand. But Porn-Chai had said that he could not bring such a holy object for someone who wasn't a Buddhist. Instead, he brought him a red silk tie with a picture of a dancing maiden embroidered on the front. Porn-Chai was quiet and gentle. His hair fell over his face when he leant forward and he kept flicking his head to send it back up his cranium. The only time Benson had seen him at all angry was when he had tried to play him his LP of *The King and I.* Porn-Chai said that it was a very bad thing, disrespectful of the Thai king.

*   *   *

31

Benson found the Brooklyn Bridge after more than an hour of walking. It was a hot day and pools of water formed in the soles of his sandals as he tried to find a route to the bridge, dodging lorries unloading fish at the Fulton Street Fish Market. He could see the bridge clearly enough but finding an approach road to it proved more difficult. One would have thought that there would be a few signs to help tourists. Aberystwyth was full of signs. Perhaps the New York Corporation should send a delegation there to learn how to signpost things efficiently.

A man riding a larger version of a child's scooter passed him, scooting away. As he passed he wished Benson peace, and Benson breezed back 'Same to you!' The man had long hair, longer even than the Beatles now wore. Benson wished he could have long hair, but after a few inches something happened to his hair. It began to curl unbecomingly and stick out oddly. If he left it, there would come a time when he could not get a comb through it and he would have to go off to the barber in Aberystwyth, who always accused him of trying to grow his hair long. This was true, though Benson had been of the opinion that the barber should not single out for disparagement the few customers he actually got into the shop. But as the barber lectured him, while Benson looked at himself in the mirror and worried that he was losing his looks, it felt like an accusation that he had been attempting to steal food from the mouths of the barber's wife and children. Though Benson asked for something stylish he always came out with an out of fashion short back and sides – a style only good for facilitating barbed comments from Meryl – and had to start the whole hopeful growth process again.

The man on the scooter had flowing locks. Dad and Alice would have accused him of being like a girl. Still, he had greeted him nicely, rather like an early Christian. That was nice. Benson wished that he was not scootering away at such speed. Perhaps they could have become friends. He also would have loved to have enquired about how he had attached a motor to the back of the scooter. With that knowledge Benson could go back to Aberystwyth, buy up – with the aid of a loan from the Midland Bank – every Triang scooter in sight, attach a motor to the back wheel and single-handedly bring about a revolution in the world's mode of transport. Yes, he thought, they'd definitely catch on. The Benson Scooter. It would knock the Mini off the road. Students could take courses that involved lectures in the town and up the hill. Old ladies stuck in tower blocks would be freed to travel around town. I could bring out a de-luxe model with a windshield and a lockable shopping basket.

As he came to the central section of the bridge he forgot the man on the scooter and the idea for a business to solve the problem of what to do with his life. A wind blew against his blue bri-nylon shirt and cooled him. To his right, in the far distance, looking no larger than the miniature statue of Our Lady of Lourdes in a plastic dome that he had been given when Mrs Stone returned from Lourdes, was the Statue of Liberty. He would have to go up her at some point. But that would have to wait. She was bound to be a tourist trap and might cost him an arm and a leg. He contented himself for the moment by smiling at her and saying, *Give to me your tired, your poor, your huddled masses yearning to be free*. There were, he noted, huddled masses of refuse in the East River. It floated along, great islands of it. Branches covered in what looked like lard, and empty oil-drums. There would probably be hundreds of used contraceptives too. It was all a bit like the Mersey between Liverpool and Wirral. Benson had often gazed down from the ferry-boat at convoys of contraceptives floating in the brown river. They had been christened Mersey Gold-fish because they seemed to swim in shoals. Opened out in the water they were huge, so huge that Benson had despaired. If there were men about who had worn one of those *and been able to keep it on* there was absolutely no chance for him. He would never even reach the sides.

Thinking how his thoughts, though aiming for the stars, always seemed to end up back on the rubbish tip, Benson descended to the Brooklyn side of the bridge. He was not tempted to continue on into Brooklyn, however. To his left a discouraging sign on the side of a building announced Christian Book Depository. Benson pulled tongues at it and turned away.

It was a pity, he thought, that Rufus in *Another Country* had not jumped off the Brooklyn Bridge. Ralph Wynn was always going on about the Brooklyn Bridge as a metaphor for America. So, to have Rufus jump off the George Washington Bridge was a tactical mistake by James Baldwin. It spoilt an otherwise perfect novel. Of course, Benson would have been much happier if Rufus had not jumped off anything, but rather had been waiting for Benson at Kennedy Airport, blowing on his trumpet and saying 'This is my friend Vivaldo,' to him. He said an *Eternal Rest* for Rufus.

The skyscrapers of downtown Manhattan beckoned in the sunlight. Benson repeated Gatsby's line. When he got back to Manhattan he bought himself a pretzel. Then, on impulse, a little bell on a leather thong from a street-seller, who was wearing one round her neck. This he put in his pocket and, munching his pretzel, he went down into the subway.

At Times Square he took the Flushing train. He sat

on the hard blue metal seat and read the Preparation H advertisement. The train screamed off. Every time it took a bend it screamed and in the tunnel out of Manhattan the sound was almost unbearable. Benson wondered why the subway people couldn't put rubber on the wheels or a dab of oil. Perhaps they should go to Liverpool and learn how a *real* underground should sound.

At Woodside station – though there was no wood in sight – he noticed another advertisement for Levi's bread. This one showed a smiling black boy eating a Levi bread sandwich. 'You don't have to be Jewish to enjoy Levi's bread.' Someone had added – 'BUT IT HELPS.' That wasn't very nice. Lots of Jewish people as they passed in the train would see that and be upset and worry about anti-Semitism and Israel. Benson considered the recent war. It had mixed him up about Israel. Until the war he had seen Israel as a place where poor homeless Jews went to make a home for themselves. There were kibbutzes in Israel where people shared everything and made the desert bloom. But just after the war an Arab student, Mohammed, had spoken to him in Pantychelyn hostel's dining room and said that the Israelis had taken his family's land, blown up his village. He had been near to tears.

Benson had sympathized and felt foolish. What did he know of life? Mohammed sat down next to Anne Frank in his mind, both crying to heaven for vengeance, while Benson preached niceness to both.

There were hair-pieces all over the dining room table in the apartment when Benson arrived back. Jung-Ja was cooking the evening meal in the kitchen. Wonderful aromas completely beyond Benson's experience wafted out to meet him. Jung-Ja was the wife of Sung-Il, who was going to study at the University of Kansas in the autumn. In the meantime Sung-Il was working with Lee-Chun in the hair-piece business.

It sometimes seemed as if the two Koreans lived and breathed hair-pieces to the exclusion of almost everything else in life. There were hair-piece trade journals all over the apartment. Even in the evening after dinner they sat smoking, dressed in shorts, comparing the different styles of hair-piece, poring over charts and invoices and bills of lading.

Benson could not get enthusiastic about hair-pieces, especially after he had learnt on the second day staying with Lee-Chun that the hair-pieces had all been fashioned from the tresses of Korean girls, who sold them as other people sold – say – sweetpeas or apples. Lee-Chun said they could get a lot of money for their hair, that they were poor and it was a sacrifice worth making. Anyway, they were in great demand in America. Benson felt like saying that just because there was a demand that didn't necessarily mean that it was a good idea to satisfy it. He also wondered whether the barber in Aberystwyth had bundled his hair into sacks and sold it at exorbitant prices to the Americans. Perhaps Frank Sinatra was going around with some of Benson's hair clippings on his daft head.

Still, there was obviously money to be made from hair-pieces. Benson had learnt from the magazines that a wiglet made from oriental hair cost $35 up and an Oriental Fall began at $99. A wiglet made from European hair, on the other hand, cost $65 up and a European Fall $135 up. Benson had complained to Lee-Chun about the odd pricing, saying that he thought oriental hair was much prettier than European. But Lee-Chun had replied matter-of-factly that the lighter the hair the more expensive. He had gone on to talk about his great worry that hair-pieces made from Dynel, an artifical hairlike fibre, would brush the real thing off the market. It was less than half the price. Lee-Chun had a sample of Dynel Fall. Benson had felt it, stroked it like one might stroke a cat as it lay there on the dining table. No, it was definitely nothing like as good as the real thing. This had not consoled Lee-Chun, however, who had gone on to tell Benson about his greatest worry: that suddenly hair-pieces would cease to be fashionable. This worry had communicated itself to Benson who had ever since been scouting about for new business opportunities that would both save Lee-Chun from penury and himself from the necessity of thinking up a boring career.

Lee-Chun was very different from the man he had grown to love at Aberystwyth. He had already been in America for a year and had grown fatter, smoked more and spoke with an American twang. He did not like New York at all, had tried to dissuade Benson from making a foray into Manhattan, saying that it was a dirty and dangerous place. Benson, however, could not see himself staying in Jackson Heights, even for the few days prior to his leaving for the Catskills and his job as camp counsellor. Every road in Jackson Heights led to the main road into Manhattan above which an elevated track carried the subway. The shops were dull and, although it had a patina of foreignness to it, Benson felt strongly that to stay in Jackson Heights would be similar to visiting Wallasey but never venturing into Liverpool.

Jung-Ja offered him a Coke, insisting that she should bring it to him at the table. It embarrassed Benson rather that Jung-Ja should serve him. He would have been happier just to reach into the huge fridge and take out the drink himself. Anyway, the fridge was an adventure. Apart from the plastic-covered bowls of Korean kimchy and left-over meals, there were half gallon cartons of milk. Americans never rinsed and returned anything as far as Benson could see. Every-thing went straight into the bin which you then took to a little room that smelled of burning, next to the lift, and dropped the rubbish down a chute. It clanked and rattled its way down ten storeys most satisfactorily, but it was a bit wasteful. In the fridge were long bars of butter with a stag on the front. There was orange juice which tasted much better than Quosh, and a huge box of bicarbonate of soda which Jung-Ja said was good to stop the fridge from smelling. The English didn't know that. Benson wondered if there might be a career for him in telling the English about the benefits of bicarbonate of soda. You could clean your teeth with it too and buff up your jewellery. He could market it as Magic Powder and make his fortune, not telling people it was just bicarb.

He heard the sound of Coke being poured over ice and decided to give Jung-Ja a fright when she came in. He put on one of the more extravagant hair-pieces and awaited her arrival.

When Jung-Ja saw him, she put her hand over her mouth and her eyes became a deep wrinkle. Benson thought she was smiling behind her hand but he could not be sure. He took the hair-piece off.

'That was a joke!' he said.

'A joke?'

'Ha-ha!' said Benson.

Jung-Ja nodded, walked off in a way which suggested that she did not wish to cause any offence to the air in the vicinity, and returned with her dictionary.

Benson found the English–Korean section and looked up 'joke'. Then he put his index finger under-neath it. He was about to show Jung-Ja when he noticed that the finger-nail had some black under it. He deftly replaced the finger with the middle one, which was more satisfactory and would not offend Jung-Ja's aesthetic sense. She looked at the odd configuration of circles, lines and diagonals which was Korean – or at least one bit of it – and said: 'Joke.' Then she said, 'What is a joke?'

'This is a joke,' said Benson, and he put the hairpiece on again. Then, as Jung-Ja gazed at him blankly, he took it off, throwing it with the others.

'No. That isn't joke. That is . . .' and Jung-Ja turned to the Korean–English section of her dictionary, leafing through it, repeating a Korean word which sounded to Benson like 'fart'. 'Ah,' she said, and showed Benson what she had found.

'Silly, foolish,' said Benson. Where was Jung-Ja's sense of humour? He had noticed this before. The previous night the men had been playing mah-jong, smoking and drinking whisky at the table. He and Jung-Ja had watched *I married Joan* and *Bilko* on the colour television. Now Benson did not think either programme was *that* funny. He did not roll about or anything, but the programmes could make him smile. Jung-Ja, however, had sat stonily throughout. Part of it could be that her English was pretty poor, but she should have laughed at the non-verbal jokes. The fat chap in *Bilko* had come on dressed as a baby at one point. But Jung-Ja hadn't found that funny. Was everything that he found funny just silly to Jung-Ja?

'I bought a record in New York,' he told Jung-Ja. He took it out of his Aer Lingus flight-bag, and handed it to her. While she was looking at the picture of Sidney Poitier, Benson took a long slug from the Coke. It almost hurt him as it went down. He felt it land icily in his stomach. It gave him a pain in the temples. The ice in this one drink would have exhausted the capacity of the silly English Electric fridge Dad and Alice had just bought. Here the fridge had a freezer compartment that you opened separately. You could have frozen at least four shoe boxes in it if you had wanted to. But the one at home was filled up by a box of fish fingers. Lots of ice bucked up Coke – a drink he had always found a bit pathetic in comparison to Tizer – into a truly wonderful experience.

'I'll put it on so's you can have a listen,' said Benson, using his left hand as a turntable and his right index finger with the dirty nail as a needle.

Jung-Ja nodded and Benson put the record on. They listened to 'To Sir With Love'.

'Good, isn't it.?'

Jung-Ja nodded and gave him a little smile. Then she stood up, slithered through the air and returned with a note-book and pencil. 'Write the words,' she said.

Benson put on the record again and started writing as furiously as legibility would allow. He had to play it a third time to get it all down, but the repetition, he reasoned, would be good for Jung-Ja. Then he presented the lyrics for her to read.

Jung-Ja underlined 'telling tales', 'biting nails', 'crayons', 'write across the sky a letter', 'To Sir With Love', and that was only the first verse.

Benson weighed in. 'Well, the song is sung by a white schoolgirl to her black teacher.' He used the record sleeve as a visual aid. 'There's the teacher. Sidney Poitier. He was in *Porgy and Bess*; and very good he was too, though I'm pretty sure he was miming ... er ... not singing himself. The girl says that schooldays are finished. They consisted of things like telling tales. That's telling stories about your friends ... and biting nails. Well this is biting nails.' And Benson bit his nails. 'Anyway, all that is finished now. Now, although they're finished, she thinks that in her mind ... in her head ... they will go on and on ... continue.'

Jung-Ja started shaking her head. She giggled and

40

placed her hand in front of her mouth. 'You don't understand, do you?' Benson asked her.

Jung-Ja shook her head. 'Some,' she said. Then she sat down again. 'Do you know Doh"?'

'Doe? Money?'

'No. Song called "Doh"?'

'No. How does it go?'

'Excuse me?'

' "Doh". Can you sing it? You know . . . la-la?'

And Jung-Ja sang the first two lines of 'Doh, Ray, Me' from *The Sound of Music*.

Benson did know the song. He knew *The Sound of Music* backwards, had seen it four times at the Odeon. For the next half hour he instructed Jung-Ja in the meaning of 'Doh, Ray, Me', thinking what a good way of learning English songs were. Much better than boring old grammar books, the sort of thing that Jung-Ja sat hunched over for hours on end. Songs were alive. Maybe he could go into business with little books explaining the meanings of songs to foreigners. Yes, that would be good. He might be able to combine it with a business making sellotape loops for hanging up posters. No, the trouble with sellotape loops was that, instead of buying what Benson had made in his little factory run on co-operative lines, where his employees called him Martin and loved him like a father, people would just steal the idea, go off and buy a roll of sellotape and make the loops themselves.

Benson completed his lesson with a flawless rendition of 'The Lonely Goatherd'. Only then did he let Jung-Ja escape back to the kitchen to get the dinner ready.

'No, like this,' said Lee-Chun.

Benson had just dropped a dumpling on the table-cloth from his chop-sticks. He just could not get the hang of them at all. He liked the aesthetics of them, of course. Who wouldn't? But it seemed to him that the design of chop-sticks could be greatly improved if one end were hinged, or better still, sprung like a pair of sugar tongs. They might be further improved if they had a spoon on each end. As it was, even efficient users of chop-sticks like his three friends had to take a spoon to rice. Either that or lift the bowl to their lips and then spoon the rice home using the chop-sticks like a brush. Another business? he wondered. If they caught on, there would be a huge market! Look at China. Of coure he would have to make sure to patent the idea before somebody stole it. He had learnt from the débâcle with the sellotape loops. A hundred employees were depending on him! Not to mention their families, all in little company cottages with gardens in the village of Port Benson, which had its own theatres, art galleries and a spanking new Homocentre.

Lee-Chun took Benson's chop-sticks out of his hand, banged the ends on the table and then held them artistically in his own hands. 'Only move the top one,' he said. Then he moved the top chop-stick so that it looked like a speaking pelican.

'That's easier said than done,' Benson said. Jung-Ja looked at him interrogatively. 'It's easier to say than to do . . . er . . . '

Lee-Chun translated.

'That's easier said than done,' said Jung-Ja as Benson tried to make the top chop-stick move while the other stayed still and the rest of the table watched him with bated breath.

'Maybe you should use a spoon,' said Lee-Chun.

'No, I'll just keep trying. Practice makes perfect.' He did not dare look at Jung-Ja.

'Did you enjoy your trip into the city?' Lee-Chun asked.

'Yes. I went to the top of the Empire State Building and walked across the Brooklyn Bridge. It's wonderful there. I'm sure there's nothing like it anywhere else in the world.'

'You didn't talk to anyone?' Lee-Chun asked.

'Well, no-one talked to me, but everyone looked all right,' Benson replied. 'They're a bit ruder than I'm used to, but it's probably cultural.'

'You have to watch yourself,' said Lee-Chun. 'The Negroes, the faggots, the Puerto Ricans.'

Benson looked at his plate. In one sentence Lee-Chun had managed to damn his two favourite peer groups. 'You can't generalize,' he muttered.

'You can in this city. Martin, I promised your mum and dad that I'd look after you while you're here. They wouldn't have let you come otherwise.'

'They couldn't have stopped me!' replied Benson militantly. 'It was me who saved the plane fare out of my grant money and by working during the holidays. I'm over twenty-one. Anyway, the word "faggot" is a nasty one. Why don't you call them homosexuals?'

'They're nasty people, that's why,' said Lee-Chun.

'They are now legal in England. I read it in *Time*,' said Sung-Il.

'How do you mean?'

'Faggots. They are legal.'

Lee-Chun started talking to Sung-Il in Korean then, and Benson was left to absorb the implications of what had just been said. He had heard that a bill was going through Parliament, though he was not quite sure what difference it would make to his life. The big problem lay in finding people who were. Once you got them back to your private room you could take your chances. It was the rest which was so difficult.

Of course, he had never said anything to Lee-Chun about his being a homo himself. But he had told him in

Aberystwyth that he wasn't attracted to women. On hearing this, Lee-Chun had commanded him to go and call on female acquaintances at the women's hostels to see if he could get one of them to yield. Benson would march off glumly up the hill. He always called on Meryl's friend Gwen because Gwen had a fiancé on VSO and was saving herself up for him. After an hour or two with Gwen, off he would trot back down the hill to tell lurid stories to Lee-Chun about his full frontal assaults on the virtues of the inhabitants of Ifor Evans. He went into quite explicit detail, hoping against hope that he was getting the anatomical bits correct. Lee-Chun loved to hear these stories. He could be as ribald as any Englishman once he had a couple of whiskies inside him, and he always had a bottle in his room. At such times, Eastern aesthetic sensibilities were ground to dust, like the stubs of his Marlboros.

But at other times he would touch Benson, hold his hand unselfconsciously on their way up to the squash courts. Nothing more, but it had been enough to keep the still-frustrated Benson enthralled. He had invited Lee-Chun home for the summer and both of them had worked in a café on the pier in New Brighton. Then, when Lee-Chun had saved up enough money for his ticket to America, he had seen Lee-Chun off at Lime Street Station, weeping copiously. He offered up his chastity during his second year at Aberystwyth in the hope that upon arriving in New York a miracle would take place and Lee-Chun would suddenly change into Dearest Him.

During that second year he had written letters to his friend almost every day and had received a reply about once a fortnight. He read Lee-Chun's letters again and again and kept them in a transparent pocket on the front of his file. He had even bought a *Teach Yourself Korean*.

Now he sat at the dinner table feeling like a faggot surrounded by strangers. A faggot in England was a cheap meat. He had eaten them often enough. Did the American expression – one that struck him as particularly ugly and uncouth – come from that? He did not want to think about it. He was glad that only the weekend lay between him and departure for Camp Manley. They were all going to go to Jones Beach on Sunday. After that he would be on his own.

Benson excused himself, picked up *Time* from the coffee table and went off to his room to read. He turned its pages at speed, past 'The World' and 'The USA' to the pathetic couple of pages devoted to England. There, beneath a picture of Oscar Wilde, he found the story that Sung-Il had referred to.

Yes, now he was legal. Hurray. But the account of the debate in the House of Commons did not cheer him much, did not go any length towards banishing the bitter taste of the dinner conversation. He read what Roy Jenkins had said:

This is not a vote of confidence in, or congratulations for, homosexuality. Those who suffer from this disability carry a great weight of loneliness, guilt, shame and other difficulties. The crucial question we have to answer is whether, in addition to these other disadvantages, they should also be made subject to the full rigour of the criminal law.

Benson could not exactly decide why the speech so depressed him. True, he had had his share of loneliness, guilt and shame. Still had. But he no longer saw himself as having a disability. There had always been homos, hadn't there? Look at Mary Renault and Michelangelo. It was typical of the English to label part of life's rich pageant as *a disability*. He read the article again. Then he turned out the light and, as he drifted towards sleep, found himself thinking that he didn't much like being English. It would be much nicer to be the citizen of an innocent country. But he was snoring mightily before he could think of one.

Benson woke up still seething about the Old World. The waterfall shower knocked sense into him. *I am not contain'd between my hat and boots*, he told himself. Fresh-dressed he ambled up to Jung-Ja, singing 'To Sir With Love' to her. Then he asked her to come to Manhattan with him.

'What we do there?'

'Well, it's hard to know where to begin,' began Benson, who had read his copy of *New York on Five Dollars a Day* from cover to cover. 'We could take a boat around Manhattan, though we'd have to get a move on . . . leave quickly to catch it. We could go to the Metropolitan Museum of Art. We could walk in Central Park. We could see *To Sir With Love*. Also there are concerts in Central Park on Saturday nights. I don't know who's on tonight but . . .'

But Jung-Ja had already started speaking in Korean to her husband and from the sound of it the trip was getting the thumbs down. She was pouting as she protested Sung-Il's decision, playing with the noodles on her plate. Then she looked at Benson sadly and said that she could not accompany him.

'What a pity,' said Benson. It was, too. He would love to have shown Manhattan to Jung-Ja. The population would have stopped in their tracks to see him with a Korean woman. It would have been good for them to hear his English accent and realize that the English could get on peaceably with the same sort of people Americans were bombing the life out of, spraying defoliants over, using most shamefully. A great opportunity for giving a good example was going to be missed.

He put over his shoulders a sweatshirt with *University College of Wales Aberystwyth* on the front and *Coleg Prifysgol Cymru Aberystwyth* on the back. Lee-Chun came out of the bathroom smoking a cigarette, his hair beautifully all over the place. Benson told him he was going into the city.

'Be careful,' said Lee-Chun.

'I will. I should be back by this evening. If I'm going to be late, I'll give you a ring.'

As he waited on the subway platform he noticed that someone had drawn graffiti on the advertisement for *Thoroughly Modern Millie*. Julie Andrews, dressed as a flapper, was looking out from the advertisment, making a big O with her mouth. Someone had drawn a penis with a pencil. It disappeared into her mouth.

Well, thought Benson. That is a bit much. It's bad enough when people do things like that in toilets, but to draw an obscenity right there where families and children can see it. It ought not to be allowed. It would never be allowed in England.

He noticed that he was all the time comparing England and America. Usually America came off rather badly. Manners had been forgotten in the rush over on the boat. There was even an advertisement on the television – television which made Commercial Television in England seem positively intellectual – 'If you don't get a hello, a smile and a thank you when you visit our bank, we'll give a crisp new five dollar bill'. Things, in Benson's opinion, had reached a pretty pass when courtesy became a commodity. Brother O'Toole had once given 3B a talk on the difference between courtesy and etiquette. The former was alive, he had said. The latter was dead. Courtesy was Christian and moral and selfless. Etiquette was self-serving. You followed etiquette when you went to see the Queen of England, whose forebears had treated the

Irish Nation so shamefully. But the Christian gentleman would treat a tramp like a queen. Etiquette was puffed-up and hollow. Courtesy was an acknowledgement of Christ in your fellow men.

Benson courteously held back to let everyone on to the subway train ahead of him. He sat down on the hard seat next to the subway policeman. There was a policeman on every train. Benson thought what a horrible job it must be, hearing that screaming for eight hours a day, having to stop people with flick knives from having rumbles all the time. Still, if all the stories that Lee-Chun had told him were true, then a policeman in every subway train was a good idea. But it was a sad comment on the American Dream. Why couldn't everyone in the melting pot of New York melt happily together? Why must people brawl?

He came up the same staircase at Times Square. The manhole was still smoking. It must be something that it did all the time. He had seen another manhole doing it outside the Empire State Building. No-one took the least notice of it. There's no smoke without fire, he thought. Where does it come from? I think we should be told.

Without making any conscious decision to do so, he was walking along 42nd Street towards the west. He was not edified by the street. A lot of people were just hanging about looking odd. There were Negroes and a few whites, but most of them were a mixture of races. Benson was a great believer in the mixing of races until everyone became the colour of coffee with a dab of milk in it. But these people did not look particularly happy. One or two looked at him with hard stares, as if they had just been sucking on a lemon.

There were cinemas showing sexy films of a kind that would never be allowed in London. A good thing too, he thought. *Sexy Teachers* – a contradiction in terms if ever there was one – and a poster showing a woman wearing a mortarboard and black underwear beating a man on the bottom with a cane as he lay across her desk. *Return to the Isle of Levant* was also on offer. Surely once was enough.

In between the cinemas were shops crammed with transistor radios, cameras, watches and televisions. They all had 'Closing Out Sale. Everything Must Go!' on the windows, and Benson stood in front of one, comparing prices with those at home. There was a rather fetching little radio at the front of the display for $3.99. That was quite good value, even if there was a dead bluebottle on it. Still, he could not afford to spend his money on such luxuries. He had to earn some first. He would earn forty dollars a week in Camp Manley. If he earned that for ten weeks then he would be able to come back to New York and buy souvenirs till the cows came home.

Then he saw the dirty bookshop. He looked to left and right before going up to the window, expecting Brother Hooper to be making his way down the road towards him. In the window there were pictures of naked men and women on the front of magazines. They all had stars over their private parts. A notice in the window invited him to come on in.

Benson did not immediately accept the invitation. He decided that a walk round the block was necessary to give him the required courage. Nobody knows me here. I can do what I like. What does it matter here what people think? He grasped his Aer Lingus flight-bag, slinging his left arm with it. Of course it's not going to do Aer Lingus' reputation any good seeing someone who has flown on a plane with them going into such an establishment. The shamrock on the badge is a symbol of the Trinity. It's probably an extra sin to take that into a disreputable place. No, the

49

important thing is what *I* think about all this. Then he thought about what he thought as he took one and a half of his longest paces along each of the paving stones on the sidewalk.

Too soon he was back outside the bookshop, his courage only partly screwed up. He stepped inside. A man sat behind a counter high up to his left. Ahead of him were racks of magazines. There were men gazing among the magazines and the man at the counter was watching them like a hawk.

'Good morning,' Benson said to the man. The man did not respond. Benson walked further in the shop. It smelled funny, like a cellar that is seldom opened. Benson walked slowly along the displays, trying to look like a journalist gathering first-hand information on low-life for *The Catholic Herald.* He frowned at the woman with the huge breasts tucked down into the top of her jeans. He paused in front of a magazine that announced: 'Twenty Effective Methods of Penis Expansion'. His hands itched to pick it up. Then he thought of Lee-Chun. If Lee-Chun could see where his guest had gone! Then he saw a display over which had been scrawled on a card HOMO. Benson walked away from it to the other side of the shop as if it were warning of a precipice. The man glowering at his customers from his raised podium seemed to represent all the people who would disapprove of what he was doing. He stopped in front of some magazines showing fat women. He picked one up and turned the pages. It would have cost him $5.99 to buy. He could have a little radio and change for that! And all it showed was a lot of fat women. Well, he could imagine what fat women with no clothes on looked like without paying all that money. Still, the time spent browsing gave him time to consider strategy. He felt the eyes of the man on him but told himself that the man was not like the people who would disapprove of him. He was working in the dirty bookshop after all. He could not afford to be sanctimonious. Benson put the magazine back and walked, a cynical, worldly expression on his face, down the display, towards HOMO.

At last he arrived. Most of the magazines had stars over the good bits. He picked one up and opened it, aware of the eyes and the knowledge they now had of him, trying nonetheless to appear to be an interested observer, interested in how low *other people* could stoop. Suddenly he felt giddy. There were no stars over the men inside. He turned over page after page and looked hard at the men on rocks holding beach-balls or throwing javelins, who were not covered up. He felt an erection split him. He panicked.

Suddenly he wanted to leave the shop, at least part of him did. Another part of him wanted to stay there all day. He had not imagined five minutes before that just opening a magazine could spark off the ineffable giddiness of showertime at the University Sports Centre. At the same time he felt the eyes behind him. They wanted him to buy something and he did not want to buy it. He wanted to look but not buy. But if I stay on here I'll have to buy. He put the magazine back and made a strategic withdrawal towards the fat women. He was now standing directly below the man. Furtively, he darted past him and out into the street.

People were passing. He tried to put on a quiet, cynical smile of the sort that a person might wear who now feels he has seen everything. He even said *My, my* to himself and shook his head.

Benson bought himself a coffee at a scruffy coffee bar on the corner. He was not shocked when the waitress treated him with total indifference. He would not be able to claim a crisp new five dollar bill from such an establishment, that was obvious. He lit a cigarette.

'Gimme one o'them,' said a voice.

Benson turned and was confronted by a black girl in a mini-skirt. Dumbly, he offered her his packet of Benson and Hedges. The girl took one. 'Thanks,' she said.

Well, thought Benson. She did not say please, but she at least said thanks. That's something.

'That's a fancy package. Real pretty, you know.'

'Yes, it's Benson and Hedges Special Filter. I got them at the duty-free shop. Usually I smoke little cigarettes.'

'I ain't never seen none in a gold package before,' said the girl. 'You ain't from aroun' here, is you?'

'No,' replied Benson. 'I'm from England. I only arrived a few days ago.'

'This here cigarette don't taste nothin' like ours.'

'Don't it . . . er . . . doesn't it? They're Virginia.'

'You don't say! Ain't that somethin'? I'm Virginia, too.'

'You mean that's your name? I'm Martin.'

'Martin. Like Martin Luther King, right? You heard o' Martin Luther King?'

Benson was shocked that anybody looking at him could think that he had *not* heard of Martin Luther King. '"Through our scientific genius, we have made of the world a neighbourhood; now through our moral and spiritual genius we must make of it a brotherhood,"' recited Benson expansively.

'Oh, wow,' said Virginia.

'I know a lot of his speeches: "When we allow freedom to ring . . . we will be able to speed up that day when all God's children, black men and white men, Jews and Gentiles, Catholics and Protestants, will be able to join hands and to sing in the words of the old

Negro spiritual, 'Free at last, free at last; thank God Almighty, we're free at last!'" There you are. I could go on and on. I've got an LP of his speeches. It wasn't cheap but I think it's more than given me my money's worth.'

'You soun' real southern when you says that.'

'Do I? Well that's because Martin Luther King is southern, I suppose.'

'You know the Queen of England?'

'No. I saw her once. We had to stand on the street when she came to our town. I nearly didn't see her at all. We had been waiting for hours and hours and just as she was passing some people came out of a pub and elbowed their way through most rudely, standing right in front of us.'

'That was real mean o' them.'

'Yes, still I did catch a glimpse of her. That's all you get unless you're a lord or something. It's a matter of class.'

'You talk real classy.'

'Do I? I don't think I do. I'm from near Liverpool . . . where the Beatles come from.'

'Are you? Wow! They was here in New York City! You never seen nothin' like it!'

'Yes, we saw it on the news. Would you like a coffee or something?'

'Yeah, I really would. Thanks.'

Benson went to the counter and got Virginia a coffee. It was lovely to have someone to talk to. Virginia looked as if she was wearing one of Lee-Chun's hair-pieces. He judged it to be Dynel rather than natural hair. It was long and straight, like Tina Turner's. Benson rather liked Ike. Virginia's thin body seemed to have been poured into her blouse, which reminded him of the fur on a bee. Black-and-gold stripes. But even Benson, who was famous for his ignorance of

53

what matched, could see that it did not really go with the little red skirt.

Virginia added two packets of sugar to her coffee and stirred it briskly with the plastic stirrer. She drank some and made a face. 'They sure make lousy coffee here. I mean, I don't want to sound ungrateful, you know. But they let it sit way too long. You English drink tea, right?'

'Yes, we do. If we drink coffee we drink Nescafé. Real coffee is a luxury for us.'

'Is that right?' Virginia seemed concerned.

'Yes.'

'What you doin' here anyway?' asked Virginia, her dark eyes wide behind her cup.

'Well, I'm just looking around the city. I've only got this weekend and then I'm going out of New York to be a camp counsellor at a children's summer camp.'

'I went to a camp once,' said Virginia.

'Did you like it?'

'Oh, yeah. It was real nice. Ev'rythin' green, you know. I helped a farmer milk a cow.'

'Are you from New York?'

'Well, I live in the city now, but I come from Brooklyn. I came to the city 'bout three years ago.'

'What do you do?'

'Oh, this and that.'

'How do you mean?'

Virginia gave Benson a funny look. He thought what a nice face she had. Her skin was very dark, not quite black, but almost. 'I think you know.'

'No, I don't.'

'Come *on*! No-one comes here without they knows what goin' on.'

Benson looked around. 'How do you mean?' he asked again.

'Yuh really don' know, do you?'

'No,' said Benson.

'You're a fag, ain't you?'

'How do you mean?' Benson asked again.

'How do you mean?' mimicked Virginia. 'Oh, I'm sorry. It's just that all you English sound like fags.'

Benson took a cigarette out of his gold packet. 'This is a fag in England.'

'What? A cigarette? You don't say!'

'It's slang of course. It wouldn't do to ask, say, the Queen if she would like a fag. You'd have to say to her, "Would you care for a cigarette, Your Majesty?" That's what etiquette demands.'

Virginia started laughing. 'Go on, say some more! I love the way you talk!'

"'I was angry with my friend. I told my wrath. My wrath did end. I was angry with my foe. I told it not. My wrath did grow. And I watered it with fears, night and morning with my tears. And it grew both day and night. Till it bore an apple bright. And my foe beheld it shine. And he knew that it was mine. Into my garden stole. When the night had veiled the pole. In the morning glad I see, My foe outstretched beneath the tree,"' recited Benson in his poshest voice.

'You *got to* be a fag.' She did not say it in a nasty way.

'I know what fag means. I just don't like the word. I am a homo though, if you want the truth.'

'Ain't I said that?' said Virginia. 'They's takin' over all round here. A girl just don't stan' *no* chance!'

Benson suddenly felt hopeful while at the same time concerned for Virginia. 'Come on, Virginia, there must be lots of nice men who would love to go out with you!'

Virginia drank some more coffee and helped herself to another cigarette from Benson's packet. Benson frowned but did not say anything. 'You know, Martin, I like you!'

'Do you? Why?'

'Hell, I dunno. You just diff'rent. Where you living? A hotel?'

'No, I'm staying with some Korean friends in Jackson Heights.'

'You ain't!'

'I am, yes. What about you?'

'I live with my mom hereabouts.'

'You're very handy for everything.'

Virginia nodded and pulled her lips over to the left side of her face while at the same time opening her eyes wide. 'You can say that again!'

'You're very handy for everything!'

'You high on somethin' or *what*?' Virginia asked him.

'Me? No, not in the least.'

'I guess you's just weird in an ongoing way.'

He didn't say anything. There was no answer to that. He would just have to worry about that later.

'Everyone's waitin' for their new album.'

'Whose?' he asked.

'The Beatles. There's a new album coming out soon. I have all their work.'

Benson supposed that Virginia was referring to having all the Beatles' records, but it was a funny way of putting it. He did not consider singing on a stage *work*. 'Do you? I haven't got much by the Beatles. I've got the single of "Strawberry Fields Forever". It's got "Penny Lane" on the back, but I don't have much to spend on LPs and what I do have I spend on Bob Dylan and Pete Seeger and Woody Guthrie.'

Virginia had finished her coffee. Benson felt he ought to get on with exploring the city. He made to stand up.

'You ain't going already, are you? We was just gettin' to know each other.'

'Yes, I was thinking of going. You see I want to see the Metropolitan Museum of Art. People say it's wonderful and it's free too.'

'Can I come along? Ain't got nothing to do at this precise moment and I never seen the . . . what you said.'

Fancy someone who lives in New York never having been to the Metropolitan Museum, Benson thought. Then he imagined what a strange couple they would make. It wouldn't be so bad if Virginia's mini-skirt were a little less mini, a little more maxi, not quite so loud. Mum would have said it was common. But he felt mean having these thoughts. Who cared what people thought? Anyway, he was abroad! He was three thousand miles away from nosey neighbours brushing their steps and watching his every move. He was in the melting pot.

'Yes, it would be lovely to go with you. To tell you the truth, Virginia, I've been a bit lonely up to now.'

Back on 8th Avenue, Benson consulted his New York street map, cursing himself that he had not thought to do it in the coffee shop when there had been space. 'Right, we go this way and then go along this street to get to the east side of the park . . .'

'You mean we's going to *walk*?' asked Virginia.

'Well, yes, I thought we might. It's the best way to see the city, you know.'

'Yeah, but look at me!' Virginia was pointing to her scarlet stiletto heels, 'I'll never walk all the way up to 81st Street in these. You're all right. You got . . .' and she looked down at Benson's practical sandals. 'Hey, what *have* you got on? I ain't never seen nothing like them things before.'

'They're English sandals. Look, couldn't you change? Are you living nearby? I mean we could take the subway, but it would be much nicer to walk. Don't you think so?'

'I guess, maybe. I live on 33rd near 9th. Yeah, why not? Let's have us a vacation.'

They walked south. Virginia kept crossing the road when the sign said DONT WALK. Benson tried to teach her her kerb drill, but she wouldn't take any notice and took frantic little runs in front of honking cars. Benson kept holding back and she had to wait for him. She called him a scaredy cat.

'Well, maybe I am, but rules are rules,' said Benson, hating himself for saying it.

They arrived at a door. Virginia searched in her shoulder-bag for her keys. Benson looked up, and noted the fire-escapes zig-zagging up the side of the building just like in *West Side Story*. She opened the door and he followed her in and up flight after flight of steep stairs.

'It's a walk-up,' she said.

Benson could see that.

At long last Virginia stopped and started opening the door of her apartment. It said 9 on it, but one of the screws had come off and the nine had fallen on to the other screw to become a loose 6. First Virginia turned a key in the top of the door, then, sorting through her keys, another at the bottom. Only then did she use her Yale to turn the last lock. She pushed but the door wouldn't open. 'Goddam!' she said and started to ring the bell.

After many rings, ending with Virginia leaning her thumb on the buzzer for at least half a minute, Benson heard a bolt drawn across from the other side. A black woman's face looked out at them. The face looked tired and sulky. 'It's you,' she said, and drew back from the door.

Benson followed Virginia into the apartment and

saw, hardly before he had passed the threshold, the woman wearing a shiny dressing-gown disappear through a door, and bang it.

'That's my mom,' said Virginia. 'She works nights. She's got this thing 'bout robbery. She always bolts herself in like that. You just have a seat. I'll go find myself some walkin' shoes.'

'Right-ho,' said Benson. Virginia gave him a fleeting quizzical look with a smile on the end, and walked down the corridor, past her mother's room, disappearing through a farther door.

The apartment was a bit dark, considering the sun was shining outside. Cream-coloured blinds covered the window, through which the sun shone diffusely, as if he had closed his eyes. The rest of the room was awash with colour and patterns. There was a framed picture of a Swiss scene with a castle by a lake and looming mountains behind. Benson had seen that print before, though he could not remember where. He dimly recalled that there was a story attached to it. Hadn't a poor prisoner been kept shackled in the dungeon of that castle for decades? You could still see his footprints, worn in the stone where he had sat. He thought that was the story, though he might have made it up. On a glass table next to the sofa he was seated on was the largest ashtray Benson had ever seen. And in the ashtray enough cigarette-ends which, complete, would have satisfied him for a week. A big television looked back at him from the corner and on top of it, next to a lamp, was a statue of Our Lady.

'Are you a Catholic?' he asked Virginia when she returned. She was wearing a pair of flat shoes and had changed her skirt. The one she now wore, Benson noted approvingly, was a few inches longer and maybe matched the black-and-gold of her striped top.

'No! Why you asking that?'

'The statue on the television.'

'Oh, *that*! No. That was a present to Mom. She keeps it there for good luck.'

'That's nice. Is your dad out at work?'

'My daddy walked out on us when I was a little girl.'

'I'm sorry.'

'What you ain't never had you don' never miss.'

Benson thought about that. It might be true, but he could think of several items in life that he had never had but would love to have.

'I'm sorry 'bout the apartment. Mom ain't too good a manager. Tell you the truth, I stay away as much as possible,' Virginia said as they walked up 8th Avenue.

'But what do you do, Virginia? Are you a student?'

'I flunked out of school when I was sixteen. I'm twenty now.'

'I'm twenty-one,' said Benson. 'I'm a student. Does your mother work?'

Virginia nodded slowly, a bored expression on her face. 'Yeah, she works. She's working now, matter of fact.'

'Is she? She works from home?' Benson saw Virginia's mother embroidering flowers on table-cloths in her room.

'Martin, you really *na-eeve*, ain't you?'

Benson did not think he was naive in the least. Hadn't Mrs Clitherow told him a while back that he was a man of the world. Of course he was not so naive as to suppose that he knew everything there was to know about everything. 'I think we should turn right somewhere here. I want to see the park. At the moment we're a long way on the wrong side of it.'

'Wish I was jus' visitin' New York, same as you, Martin,' said Virginia.

'Why? It must be a jolly interesting place to live in.'

Why had he used 'jolly'? Why had he suddenly used an adjective which, in England, he wouldn't have touched with a ten foot pole? He knew why. He was trying to impress. To be more English than the English in order to seem special to Virginia. Why did he want to do that? She hadn't tried to impress him with her *Negritude*. Virginia could probably give him all sorts of insights into the Negro novelists and Leroi Jones and Black Muslims if she wanted to. But she didn't. She stayed quiet, a little sad, always surprised by small things. Why couldn't he be like that? Why couldn't he just be himself – whatever that was.

'It prob'ly is "jolly" for folks with money. Rich folks prob'ly really get off on New York. Me? I think it sucks.'

'But there seem to be lots of opportunities here.'

'For white folk. Black folks too if you got a education. I ain't got no education. Ain't nothin' for me or Mom here, 'cept for what we do.'

'What's that?'

'Mom prob'ly thinks you and I is getting it on right now. She be angry if she knew we's going to a art museum.'

'How do you mean?' he asked.

'Don't you know nothin', Martin? Me and Mom we turn tricks. Why you think I was in that place? Why you think I axed you for a cigarette?'

'I see,' said Benson. 'So your mother thinks I'm one of your, er . . .'

'I reckon. Still, it don't matter. I need a day off.'

Benson did not have the least idea what to say. He was not shocked exactly. The thought had entered his head on several occasions since meeting Virginia, but he had dismissed it as unworthy, perhaps also as prejudiced. If he had bumped into Meryl in the coffee bar, would he have at once thought Meryl was a

61

prostitute? No, he wouldn't. He had tried to think the same about Virginia.

There were lots of questions he would love to have asked her, but they seemed somehow indecent – as many of them were. On some days, when sex reared up like a monster from the deep, he had felt that he could quite happily have been a prostitute himself. There would have been nothing nicer. He might not even have charged. But he had read enough about prostitutes to know that usually they did not enjoy their work. Still, fancy your own mother!

As if divining what Benson was thinking, Virginia said, 'It ain't my mom's fault. She's had a hard time, you know. She used to work real hard in a respectable job but one of her boyfriends got her on drugs. Now she gotta turn tricks to keep up.'

'But can't she get some help to stop the drugs?'

'She don't want no help. *She's* happy. It's me that ain't happy.'

They had reached Columbus Circle and the south end of Central Park.

'Down there's where all the faggots go,' said Virginia pointing up Central Park West and allowing Benson to fill in some of the holes left in the otherwise comprehensive *New York on Five Dollars a Day*. He filed the information away.

'Let's walk through the park,' said Benson, trying to lift the mood. The thought had just struck him that his confession about being a homo would, in many circles, be seen as just as bad as Virginia's saying that she was a prostitute.

'No, I wanna see them horse-and-carriages,' said Virginia.

Obediently Benson walked east along Central Park South, though he did insist that he and Virginia cross over to the side of the road fringing the park. 'Imagine livin' in an apartment up there, Martin!' she said, pointing up to the high buildings to their right.

'Yes, it would be lovely, but there's quite a bit of traffic noise, isn't there? I think if I had money I'd want something really quiet too.'

'No sir, not me. I want to know life be right there near me so's I can lean over my balcony and touch it . . . there's the Plaza Hotel!'

There were horses and carriages parked opposite the Plaza. Several of the horses had left manure on the street. He thought it a surreal sight in the circumstances. The cars whizzed past them but there they were, behaving as if they were in the middle of the country. If Mum had been there she'd have told him to go out with a shovel and collect the manure for the garden. But she wasn't. He looked upwards.

Finally, in the Metropolitan, Virginia's enthusiasm soared still further. They stood in front of some stained-glass windows and Virginia said that looking at them she felt like she had died and gone to heaven. Benson thought them rather overdone, but did not say so. They wandered randomly through the huge museum but no object could Virginia pass without an enthusiastic comment. 'I can't even paint a wall,' she said. 'Imagine bein' one o' these here artists and goin' to bed at night after painting a picture like that there one!'

Benson did not say much. He was delighted that she was delighted. He was grateful to Virginia for being with him, though he felt some unease that he could not put his finger on.

They came to the American Gallery. Benson had not been too keen about going into this one. He felt that all he would see was cowboys and rodeos. But almost the first picture he saw took him and held him fast. Virginia came and stood next to him.

'He's a goner,' she said.

'I don't know. There's a ship in the distance. Look, up there!'

'Yes, but those sharks is gonna get him. And look at that twister right near him. And that there rough ocean! That poor nigger gonna be chop meat.'

'Don't use that word!' said Benson severely.

'What word?'

'You know what word!'

Virginia looked at Benson oddly, then returned to the picture. 'Ain't no hope for him,' she said. 'He ain't even got no sail. That there ship is way too far away. Look how hungry them sharks are! And look there! There's blood in the water! Maybe there was somebody there before and the sharks got him. Oooh, real spooky!'

'I think he looks indomitable,' said Benson, admiring the Negro's feet. 'There's resignation there. He is definitely thinking *que será, será,* but I think what will be is that the ship will save him.'

'No, you wrong, Martin.'

'It's a matter of opinion. We'll never know, will we?'

'Why it called *Gulf Stream*, you think?' asked Virginia.

'Don't know. But the Gulf Stream is a warm current that starts in the Gulf of Mexico, winds up the eastern seaboard of the USA and then goes across the Atlantic. It washes round Britain, in fact,' Benson informed Virginia.

'Wow, it's gorgeous. It tells a whole story, don't it?'

Benson agreed with her that it did. He could hardly wait to find the museum shop and buy some postcards of *Gulf Stream*.

'Why you buyin' so many?' asked Virginia.

'I'm going to send them to all my friends.'

She nodded. 'Where you want to go to now?'

'I'm not sure,' Benson replied. 'What are you doing?'

'Oh, nothin',' said Virginia in a sad voice. 'I guess I have to go home sooner or later and face the music.'

'Why face the music?'

'Well Mom expect me to make me some money. She ain't gonna wanna hear 'bout no Metropolitan Museum.'

'Are you short of money? I could give you some,' he said, wondering if he could.

'You could? That'd be swell!'

'Would five dollars help?'

'Sure would. Thanks. You're a pal.'

He reached into his back pocket and pulled out five dollars. He thought of a little white transistor radio. 'There you are,' he said.

Strangely, Virginia said she had to be going shortly after that. He asked for her address, saying that he would like to see her again when he got back to the city. He rooted in his flight-bag. Then he found B in his new address book and took down her address to her slow dictation.

'You're my first,' he told her.

2

EDUCATION

And when we find ourselves in the place just right.
'Twill be in the valley of love and delight.

Shaker song

Benson held his breath as the Liberty bus crossed the bridge out of Manhattan. He succeeded in not breathing until the bus had reached the continental United States.

He frowned at the continental United States, thinking how most of what he was seeing would never have got planning permission in England. And quite right too. The big signs everywhere were definitely an eyesore. Everything screamed 'Buy! Eat! Fill up!' He told the spirit of Walt what a falling off there had been. Walt nodded and hugged him, tickling him with his beard, weeping great tears all over Benson's shirt.

He had already had plenty of time to pass judgement on Harlem, doing his best then to look Negroid and sympathetic as the famous fronts of the tenements flew past. White people didn't go to Harlem. It was one of the things he kept hearing. They had gone there once – for the music mainly – but now it was far too dangerous. Honkies were not welcome. It wasn't very nice calling him a Honky. No doubt there were lots – perhaps the majority of white people – who deserved to be so called. But surely not him. It was a pity he could not wear a badge which encapsulated his enthusiasm for the race and his excellent record in improving race relations throughout the length and breadth of Aberystwyth. But, if a black man came up to him in Harlem determined to do him to death for the sins of his race, he was not sure he would have time to explain that he was trying to be as nice as Pete Seeger. Would his attacker pause for Benson to tell him that he had shown a complete stranger – also black – around the Metropolitan Museum? Would he hold back the blow long enough for Benson to sing 'No More Auction Block For Me?' Probably not.

Virginia had been the first Negro he had spoken to in America. That had gone well. But meeting Virginia had not managed to banish the thought that the people he so wanted to be accepted by, to be loved by, would never, because of history and prejudice, riots, black power politics and, of course, his spare tyre, love him back.

Still, Harlem passed uneventfully enough. The papers were saying that this summer it would catch fire. People in England had tried to discourage him from going to America. Even Meryl had tried.

Riots always seemed to begin either with a policeman firing off a gun or with a fire-hydrant exploding. There were plenty of fire-hydrants in Harlem. But none of them seemed to be spraying water. Rather they were providing perches for old ladies to rest on.

The bus stopped at a traffic light. Fortuitously, a rotating doughnut on top of a pole lit by red-and-white neon reared up into his vision to test his tolerance to its uttermost. He bit his lip. It's a kind of art in a way. It brightens things up no end. Above all, it's different. I've never seen a huge doughnut rotating on top of a pole before. Neither have I seen a hamburger at the roadside that opens up and steams real steam. It's really quite clever. I wonder if it is art?

Benson lit a Benson and Hedges Special Filter. Then he placed the gold packet prominently in the little string mesh receptacle on the back of the seat in front. People behind would therefore know that Benson was an exotic specimen of humanity. Perhaps the black woman one behind him on the other side of the aisle would realize that he was British and not think of him as your usual American Honky. Still, that might not help. If she knew anything about history she would know that the English could only afford gold cigarette packets because of the way they had exploited her forebears. He puffed on his cigarette and leaned back in his seat.

He was sorry to be leaving New York. A part of him would have liked to stay much longer. Still, he was in America for a purpose. Money had to be earned. That was how life was. Dad had given him a lecture. You couldn't just sponge off friends the whole time. He thought of the future. I am going to be a camp counsellor. For two months I am going to be *in loco parentis* for a group of American children in a log cabin. We'll go swimming and rambling. We'll canoe on lakes and sing songs round camp fires. I'll sing them English madrigals and thrill them with my encyclopaedic knowledge of the *Bob Dylan Song Book*. Yes, it should be fun.

He had spoken to the owners of Camp Manley, Mr and Mrs Manley. Mr Manley – 'Call me Bill!' – had sounded nice enough, saying that he would pick Benson up on his arrival in Liberty and take him out to the camp. Everything would have been most reassuring except that Bill kept interrupting their conversation to tell noisy people in the room with him to shut the fuck up. Benson frowned at that. A good example needed to be given. He would try to give a good example.

He stubbed out his cigarette and sat back. But then he had to return his attention to the ashtray because he had somehow managed to ignite a sweet paper buried at the bottom. He poked around for a while, using his stub as a damper. Then he clicked the lid shut, frowning at the ashtray for a moment. He sat back, reassured that the flames had died.

The bus had left the city far behind and was passing along a wide dual carriageway road meandering through fields and woods. Only the occasional detached house intruded. Benson relaxed to the curving rhythm of the bus but then noticed that the ashtray was smoking again. He leant forward and started prodding at the invisible source of the smoke.

Then he was pulling his hand away, shocked by the feel of a cold liquid. The man behind had leant over the back of Benson's seat and was pouring a bottle of Pepsi Cola into the ashtray. The ashtray was awash and some of the sticky liquid had leaked over Benson's C & A trousers. Benson looked back over his shoulder angrily but was disarmed by the smiling face of a man he judged to be about his age. He had curly blond hair and the widest mouth Benson had ever seen, into which he now stuck the neck of the Pepsi bottle, pulling a slug which made his prominent Adam's apple go up and down. Benson, preoccupied though he was, remembered that he did not have an Adam's apple. If I lose a few pounds will it appear? It's supposed to be a sign of manliness. But if I don't have one, even after I've got rid of some weight, what does that signify?

'That should fix it,' said the man.

'Er . . . you've spilt some of that stuff on my trousers,' said Benson accusingly.

'You weren't doing such a great job on putting it out yourself. Your smoke will be ruining my clothes too. Cigarettes are a stinking habit. Why do you smoke anyhow?'

Benson knew why he smoked. He liked smoking. Smoking relaxed him and made him feel suave. Anyway he had tried not to smoke and had been most irritable, going so far as to refuse to fit in with Meryl's babysitting schedule. She had ordered him to start again at once.

'Well, I don't know really. I like it,' he replied defensively, guiltily, angry with himself for feeling defensive and guilty.

The face had disappeared. Suddenly the man was sitting down next to Benson making the springs of the seat twang and catching Benson's jacket under his bottom. He stuck out his hand. 'Rod. Happy to make your acquaintance.'

Benson, bending to the right to remove his jacket from under Rod's bottom, took his hand and was suddenly wincing from the intensity of the grip. Rod noticed Benson's pained expression and smiled widely, causing the sides of his mouth almost to disappear behind his ears. 'Not bad, huh? I used to smoke like you . . . what's your name by the way?'

'Martin.'

'I used to smoke, Martin. Now I take care of myself. I used to have a grip as flabby as yours – you know you shake hands like a fag? – but now I use my click-grip. The best dollar ninety-nine I ever spent. Look!' He held out a thing that looked a bit like a stapler. 'While you were smoking I was doing my hand-strengthening exercises. I do two hundred and fifty of these three times a day. Both hands.'

'Really?' Benson asked, wondering if he really did have a weak handshake.

'That's right.' Rod looked at Benson quizzically. 'You're English, aren't you?'

'Well, yes I am, actually. That's jolly . . . er very clever of you.'

'I was there one time. With my folks. We stayed at these bed and breakfasts. All I can remember is the awful bathrooms. Tubs with crud around the sides. The owners were really shocked when we told them we wanted to bathe every day. Some of them even *charged* for it! Can you imagine that? Coming from the US of A, it was hard to believe. Still, London was pretty interesting.'

'Friday night is bathnight,' said Benson pedantically.

It was a bit much this American pouring Pepsi Cola down his ashtray, joining him without a by-your-leave, crushing his fingers, then judging the English and accusing them of uncleanliness. Benson took a shower every day at Aberystwyth. He was always as clean as a whistle, though cleanliness was not necessarily his main motivation.

'Christ, well I'm glad I never balled an English chick on a Thursday! Hey, I also remember the houses smelt like burnt toast, boiled cabbage, cigarettes and damp laundry! Yuck.'

'Well, all I can say is that my house . . .'

'Yeah! I remember now! It's all coming back to me like some unreal nightmare! They'd put their clothes in front of the fire and dry them on a wooden rack. You'd be sitting there telling the bed and breakfast owner that you liked Stonehenge but the wind off of Salisbury Plain had left you feeling like a block of ice, and all the time there were these grey sheets and shirts with ring-around-the-collar and steam rising off of them, just sitting there between us and the fire. Wow, even British dogs smelled weird.'

'How long ago was this, may I ask?'

'Nineteen-fifty-nine. Summertime. Well, they called it summertime. Rained most days.'

'We were still recovering from the war,' said Benson. 'If you went there now you'd see some changes. My stepmother, for example, has a Hoovermatic.'

'And then there were these crazy contraptions on the ceiling. One place we were eating our breakfast, water dripped down on us right there at the table from this thing. They put the wet clothes on the whatchamacallit and hoisted it up with a rope – a rope for Christ's sake – right up to the ceiling. Then they let it stay there for days on end dripping on the people. That was in York-shire.'

'Yorkshire. Yes, I know them. They're called pulleys. Anyway, as I said, things have changed since then. Perhaps if you Americans had joined the war before the Japanese bombed Pearl Harbor we might have got it over quicker. As it was you left us to do all the hard work, only deciding to come in when the thing was practically won.'

'Oh, come on! What's your name again . . . ?'

'Martin.'

'Come on, Martin! We saved your Limey skins! And look at the Marshall Plan!'

Benson decided he wanted the subject changed. He was still holding Rod's click-grip, trying to press it in. It hardly moved. 'This is yours,' he said to Rod.

Rod took the click-grip from Benson's hands and commenced pressing it. The grip concertinaed to half its size and, as Rod puckered his lips with effort – though Benson thought they were still wider than his when smiling – the grip let out a loud click. 'There. Nothing to it. Now you try!'

'I've already tried and I can't do it,' Benson replied.

'Christ, you *are* a fag! Come on, just try!'

'I *did* try!'

'Nah, you didn't. I don't mean try like an English *try*. I mean try like we try in the US of A! TRY!'

Benson sighed, took the grip and tried.

'Try!'

He frowned and puckered his lips. The grip moved a bit but was still a good inch away from a click.

At last, seeing that Benson was a hopeless case, Rod snatched the grip from his hand and held it up in front of Benson's face, making it click, and grimacing. Then he threw it into the air, caught it and put it into his top pocket, giving Benson a wink.

A thought had struck Benson as Rod was throwing the grip into the air. Here he was on a bus travelling at about sixty miles an hour up a dual carriageway. Why did the grip return to Rod's hand? Why did it not come down further back in the bus? Well, he thought, obviously the air is contained by the bus. Still, even if they had been in an open-topped bus the grip would still have come back to his hands. Or would it? Mystery! He didn't know basic science, his hands were weak, his clothes smelt . . . 'You know, I was feeling quite cheerful until you poured Pepsi Cola into my ashtray,' said Benson.

'I have that effect on people,' replied Rod. 'People don't like honesty. And I pride myself on my honesty.'

'Well, honesty is a virtue sometimes, but pride is usually a vice,' Benson informed Rod in his best Dr Griffiths voice.

'You English are a lot more foreign than you seem at first.'

'Was that honest or just rude? You know honesty can be rudeness. It is sometimes better to do without the hygiene than offend the washer-upper.'

'Where you headed?' asked Rod. Benson felt a click of satisfaction pulse through him. He had won. He was not as thick as he had thought. His little aphorism – home-made and consigned to his 1967 diary in February – had worked its tongue-tying magic.

'I'm going to be a camp counsellor outside Liberty. I'm taking this bus as far as Liberty and then I'm being collected by a Mr and Mrs Manley.'

'Christ! That's where I'm going. Don't tell me they've started hiring cheap foreign labour.'

Benson's heart sank when he thought of two months in the company of Rod. He felt he had better continue standing up for himself, though the need to have to do so depressed him. 'You know, what you just said might have been the first thing to bubble up into your Yankee brain, but it is also extremely hurtful to be referred to as "cheap labour". You might find, were you to reflect, that second thoughts are often better. Also,' Benson continued, suddenly finding an apt dagger to twist over an earlier victory Rod had had over him, 'you Yanks would not have been able to afford the Marshall Plan if you hadn't exploited cheap labour throughout your whole history. Look at United Fruit! And what about King Cotton? Not to mention your shameless genocide against the American Indian!'

'Are you going to talk like that to your kids at camp? I give you three days.'

'How do you mean?'

'Three days. Max. They'll swallow you up in one piece. No, kid, you'd better stick with me. All you Limeys sound like faggots. You shake hands like one and talk like a triple one. Without me you're a goner.'

'Have you done this before?'

'Nope, but I was sent to enough camps when I was a kid. I know how they operate.'

'Do you?'

'Yeah.' And Rod looked ahead of him towards the front of the bus. 'We're heading for the jungle up there, boy. You're on your way to 'Nam, New York State style.'

'You keep saying that sort of thing, but why?'

'Well, seeing as you're a foreigner, maybe you don't know. Summer camps exist so as parents can get their kids out from under their feet. And away from the city heat in summer. Anything to be rid of the little brats and keep them off amphetamines. How did you get the job, anyway?'

'Through the British Universities' North America Club. They're the people who arranged my flight over too. It was a charter. The plane actually belongs to Aer Lingus.' Benson readjusted his flight-bag.

'You don't say. I answered an ad in the *New York Times* two days ago. I just phoned whatshisface Manley and he told me to get my ass up there on the double.'

'Didn't he take any references? What about a resumé?' Benson asked.

'No, nothing like that. That guy sounded so deep in hot water he'd have taken a corpse. I mean, look at you!'

Benson was about to cut off communication when Rod touched his arm. 'Only joking!'

'The resumé took me ages. I hope it isn't going to be as bad as you say.'

'Well, you'll find out soon enough. Hey, don't get offended if I take a little shut-eye now, all right? I know how sensitive you English guys can be. Wake me up when we get there, OK?' And Rod closed his eyes. He was soon snoring quietly, much more quietly than Benson would have expected.

Benson looked over at his companion. While Rod had been laying siege to him he had not noticed how startlingly handsome he was. The mouth in motion tended to absorb all attention and he had missed the perfect, lightly tanned skin on his face, the down that covered his cheeks and the thickness of his naturally blond hair. Benson envied Rod his hair. If he was doomed to be a white man, it would be nice to be a spectacular one with blond hair like his. Blonds had more fun and would be fêted as sun gods when they walked into dark countries. He saw himself arriving in Africa all blond and tanned and without a blackhead or pimple anywhere. He would not have got out of the airport before some ideal would have offered to share his hut and his cattle with him and cleave to him for ever. As it was, in his less than perfect state, he might find someone. There must be people who liked white men with mousy hair. But how much better it would be to look like Rod! Rod was a really golden child. Until he opened his mouth.

The driver called 'Liberty!' at great volume but Benson had to shake his companion awake.

Benson and Rod shambled to the front of the bus as it headed into the open bus station. It drew suddenly to a halt, sending Benson into Rod's back. 'Don't die yet. Save it for the camp,' said Rod over his shoulder.

Once off the bus, Benson looked around for Mr Manley but could see no likely candidate. 'We'll just have to wait, I suppose,' he told Rod and made a bee-line for a bench next to a chocolate machine. He put down his heavy suitcase, noticing a strange Volkswagen camper parked nearby with a man in faded jeans, a bandanna around his head, sitting inside, asleep. Then he forgot the van until he had fished out a quarter and obtained his Hershey bar.

He sat down on the bench and looked at the camper. Half of it was white, as the Volkswagen people had intended, while the other half had sunflowers painted on the front, held by a nude woman whose body went down the side, her golden tresses splayed out all over the place, strands even curling over the roof. Benson thought of Lee-Chun. All around her were daisies and bluebirds and strange objects: an open palm, a single eye, Chinese writing.

Benson thought how taking such liberties with the bodywork of a camper would be bound to severely depress its resale value. When, a couple of years before, he had scratched the bodywork of Dad's new second-hand Vauxhall with his bike, he had offered to touch it up with gloss paint of the same colour. But Dad had given it to a friend to do, saying that amateur painting always showed.

Rod had disappeared. Benson minded his suitcase

79

and munched on the Hershey bar. It was definitely chocolate to chomp rather than suck. Sucking Hershey bars just did not pay back the initial effort. No great rivers of sweetness flowed from the mass of each piece. Benson pondered the problem. They've gone too easy on the sugar and too heavy on the cocoa, he decided. Americans just do not have the hang of sweets at all.

Rod returned and stood in front of him. Benson surveyed his crotch for a moment but Rod was not giving anything away. 'Er . . . where were you?' asked Benson.

'In the head.'

'That's the toilet, isn't it?'

Rod didn't deign to .reply. He looked around him. 'Christ, what a dump! If I weren't short of bed and bread, man, I'd hightail it out of here. You know, I think I have an allergy to open country.'

Benson could not see much that was open country about the Liberty bus station. But he had to agree with Rod's sentiments. He was already yearning for his new friend Virginia, the Brooklyn Bridge. He wanted to count the floors of each skyscraper until they blurred into heaven . . . 'This could be Aberystwyth,' he told Rod.

Rod sat down next to Benson, once again trapping his jacket underneath his bottom. 'Where the fuck's Aberwhatchamacallit?' he asked.

Benson began telling him, but in the midst of their conversation he saw the man in the Volkswagen camper approaching them and his heart started to sink. The man looked dishevelled, his jeans patched, a hole in the sleeve of his shirt. Benson searched in his pocket in case the man asked him for enough money to buy himself a cup of coffee, as a similar figure had done at the bus terminal in Manhattan.

'Hi,' said the man.

'Hello,' said Benson. Rod just looked at him.

'I'm Bill Manley. You're not the guys I'm expecting, are you? I must have dropped off.'

'Yes, I think we are,' said Benson. 'I'm Martin Benson.'

'I'm Rod Nicklin.'

They shook hands. Benson saw Bill Manley wince when he shook hands with Rod. Then he noted Rod's sadistic smile.

'Let's get your stuff in the back of Angelina,' said Bill. He picked up Benson's suitcase and Rod's knapsack, walking off ahead of them towards the painted lady.

'Angelina! He calls the fucking thing Angelina!' whispered Rod.

But Benson was busy trying to assume sanguineness, despite all the evidence before him. The deep-green summer trees passing by the camper left him unimpressed. Rod talked to Bill Manley about things Benson could not take in. What would Virginia be doing now? Would she return to the Metropolitan to view the pictures Benson had introduced her to? Would they ever meet again?

Then the Volkswagen passed a sign which said: 'Camp Manley for Boys Who Love the Great Outdoors'.

'Just a mile to go,' said Mr Manley. He was lighting a very untidy roll-up cigarette. 'Let's all have a pull on this before we face the music,' he said.

'Right on,' said Rod, apparently warming to his employer.

Emily Manley was sitting in a rocking-chair on the deck of the reception cabin, wearing a green plastic eye shade. As Bill Manley approached with Rod, Benson and their luggage, she looked up, frowning, chewing a pencil. Then, just as Benson was about to present her with one of his prize-winning beams, she looked back at the clipboard on her knee and said in a monotone, 'Where the hell have you been?' to her husband – or so Benson hoped as he fluttered, trying not to forget to remember to give a firm handshake.

Bill Manley looked uncomfortable. 'The bus was delayed, hon. They just get worse and worse.' And he looked at Benson for support.

Benson nodded. 'Shocking.'

'This is Martin, the counsellor from England . . .'

Benson let out his smile. Emily Manley nodded at him, but did not loosen her pout an inch.

'. . . And this is Rod, the guy I hired a couple of days ago.'

Another nod. Then Emily seemed to forget them. 'I can't make any sense out of these cabin assignments. Why, for heaven's sake, have you put all the bed-wetters in Kerouac this year? I thought we agreed there's no use in taking the parents' word for it. You know they're too tight-arsed to tell the truth.'

'We can always move them around later,' tried Bill, swaying slightly.

'But by then the sociometric bonds will have been formed, Bill. Darn it, why didn't you just arrange them alphabetically like I thought we agreed? And what's the point of putting everyone who stated a preference for a low-calorie menu together. It's not as if they're going to swap recipes.'

'But they'll be the fatties. That's the way it was last year. They all stuck together.'

'Alphabetical, Bill. Alphabetical. And what do these stars mean next to the names?'

'They're the ones who haven't paid their deposits.'

Emily looked down at her clipboard, then up into Bill's face. Her eyes narrowed for a moment. Finally, surprised that Bill could have done anything so obvious, she looked down at the clipboard again, her face marginally clearer.

Bill started smiling like a schoolboy. Without looking up, Emily said: 'Take them to their cabins. You finished the list, didn't you?'

'Sure I did, hon. Martin, you're in Longfellow. Rod, you're in Hawthorne.'

'I never made it through *The Scarlet Letter*,' said Rod.

'Who has?' said Bill.

'Dexter Bulkington has,' said Emily. 'He arrived while you were away. He's in Whitman.'

Benson had been wondering if there was a Whitman hut. He would have liked to have bagged it for himself. He could remember nothing of *Hiawatha* except the rhythm and the fact that Minnehaha had been Hiawatha's girl friend. He also had the feeling that a wet mountie came into the proceedings at some point. Then he remembered a joke about Minnehaha. He dithered about presenting it, but suddenly the question was coming out: 'Why is Minnehaha called Minnehaha?' he asked the group expansively, trying to give the verbal equivalent of a firm handshake.

Emily looked up and he suddenly felt sorry he had started his joke.

'OK, tell us why,' said Bill. Rod looked at his fingernails.

'Well, she was to have been called Minnie, but the vicar got the giggles.'

The three looked at Benson. 'Why on earth did he get the giggles?' asked Emily.

'Well, I don't know really. I suppose Minnie is a peculiar sort of name really.'

'I have an Aunt Minnie,' said Emily. 'She brought us kids up singlehandedly.' And she looked back at her clipboard, rearranging the order of papers. 'She was a great nurturer.'

Bill started laughing. 'I get it!' he said. Rod was smiling a quiet smile and nodding his head. Benson looked at him.

Emily said: 'We still don't have anyone for Dickinson or Kerouac, and that's no laughing matter, Bill. The invasion begins tomorrow. Warm bodies! Round up warm bodies, Bill! Like pronto!'

'Everything's under control, hon,' Bill replied. 'The other two are coming up on the evening bus.'

'They'd better be! They'd better be!' said Emily. And she cut off all communication, burying her head in the clipboard.

'Don't pay no mind to Emily. She's stressed. She's always like this before camp starts. Once we're under way you'll see she's a whole different person. She's basically the earth-mother type. Hey, why don't I take you to your cabins, then I'll show you around. We've got a counsellors' lodge.'

'That's nice,' said Benson.

Bill was leading Benson and Rod away from the reception cabin along a path covered in what looked like chipped tree bark. The path led downhill at a shallow incline between trees. Log cabins, identical to the one where Emily was, had been built in little clearings among the trees. At the bottom of the shallow incline Benson could make out a stretch of water glistening in full sunshine. The sight lifted his spirits somewhat.

'The cabin over there is Whitman, just in back of Dickinson,' said Bill.

'I wonder if they ever met?' Benson asked, carried away by all the literary references.

'Well if they did,' said Rod, 'that's where Whitman would have been really at home.'

'How do you mean?'

'In back of Dickinson.'

Bill and Rod laughed together. Benson didn't, though he had understood the joke. Hardly the sort of humour camp counsellors should give way to.

'Whitman is your greatest poet!' Benson informed his erring New World companions.

'Sure, sure,' replied Rod. 'I just love Ginsberg's send up about Walt Whitman down among the sailors and all.'

'Parody, like thieving, impoverishes the perpetrator,' said Benson.

Bill looked at Rod and Benson. 'Then there're the two girls. Debby and Becky. They're in the same cabin. Thoreau. Debby's Thoreau's Big Sister and Becky's Chow Mother.' Seeing Benson's puzzled expression – he was still trying to heat up verbal lead to pour over Rod's thick head – Bill added: 'The Chow Mother is the person in charge of the dining hall. We find these names appeal to the kids and the kids' parents. We also encourage the kids to choose new names. If they want to stick with their own, fine, but some want a rest from their names. Well, you can understand that, can't you?'

Rod nodded understandingly, leaving Benson feeling even more foreign. 'How do you mean, Mr Manley?'

'Bill. Well, Martin, perhaps this is a good time to explain a little of the philosophy behind Camp Manley. Emily and I met at college. U. Mass. We were both psychology majors and the products of broken homes. We had also spent our summers very unhappily at a succession of summer camps in New England . . . Er, hold on there. Here's Hawthorne cabin. This is yours, Rod, I believe. Let's go inside. All the cabins are identical.'

They walked up the three steps on to the deck. A

broken bench sat on it like a child's slide. Bill opened the door. It creaked alarmingly. Inside it smelt damp. There was a narrow single bed by the door. Arranged down each wall, four wooden two-tier bunks. 'The washroom and the head are through there. You'll sleep there, Rod. As you see we haven't made up any of the beds. First thing the kids have to do is make up their beds. They're expected to make them every morning, by the way. Any accidents, well, you just take them around to the laundry.'

Rod put his knapsack on his bed and left the cabin with Benson and Bill. 'Longfellow's at the end, just before the lake. It makes it a longer walk back to the cafeteria but you're handy for the lake.'

'That's nice,' said Benson again.

'Yeah, you'll be able to jump right in when you see what you're in for!' said Rod.

Bill was suddenly serious. 'That was a negative comment, Rod. Cut it out, OK? If you feel negative don't verbalize it.'

'Yes, sir,' said Rod.

Benson, while wondering why Bill hadn't said that to Emily, was hiding the satisfaction he felt at seeing Rod getting a good telling-off by reading a wooden sign next to the path. Below the picture of a bear in a scout hat like Baden Powell's was written in big red letters,

SMOKEY BEAR'S ABC
Always hold matches till cold
Be sure to drown all camp fires, stir the ashes and
drown them again
Crush smokes dead out.
PLEASE!
Only *you* can prevent forest fires.

That's ABCPO, he thought.

'Anyway, we were in the psych department together. Emily's honors paper was on peer group competitiveness and mine was isolation and alienation. Our family backgrounds inspired us to talk for hours. Eventually we worked out the idea for Camp Manley. You could say that the camp is a laboratory where we put our ideas into practice. You'll hear all about that when we all get together for the orientation seminar tonight.'

Benson nodded. He felt that he could do with orienting. At this precise moment he felt very disoriented indeed. Still, he was bound to feel out of his depth at first. He had felt strange to be with Sung-Il and Jung-Ja for the first few hours but that had soon passed. No, I must be positive. I am going to be an ideal big brother for the boys in Longfellow cabin. Long after this summer camp is over and my boys have grown up and become lumberjacks and policemen and lawyers and television personalities they will look back on their time with their big brother, Martin Benson, realizing that they were put on the right road at Camp Manley, that all the negative things in their childhoods were put into some kind of perspective. I wonder where I can find a copy of *Hiawatha*.

Longfellow cabin was just like Hawthorne, except that the bench on the deck was in better order. Benson cast an expert eye over the bathroom while Rod and Bill walked down to the lake. There were three washbasins, a shower and two toilets divided by a four foot high screen made of plywood. At first he did not perceive what was wrong. He stood there looking at the toilets for a long moment, trying to see what he knew was obvious but somehow could not perceive. Then he perceived.

Bill and Rod were seated at the end of the jetty, their

legs dangling down towards the water. They were smoking, passing the reefer between them.

Benson lit a cigarette and sat down next to them. 'Have a drag on this,' said Bill. 'It's home-grown.'

'I don't think I ought to. It makes me funny.'

Bill and Rod laughed together. It was not a laugh which, Benson felt, included him. He felt distinctly alienated and on the losing side in an example of peer group competitiveness. 'I was just wondering, I was in the toilets at Longfellow and there don't appear to be any doors on them. Has someone forgotten to er . . . fit them? I thought I should tell you before it becomes a problem.'

Rod and Bill broke into splutters of laughter, laughter so loud that it frightened a flock of Canada geese basking on a raft a hundred and fifty yards out in the lake. They ran across the water and took off, calling sadly to one another. Then they wheeled off in formation towards the west.

Benson watched them wistfully.

'We really shouldn't laugh,' said Bill. Rod immediately became serious and Benson realized that Rod was sucking up to Bill and acknowledged what his instinct had been telling him since they had first met on the bus. He did not like Rod Nicklin one little bit, apple cheeks or no apple cheeks. 'Martin, we don't have doors on any of the heads. We like to encourage, well, a certain frankness about physical matters. You see, many of our kids come from very over-protected homes. Camp Manley is an opportunity for them to confront some of their problems. Here at Camp Manley we help the youngsters to lose their inhibitions, both physical and mental. We also have a nude bathing policy.'

'Hey, talking about swimming, I sure wouldn't mind a dip right now. It sure as hell looks inviting,' said Rod.

'Go right ahead,' said Bill. 'You too, Martin.'

'That sounds nice, Hold on a sec. I'll just go and get my trunks,' said Benson.

Bill shook his head. 'Uh-uh', he said. 'You weren't listening, Martin.'

'Er . . . but I thought that was just for the boys. I mean, what if Mrs Manley wants a swim. Or the Big Sister of Thoreau?

'Skinny-dip or no-dip. It's one of the rules of Camp Manley. No exceptions. It was in the brochure. Didn't you get a brochure, Martin? We sent a whole bunch to BUNAC.'

'Did you? Well, I didn't get one.'

Bill frowned. 'That's a damned shame. It contains our *desiderata*.'

'Does it?'

'You read it to me over the phone. It sounded . . . like . . . liberating,' said Rod, taking off his pants.

'That's the word, Rod. I'm glad you used that word. It's a word you'll hear a lot of here at Camp Manley. It's our whole *raison d'être*, you know. Liberation.'

Benson was busy twisting one of the braces buttons off his trousers. If you kept twisting in one direction the button came off like an apple off a tree. It must be some sort of fatigue that causes that.

'You look unhappy, Martin,' said Bill. He too was taking off his clothes. Rod had already finished undressing and was waving his arms about, stretching, showing off his torso. 'Come on, don't be ashamed. It's easy after the first time.' Bill reached over and tousled Benson's hair.

'Well . . . er . . . I suppose I can have a go,' said Benson. 'It's just I'm not used . . . I mean I'm a bit self-conscious.'

'Hold it right there,' said Bill. 'I understand exactly where you're coming from. Don't be self-conscious about being self-conscious, Martin. That's how you'll be able to empathize with the kids. They feel exactly the same as you.' And Bill took off his pants and slip, then his T-shirt, and stood naked in front of Benson. He started to sing 'Oh Freedom' – under happier circumstances one of Benson's favourites – holding his arms above his head and slowly rotating, giving time for Benson to imbibe the sight. Rod joined him. Benson was gratified to note that Rod had a bit of a spare tyre.

Benson, debating whether his spare tyre was better or worse than Rod's, prepared for the inevitable. He decided he would just have to try not to worry. Pretend you're alone, he told himself. They are an illusion. They have ceased to exist. You are alone with the trees and the jetty and the lake. He started to undress.

In no time at all he was nude. The breeze blew against his body, cooling it. He glanced over at Bill and Rod. Rod was regarding Benson.

'Christ, you're not cut,' he said.

'Er ... no. You are, aren't you?' Benson asked tentatively. He had noticed straight off but to admit that he had noticed was to admit that he had looked. Also – and he had thought this before – how would he know if he had never seen anybody nude before? They were not to know that such matters were an obsession.

'How does it feel?' asked Bill. 'You see, almost everyone is circumcised over here. Doesn't it make sex difficult?'

'Er ...' said Benson. Sex had always been difficult, but not because of foreskins. 'Aren't we going to have a swim?' he asked, his hand jittering around his privates like Adam, longing for the lake to clothe him.

'Sure,' said Bill. 'We'll talk it through later.'

'Can you dive here? I mean, is it deep enough?'

Bill said, 'Sure,' and Benson ran towards the end of

the jetty, aware that his bottom was probably wobbling. Still he would banish their contempt by the quality of his running dive.

He launched himself into space. In the air he tried to savour the feeling of flight but it never lasted long enough for his brain to register it properly. He was ripping through the cold, effervescing water of the lake, swimming great breast strokes underwater. He kept on and on, thinking that Bill and Rod would be worrying. Finally, he made for the surface and swam a few fast strokes to show Rod and Bill he had plenty of puff left, and then looked back to receive the acclaim that was, he felt, his due. But Bill and Rod were swimming too and had not even noticed his prodigious ability to swim underwater. He lay on his back, his penis lolling above the surface. It did not look bad. It didn't dangle like Bill and Rod's but it was nothing to be ashamed of. He was in America and had broken a big taboo. He was swimming in the nude and the world had not ended. Walt gazed down on him, slipped him a wink.

'You're a damned good swimmer,' said Bill to Benson as they lay in the sun to dry off. 'You'll be our lifeguard. Everyone has to take on an extra responsibility apart from Cabin Brother. I've already got Rod taking charge of the kids' allowances. Debby's in charge of the shop. Dexter's camp fire entertainment.'

'Yes, I don't mind that. But will I have to be nude all the time? I don't know that I fancy being around the kids in the nude.'

'Now, that's very interesting, Martin,' said Bill. 'Why do you say that?'

'Well, it . . . er . . . just doesn't seem right. How old are the kids?'

'Ten to fourteen. But I'm really interested in your hang-ups. Do you feel you want to talk about it?'

'How do you mean?'

'Well, why are you worried about being nude around the kids?'

'Well, it's just embarrassing,' said Benson.

'Are you embarrassed now?'

'Yes, I am, to tell you the truth.'

'And why do you think you feel that way?'

''Cause he's English that's why,' said Rod. 'They spend their whole lives being embarrassed. Have you ever been to a dance there? Christ, they're all so uptight it hurts.'

Bill – to his credit, Benson thought – ignored Rod. 'Didn't you ever shower with other boys in school?'

'No, I wore a bathing costume when I showered. I went to a Catholic school, you see.'

'Ah,' said Bill. 'I didn't notice that on your resumé. Not that it would have made any difference. No sir, you're going to be very helpful around here. Lots of the kids are Catholic. You can take them into Liberty for Mass on Sundays. But I can empathize with what you're going through. Christ, I'm amazed you're as relaxed as you are. Still, you have to try to overcome this embarrassment stuff. Seeing you in the nude will *help* the kids. Emily and I believe strongly that hiding the body is the root cause of a lot of hang-ups in kids. They should see their parents in the nude starting from an early age. Jupiter X – that's our kid – he always takes his shower with his mom and dad. He'll grow up used to the human body, knowing that it's nothing to be ashamed of.'

'Jupiter X? Is that your son's Christian name?'

Bill nodded. 'We added the X to give him a growing space. He can fill it in himself later. You can understand that, can't you?'

Benson nodded. He could in a way.

'Like Malcolm X,' Rod said. 'You heard of him, Limey?'

92

'Yes, of course,' snapped back Benson. 'He was killed earlier this year by the Black Muslims. I'd much rather have Martin Luther King, though. He's non-violent.'

'Non-violence is un-American,' said Rod.

'Anyway,' continued Bill, 'we're hoping that Jupiter X will grow up without any hang-ups.'

'That would be nice.' It would be too. He wondered how different his life might have been if he had been Jupiter X and brought up by Bill. He'd have got ragged in the playground, that's what. Carrying a name like Jupiter X around would have been a heavier burden than the couple of stone of wobbly bits which had, in fact, been his lot.

'You know, I think Emily is going to be very interested in you, Martin. I'm sure she'll be in touch when things get . . . er . . . less stressed.' Bill stood up, dried himself with his T-shirt and then put it on. 'Now I'll show you the rest of the place. Maybe we'll be able to find your Brothers and Sisters too.'

The orientation seminar started that evening with a presentation by Bill. The seven counsellors – swelled by the arrival of Louise and Simon on the late bus from Philadelphia – were told by Emily to form their benches in a semicircle around the Conference Tree. Bill stood up, then leant against the tree, introducing himself and welcoming his 'Brothers and Sisters' to the summer camp. The camp was going to be a life-enhancing experience.

Benson was about to enter into the spirit of things and clap but just in time the counsellor Bill had pointed out as Dexter caught his eye. Dexter's look was eloquent. The raised eyebrows above the pebble spectacles, the steady stare through them, the curly, unkempt ginger hair raised in question marks and exclamations, the downward-pulled mouth when he registered that Benson was looking back knowingly at him, all told Benson that Dexter was casting a cold eye on the proceedings. The thought dawned that alienation had its consolations when shared. He looked at Bill, who was running around being positive, then back at Dexter. He did not clap.

Bill continued, 'First of all, I'd like each of you to sing a song. But before you sing your song tell everyone your name and give a sentence or two about yourself. Now I don't want a long song, just one verse is all, enough to show yourself and the group how you can loosen up. I'll get the ball rolling.'

And Bill stood up, repeated the information he had given Benson earlier in the day, and sang a verse of 'This Land is Your Land'.

Bill then chose the next contributor. 'I'm Rod Nicklin. I'm twenty-four and I live in New Jersey. The last couple of summers I worked at the World of Rubber Museum in Akron, Ohio, but I got tired of telling people not to squeeze the exhibits. I start college in September. Between you and me I hope to escape the draft.' There was a rustle of applause, led by Bill. Rod then sang a blasphemous version of 'Blowing in the Wind', missing every note by a hair's breadth. Rod chose Becky.

'Hi. I'm Becky Feinstein and I'm a poly sci major at Smith. I live in Northampton where my father is a doctor. My mom teaches piano. I hope to go to Africa with the Peace Corps after I graduate.' Becky received a high approval rating too and went on to sing 'If I Had A Hammer' in a wobbly contralto. Becky chose Benson.

Benson stood up nervously. He had hardly listened to the other presentations because he was having a hard time trying to think of the right song to sing. At first he thought he would sing 'Maria', but that might go on too long. Then he had wondered about trying 'Desolation Row'. No, a bit negative for the Manleys. 'I'm so Lucky To Be Me'?, 'The Leaving of Liverpool'? When he stood up he still did not have the least idea of what he would sing. The thought also struck him that he had not the least idea what he was going to do with his future. Still, he would have to worry about that later. He slammed the drawer shut and said, 'I'm Martin Benson and I'm from a town across the river from Liverpool in England. I'm twenty-one and I study American literature at the University of Wales, Aberystwyth. This is my first time in America. I don't have the foggiest what I want to do when I finish university but I'm open to suggestions.' This thumbnail sketch was received in a rather muted way. He decided on 'To Sir With Love' and that went down well. He chose Dexter.

'I'm Dexter Bulkington and I come from Butte, Montana. I'm majoring in English at the University of Chicago and I want to experience life in appropriate surroundings conducive to considering my life at leisure, because it is my belief that the unconsidered life is not worth living.' Dexter's statement was received in utter silence. Dexter did not seem in the least fazed, but stood ramrod straight and sang in a fine baritone voice that sent shivers through Benson,

> *Ist auf deinem Psalter,*
> *Vater der Liebe, ein Ton*
> *seinem Ohre vernehmlich,*
> *So erquicke sein Herz!*
> *Offne den umwölkten Blick*
> *über die tausend Quellen*
> *neben dem Durstenden*
> *in der Wüste.*

Then he sat down, forgetting to choose someone to follow. There was a silence, which Benson broke with loud clapping just as Bill was about to tell Dexter about his omission. The clapping did not catch and Benson knew it had not caught but did not stop at once. He had liked what Dexter had said, loved the sound of the voice, though he had never heard the song before.

'Christ, what a downer!' said Rod.

Benson turned round and glared at him.

Bill nodded to Debby, who said that she was at Teachers College, Columbia and hoped to teach in the ghetto. She sang 'Twenty Four Hours From Tulsa' in retching imitation of Gene Pitney, and got clapped. Again Benson caught Dexter's eye.

Debby chose Emily and Emily said that she was Bill's wife and hoped that everything would run smoothly and if anyone had any problems would they please go to Bill rather than her at least for the first few days because she was up to her neck in accounts. She apologized for her voice before massacring a verse of 'I Wanna Hold Your Hand' which was received warmly, especially by Rod, who whooped. Benson curled his lip. Emily chose one of the late arrivals, Simon, who vouchsafed that he was a draft-dodger, got loudly cheered and sang a verse of 'Ramblin' Boy'. He chose the only person remaining, a tiny girl in a long dress. 'Hi, I'm Louise and I'm just hanging out. I plan to go out to San Francisco when I have the bread. I don't sing but I DO dance.' And Louise began to dance about without benefit of music. Then she sat down to much applause.

Bill stood up again. 'I can see we have a swell team this year! A real out-front set of freaks!' Bill nodded at his audience and Rod started a cheer which was taken up by everyone except Dexter, Benson ad Emily. 'Now things start getting really interesting. We're going to do a role-play. It's fun and serious at the same time, like all the best things in life. But before we do that how's about someone getting that fire going. I do believe we've got a couple of pounds of marshmallows to toast.'

More cheers. Rod set about making a fire and Becky walked off towards the kitchen. Benson noted that the loose cotton dress could not disguise her fat bottom. Surely she wouldn't dare swim in the nude, would she? 'Now, I'm going to choose pairs of Brothers and Sisters. Each pair will come into the middle, sit down opposite one another and act out a problem one of the kids might have. As some of you are new to camps, I'll give you the problem. Now I don't want no intellectualizing. You've got to put yourself in the shoes of your kid, OK? First Rod and Louise.'

Benson thought Rod's impersonation of a bedwetter pretty lame. He cried a lot and Louise patted his head. But he didn't manage to produce one tear. Mum had told him that she had watched Rachel Kempson at the Liverpool Playhouse and Rachel Kempson had produced real tears.

Still, the marshmallows were good and he mentally role-played himself selling them at vast profit in England. Then, after making his pile, he'd live in appropriate surroundings and consider his life.

Benson was busy considering Dexter's life on the steps of Whitman cabin later that night.

'I should have gone fire-watching back in Montana, same as I did last year,' Dexter said. 'It was completely isolated. I was alone for weeks at a time. I read book after book. Twenty-five books I read last summer. I just had to glance up and check the forest for fires every once in a while. I didn't realize how lucky I was. I wonder if we ever do appreciate happiness when we have it.'

'But you can't have appreciated it afterwards either, Dexter. If you had, you'd have wanted to repeat the experience,' said Benson.

Dexter nodded slowly. 'You're right, I suppose. What a funny species we are. Only when we are faced by something really awful do we appreciate the joy of *then*.'

'But why do you think this is unpleasant? It hasn't started yet!'

'But how about the Manleys? My morale just hit bottom during that God-awful orientation. It may not have struck you that way, but I've been around types like the Manleys my whole life. Emily with her damned ledgers and money-grubbing and Bill with that camper and the psychological stuff.'

Benson nodded, though he had rather taken to Bill, thought the psychological stuff interesting. Also, he had to try to be hopeful and Dexter Bulkington wasn't helping him to move in that direction. They sat smoking, the only sounds a distant thump from Camp Manley's generator and a Joan Baez song coming out of Thoreau cabin, where Debby and Becky were staying. The stars overhead were the densest Benson had ever seen.

'So what are your duties in the morning?' asked Benson.

'Parent car park. What about you?'

'I'm assistant Chow Brother.'

'I'd rather be fire-watching again. Bears passed the cabin. They were quite tame,' said Dexter. 'Care for a joint?'

'Why not? What were you singing at the orientation, Dexter?'

Dexter was lighting a reefer. 'It was a piece from Brahms' "Alto Rhapsody".'

'I haven't heard it before. It sounded nice. Do you know what the words mean?'

'It's about being lost and found. Hey, do you know Kathleen Ferrier?'

'She's dead, unfortunately. But I know "Blow The Wind Southerly". It was often chosen as Bumper Bundle on *Family Favourites.* I heard that when she opened her mouth you could fit an apple into her throat.' Who had told him that?

'You know, you're the first person I've ever met who knows her, apart from my English professor at Chicago.'

'Then there's "What is Life to Me without Thee?". That's good too . . .' said Benson, chuffed to have neatly caught a dropped name.

'She sings the "Alto Rhapsody" on my record. I've also got an album of her doing *Das Lied von der Erde,* "The Song of the Earth".'

'Do you have it here?'

'No, why?'

Benson took a puff of the reefer. 'I've got a portable Philips in my room in Aberystwyth.' That was not quite accurate. His Philips was in the trunk room. As he sat amid the alien corn his possessions were lying in the dark so far away. Unbelievable!

'Where's Aberystwyth?'

'Well, you know Wales? It's the bit that sticks out on the west of Britain. Hard to draw in geography. Aberystwyth's half way down there. It's a small town, but interesting. I'm enjoying my time there. I'm president of the Overseas Students' Society.'

'But you're English.'

'Everyone says that. Well, it all just sort of happened. I was vice-president in my first year and then the president resigned at the beginning of my second year and they insisted that I take over. But tell me what the words mean on that Brahms' "Swedish Rhapsody".'

'"Alto Rhapsody". I can't remember exactly.' Dexter handed the joint back to Benson.

Benson felt like he had only just handed it to Dexter. He was beginning to feel funny. 'I think I've had enough.'

'Me too. That's the trouble with the oral tradition,' said Dexter.

'How do you mean?'

'Remembering. Imagine having everything spoken to you, like they did before printing. If you let your mind wander, you'd miss something that might not be repeated for the rest of your whole life. We can go back again and again to a piece of writing that moves us. But before, if you didn't listen and retain, you'd miss it.'

'It makes you think,' said Benson, thinking how much he forgot, even though *everything* seemed written down.

'Have you ever heard about the War of the Book?' Dexter asked. 'God, I'd love a Coke!'

Benson shook his head.

'There is an island off the west coast of Ireland called Inishmurray. On the island, St Molaise founded a monastery in the sixth century. You can still see the remains. In the early days of the monastery a scribe, St Finian was his name, lived on Inishmurray. He was known for the beauty of his illuminated manuscripts. St Columba, also an accomplished scribe, visited the island and, under the cover of darkness, copied St Finian's book, *St Jerome's Psalter.* This was discovered and the monks got very angry. They appealed to the King of Sligo, who decreed that the copy of a manuscript is like the calf of a cow, and belongs to the owner of the original. St Columba refused to accept this verdict and organized an army. They fought a great battle under the mountain of Ben Bulben. Three thousand men were slain. St Columba was victorious, but he repented the slaughter he had caused, and left the place. The battle was known as "The War of the Book".'

'That's typical, isn't it? Call themselves Christians! And both of them saints after all that. That sort of story makes my blood boil! Fancy all those lives wasted over a book,' said Benson.

'Yes, it sounds amazing now. Double amazing when you think that the book they were fighting about advocated peace and love. To tell you the truth, I'd like to have been living then.'

'No Cokes, though,' said Benson.

'Yeah. No Cokes. No summer camps either. Maybe there was fire-watching, though. Or looking out for Viking ships. I think I could have stood the cold. God, Martin, I've made a bad mistake coming here.'

'Give it a chance! I know it's a bit odd. But everything will be all right when the kids arrive. It's just a matter of getting into a routine. Also,' he added, in his High Moral Tone, 'you ought to try to get on with the others. What will they think of you if you stand all aloof?'

'Never worry about what other people think of you. Only worry about what you think of other people,' Dexter replied.

Benson thought about that in the moments between wondering why the sky seemed to be swaying above him. Then he remembered that Jung-Ja had packed him a bottle of orange juice. 'I've got something we can drink,' he said.

They walked towards Longfellow cabin. And as they walked the sound of the generator died. The small lights all around slowly faded and they found themselves in the middle of darkness. Joan Baez sank and stopped.

'That's more like it,' said Dexter.

*   *   *

'Right, Booboo, I want you to tell us about yourself,' said Benson.

'Don' wanna,' said Booboo.

'How about you, Yogi? Will you start the ball rolling? Then maybe Booboo will change his mind.'

'I don' wanna neither.'

Benson sighed. 'You really aren't entering into the spirit of the thing, you know. Go on, just tell us a couple of things. It won't hurt that much, will it? I'll let you off singing a song if you say a few words. Really you're supposed to sing a song too, you know.'

But Yogi shook his head resolutely and Booboo followed suit. Benson had noticed several times that Yogi was Booboo's mentor. They had been the only two of his seven charges who had opted for a new name. The odd thing was that Yogi, although he was definitely the leader, was Boobooish in stature. He was a tiny twelve year old, whereas Booboo, though the same age, was tall, gangly. Still it was definitely Yogi who was the leader. Booboo followed Yogi in everything.

Benson decided to put Yogi and Booboo on the back burner for the time being. The others were getting restless. For the past few minutes Benson had noticed kids from other cabins wandering about free, searching out the names of every building and site in Camp Manley and marking them on their maps so that they would know where everything was. He gave out the maps to his boys. 'Here you are, Velvel. Here you are, Peter. That's for you, er . . . Jim. Here's yours, Leroi . . . with an i. This is yours, er . . .'

'Reggie.'

'Yes, of course. Reggie. This is yours, Reggie. And here's yours Yogi. And yours, Booboo.'

'What is it?' asked Yogi, holding the paper out in front of him.

'It's a map of Camp Manley. What you have to do before dinner is fill it in.'

'You mean fill it out?' asked Reggie.

'Er . . . you just write the name of all the places in the spaces. For example, A is the cafeteria. So you can write "cafeteria" after the A. Now what's B?'

'That's us,' said Velvel, a petit child with black-framed glasses.

'Good, Velvel. And what's our name?'

'Longfellow,' said Velvel.

'That's it. So write "Longfellow" after B. And you do the same for the rest. Now in order to find the other names you'll have to explore the whole of the camp. There's a prize for the first correctly completed map.'

'What's the prize?' Yogi asked.

'Yeah, what's the prize?' echoed Booboo.

A clip round the ear, he thought. 'I don't know. Brother Bill and Sister Emily have them. It's a surprise, I expect.'

Yogi mimed wiping his bottom with the map and Booboo yucked unpleasantly. Benson frowned at them, thinking dark thoughts. 'Right, off you go! See you at dinner! Try and get to know some of the other campers!'

'Mister,' said Leroi, a formally dressed black child of ten who came from Brooklyn. 'I don't understand what I have to do.'

'I've told you twice,' said Benson teacherishly. Then, seeing Leroi's chin quiver, he added, 'Come with me.'

By the time they came to the HQ, Leroi was getting the hang of the activity and was not stopping to have his answers checked. Between the HQ and the cafeteria, Benson noticed Bill Manley crouched down by the side of his Volkswagen camper, which had been driven into the narrow space between the two cabins to be out of sight of the arriving parents. He was drawing the outline of a galloping horse down its right side.

'That's a nice horse, isn't it, Leroi?' said Benson.

'Christ! Christ, it's you, Martin. You startled me. I thought it was Emily. I've come out here to relieve the tension. Painting Angelina relaxes me. It's been hassle-time. Still is as a matter of fact.'

'I've noticed that Emily looks a bit worried.'

' "A bit worried" is one way of putting it, Martin. But it doesn't really cover the territory. You know we're twelve campers short? Emily's as mad as hell. It's a bitch. Still,' and Bill looked at his camper with pride, 'there's always Angelina when things get too bad.'

'Yes, it's good to have a hobby. It can't be easy organizing a camp. It would make me dizzy.'

Bill nodded and turned his attention to Leroi. 'Cute kid,' he said. Leroi pulled back from Bill's approaching face. 'What's your name?'

'Leroi. With an i,' said Leroi.

'That means "the King". He's Martin. You're King. All you need is Luther and you've got a civil rights movement.'

'We've still got some places to find, mister,' Leroi said to Benson.

'Martin. I'd better be going, Bill. See you later.'

Bill, nodding a goodbye, got back into his horse.

'Now where?' Benson asked Leroi.

'This way. This thing by the lake. What's that, Martin?'

'Well, I can't help you, can I? That would be against the rules. Look, we'll go down to the lake and you can ask someone what it's called. Maybe you know yourself.'

Leroi nodded sagely. Yes, that was right, Benson thought. I'm teaching him that he has to find his own answers. Learning by doing, isn't that what Emily said? Maybe I'd make a good teacher. Being with Leroi makes me feel good. But then he thought of Yogi and Booboo. Being with Yogi and Booboo did not make him feel good. No, maybe what he was feeling were fatherly instincts coursing through him. It wouldn't do to mistake those for the urge towards pedagogy. He had felt fatherly before, though that was always alloyed with other feelings when he wheeled Carole around in her pram during the holidays and Hugo around in his during term-time. Whenever he did this he noticed that people – women especially – were curious about what was in the pram. Without shame, they would glance in, coo at the contents, then ask Benson how old the baby was. That felt good. He did not tell any of the women that he was not the father. Rather he took the credit. Of course, when the time came for changing nappies he couldn't be seen for dust, but there was no denying that wheeling a pram had lots of the ingredients for a good time. The populace approved of him. It made him feel comfortable, right in the middle of what made the world turn. If he were a father it would focus his life straight away. He would work hard to buy nappies and talc for his children. But, he thought, if I were a father I'd have to do the necessary to a wife every night. Lummy! The trouble was that he didn't possess the biological qualifications for a pram licence. And never would, unless something really strange happened.

'Are you married, Martin?' asked Leroi, as if divining what Benson was thinking.

'No, I'm just a student. Anyway, don't you think I look too young to get married?'

105

Leroi appraised him. 'No,' he said.

They arrived at the jetty. 'This is it,' Benson told Leroi.

'But what's its name?'

'Don't you know?'

'Harbour?' tried Leroi, looking up into Benson's eyes.

'Well, it could be called a harbour but a harbour is usually much bigger. It begins with J.'

'J . . . J . . . No, I don't know.'

'Jetty. That's j . . . e . . . t . . . t . . . y.'

Leroi knelt down on the jetty and wrote down the word.

They returned to the cabins and Leroi wrote down the names while Benson gave him a thumb-nail sketch of the accomplishments of each of the writers after whom the cabins were named.

'Write your name and your cabin name on the top, Leroi. We'll give in your map to Sister Emily.'

Leroi slipped his hand into Benson's as they were walking towards the HQ. Benson felt hugely self-conscious and after a decent interval excused himself and scratched his nose with the hand. Then he put the burning hand in his pocket.

Emily was rubbing her eyes when they handed in Leroi's paper. He was anxious to be gone and pulled at Benson's hand, a hand only recently released from his pocket.

'You've got a friend there,' said Emily, and she smiled. Yes, he thought. If he wants to hold my hand, why not? Emily looked so much better when she smiled. Everyone did. He would write that down. Benson went out of the office with a smile sprawling across his features, his hand almost at ease in Leroi's.

'I think we'd better see what the others are up to. None of them have handed in their maps yet.'

'Do you think I might win the prize, sir?' asked Leroi.

'Martin. I don't know. You might. Still, the reward is not in the prize, more in just taking part. Where are the others?'

After dinner that evening Bill Manley stood up to talk to everyone. He told the boys to have a good time, to seize the present moment and squeeze all they could out of it. He made Benson stand up, saying that Benson was the lifeguard and that nobody was to swim without Benson being around. Leroi looked up at Benson admiringly.

After wash-up – something that each cabin in turn had to undertake – everyone would gather round the camp fire for songs organized by Dexter, who was also introduced. The following day there would be a day's hike beyond the lake through the Catskills. Anyone who did not want to go should inform their cabin Big Brother . . . 'Or sister,' . . . added Becky pointedly. Benson would be staying around the camp the following day for anyone who did not want to take a nature walk. That was news to Benson. He had rather fancied a ramble.

'I'll stay with you,' said Leroi. Oh, no you won't! thought Benson.

'And now the prize for the best filled-out map. And the winner is . . . Leroi from Longfellow. Take a bow, Leroi.'

Leroi beamed at Benson, stood up and went and collected a gaily wrapped package from Emily.

Yogi leaned over and said to Benson, 'That's not fair! You helped him.'

'I did not,' said Benson. 'I just accompanied him. I'd have accompanied you if you had wanted me to.' Then he remembered all the hints he had given Leroi. Still, it was too late now. He couldn't admit it. Teachers never admitted their mistakes. It was the rule.

'You helped him!' added Booboo, while Yogi spread dissension around the table. The whole cabin looked at Benson darkly while Leroi returned, unwrapped his prize, oblivious to the dark looks aimed in his direction, and took out a mug which said 'Camp Manley '67' on it.

'Well done, Leroi!' said Benson warmly. He frowned down the table at the boys, silently ordering them to congratulate Leroi. They looked at their plates.

In the interval between wash-up and sing-song, Benson felt strongly that he had better answer a call of nature. He could not possibly go when anyone was around. That was just beyond the realms of possibility. He disengaged his hand from Leroi's telling him to mix with the other boys while he went away for a moment. Leroi asked him to put his mug in the cabin for safe-keeping and not to be long. Benson took the mug and walked off towards Longfellow in the dark.

Benson put Leroi's mug in the bottom of the boy's locker, took his towel from his suitcase and went to the bathroom at the back of the cabin. He chose the toilet on the end and hung the towel over the entrance, just in case somebody came in unexpectedly. Then he set to work. This was rather more difficult than he had anticipated. He had still not got back into a daily rhythm after his long flight across the Atlantic. And the catastrophic news of the toilets without doors had not helped matters. There was lots just waiting for release if only he could coax it to come out. He sat on.

There was no pleasure in the waiting. At home he could read the Domestos label, or, if he had had the foresight to bring a book in with him, a few pages of something worth while. Even at Aberystwyth, though the lighting in the toilets was not the best, he would sometimes take time to read.

Then he heard voices. Some of the boys had come back to the cabin. He could hear Yogi making uncomplimentary remarks about the dinner and Booboo backing them up with choice expletives of his own. Well, boys will be boys, I suppose. He sat very still, praying to the Wisdom and Spirit of the Universe that no-one would come into the bathroom.

Benson couldn't hear anything else for a long while. But the silence ended with a gale of laughter from the boys. Then footsteps and silence.

That was a close shave, he thought. The excitement moved him and he produced an excellent stool which amazed him. As a small child he would have summoned Mum in order to receive congratulations. It disappeared round the bend and took three flushes to get rid of. Lots of that must have started down me while I was still in England! The dinner on the plane is probably there. From now on everything will be made in America.

Benson wafted his towel around the bathroom a few times. He was about to leave the cabin when he noticed that the cover on Leroi's bunk did not seem as neat as it had been, and he smoothed down the wrinkles. It was soaked through. He thought of the silence and the laughter. Could it be that Yogi and Booboo had done this deliberately to Leroi's bed? Had they poured water on it out of spite? He sniffed. Was it just water?

Benson stripped the bed and took the mattress off. Then he took a dry part of one of the sheets, wet it under the tap in the bathroom and rubbed down the mattress. He took the mattress off one of the spare bunks and replaced it with the wet one, remaking

Leroi's bed with the sheets and bedding from the spare bunk. Finally, he stuffed the wet bedding into the pillow-case and left it outside the laundry.

'Hello, Leroi, are you enjoying yourself?'

'You were gone a long time, Martin.'

'Not that long. Did you make any friends?'

'I sat with Velvel,' said Leroi.

'That's good, where is Velvel now?'

'He didn't talk to me, though.'

'No, well he was probably singing. That's what we should be doing.' And Benson started singing 'London's burning! London's burning!' In his mind's eye, flames engulfed the Houses of Parliament and all the snobby MPs who had made ribald comments as they made him legal ran out with their fat bottoms on fire.

At bedtime, Benson kept his eye on Yogi and Booboo to see how they would react to the dryness of Leroi's bed. He thought he detected an exchange of glances between them when Leroi got into bed, but it was not enough of a reaction to convince him of their culpability beyond reasonable doubt. He waited until everyone was in bed, then said good-night to the boys individually, switched off the light and felt his way to his own bed.

Benson was shocked to discover that it was soaking wet. Why hadn't he thought to check? He found himself a dry bit and sat on it, trying to think what he should do. He could switch the light on and make a fuss, but was that going to achieve anything? Instead, he waited for a few minutes, then got up and searched around in the dark for one of the spare beds. He did not make it up but took the sheet, wrapping it around himself, pulled the blanket up and set off on his quest for sleep.

He was woken by the bell wielded with great sadism by Debby. Everyone slowly stumbled out of their bunks. 'Now everyone wash and make up your beds before you go to breakfast!' Benson told his cabin. Yogi and Booboo were the last to leave. They hung around the bathroom.

Only when everyone had gone, did they come up to Benson where he sat doing up his sandals. 'Martin,' said Yogi, 'we've wet the bed.'

'You *and* Booboo?' Benson asked.

Booboo nodded.

'Well, don't worry about it. I used to do it a lot too. Nothing could stop me. It's just one of those things. Now gather up the sheets. I'll put them in a pillow-case. Mine seems to have got wet too. That's why I slept over here.'

They did as they were told. They looked up at him as they trundled the stained sheets into the pillow-case he held open. Benson wondered. Hmm, definitely something psychological going on. Still, they seemed very different, much nicer. 'Don't worry about it. By the way, you were right. I *did* help Leroi with one of the things on the list. I just didn't have the courage to admit it last night.'

The two boys looked at one another, then back at Benson.

'That means you've got to help us next time!' Yogi said.

'Even Steven!' added Booboo.

Benson wondered about that. This is where corruption starts, he thought. 'Off you go to breakfast.'

Then he set about sponging down the mattresses before heaving them outside to dry anonymously on the deck. And as he did these chores, he thought of himself less than a decade ago concealing his own stains. Was he any different now? He supposed he was rather. Yes, I'm definitely an adult. Everything in the garden's lovely.

*   *   *

As time passed at Camp Manley things slowly began to settle down into a pleasant routine for Benson. Yogi and Booboo reverted to their normal names – Paul and Norman – on the third day and Yogi-Paul stopped bed-wetting on the fourth. Booboo-Norman did not manage a dry night until the fifth day, but both seemed to discard much of their oddness with their names.

Benson spent some hours each day in his lifeguard's chair, with a book and a towel covering his private parts. But he soon noticed that several of the boys were wearing their trunks and he did not have the courage to tell them to take them off. There was no danger that the Manleys would descend upon them to enforce their dogmas. Bill and Emily seemed to be growing increasingly distracted as the days wore on. With no sign of any further boys arriving, Emily fretted in her office, while Bill painted the camper.

One very hot day, several of the boys from Long-fellow had gone off on a ramble with Dexter and Debby, leaving behind Paul, Norman and Velvel and a smattering of boys from the other cabins. Most of them were canoeing on the lake with Rod and Becky over-seeing them. But a few stayed to swim, play ball or shoot at a basket.

Benson on his elevated chair, wearing his trunks, his book and towel concealing his clothedness, was watching the three Indian-style canoes nosing out into the still lake. Their presence startled the flock of Canada geese who had not, in fact, flown west on that first day. A breeze blew in off the lake. Birds twittered in the trees on its edge. Benson, reading Dexter's copy of *Walden*, then looking up to survey the peaceable kingdom at his feet, felt that this was pretty near heavenly. Would he be more happy if he had no responsibilities at all? No, he did not think so. He had to keep looking up to count the swimmers, to glance around at those playing near the cabins – though Louise and Simon were supposed to be in charge of that. Things could only have been better if he'd had Dearest Him beside him. This was as comfortable and leisurely as life could get without becoming tedious. Take away the easy labour of the lifeguard and he might get bored with *Walden*. As it was he was taking it in snatches, repeating lines of it to himself as he guarded his charges.

He wondered again whether he ought to be a teacher. He couldn't think of anything else to be, offhand. The BBC would never take him on as a trainee news-reporter. He wasn't high class enough. He didn't think that newspapers would have him either. Anyway, he wasn't sure he fancied interviewing people, rushing around after a story. It sounded rather wearing. It might be all right to write a wise column every week like Katharine Whitehorn – his favourite journalist – did. But those jobs didn't grow on trees. Anyway, he had heard Katharine Whitehorn on *Any Questions*? and she sounded as posh as anything. It was too late to be a pop star. Who wanted *another* singer from Liverpool? It might be nice to be a folk singer like the Spinners. They were good, but he didn't play anything. He had tried but just couldn't get the hang of it. His singing voice was all right for folk songs. He could be quite raucous when he wanted to be – his 'Dirty Old Town' was positively fishwifeish, Meryl said – but you had to be able to offer an instrument, or even two.

He turned back to Thoreau for guidance: *Why level down to our dullest perception always, and praise that as common sense? The commonest sense is the sense of men asleep, which they express by snoring.* Yes, that was good. He was glad that Dexter had introduced him to *Walden*. In fact, meeting Dexter had been the best thing that could have happened. There was something about Dexter that he knew fulfilled many of the demands he made on friendship. Meryl had it too. Benson was really not that different from Leroi. He needed to hold on to a hand, confident that it belonged to a teaching body. He did not feel that he wanted to either hold hands with or sit at the feet of Bill and Emily, though they had set themselves up as teachers. No, the teachers he liked were self-absorbed, totally taken up with their own learning. Benson drank at the spring overflowing from them, opened his mouth and caught the big bubbles of enthusiasm they blew over him. He did not want to imbibe what had been dredged up for mere public consumption.

That day by the lake was almost ideal. Once he had to get up and dive in to stop Norman from ducking Velvel, then get them to make up. But that was all.

He noticed some of the boys casting about, furtively glancing at the penises of their contemporaries and the glances echoed in his memory. He wondered if he should tell them not to worry, not to let guilt and its brother, obsession, enter their heads. Curiosity was natural, wasn't it? If they were curious about how their friends were doing, even about how he was doing, that was as natural as being curious about why the luminous paint on his watch shone in the dark, or why you got a pain in your ears when a lift ascended.

But then he thought about himself at that age. If he had decided to let his charges rely on their own wisdom, then might not his teachers have been of the same opinion? He thought about that. Usually he felt that things had turned out quite nicely.

Usually. But it was strange how, just when you started getting comfortable about something, thought you knew the road ahead was clear, allowing you to pedal confidently towards the future, something would come out of a side street and biff your bike.

Dexter had biffed Benson towards the end of the second week. Benson had been about to turn in and had said that he was retiring for a bit of self-abuse. He had said it as a joke, but Dexter had not taken it in that spirit. 'If what you are saying is true I would strongly discourage you.'

'It was just a joke, but I do do it. What's wrong with it? It's either that or blow up.'

'Masturbation is the ultimate in laziness,' Dexter replied. 'It is selfish and leads one away from the search.'

'What search is that?'

'The only search. The search to love and be loved. To connect. If you spend all your energy on solitary pleasure you let the spring go slack, the spring that, at your age, should be taut, pushing you towards the Other.'

'But say no-one wants my taut spring, as you call it? What then? Say my spring propels me towards Others who don't reciprocate. You know I'm homosexual, don't you?'

'You've made it clear on more than one occasion, Martin. I don't think that alters matters in the least. We all have the same responsibility. You know what Forster says, don't you? – and he is homosexual?'

'No. What?'

'Only connect.'

'Well, I'm trying to. I've been trying to for years. But usually what happens is that people want to connect with me just the once.'

'Well, maybe you're looking for the wrong people.'

115

'Usually, Dexter, I am looking for *any* people. I don't have a great deal of choice. It's all right for you lot. Any woman is potentially a lover. I've first of all got to find a man who shares my inclinations – no easy matter I can tell you – and then make sure he is *suitable*! Usually I'm too giddy with lust to check into his credentials.'

'So you go to bed right away, do you?'

'If there's a bed in the vicinity, yes. But I spent most of my adolescence fumbling in toilets and bus-shelters. Most of the time I'd have been better off staying at home and tossing off.'

'Tossing off?'

'Masturbating.'

'No, I can't accept that. You would have probably been better off doing nothing.'

'That was a physical impossibility.'

'It was a physical impossibility because of your lack of discipline.'

'Well, maybe it was.'

Maybe it was. At the time he had thought that his drives were just too strong to be resisted. Had he tried hard enough? He thought he had tried far too hard, so hard that it had made his whole adolescence a headache.

'Perhaps I had urges that were too strong to be resisted.'

'Then,' said Dexter unforgivingly, 'you should have risen to the occasion with self-discipline commensurate with your urges. If you had a bad temper, a tendency to lash out at people with little provocation, you would have had to control it or face arrest and incarceration. Life, Martin, is struggle.'

'And have you always been so virtuous, Dexter? Have you always mastered your flesh?'

'No. But every day I struggle for mastery. Your going

off to "toss off" before turning in sounds to me like the action of someone who has definitely decided that the struggle nought availeth.'

'In that department I think I have. But I do try to be nice.'

'Nice to be comfy, nice to be nice,' said Dexter sarcastically. 'Is *being nice* the farthest limit of your ambition?'

'Well, maybe nice is the wrong word I . . .'

'Because it isn't *nice* to take someone's body and ignore the fact that there is a soul there too.'

'No, but . . .'

'Once the body has been used – once the strong physical sensations have been plundered – connecting, meeting of minds, getting on, being *nice* to someone is pretty thin beer.'

'All right, all right. I'm going back to the cabin to check up on the kids. They should have finished tossing off by now. I won't. I wouldn't have anyway. It was just a joke,' lied Benson.

'Yes, but jokes can be revealing. I like the expression "toss off". You toss off an essay for a prof when it's overdue. Taking little care. You turn something very important into a thing of no importance.'

Dexter had touched a raw nerve by attacking masturbation. Masturbation had been the first thing that, by dint of repetition, Benson had managed to feel completely at home with. To say it was a habit would be saying less than the full truth. Masturbation, just as it had been his first signpost to the realization that he was an erring son of Adam, the harbinger of guilts beyond number, had become, as it lost its halo of guilt and remorse, a daily sign that he had managed to shrug off the Catholic strictures which ran so directly contrary to his inclinations. But now Dexter had attacked this lynchpin of the new Benson. Worse,

117

he had launched his attack from an obtuse angle which had taken Benson completely by surprise.

Benson's unloving experience with a Welsh farmer – though it had ended after only two encounters – continued to figure in his fantasies. But the bald fact had become decorated as time passed. The farmer brought his friends, first to watch, then to participate. Whole Welsh valleys were denuded of their male population to play their increasingly wild roles in Benson's nightly stories. He was getting a little ahead of himself, he felt. But what if one day he wanted real life to mirror fantasy?

Dexter that night had attacked him from a new angle. And because it was Dexter who had said it he knew that it would enter his consciousness. He wondered if Alcibiades had been similarly influenced by Socrates. Had he amended his life as a result of his conversations with the great philosopher, or had he gone back to his own ways? There was no way of knowing. But probably Alcibiades had had a go at being a bit better.

But Dexter's Socratic dialogue with Benson was not given much time to bear fruit before Camp Manley folded.

Benson was awoken by Debby's bell, shook his boys awake and saw them through their routine. Then, when the cabin was ship-shape, he accompanied them to breakfast. In the cafeteria the other camp counsellors were huddled together at the table where Emily and Bill Manley usually sat, reading a note. Benson walked up to them, observing as he passed the tables, that it was Generic cornflakes again. And the Generic Cornflake Company were not very good at cornflakes.

'The Manleys have split,' said Rod.

'How do you mean?' asked Benson.

'They've taken Angelina and left,' said Dexter.

'God, what are we going to do?' said Louise.

Benson read the note that everyone had been looking at.

To all our Brothers and Sisters: Sorry we have been forced to do this. We're leaving you. Though camp fees fell short, we used what we had to keep you going as long as possible. Now there is nothing left. Peace.

Emily and Bill

'Does that mean the camp is over?' asked Benson.

'You're getting there,' said Rod. 'Christ and to think I lent Bill my *Book of Changes*.'

'Can't we do *something*?' said Simon. 'Aren't there any people we can contact for help?'

'Only the police,' said Dexter.

'But what about the boys?' asked Benson.

'What about *us* for Christ's sake! We're stuck same as the kids. Leastways they've got loving homes to go to. We're supposed to be earning bread!' said Rod.

Dexter said, 'I think we should carry on today. We've got enough supplies, haven't we, Becky?'

'Sure.'

'I'll notify the police, I guess,' said Dexter.

'Then what?' asked Rod.

'Then the parents will come and take their kids back. The police may be able to find the Manleys, though I can't see how that will help much. They must have been desperate.'

'But don't they own this whole camp and the cabins and everything?' asked Benson.

'No, this was their first year here. These places are set up as summer camps by local farmers and then rented out.'

Benson looked out over the boys as they tucked into

their cornflakes. 'Who's going to tell them?' he asked. Then he spotted Norman pouring salt over Velvel's cornflakes while Paul, wearing a smirk, distracted Velvel by pointing to the ceiling of the cabin.

'Norman! Stop that!' Benson called out in his teacher's voice. The room went quiet and all the boys looked in his direction. He smiled lamely at them and slowly the boys turned back to their breakfasts and the hubbub rose. I can control them, he thought. Then he wondered if he was pleased about that. Perhaps, were he to become a teacher, he would be striding down dinner rooms to pick up erring kids like Norman by the ears without a second thought. He might have grown used to the exercise of power over the weak, like Ian Smith or George Wallace. That way lies perdition, he thought. But if not teaching, what? I've got to do something . . .

'You missed your great opportunity. You could have told them the glad tidings,' said Rod at his elbow. 'Christ, most of my bunch are going to cheer.'

Benson, as had become his custom, barely reacted to Rod.

'You know what I think?' said Becky. Everyone looked at Becky. Benson thought that she had never once come down to the jetty for a nude swim. Now he was never going to see her bottom. 'I think we should give the kids a real day to remember. There's some great chow in the store. We could have a wild cook-out and there are marshmallows enough to feed an army. All the fixings for cakes and cookies. Let's do it!'

'Christ, Becky,' said Rod, 'we've already been taken for suckers. Every day we spend here is a day wasted in getting bread. I'm gonna high-tail it out of this armpit.'

'I think that's a great idea, Becky,' said Dexter, ignoring what Rod had said. 'It's going to take us at least a day to get in touch with the parents anyway. We can't just leave now. Why don't we give them one perfect day?'

'No way. I'm heading out,' said Rod.

'See you around. All in favour?' asked Dexter.

Everyone put their hands up at once.

Debby said that she would keep the kids amused with a treasure hunt, the clues of which she had planned out with Becky already.

Becky said that she'd spend the day getting everything ready for the cook-out.

The other camp counsellors sat round the table as the boys cleared up their breakfast things. When they had finished they left and Debby's voice could be heard loudly issuing instructions from the vicinity of the Conference Tree. Benson looked up at one point and saw a small boy standing in the doorway. The light coming through the door was so bright that it made it difficult for him to see who it was. But he knew. He excused himself and walked over to Leroi.

'I can't come, Leroi. We're having a meeting. You join the others for the treasure hunt. I'll be finished by the time you get back.'

'Is everything OK, Martin?'

Leroi was looking up at him, lifting his hand towards Benson's, then lowering it again.

'Of course it is! Grown ups are always having meetings. They get things done properly for people like you!' Another lie, he thought. Is there no end to them?

Leroi nodded and ran off to join the group. Benson felt his chin quiver.

When he got back to the group at the table, they were busy planning a sports day event for the afternoon. Canoe and swimming races were suggested, running. Dexter asked for further ideas.

'Sack races, three-legged races and egg-and-spoon races. They're a must,' said Benson.

The group looked at him.

Late that night, sprawled amidst the wreckage of the cook-out with Dexter and Becky, Benson had to admit that it had been a wonderful day. Becky had surpassed herself at the cook-out. There were hamburgers and steaks, water-coolers full of juices, trays of brownies and cake, troughs of salad. All the counsellors had slaved over the griddle-covered wire, cooking the meat, while Debby got the kids singing, then lined them up with their plates and cutlery. During the meal, as the boys sat about on the grass, she had revealed a totally unexpected talent. Taking a brand of flame from the fire, swigging from a bottle, she had commenced blowing great plumes of fire from her mouth, to the accompaniment of whoops of delight from all assembled.

After the meal each cabin went its separate ways armed with a piece of paper on which were written their entrance and exit lines for an improvised version of *Cinderella*. Longfellow had, 'Oh, dear! I wish I could go to the ball!' as their entrance line and, 'Cinderella, now you CAN go to the ball!' as their exit line. With the contributions of chunks of the story from the other huts, this built up to a telling of the whole story, enacted on the deck of the administration cabin.

At the conclusion of the show some more songs were sung, more juice drunk, and the boys trailed off to their cabins.

'How did you do with contacting the parents?' Benson asked Dexter.

'Not too bad. I've got a list together. Most will be coming in the morning. Some of them are really pissed off. You can't blame them. Still, they can't blame us.

The police will be here. They say they've put out an alert to find the Manleys.'

'They shouldn't be too hard to find,' said Benson. 'I feel sorry for them in a way.'

'Maybe, but what they did was really wrong, Martin.'

'I know, but I just don't think they knew what to do. You remember how distracted Emily was all the time?'

'They took the cowards' way out.'

'You really are as hard as nails, aren't you, Dexter?'

'Well, I wouldn't have put it that way myself, but I do expect ethical conduct from people. What the Manleys did has really turned a lot of lives upside down.'

'Yes, I know.' He did too. He was dreading the following day, dreading too the prospect of returning to New York without having earned a cent. What would Lee-Chun say? He had hoped that the money earned at Camp Manley would finance him on a trip through the Southern States but his time at Camp Manley, while it had given him lots of worthwhile experiences, had left him almost completely bereft of funds. He had twenty dollars back in Jackson Heights. But that was it. 'What are you going to do, Dexter?'

'It's back to Montana. I'll take a bus from New York. In a week I'll be fire-watching.' He stubbed out his cigarette, then looked at Benson. 'You could come along if you like. My folks are always pleased to see a new face, and you could get a job with me probably.'

'Could I? Thank you very much for asking. I'm not sure, though. I'll have to talk to my friends in New York.' But he knew that he wouldn't be going to Montana. He did not have the bus fare. 'Will you give me your address?'

'Of course I will. When do you think you'll be leaving for New York?' Dexter asked.

'As soon as possible, I suppose.' Benson looked past the embers of the fire, down to the jetty and the lake where an almost full moon was sailing. 'I've been happy here.'

'But in the middle of it all you couldn't have said that, could you?' asked Dexter.

'Yes, you know I think I could have,' said Benson. 'In fact, I'm absolutely positive I could have.'

They set about clearing everything away.

3

INDUSTRY

When true simplicity is gained,
To bow and to bend we shan't be a-shamed.

Shaker song

'So what will you do now?' asked Lee-Chun.

'Er . . .' He had had that question on his mind for forty-eight hours. Now, rather than confront Lee-Chun, his first American Dream a failure, he would have preferred to get on a plane home that evening. But that was no good. Even if he went to the Aer Lingus offices, holding his flight-bag prominently, clutching a rosary, he was sure they would not change his ticket. It was only good for one flight on one particular date.

He had spent a further two days and nights at Camp Manley. At breakfast that first day, Dexter had told the news to the assembled boys, bleary eyed from sleep and the exertions of their perfect day.

The boys trailed off disconsolately to pack while Benson took aside those boys whose parents they had been unable to contact.

These were joined by Leroi, who was not on Benson's list. 'Shouldn't you be packing, Leroi?' he asked.

'I don't want to go, Martin. I'm happy here!'

Benson, flustered, made Leroi look at him. 'Worse things happen at sea, Leroi. It's not as if it's the end of the world. You've really got to try to look on the bright side. You're a big boy now,' he said mechanically.

Leroi nodded, quite composed. He sniffed some snot back into his nostrils. Benson searched in his pocket for a paper handkerchief, wondering if he might find a strap and a detention book there too.

Then the boy turned and ran off, leaving Benson certain that the benign man he hoped he was on his back-slapping better days had turned into a monster teacher. How had it happened? Was it something they put in the water-coolers? Had Leroi actually been consoled by his clichés? Or did he feel Benson had let him down?

By five the following evening, all the boys had been collected by relatives. Becky too was led away by a group of long-haired youths in a camper not dissimilar to the Manleys'. Dexter and Benson, their bags at their feet, locked the door of the office hut and handed it to the owner.

'I got paid in advance. It's you I feel sorry for,' he said.

'Thanks,' said Dexter. 'You couldn't give two indigents a ride to the Liberty bus station, could you?'

'Sure.'

Benson sat in the back of the station-wagon, while Dexter sat beside the driver. He noticed that the owner of Camp Manley had a bald spot, and felt his own head. No, it's still as thick as anything. When he remembered to turn around to bid a tearful farewell to Camp Manley, it had already disappeared from view.

On the bus neither had anything to say at first. They looked up the aisle of the bus at the road ahead. Then both came to themselves and Dexter smiled at him. 'You certainly made an impression on those kids, Martin.'

'I don't think so really,' he replied modestly. 'I liked them, though.'

'So why don't you get married?'

'That's a bit of a jump, isn't it?'

'There's no reason why you couldn't find a woman who likes kids too, but isn't that interested in sex. They probably exist.'

'Yes, but I'm rather keen on sex, on sex and love in combination. In theory anyway.'

'But you can't have any children that way.'

'No.'

'So there you are then.' What did that mean?

'What about you, Dexter? Do you think you'll marry?'

'I suppose so. But it isn't going to be easy. I've got to find someone who will be able to get along with me. No easy task, that's for damn sure. Did you know, by the way, that after Whitman's death the doctors removed his brain to weigh it and a lab assistant dropped it on the floor?'

'No! What happened?' asked Benson, appalled, trying to work out what had led up to that piece of information. Dexter's changing the subject, that's what.

'It smashed.'

'How do you mean?'

'Smashed to smithereens.'

'Why did you have to go and tell me that?'

'I'm not sure. It just seemed appropriate. Whitman was no hero.'

'Wasn't he?' But Benson was still squirming from the thought of Walt's brain smashed on a laboratory floor. *I am not contain'd between my hat and boots.*

'He puffed up his poetic self with health and strength and lofty love of comrades, but really he was a mixed-up neurotic.'

'Yes, but – *Do I contradict myself? Very well then I contradict myself. I am large, I contain multitudes –* the character of the writer doesn't invalidate the truth he expresses in his art,' said Benson. Then he wondered what had made him come out with that. He did not really believe it. At least he had not believed it before. The character of Wagner kept him away from Wagner, that and the dreadful din. It would not keep him away from Whitman, however. 'All you're saying is that he was a real human being. Feet of clay and all that.'

'Yes, maybe that's it.'

129

'Ah, but the rest of Walt was made of everything precious!' said Benson. And he changed the subject.

He stayed with Dexter until his Greyhound drew away from the bus terminal, waving at the darkened windows until it disappeared down a ramp. Then he walked back into Manhattan, grieving for the way the present had of disappearing into the past. Of course it happened all the time, but it had not struck him so forcibly before. He recited the names of his boys as he walked. Then of the counsellors. But by the time he had passed the shoeshine men in Times Square subway station his thoughts were completely taken up with the problematic future.

* * *

Lee-Chun said that the Manleys' lack of responsibility was a sign of the times. Benson, he said, should forget summer camps and get himself a social security card. That was a passport to a real job. All Americans had a social security card with a number on it. With a social security card no-one would ask him whether he was an American. Half the population of New York City spoke with a foreign accent anyway. Benson could blend into the melting pot as easily as anyone.

'But how easy are they to get?'

Lee-Chun clicked his fingers to show how easy it was.

And it had been easy. Lee-Chun took him down to an office where lots of lost-looking people were milling about. He helped him fill in a form. They waited for an hour on a bench and then a clerk shouted 'Martin Benson', and gave him a little card with his name, address and a number on it. She even smiled at him as he took it, his hand shaking.

130

'That is yours for life,' said Lee-Chun. 'Keep it carefully.'

The little card did not look like something of value. It was hardly more substantial than a train ticket. Benson had been hoping for something more monumental. Above his name and address was the number: 055–44–2889. Still if it would help him find a job it was worth holding on to. Benson put it into his wallet, pleased to have something important to put behind the transparent plastic. He threw away some Embassy gift coupons.

The following day – after scanning the pages of the *New York Times* to no avail – Benson left the apartment with Jung-Ja and walked with her to the local Macy's.

They wandered around the store for a while. Jung-Ja bought a garlic press in the kitchen department. On their way home they passed an office with 'Manpower' written on the window. A sign stated that Manpower was looking for temporary staff for all kinds of jobs and that the pay was good.

Jung-Ja didn't want to go in with Benson, but neither did she want to stay outside alone. Inside there was a counter with a glass partition above it. Benson walked up to it and asked what jobs were on offer.

'Fill this out,' said the girl.

He wrote his name, address, phone number, social security number. Then he had to tick the boxes, scores of them, next to the skills that were listed.

'I don't seem to have any skills,' he told Jung-Ja. He had got to the bottom of the first column without writing one tick. Why, he wondered, isn't there a box for 'winning smile', or 'well-read', or 'good at holding people's hands'? He almost ticked 'typing' but then recalled that he could only do it with two fingers. Anyway they wanted to know how many words per

131

minute and he did not think that four or five would impress the Manpower people.

He got to the bottom of the second column too without ticking anything. Well, he hadn't had any chance to be a receptionist or a filing clerk or any of the other things. He handed his very empty-looking form back to the assistant, thinking that she would say she couldn't help him.

Instead she wrote something on the form and said: 'Minimum wage,' to him.

'How do you mean?'

'We can offer you manual labour – kind of non-skilled. You just don't seem to have any marketable skills. Can't you type?'

'No, not really.'

'Well, are you prepared to accept manual labour?'

'What's the pay?'

'Minimum wage. That's a dollar fifty an hour. You might get a dollar seventy-five.'

That's about twelve shillings an hour! If that's the minimum I wonder what I'd have got if I'd managed to tick some boxes! 'Yes, that would be all right. I need a job. If you can find me one, I'd be very grateful.'

The girl smiled at him, as if gratitude was something she did not get every day. 'OK. Come back tomorrow at seven a.m. We'll tell you the name of your employer and give you directions to get there.'

'Thank you very much,' said Benson. Another smile. Benson opened the door and stood aside for Jung-Ja to pass.

'That's good, isn't it, Jung-Ja? Lee-Chun will be pleased I've managed to get something so quickly.' Jung-Ja nodded. He was not sure she had understood. The garlic press had only been seventy-five cents! He could buy Jung-Ja a garlic press every half hour if he wanted to!

They walked back to the apartment in silence. Benson was thinking of a time during childhood when he had been walking with Mum. Their conversation had worked its way round to what he would do when he grew up. He could still remember saying to Mum, 'Well, if I get twenty pounds a week I'll give you and Dad ten pounds and then I'll save five pounds and spend the other five pounds.' He could still remember computing how many Mars Bars he could buy with five pounds. Two hundred! Enough liquorice shoelaces to tie the earth in a parcel. You got four Fruit Salads for a penny, nine hundred and sixty for a pound. Four thousand seven hundred and forty for five pounds, and ditto for Black Jacks. Each week he could build a house of Fruit Salads and Black Jacks.

His horizons had changed little in the intervening years. He still changed salary into the number of edible favourites it would buy him. He tried to mature. A Greyhound bus ticket cost $99 for ninety-nine days unlimited travel. He could earn that in less than two weeks working for Manpower. But then he remembered that those tickets had to be bought outside the United States. Anyway, even if he could have bought one, would he want to? Wasn't he happier staying in New York?

Lee-Chun seemed pleased that Benson had found himself work so quickly, but was not particularly impressed by his wages. 'You couldn't make out on that. Even a room costs fifty dollars a week. Except at the Y.'

The YMCA, he thought. 'Oh, dear. Does it? I feel really bad about this. I think I should look for a place, though.'

*   *   *

Benson turned up at the Manpower office a few minutes before seven. There was a group of men standing outside, waiting for the office to open. Benson greeted them, noting that he was the only white. One or two nodded back to him. They were all smoking. Benson lit a cigarette too. He looked around. Traffic was already heavy. He wondered how he must appear to the drivers in their comfortable cars. He felt like a journeyman about to be hired for the day, and quite liked the feeling. Here he was in the middle of a group of real working men! They should be singing Woody Guthrie songs and sticking to the union! Benson walked up and down, holding his cigarette between thumb and index finger. Then he stood, legs straight and apart. *The press of my foot to the earth springs a hundred affections.*

Walt would have been as comfortable as anything in the company of these waiting men. He would probably have gone up to all of them and given them each a big bear hug, tickling them with his long, white beard. Walt would have seen such a group as brothers in democracy. And – oh joy – Whitman had definitely been a homo. He started searching in his flight-bag for a pen and paper to consign a sudden thought to immortality. Then he looked up at the group of men. No, better not, he thought.

Benson plucked up courage and expansively nodded at his brothers in work. One black man nodded back. Benson seized the opportunity and paced up to him. 'This is my first day. They should be opening soon, shouldn't they?'

'They take their own sweet time,' said the man, whose voice was not as deep as Benson had expected it might be. 'What's your job?'

'I don't know. I'm minimum wage. Unskilled.'

The man nodded. 'You a student?'

'Yes, I'm over from England for the summer. I was working on a summer camp but the people who ran it went off with all the money. So I need a job.'

'Run off with the money, did they?' asked the man, laughing.

Benson was not sure that it was a laughing matter. 'Yes, but it caused us a terrible amount of upset.'

'I'll bet.'

'What about you? Have you worked for Manpower before?'

'Yeah. Like odd days, you know. I'm a student too.'

'Are you? I expect you're skilled, though, aren't you? I was ashamed yesterday. I couldn't tick any of the skills boxes.'

'Me neither.'

'So we might be put on the same job?'

'Could be. Hey, England's near Scotland, right?' said the man.

'It adjoins it along its southern border. You see England is part of the United Kingdom. That includes England, Scotland and Wales. Yes, and sort of Northern Ireland.'

'You all have too many names for your country.'

'Yes, I suppose we do a bit. My name's Martin, by the way.'

'Earl.'

At this point, in a perfect world, Benson mused, now would be the time to invite Earl to one of my coffee mornings. Wouldn't it be nice to be a housewife and go out meeting people all day and then have them back for coffee?

The office opened and Benson waited with Earl at the back of the queue. When their turn came Earl went up to the counter and gave his name to the woman.

'Right, Earl, you been to the Woodside Industrial Coathanger Plant before?'

135

'No.'

'It's real easy to find,' and she took out a map. 'Here's Woodside station. Then you go down Twelfth Street and make a left on to Pine. It's straight down Pine on the right. I think someone else is going there too. They want two workers. They're taking inventory.'

'Maybe that's me. I'm Martin Benson.'

'That's right.' She handed a letter each to Earl and Benson. 'Just take the subway to Woodside. You'll be all right after that. Hand Mr Trabulsi this letter. Come back Friday evening for your pay. Good luck, gentlemen!'

Benson left the office behind Earl, feeling immensely cheered that he was going to be working with him. He had already allowed a fantasy to grow in his mind that Earl – perhaps over lunch – would reveal that he was a homo who had been looking for a nice white man for ages; someone who would read Whitman to him and never leave him. Of course it was too early to be having that sort of fantasy about Earl. He had absolutely nothing to go on, after all. Still Dexter would approve. He was not being lazy. No, he was trying hard to connect. He hadn't masturbated since he came to America either. This was due more to lack of opportunity than any self-control on his part. Still, he thought, when the time comes, when I do meet someone nice, I'll certainly be at my very sexiest.

'This is it,' said Earl. Benson followed him off the subway. They passed by rows of little wooden houses, each with their own patch of garden but without any fences. They turned right on to Pine and walked along the concrete-slab sidewalk until they saw what looked like a warehouse, atop which was a gigantic coat-hanger with a suit made of wood hanging from it and 'Woodside Industrial Coathangers' painted on the front of the jacket.

They went through the open double-doors of the factory, looking for Mr Trabulsi.

'Martin, you see them rows of metal containers?'

Benson nodded. You couldn't miss them. There were at least a hundred of them stacked five high along one wall of the factory.

'OK. Now I'll tell you what we want. We need to know how many parts we've got. Things have really gotten mixed up around here these last few months. You need to sort everything so when you've finished the bins will be just like you see them now, except they'll be labelled correctly and only one kind of part will be in each box. How you count them is like this: take an empty box and weigh it on those scales over there. Then, weigh a sample box with a certain number of parts in them. Next, weigh all the boxes with that part and you should get the answer. It's faster than counting them by hand, believe me. Now you don't have much space to work in. Business as usual in the factory and there's a lot of traffic passing back and forth. So you have to use a system that doesn't take up too much space. You get me?'

Benson nodded. It seemed like a terribly complicated job for someone who hadn't ticked any of the skills boxes in Manpower's questionnaire. Also he was to be alone in the job. A dark-haired man, who looked like Bernardo in *West Side Story*, had stolen Earl away. Earl was having to organize long metal poles, count them and put them against the wall in little partitioned enclosures. He was across the factory floor from Benson on a raised section. He had already set to work.

Now, I must think logically, he thought. I've got to do a good job. They'll sack me if I don't. It's as simple as that. I've no union representative who is going to rush to my aid if I make a mistake. Vic Feather is thousands of miles away. I'm on my own.

Benson made a tour of inspection along the stack of bins. His heart sank as he walked. There were washers, different sizes of screw, hooks, pieces of tube – some with a screw attachment, some without – round rubber things that looked like doorstops, transparent plastic semicircles, nuts, bolts . . . there seemed no end to the components. How could a coathanger be so complicated! Never again would he wander through Peacock's and take them for granted. No, he would tell Meryl exactly what had gone into them and if her eyes glazed over and she wanted to talk about different kinds of talc he would chide her for her blindness and tell her that there was an important lesson to be learnt. Yes, that's what he'd do.

He made a second tour of inspection, taking his jacket off as he did so. Although Mr Trabulsi had said that things were in a state of disorder he was relieved to see that most of the bins contained the same component. He took a sampling. In one containing washers he found a number of black bolts but not enough to make added complications. The black bolts were just the sort that a monster on the television had bolted into the sides of his head. He wondered if Mr Trabulsi might miss a couple. He could take them home and terrorize Jung-Ja with them.

Now what I'll have to do first is move the stack away from the wall so that I can separate the bins and then replace them correctly stacked.

Each bin had to be lifted one at a time. Benson had soon lifted half the row, placing it at right angles to the old row. He thought he would inventory the metal washers first and separated all the bins containing washers. He emptied one on to the floor, picked up one of the bins and weighed it. 9lb 7½oz. Then he counted one hundred washers into the bin. The bin now weighed 10lb 4oz. Now what do I have to do next? Think logically. It's a small job as jobs go but it is definitely a cog in the great wheel that keeps America turning. If Walt could see me now – and probably he can – he would be writing a poem about me. He was very fond of labourers. I have to weigh all the washers, making sure that I am weighing washers *and only* washers.

The washers were carefully subjected to Benson's gimlet inspection. He ran his hand through them like Long John Silver, thinking *Gold! Eh, Jim Lad and it's all mine!* as he did so. He found a nut and pounced on it like a hawk on a rabbit. He looked through the other bins for more washers, found a few in the bottom of an otherwise-empty one, along with half a comb and a paper cup. Well, he could see what Mr Trabulsi had been talking about. It was obvious that housekeeping had become somewhat lax. It really was time they invited a new broom to restore order! He would go through the Woodside Industrial Coathanger Factory like a White Tornado.

With a grunt of manly effort Benson lifted the bin filled with washers on to the weighing machine, wondering as he did so why he had taken the bin off the scale. That had been an inefficient move. He hoped no-one was watching. The bin tipped the scale at 41lb exactly. Now comes the hard bit, the bit where I have to have my wits about me. And he subtracted the weight of the bin from 41lb, coming up with 31lb 6½oz. Now, if one hundred washers weigh 2lb 6½oz, what I have to discover is how many times 2lb 6½oz goes into 41. Now I wonder if I should decimalize. He thought for a bit. No, maybe I won't. Er . . . I could round it off to 2½lb. I can do that in my head as easy as anything. If I round the 41 up to 42 I can. Now let's see, half of 42 is 21. Now, a quarter of 21 is 5¼, so a half is 10½. So the answer is 31½. Er, no it isn't. Gosh, I can't do this! Yes, you can! Did the builder of the Brooklyn Bridge give up because he couldn't figure out a little sum? No, he didn't! Bridges flow from the fingers as a result of a million menial tasks. *The same old role, the role that is what we make it, as great as we like, or as small as we like.* Get on with it! He got on with it and decided that there were approximately 1600 washers in the bin. Sixteen hundred! And it's all mine! Mine!

He had sorted about twelve bins, stacking them neatly along the wall, when the hooter went for the coffee break. Everyone seemed to be making for the big doors. In fact he wondered where all the people were coming from. The actual coathanger bit must be through the funny rubber door below the raised section where Earl's working. I'll have to pay the factory floor a pastoral visit at some point.

Outside it was sunny. Most of Benson's co-workers were sitting with their backs against the wall, eating things they had brought with them from home. But there was a big food wagon parked on the street right outside. It was a vehicle completely outside Benson's experience, a bit like a large shooting-brake, but completely faced with stainless steel. The side had been cut away and a rolling top, also made of steel, lifted up to reveal a cornucopia of sandwiches. The sandwiches too were exceptional. They were not the usual squares or triangles you got at home. These were huge things, all wrapped in plastic and overflowing with a generous filling.

Benson gawped.

'Hey, I haven't seen you before,' said the owner of the travelling café.

'No, this is my first day. I'm only temporary,' Benson replied.

140

'You sound English, too,' said the man.

'Yes.'

'Hey, I've been to England.'

'Have you? On holiday?'

'Hell, no. I was stationed at Bent Waters Base, Suffolk in the fifties. You don't happen to know a Lilian Jones at the Live and Let Live pub in Orford, do you?'

Benson thought for a moment. 'Er . . . no. Well you see I haven't ever been to Suffolk.'

'Well you wouldn't know her, would you? I always send her a card at Christmas but I never hear anything back.'

'That's sad.'

'What can I do for you?'

'Well, I was just looking, really. Are you here at lunchtime too? I don't want anything to eat just now, but those sandwiches look very good. Much better than we get in England.'

'Sure I'm here at lunch. How about a coffee now? You look like you need something to help you through it. You're sweating, baby!'

'Yes, a coffee would be nice,' said Benson, reaching round to smell himself. *The scent of these armpits aroma finer than prayer.*

'Cream?'

'No, just black please.'

'Sure thing.' The man poured Benson a coffee from an urn on the back of his truck.

'This is an amazing . . . er . . . vehicle you have here. I've never seen anything like it before.'

'Yeah, she's my pride and joy. Guess how old she is.'

'I don't know. Two years.'

'Nine years old. Yes sir. I never let her down and she never lets me down. Built to last. Beats a woman, you betcha! Only twenty-five thousand on the clock.'

141

'Do you have far to come?'

'Flushing. 'Bout six miles. Say, what you doing in the States?'

'I'm just here on holiday.'

'Some way to spend a holiday.'

Benson told the man about Camp Manley. He commiserated.

Earl came up and Benson asked him if he would like a coffee. Earl consented to a tea which he milked with a packet of Coffeemate. 'This is Earl. He's temporary too.'

The man nodded at Earl. 'Well I'd better be off. They stagger the breaks so's I can get round. I'll see you at lunch.' Benson waved the café-truck around the corner.

'How are you doin'?' asked Earl. 'I've been watching you working your butt off. You sure as hell seem anxious to finish.'

'No, it's going to take me days. But you know, Earl, I'm really enjoying it. I've never done work quite like it before.'

Earl gave him an odd look. Then he said, 'I think the work sucks. It's boring, man!'

'I'm not bored. Not yet anyway.'

'So if you're not bored, take your time. At the rate you're going you'll finish a five-day job in three.'

Benson thought about that. 'I don't think I'm hurrying. I'm really quite comfortable with the pace. The thing is, if I slow down, it would probably become boring.'

The hooter for the end of the break blew and Earl, crushing his coffee cup, turned on his heel and started walking back towards the factory door without another word.

Benson returned to the mayhem of bins and components wondering what Earl was talking about. He got down to work again, deciding that he would audit the pretty plastic semicircles first. There were enough of them to fill several bins, yet on their own each piece hardly weighed anything at all. He held one up and thought how with a clasp through one end they might make nice ear-rings for Meryl. Then he emptied a bin, put it on the scales and counted five hundred of the pieces in order to add half a pound to the empty bin's weight. Mr Trabulsi passed by, giving him a nod. Benson smiled and ran his hands across his streaming brow, before tipping another binload of components into the bin on the scales.

He thought as he worked how odd it was that Earl should want to slow down his rate of work. To have to think every five minutes, 'Am I going too fast?' robbed the labour of the best thing it had to give him. He had been in a bit of a dream as he walked out to take his break. The lifting, moving, weighing, computing, had completely filled him up. The passing of other workers he had noticed, nodding to them, gaining more satisfaction from the fact that they could see that he was doing a good job. As usual, his motives were mixed. *Worry about what you think of other people.* But that was not the main motive. Mainly he was taking satisfaction from the work. The work made its own demands, created its own logic and, finished section by section, bestowed its own rewards.

He collected three and a half bins of plastic semicircles. They shone. There were 42,000 of them. Yes, they'd make nice ear-rings. How much would each one be worth? Maybe five cents. He could get an ear-ring attachment for another ten cents. He could probably make a pair for less than fifty cents, sell them for ninety-nine cents. If there were 21,000 pairs in his bins here that would be a profit of over ten thousand dollars! Still, imagine if no-one wanted to buy them, if no-one shared my vision of them as fitting compliments to women's ears! I'd be stuck with them. Yes, that is what would probably happen, and when he died loving nephews and nieces would come to pack up his things to take them off to the St Vincent de Paul Society and would come across 21,000 pairs of ear-rings in the bottom of his wardrobe. They'd go to Alice in her rocking-chair to ask what they were:

'Your Uncle Martin's attempt at business. He just couldn't shift them, children. I wore a pair to show willing but they were greeted with total indifference up and down the county borough. But I want you to read his journals. For fifty years he made sandwiches which he sold from the back of a Morris Minor Shooting-Brake. The current health of the workers in South Lancashire and North Cheshire is largely due to the quality of Uncle Martin's sandwiches. They were as generous as he was, children. And all the time he kept a journal. Open it, children, and read Uncle Martin's wisdom.'

'What does this mean, grandmother?'

'Read it to me, child.'

'Masturbation is the ultimate in laziness.'

'Never you mind. Just go and put the kettle on.'

Benson switched his attention to a set of heavy rivets, rivets so heavy that he could not imagine them having any part to play in the putting together of a coathanger, even the most industrial one. These he counted by hand. Their shape and weight satisfied him as they moved through his hand. There was no denying that they were phallic. Rivets held bridges together. They held everything together. The shape was elemental. Skyscrapers and church spires. Door-posts. The phallus was everywhere. Everyone's dead fond of them but they'd never admit it. Hypocrites!

The morning passed in a flash. He bought himself a

submarine sandwich from his new friend, who talked some more about his time stationed in England. Apart from Lilian Jones at the Live and Let Live, English girls had been cold. Benson pulled manfully on his large sandwich while nodding sage agreement. He took a swig from his bottle of Pepsi and told the man that French and Swedish girls were a much better bet. Then he wiped his mouth on the back of his wrist ignoring the painful biff his Timex gave his front teeth because he could see that the sandwich-man was definitely warming to him.

'The name's Harry. Don't think I told you that. What's so good about French and Swedish women, Martin. You know, man to man?'

Benson swallowed his hunk of sandwich, screwed up his eyes like John Wayne looking across the prairie, and tried to think of ways in which French and Swedish women might be better. 'They've got long legs,' he said, suddenly shocked because it felt as if the statement had come out in an American accent. Why had that happened? Whatever next?

Harry nudged him and confided, 'Yeah! And they can grip you like a vice!'

'They certainly can and they're just not inhibited, not in the least self-conscious. There's nothing they won't do for a fellow. If you get my meaning.'

'I love it! I love it! "If you get my meaning!" Christ, you English sure have a way with words.'

Benson was getting into his role. 'They like a bit of fellatio. Not like English women. It's the devil's own job to get an English bird to give you a gobble!'

'"Gobble!" You're killing me! Yeah, that's right. I never got an English girl to French me! Still, what about the melons on Swedish girls?'

'You can lose yourself in them,' said Benson.

A couple of workers came along for sandwiches.

145

'That new guy. You should have a talk with him. He'll make you cream your jeans!'

The men looked at Benson, smiling broadly. 'He's a real ladykiller! You want ketchup on that?'

The men declined the ketchup and went back to sitting against the wall of the factory, where, Benson noted, Earl was sitting alone.

'Where you living, Martin?' asked Harry.

'Jackson Heights. I'm staying with some Korean friends.'

'Great fighters, those Koreans. Ruthless killers.'

Benson nodded.

'Ever had anything to do with oriental women?'

Benson was non-committal.

'Cat got your tongue?'

He thought of Jung-Ja. 'You know, Harry, I think I'll go and have a rest before work starts again.'

'Sure thing. Catch you later.'

Benson went and sat against the wall a couple of yards away from Earl. The sun shone down pleasantly. He closed his eyes, wondering why he felt the need to enter into such a conversation with a sandwich-salesmen. Mind you, he wasn't demeaning sandwich-salesmen. Salt of the Earth. But it was not the first time he had rambled on about saucy matters of which he did not have the least personal experience. He was always going along with men and the way they talked, chipping in lines of his own that reflected well on his own masculinity. He knew why he did it too: he was afraid not to do it. He also did it because such confidences released a ribbon of camaraderie which wound itself round him and formed a bond between him and the man or men he was with. He did not mind making up sexy stories. That was easy. He would have to be dead or daft not to be able to do a good impression of a lusty man. But there were other areas of masculine experience which Benson just could not make the required leap into. Sport was a closed book. He could not understand it. There seemed no point to it, except in as far as it stopped your spare tyre from overhanging your trousers. Cowboy and war films were another closed book. The genres might have come from Mars for all the effect they had on him. He quite liked Ward Bond in *Wagon Train*, had often imagined himself being led across the prairies by Ward Bond, had not, in his fantasies, been above getting below a wagon with him at dead of night when lonesome coyotes called. But as for all the saloon-bar stuff and the fights and the shoot-outs, well, he just didn't get it.

'You're still working like a field-nigger,' said Earl.

Benson looked over at Earl, ready to chide him. 'How do you mean?' he asked severely.

'Just what I said. How you think it makes me look?'

'Frankly, Earl, I don't think anybody notices. They're just letting us get on with it.'

'Frankly I think they all notices,' said Earl, putting on an English accent. 'Dollar fifty an hour just isn't worth the kind of sweat you're putting in.'

'Well, a dollar fifty is quite a lot of money to me. It's twelve shillings.'

'Well let me tell you that I live in America. I am a citizen of the USA and I know that a dollar fifty is chicken shit.'

'Money isn't everything,' said Benson.

'Here it is. You'd better believe that it is.'

'But what you want me to do would just make the work harder. Can't you see that, Earl?'

Earl did not reply, just closed his eyes against Benson and the sun, leaning his head back against the wall, leaving Benson watching him, thinking how how beautiful he was, but that, though – or maybe

147

because – he was beautiful, he did not think much of Benson.

By the time the hooter blew for the end of the working day, Benson had sorted a third of the bins. He was covered in sweat. Dust had attached itself to the sweat. People on their way home nodded to him. He lifted his arm to say goodbye, feeling satisfied and not a little manly. He saw himself going just as he was into a pub and drinking a pint of Red Barrel while the barmaid looked at him admiringly. Yes, he was one of those men who kept the fires stoked, the wheels of industry turning. If I'd been here in Walt's time, he'd have been all over me.

He put the piece of paper with all the information of his inventory into his pocket, washed his face in the bathroom, and got ready to go.

At the door of the factory, Mr Trabulsi was talking to Earl. Benson stopped, thinking that Earl would want to walk with him back to the subway, but Earl just looked in his direction, gestured towards him and said: 'You firing him too?'

'No, we can still use him,' Mr Trabulsi replied.

'How come you can use him and not me?'

'I don't plan on getting into no big discussion,' said Mr Trabulsi, turning away. 'I've told you. You were marking time up there. Martin here put in a fair day's work. That's it. Take it up with the agency if you want to.'

Mr Trabulsi was holding out a paper. Earl grabbed it from him and walked off.

Benson wondered whether to follow him, but was worried that Earl might be waiting for him at the top of the street. Instead he said good night to Mr Trabulsi and walked politically the other way. But, he thought, as he walked into unknown sections of Woodside, race riots have started with less cause than this. Being sacked from your job beat by a million miles a leaking fire-hydrant. Perhaps Earl was getting a vigilante group together at this very moment to seek him out! He quickened his pace.

He turned left, soon coming to the main street over which the subway tracks led to Manhattan. He passed an electricity pole with all sorts of boxes and pieces of heavy equipment on top of it. A bit too much, he felt. It could easily cause the pole to crack under the weight. Think of all the components! He walked along the right side of the street, heading towards Jackson Heights. He passed a bar called O'Toole's Irish Tavern. He went in, deciding to test his working man's image by asking for a Guinness. 'Give me a Guinness,' he said. With difficulty he held back the please. Obediently the man poured him his drink. Benson sat down, lit a cigarette, squinted, regarded his grimy face in the mirror behind the bar. The barman placed the drink on a napkin in front of him. 'Thanks,' Benson said and handed him a dollar bill. Then somebody came in. Benson turned to see who it was. When he turned back his elbow upset his Guinness. The black beer fizzed along the bar. 'Oops! I'm terribly sorry,' he said. The barman looked at him. He ordered another Guinness, wondering whether his voice had gone as high-pitched as he thought it might have. He felt sure the barman knew that he was a homo with a dirty face. The barman confirmed his worst imaginings by going to the other end of the bar, where he stood watching a netball game on television, looking, though surrounded by teatowels, napkins and draining glasses, like a real man.

* * *

By the end of his first week at Woodside Industrial

Coathangers, Benson had completed his inventory of all the components. The bank of bins looked much as they had been upon Benson's arrival. Inside each, however, a complete reformation had taken place.

Benson had expected that Mr Trabulsi would tell him he was no longer needed, but half way through Friday afternoon he had asked Benson to return on Monday.

'There's more?' asked Benson, smiling assent.

Mr Trabulsi gestured towards the lengths of aluminium rods where Earl had spent his first day. 'Yeah, plenty. The black guy hardly even started.'

Benson nodded, trying desperately to dredge up something positive to say about Earl. Perhaps he should defend him on principle. But he looked at Mr Trabulsi and remained silent. Praise, like pedagogy, had to overflow.

At six p.m. he arrived at Manpower to collect his pay, his mind anchored on Manhattan. He would shower, change and go off to the city. The subways ran all night. He had earned a good time. *Crowds of men and women attired in the usual costumes, how curious you are to me!*

He stepped inside the office only to be confronted by the sight of Earl leaning against the counter in company with three other black men. Benson mentally kicked himself for not having peered in to make sure the coast was clear.

'Hello, Earl,' he said uncertainly.

'Hi,' said Earl and he turned back to the counter. Well, that was a relief in a way. Earl obviously did not think much of him but at least he didn't seem inclined to be rude. And why should he, after all? Benson had done nothing except his job, had he? The trouble was that Earl would probably see him as just another white

150

man, a Honky, who was out not to give the black man an even break. He probably hated him.

From Monday evening to Wednesday, Benson had kept a weather eye out in case Earl and a gang of Black Muslims should descend upon him. He had gone for a drink each night too. Mr O'Toole at O'Toole's Irish Tavern had been quite hospitable once Benson had lived down the spilt Guinness and told him that his dad had Irish connections and that he was a Christian Brothers' boy.

Earl left the Manpower office with his friends. He did not give Benson another look. Benson sighed, but smiled as the girl passed him his pay. He cheered up and wished her a happy weekend.

Jung-Ja was cooking for the usual Friday night Korean get-together. After the meal the mah-jong set would come out, a bottle of Teacher's whisky be placed on the table and everyone would get down to an evening's gambling. Benson had sat with Jung-Ja in front of the television before. But tonight he would not. Tonight he was bound for Manhattan!

Actually, Benson had fixed his sights on going to the cinema that night. He had read about a scandalous film by Andy Warhol called *My Hustler*. It sounded rude, but it was probably art too. That was the main thing. Anyway, *My Hustler* was waiting for him at the Hudson cinema on 44th Street.

He made his excuses and left the apartment, running to the subway. On the ride into the city he read his copy of *The Confessions of Nat Turner* until, after Queensboro Plaza station, Manhattan's skyline came into view. He thought of the week that had just passed. All that time the Magic Land had been so close and yet he could have been a million miles away from it. Woodside might have been anywhere. The wonderful thing was that it was not just anywhere, it was *here*. He concentrated on the view to his left until it disappeared as the subway screamed into the tunnel under the East River. Benson held his breath.

'When's the second house?'

The woman in the cinema kiosk looked at him.

'Is it continuous?'

'Two fifty.'

Two dollars fifty cents! he thought. I bet they've bumped up the price because it's supposed to be rude. Well, it had better be very rude for two dollars fifty cents.

Benson handed across his money. He wondered which film he should say he'd gone to if Lee-Chun asked. He rehearsed.

'I went to see *Barefoot in the Park*.'

'What was it about?'

'Well, it was a bit boring, actually. There were these two people who went into the park.'

'Who was in it?'

Who *was* in it? He mounted the stairs towards the circle. In American cinemas the circle cost the same as the stalls, not like in class-ridden England where the posh people had to pay more to be out of range of the common lot and could open their box of chocolates and place them on the plush ledge.

The film was on, but it was rather dark in the cinema and Benson had to feel his way carefully to a seat. He hadn't come in during a very rude bit. An elderly man in a bathchair was talking on a beach. Benson sat, paying close attention.

As his eyes grew accustomed to the dark he saw that not many New Yorkers had thought it worth their while to part with two dollars fifty cents. There was a man seated to his right on the far side of a pillar. There were three or four others in front of him. As the film

152

went on Benson became more and more depressed. It didn't seem in the least bit rude. There wasn't even a story that he could detect, just odd types talking away. Even the cameraman couldn't seem to be bothered to keep the camera still. It jiggled around like mad. What could have got into Andy Warhol to neglect to find a decent cameraman? Probably he found someone who had ticked the wrong box at Manpower and then didn't have the heart to sack him. No, he thought, this is all snooze and boredom signifying nothing. Even Dr Clitherow's holiday film from the Tyrol had been much better than this, and Dr Clitherow had done it all himself, apart from the developing. He wondered briefly whether he could get his money back and go and see *Barefoot in the Park*, but he knew his plea would get short shrift from the woman at the kiosk.

A man with bleached hair appeared in a bathing cos-tume. He was well-built. Ho took off his bathing costume and got into a pair of trousers. For about three seconds Benson was treated to a not particularly attractive penis. Then the man was zipping up his jeans. Surely that couldn't have been the rude bit, could it? What a swizz! I ought to write to my MP. You got more rude bits in the average Armand and Michaela Dennis film.

Still it looked like that was going to be the lot. They were now back to the old fellow in the bathchair. Just because Andy Warhol had come up with the idea of painting a soup tin, he thought he could produce anything and call it art! Why his ear-rings made out of semicircles of plastic would have more art to them than *My Hustler*.

Then Benson felt something against his leg. It gave him a fright. They had rats in New York which bit babies in Harlem. He jerked his leg away and felt down gingerly, wondering what he would do if he came into contact with a rat. His right hand touched a shoe. He drew his hand away, saying, 'Excuse me.'

He returned to watching the film, but his attention was centred on the foot. It must belong to the chap on the far side of the pillar, but why had he put it right over here? *How* had he managed to do it? The pillar was pretty wide. He must have stretched out to the limits of his reach in order to make it across the distance.

The question was, why had he stretched across?

Benson could not see what the man was like. Was he trying to make contact? He might be. He could imagine that a person as bored as he was by *My Hustler* might well stretch extravagantly like that. Benson returned his foot to where it had been. The object was still there. Benson, by accident, put his foot on the shoe. 'Sorry,' he whispered and moved it slightly. The shoe chased his and placed itself on top of his sandal. It pushed.

Benson did not move his foot away, but neither did he move it one iota. He felt that just the merest twitch in his big toe would signify consent to unknown orgiastic procedures. And he hadn't even seen who the foot belonged to.

The shoe started tapping on Benson's sandal. He thought, I should move my foot. Every second I stay under his shoe is giving him more time to think he has got me. He's probably thinking I'm his Mr Right. The thing is that he's at an advantage because his eyes had got used to the dark by the time I came in. But still Benson neither moved his foot nor peered over to see who it might be behind the tapping.

He got used to the tapping and tried to pay attention to the film. But the film wasn't helping. It was a waste of time. At last he raised the big toe inside his besieged sandal. Alice would be dreadfully upset if she knew he had allowed a complete stranger to step on his new sandals. Well, he thought, Alice is far away. I've paid all this money so I may as well enjoy what is on offer.

Benson, hot and cold and dizzy, started to return the signals. He felt that he was getting into deep water but could always swim back into his depth when the lights went on, if the person was unsuitable.

He felt, though, that it was unlikely that he was going to find Dearest Him in this manner. But then where was he going to meet *anyone* if not somewhere furtive? He thought of Roy Jenkins: *Those who suffer from this disability carry a great weight of loneliness, guilt, shame and other difficulties.* There were no parish dances for him to go to and meet suitable people. If it were ever going to happen, it would probably happen in a place like this.

At last the film ended, though it did not really end. It just stopped, and the lights went on. Benson knew that a long interval would follow and that then he could see the film round again until the point when he had entered the cinema. He thought of Manhattan outside. No, he would not stay. He got up. He looked to his right and saw that the person who had been banging his sandal was really quite nice, an oriental. As Benson looked, dark brown eyes stared back at him.

'I didn't like the film much. Did you?'

The man shook his head. 'Are you leaving? I'll come too,' he said. He had an accent. Partly American, partly something else that Benson could not put a name to.

Outside Benson walked beside the man. 'Where are you from?' he asked him.

'Brooklyn. What about you?'

'England, but I'm staying in Jackson Heights. But you weren't born in America, were you?'

'No, I'm from the Philippines.'

'I've never met anyone from the Philippines before,' Benson said, imagining another flag of friendship stuck into his map of the world. 'What's your name?'

'Pablo.' Benson wrote 'Pablo' on his Philippines flag.

'I'm Martin.'

Pablo did not say anything else. They walked on. Pablo seemed to know where he was going. They were walking uptown along Madison Avenue.

'Er, where are we going?'

'The park,' replied Pablo.

'Are we?' He had then wanted to say that he thought Central Park was dangerous at night. Still, maybe the bourgeois writers of guides felt that people like him and Pablo were the chief danger. Anyway, it had not been firmly established what Pablo wanted. Yes, it had. The wandering shoe was unambiguous, wasn't it?

Pablo said that he lived with his sister.

'I'm with a Korean friend.'

'Is he your lover?'

'No, worse luck,' Benson replied.

And that was the end of Pablo's conversation. They passed the Plaza Hotel, walking west on the park side of the street, past where Benson had seen the horses on his walk with Virginia. Then they turned right at Columbus Circle, past a newspaper kiosk, and along Central Park West.

'Those buildings look nice. I mean, the people have a lovely view,' said Benson.

'Barbra Streisand lives in that one.'

'Does she? The lucky thing! I like "People" and I rather like "I'm Five" as well. She's got a good voice, but some of the things she sings I don't like much. A bit soppy.'

Pablo did not respond. He was looking over the low

wall into the park. 'You got to watch out for the police,' he said.

They walked as far as West 63rd Street . . . The paving stones, Benson noted, were six-sided and tiny. He could cover two with an easy stride. They must have been hell to lay, the artisan in him thought. Pablo was glancing sternly over the wall still. Then he jumped up on to it and was gone.

Benson stopped. Pablo whispered from the far side of the wall, 'Come on.' But Benson didn't. He was suddenly afraid. He didn't really know Pablo. To go into the park with him might be nice but it might also mean being stripped at knife-point, forced to part with his Aer Lingus flight-bag, his money, his clothes, his sandals. What would he do in the middle of Central Park with no clothes on? If he could attract a passer-by or a policeman they would obviously assume that he had gone into the park for some nefarious purpose. They might take him to the Tombs. There dreadful things would happen to him. He stopped, looking back at Barbra Streisand's apartment building, at the lights winking so homely back at him from there. Barbra Streisand could be sitting there now, tinkling away on a white piano. What would she think if she knew?

Then Pablo was beside him again. 'Why didn't you come?' he asked accusingly.

Benson didn't like to say he was scared, so he said, 'It all seems a bit sordid. I mean, a park is not the place for . . . well . . . you know . . .'

'You're scared. There's no need to be. It's perfectly safe. If I had a place I'd take you there.'

'Why don't we sit down on this bench for a mo?' Benson said. They sat down and looked out, across the sidewalk with its clever six-sided paving stones, across the traffic, to the buildings on the west side of the street. Benson read the name on the building opposite,

The Society for Ethical Culture, Founded in the City of New York, May 1876. Below that there was a plaque with more writing on it, though he could not quite make out what it said. 'Er . . . what do you do?'

'I work in a hospital, the Unitarian Medical Center in Brooklyn.'

'I'm a student,' said Benson. This is the sort of thing we should have been talking about on the way here, he thought. It reassured him greatly to know that Pablo worked in a hospital. Of course, he could be lying. He might be a male prostitute with psychotic tendencies. And psychotics could be very plausible. Look at Antony Perkins. Peggy Lee didn't have the least idea what was in store for her at the motel. Benson wondered how he should continue his interview. He took out his packet of Pall Mall Gold 100s 'The 7 Minute Cigarette. If you think it's just another cigarette, time it!' and offered Pablo one. Pablo said he preferred his own and took out a soft-pack of Salem. Benson lit Pablo's with his Imco, thinking furiously. He stared over at the plaque on The Society for Ethical Culture building. He was now able to read it, 'Dedicated to the Ever-Increasing Knowledge and Practice and Love of the Right.' Why, he wondered, couldn't he see it before?

'I suppose I am afraid, a bit. You see, I've heard horrible tales about Central Park. Er . . . what do you do at the Utopian Medical Center?'

'Unitarian. I'm a nurses' aide.'

'That's nice. What do nurses' aides do?'

'All kinds of things. Same as the nurses really. I'm taking courses at Brooklyn College. In two years I'll be a nurse myself. My sisters are both nurses.'

'How many sisters have you got?'

'Two. I live with Theresa in Brooklyn. Anna Maria lives in a hospital apartment building on the Upper West Side.'

Benson found the names of Pablo's sisters immensely reassuring. 'Are you a Catholic?' he asked.

Pablo nodded. He opened his shirt and showed Benson an Immaculate medal on a piece of string. Benson looked at it admiringly. Pablo kissed it as he put it back inside his shirt.

'I am too,' said Benson. No you're not! he thought. Pablo had passed the interview with flying colours. They finished their cigarettes. Benson said, 'I'm sorry I was such a ninny just now. I'm better now. You lead and I'll follow.'

They stood up. Pablo looked around for a moment, then jumped over the wall. Benson followed, knocking his knee as he did so, but too excited to notice, and Pablo took his hand.

The undergrowth was wild, their footsteps caused saplings to break, dead undergrowth and last year's fall leaves to crackle. Pablo kept stopping, increasing the pressure on Benson's hand. Benson held himself as still as a statue. Somebody coughed nearby. Pablo seemed to know where he was going. The traffic noise had receded even farther. The park had taken over. A bird was calling. They startled some crawling animal nearby and stopped again in fright. Pablo's hands were sweaty, or was it his hands? He could not tell. Any moment, he knew, a gang of marauding Black Muslims could catch them, the beam from a police trap shine on them. *You faggots, come out with your hands up!* That would be terrible. Still, following Pablo was a bit like being guided by Tonto through a jungle. He could trust Tonto, couldn't he? Tonto had an Immaculate medal on. Truly the badge of a gentleman. No, he had nothing to fear except fear itself. He allowed himself to wonder what Pablo would be like. The prevailing wisdom had it that orientals were very petit. He did not know where he had acquired that idea. He could not, offhand, recall a joke that had let the thought lodge itself in his brain on its twin prongs of sexiness and foreignness. He had seen Lee-Chun, but only in its normal state. It was hard to tell. Still, if it did turn out to be true and that he was much bigger than Pablo, he would have to be very careful to be sensitive. It would not do to let his disappointment show. Anyway, he did not know that he would be disappointed, did he? The same preconception that had endowed orientals poorly had also endowed them with vast spirituality, sensitivity and technique. He suddenly remembered where he had found out about oriental penis sizes, from a book on the techniques of love-making which he had perused in Wilson's bookshop on Renshaw Street, Liverpool. Well, he thought, books were often wrong. Look at the Catechism! And anyway er . . .

They crossed Park Drive North. He suddenly fancied a cigarette. The street was empty of traffic. Benson imagined himself alone and dancing to the prologue from *On The Town*. He could close his eyes if he wanted to and not bump into anything. But if he closed his eyes he would miss the whirling sparkling columns of twinkling buildings.

They came out of the undergrowth and were walking in the dark across what seemed to be an open field. Pablo stopped in the middle and sat down on the grass. Benson looked around. 'Here?' he asked.

'Yes,' said Pablo.

Benson sat down next to Pablo. 'Isn't it a bit . . . well . . . open?' He looked around. The tall buildings on the south side of the park loomed over the dark trees.

'Yes, it's open. That's what's so great about it. No-one can sneak up on us. All the gays make for the undergrowth but that's dumb. Here we have everything to ourselves and we're safe. Can you see me?'

'Well, just about,' said Benson.

'OK. Tell me what I'm holding in my hand.'

'I can't see.'

'It's right here. Next to your face.'

Benson felt. Suddenly everything else was forgotten. His sensitive excuses, his worries, evaporated. He lay down in the middle of the park with Pablo while the city stared benevolently down on them.

'It was a lousy film, wasn't it?' Benson said as he and Pablo walked down Eighth, towards 42nd Street and their subway station.

'Yes, I thought it was going to make me horny. Such a piece of shit.'

'Yes. That's a good way of describing it. Do you think Andy Warhol is homosexual?'

'Natch!'

'Well, I wonder why he doesn't make a nice film about us? You know, boy meets boy. That sort of thing. Like us.'

Pablo looked hard at Benson. 'Don't flutter your eyes like that. It gives you away.'

Benson, though not aware that he had been fluttering his eyes, was in a mood of uncaring about what people thought. He felt much better since his time in the park with Pablo. The experience had enlivened him, washed away the bad taste of Earl and three garlic presses down the drain for *My Hustler.* Also, he had not had any need to be sensitive. Pablo was very well-built.

They were approaching 42nd Street and the corner café where Benson had met Virginia. Benson wondered whether he might find Virginia there again. He hoped he might. It would be nice to show Pablo that he had other friends in the city. He asked Pablo if he would like a coffee or a Coke.

They found a table in the café. Benson went up and bought two coffees and, as an afterthought, two large biscuits. These he brought back to Pablo, while trying to keep his eyes wide-open, only blinking when he absolutely had to. Fluttering's out from now on, he thought.

'Your shirt-tail's out at the back.'

'Is it?' He tucked it back in, noting that it had a green stain on it.

'So how long are you going to be in the States?'

'Until September. I shouldn't be here by rights. I was working at a summer camp for children but there were problems and I came back to the city.'

'You have a job?'

'Yes, I'm with Manpower. At the moment I'm doing an inventory of components at a factory in Woodside.'

'I worked for Manpower once. They're thieves,' said Pablo.

'Why?'

'Because they pay you a minimum wage but the factory has to pay them a big commission. It's a rip-off.'

'Is it?' Benson had been feeling that Manpower were nice. They had taken him on even though he had not been able to fill in any of the skills boxes.

'You could get a job at the Unitarian Medical Center. They always need nurses' aides.'

'Could I? But I don't know anything about aiding nurses.'

'They'd teach you.'

'Even if I'm leaving in September?'

'They don't have to *know* that, do they?'

'No, but . . .' It seemed a bit rotten to accept training and then just disappear. 'I mean, what's the point of them training me if I'm going away?'

'There's a big shortage of nurses' aides. They don't

pay well. Two twenty-five an hour. Do you have a social security number?'

'Yes, I do. Lee-Chun, that's my Korean friend, he got me one.' $2.25 an hour! That was a little white radio every two hours!

'Then you can have the job if you want it. And you'd be working near me.' Pablo broke his biscuit. 'I haven't finished with you yet.'

Benson felt his eyes aching to flutter. He looked out of the window and indulged himself in a quick flutter at the passing traffic. Then he looked back and fixed Pablo with a wide-open gaze. 'Yes, I'd like to see you again. I really enjoyed myself with you. I haven't done anything for ages and ages.'

Pablo looked concerned. 'You shouldn't let your seed build up in the body,' he said. 'It poisons the system.'

Benson had never heard that before but he bowed before Pablo's superior knowledge as an experienced nurses' aide and trainee nurse. 'Well I don't really let it build up. I sort of . . . well . . .'

'Jerk off.'

'Yes.'

'It's not the same thing.'

'No, it isn't. It doesn't make me feel like I felt with you. Er . . . do you often go there? I must say it's a wonderful place. But it takes getting used to. I kept thinking that someone would switch the lights on and there we'd be in the middle of Central Park with everybody looking at us.'

'It's the darkest part of the park. I only go in the undergrowth on nights when there's a full moon. That's when I can't find a bed. I usually try to find a place to go. I'd like to get you in a bed.'

'Same here,' agreed Benson. 'It's miserable when you think about it. I always have a bed to sleep in but

163

the one time I find a friend there's nowhere to go. Yet all around the park there are beds galore. It doesn't seem fair.'

'The world isn't a fair place.'

'No. Did I tell you I'm president of the Overseas Students' Association at my university? I hear a lot of stories about injustice, I can tell you.'

Benson had been about to launch into a tale a Biafran student had confided to him when Pablo pointed to the window. Benson followed Pablo's finger and saw Virginia standing outside, her arm linked through the arm of an elderly man with a moustache. Benson waved and gestured Virginia to come in. She shook her head and mouthed 'You come here!'

'Excuse me a minute, Pablo. That's Virginia, a girl I met here a few weeks ago.' Pablo nodded, and Benson got up and trotted round to where Virginia was standing. She was deep in conversation with her companion, who looked grumpy.

'Hi, Martin! What you doin' here? I thought you was out at summer camp!'

'It's a long story, Virginia. The people who owned the place ran away. Something to do with money.'

'So you back in the city, huh? You get to milkin' a cow?' Virginia's companion was whispering in her ear and pulling her by the arm. 'Hey, what's the hurry? Martin, this is Tom. Tom, Martin.'

Benson put out his hand but for a long moment Tom did not take it. When he did he was looking the other way, out to the traffic, mumbling half to himself, half to Virginia, who said to him, 'Honey, you is the most impatient old goat I ever done met *in my life*! Can't you see I'm talkin' to a *frien'*! Johns is two a penny. A frien's *hard* to find!'

'I'm sorry, Virginia. Are you in a hurry?'

'Don' pay no mind, Martin. Tom's only in the city for

a little time. He's from Jersey. He anxious to get back to civilization 'fore some fairy turn him into a pumpkin.'

Tom was trying to laugh but was not making a very good job of it. He was plainly embarrassed about something – about being with Virginia, Benson thought. Well, that's his problem. He had been thinking up things to say to Tom to make him more comfortable, but decided not to bother.

'I'm working in Woodside now. Counting components in a factory. It's not much of a job but it pays the rent – well actually it doesn't – still it's interesting.'

'And you foun' a friend?' asked Virginia, going up to the window to inspect Pablo, waving at him, her fingers pianoing the pane.

'Yes, that's Pablo.'

'He Puerto Rican?'

'No. Filipino.'

'He treating you good, Martin?'

'Yes. We only met tonight but he's very nice. He says he can get me a job as a nurses' aide.'

'You don't say?'

Tom had begun pulling on Virginia's sleeve again, like a young Benson out shopping on his mum's coat. Virginia gave him a look. 'I guess I'd better be going.' And she came close to Benson, kissed him, then rolled her eyes. 'Work!' she said. 'Don' it jus' kill yer?'

'When can I see you again?'

'Honey, I'm always here. I bet this only your second time in that greasy spoon, right? Now, how many times you run into Virginia?'

'Twice.'

'Right. By the way, I still remember our trip to the art museum. We got to do it again real soon. Check out that poor nigger!'

Benson frowned. 'OK, Virginia. I think you'd better go. Bye! Bye er . . . Tom.'

Benson watched as Virginia was led away by Tom.

'Sorry about that,' Benson told Pablo. 'That was Virginia. I met her last time I was here. We went to the Metropolitan Museum of Art together.'

'What does she do?' asked Pablo.

'Can't you guess?'

Pablo nodded. He looked disapproving. Benson thought it ill-behoved Pablo to be disapproving of Virginia only an hour after they had been cavorting together in a public place.

'She's a lovely girl, though! Heart of gold. Anyway, I like prostitutes,' he added, thinking of Melina Mercouri in *Never on Sunday* and of the sensitive way she had helped the impotent young sailor. Benson could imagine himself with Melina Mercouri, feeling that he was not big enough, all shrivelled up and useless and anxious. Melina would have reached over and talked softly to him, made him feel like a real man. She would have told him that she had had half the world in this room in Piraeus and that Benson was the best by a long chalk. Of course, it might not have been true, but Melina could have made him believe it. He felt that with Melina's encouragement he could have performed quite adequately, even though, deep down, he would have preferred the sailor.

'Yeah, but your Virginia's a man,' said Pablo.

'Sorry?' asked Benson.

'She's a man,' Pablo repeated.

'Sorry?' Benson repeated.

'Like I said, she's a man. You can always tell.'

'How can you tell?'

'How can you *tell* anything?'

That was no answer, Benson thought. 'Well, you've just said something pretty strange, you know, Pablo.

Now you've got me wondering. I mean, I know there are people who like to dress as women, but I've met Virginia before. We spent a whole afternoon together and not once did I think that she might not be a girl. She's got breasts, anyway.'

'Falsies. Hey, Martin, you sure can run off at the mouth, can't you?' Then, seeing Benson's expression turning from uncertain to stormy, he added, 'Just kidding. Hey, it was sad about Jayne Mansfield, wasn't it?'

Benson agreed that it was, happy to go along with the change of subject.

'They say the crash knocked her head right off.'

'Did it?' Poor thing, he thought. Eternal rest give . . .

'And Vivien Leigh died too. My sisters were real upset. They went to see *Gone With The Wind* three times the week after she died. I made out like crazy. *Gone With The Wind* goes on for ever.'

'I've never seen it. I saw her in something about Lady Hamilton. She was married to Laurence Olivier, you know.'

Pablo nodded. 'Let's go!'

They walked along 42nd Street. Benson looked at all the women in skimpy skirts, wondering if they were quite as they appeared. Maybe New York homos were able to find more friends by dressing as women. He wondered if he should have a go. He tried to imagine himself in a dress. No, that way madness lies!

'Can I see you again?'

'Sure you can. Think about becoming a nurses' aide,' said Pablo. They swopped addresses next to a cinema showing a double bill; *I, A Woman* and *Night Games*. And it was only a dollar fifty to get in!

'I really enjoyed our time in the park,' said Benson, fishing his address book from his flight-bag.

167

'Stop fluttering your eyes, yo-yo!' said Pablo.

Benson left Pablo at the 42nd Street subway station. He asked him what he was doing the following evening, but Pablo said he was working.

'That's a pity,' Benson said. 'There's a Pete Seeger concert in Central Park tomorrow. It's organized by the Rheingold Beer people and it only costs a dollar.'

'I'll call you Monday,' Pablo promised. As he handed Benson his pen back, he pressed his hand. Benson pressed back, attempting to make the gesture eloquent – full of hope, romantic rhymes and Khalil Gibran.

On the subway he wondered about Virginia. What had made Pablo think she was a boy dressed up as a girl? True, her face was a bit on the masculine side, but that often happened. Pablo's face under certain lights could have been that of a girl. But surely, if Virginia were a boy, Benson would have noticed, wouldn't he? He wasn't that thick, was he? Maybe he was.

He knew why he was slow. He was a latecomer to the party of independent thinking. Until the age of eighteen he had let the Catechism do the thinking for him. He was way behind. And perhaps that was why he also tended to fall under the influence of strong personalities too. He often trotted out Meryl's opinions about life and art as if they were his own. It was sometimes enough that Meryl had said it for it to become part of his arsenal of truth. Katharine White-horn had the same effect on him. And Dexter had now been added to the list.

This queer twist to his character worried him rather. If a priest or a politician appeared on the television Benson was busy firing off counterblasts to everything they said. If Dad and Alice had been able to hear his silent reponses to what was said on the boring religious programmes on a Sunday night, they would have said that he was cynical. But he wasn't cynical about anything Joan Bakewell said on *Late Night Line Up.* And, though his experience of the London theatre was non-existent, if Harold Hobson said a play was good, then the play at once got Benson's *imprimatur* and *nihil obstat.*

If Virginia were to turn out to be a man, what did that mean? Had she actually had her penis cut off? What a waste that would be! But perhaps she just put on ladies' clothes and left the rest as nature intended. But what did nature intend? Perhaps Virginia felt like a woman and had therefore felt more comfortable, more herself, in skimpy leather skirts and tight tops, talking like a lady. Nature had played a cruel trick. And what about him? If he were honest with himself – and what did *that* mean? – then it was obvious that nature had intended him to be a man. He had all the physical characteristics of a man. But then he thought of his time lying in Central Park with Pablo. There, in the dark, at his most honest, he had wanted to be taken, to be penetrated, to be possessed, as surely as any romantic heroine. His penis at its most erect gave the lie to his desires. In his way he was as split as Virginia, assuming Virginia was a man.

In England they made you manly by forcing you to play rugby and criticizing you every time you did something 'unmanly' – if commonsensical – like running away from the ball or throwing it up in the air in a panic as the pack of brutish forwards from the other team descended upon you like Viking hoards. But was not that mould into which they tried to force you perhaps a perversion of real manliness? It definitely, in Benson's opinion, conflicted with the notion of the Christian Gentleman. The Christian Gentleman was someone who never knowingly caused offence.

169

Well, he had been caused great offence by all these manly antics while growing up. He could not imagine that Christ would have come off very well on the rugby pitch at St Bede's. Still, maybe He would have if He had been in the mood He had been in when He expelled the traders from The Temple. If the PE master had been able to go over to Christ and say, 'Now when the whistle blows I want you to remember how manly you were when you expelled the traders from The Temple. Go and do likewise.' What would have happened then?

By the time Benson came to, the train was pulling out of Jackson Heights station and he had to wait until it stopped at Elmhurst Avenue. He decided that he would walk home and give further rational thought to the problem of manliness.

Back at the apartment, the atmosphere was distinctly manly, though it did not particularly jive with Benson's new definition of the term. On his walk home he had remembered the way the doors of the subway had closed on the policeman and he had thought how the man courted dreadful confrontation with drunks, gun-toting robbers, with rapists. Yet he quietly stood and did his duty, accepted everything that life threw at him. Like the soldier in *Faithful Unto Death*, like the black man in *Gulf Stream*. Perhaps that was it. Courage, either moral or physical, or perhaps a bit of both, was what manhood was about. According to this definition Virginia – if she was a man – must be very manly indeed. To be courageous enough to go out in a dress and suffer the looks and jibes of an outraged populace had to take as much courage as a soldier under fire. Benson did not think most of the time that his homosexuality showed. When told by Meryl that he walked funny, he had gone to great lengths to correct his gait.

170

But would it not be more courageous to behave in the way that nature intended? Was it not a lack of courage that caused him to appear as manly as possible and therefore escape being made fun of – or worse?

'You're late,' said Lee-Chun. 'We were worried about you.'

'I went to the pictures and then I walked about.' He did not think that Lee-Chun looked particularly worried. He was sitting at the table with three friends, a cigarette between his teeth, a glass of whisky at his elbow, one leg up on the chair, looking at the state of play in the mah-jong game. Sung-Il was on the opposite side of the table and between them were two Koreans whom Benson had not met before. He was introduced and the two strangers stood and bowed to Benson politely, though one of them was swaying a bit. There was no sign of Jung-Ja anywhere. He felt a sudden pang of guilt for having left Jung-Ja all alone to get through the mah-jong evening without any company. Still, he thought, maybe there is satisfaction there too. He could imagine himself happily taking Jung-Ja's part, cooking and bringing wonderful food to the table so that her man would be pleased. Women everywhere seemed to do it for their husbands as if it were the most natural thing in the world. Yes, he could understood the satisfaction of that rather more than the satisfaction of being served and treated as king of the castle.

Benson grabbed a bottle of Coke from the fridge, surveying the state of play inside, then took his writing things into the living room. He wrote his address at the top of the letter, then wondered who to write to first.

Dear Gareth,
    I am sorry to be taking such a long time to write to you. Will you still speak to me when I get back?

I've hardly written a letter to anyone since I arrived. Anyway probably you are too busy with all the summer trade at the chip shop to worry about a letter.

I am back in New York. Camp Manley did not work out. The owners left us all high and dry at the end of the second week! They could not pay their bills. I had to come back to New York and find a job pronto. I'm working at a factory at the moment. The work is hard and makes me sweat but I like it in a way because I can let my mind wander while I'm doing it and at the end of each day I can look at what I've achieved.

Nothing had happened to me that was really 'exciting' – if you get me – until tonight. I met a really nice chap called Pablo. He is from the Philippines. We are going to meet again. I won't go into details (but I'll tell you everything when I get back!). It was really romantic.

How's your love life? I hope you have kept to your promise to yourself not to see Howell any more. He is someone who uses people as a means to an end rather than as an end in themselves. THIS IS WRONG!! He is incapable of returning the love you offer him. Still, we've been through this many times. And, of course, I understand why you keep falling for him all over again. I've had plenty of time to think about it all. I know it is hard to find someone and when Howell comes in all rude it must be tempting to go off with him just to get sex off your mind. But you know how miserable he makes you. I know how miserable he made me. Men can be brutes. Why can't we settle for nice people who would be easy to be around. Still, I have high hopes for Pablo. Are you still seeing John? I know he is not very sexy, but he is very fond of you. He has a steady job at the National Library, a house of his own, a Ford Cortina! Why not give it another go?

New York is wonderful, of course. I still haven't been up the Statue of Liberty but I read in my guide book that she only ended up in New York because the original purchaser, an Egyptian king, backed out because of the expense. Apparently the Statue of Liberty should have been put at the Mediterranean end of the Suez canal. I bet you never knew that! Americans, however, are far more foreign than you would think. I hope you are managing to think positively. If you do fall for Howell again try not to allow him to disturb your calm. You know what Whitman says: *When we become the enfolders of those orbs, and the pleasure and knowledge of every thing in them, shall we be fill'd and satisfied then?* . . .

Think about it, Gareth!
Lots of love,
Martin xx

In bed he read a few pages of *The Confessions of Nat Turner*. It was a good read. William Styron had got into trouble with some American Negroes because he had written a scene in which Nat Turner had sex with another man. Benson hadn't come to that bit but it was, if he was honest, the main reason why he had paid out good money for the paperback. However, he closed the book after only ten minutes, his eyes heavy, reasonably sure that Nat was not going to get to the good bit tonight. He switched off the bedside light and closed his eyes, thinking what a wonderful day it had been. It wasn't everyone who had put in a full day's work, seen Manhattan, watched a film, met a Filipino, made love in the middle of Central Park, meditated on matters of great pith and moment, written a letter . . . ah, life!

Then, not knowing why, not willing to think why, he began, 'God bless Dad, God bless Mum, God bless Auntie Muriel, God bless Alice and Carole, God bless Omar, God bless Lee-Chun, God bless Sung-Il, God bless Jung-Ja, God bless Gareth, God bless Virginia. God bless Meryl and Hugo, God bless Pablo, Dexter, God bless . . .' But fell asleep before he could get around to asking a blessing on himself.

* * *

Benson watched Pete Seeger playing the banjo, fascinated by the way his hands moved to produce such a sound. Of course he had Pete Seeger's *We Shall Overcome* LP but that had not prepared him for the treat of seeing his hero in the flesh. He stood in the middle of the stage, a powerful spotlight on him, wearing a tartan shirt rolled up past his sinewy biceps, a pair of faded jeans, and sang song after wonderful song. Behind him stood the skyscrapers of Fifth Avenue and Central Park South. In front of him an amphitheatre of adoring fans, none more adoring than Benson.

This is the best dollar I'll ever spend, he told himself. He had been lucky in the matter of seating. At first he had been right at the back of the open-air theatre, the Wollman Memorial Skating Rink, where the dollar Rheingold concerts took place. But then a group of four had moved from their place in the second row. A couple quickly took two of the seats but there were still two empty and Benson had leapt forward.

Pete Seeger started with 'This Land is Your Land'. Benson knew that the man he was watching had actually sung this same song in the subway — perhaps the same subway that Benson travelled on daily. The hand that worked magic on the banjo had touched Woody Guthrie's hand, probably worked itself in the friendly manner of comrades around Woody's shoulder. Benson thought of Woody Guthrie and wept some tears for his hero anchored to a hospital bed with Huntington's Chorea. Probably Pete Seeger visited him regularly.

Then Pete Seeger, saying it was his favourite song of all time, sang 'Oh What a Beautiful City' and Benson looked behind the singer to the skyline, to the million twinkling lights and the flame border of the horizon where the sun had set over a continent of liberty and dreams. Yes! This was art. This was words and music and ideals and visual beauty coming together on a perfect evening in the spring of his life in the same park where outrageous love had been a mere twenty-four hours earlier.

The audience clapped, stamped and whooped their applause. Pete Seeger seemed embarrassed by the adulation, behaved as Benson felt he would behave were he ever in a similar situation. He was humble and dignified.

Pete took off his banjo and put on his guitar. He sang a little ditty while tuning it – which made everyone laugh – and then started *Viva La Quince Brigada!* When he said, 'It was our only desire to defeat fascism' everyone clapped spontaneously. Benson knew exactly what Pete meant. He hadn't mentioned J. Edgar Hoover, but he didn't need to. Anyway there were probably witch-hunting FBI and CIA agents in the auditorium recording his every word. Benson knew what a terrible time Pete had had during the McCarthy era. Joseph McCarthy had been a Catholic. Typical. He would remind Meryl about that.

On and on he sang. He listened to requests from the audience and at once sang them. He did not need music. Benson asked for, 'The Bells of Rhymney', but not loudly enough. Pete sang 'Little Boxes'. I won't get anywhere if I don't push, Benson thought. Before the applause for 'Little Boxes' had died down, Benson was shouting, '"The Bells of Rhymney" . . . please!'

'Oh, what will you give me?' sang Pete and the woman next to Benson gave him a smile. Benson knew that the singer was doing the song just for him. He looked up at Pete Seeger and Pete Seeger looked straight back at Benson. Benson adjusted his quiff.

Pete Seeger sang for two hours without stopping. Then he went towards a curtain at the side of the stage and waved goodbye. But the audience would not let him go. He came back and sang 'We Shall Overcome'. Then a Turkish folk song about nuclear annihilation. The audience stood to him. They were still unwilling to release him, but Pete said his wife would be worried about him. The audience understood, though they could not resist a gigantic sigh. To console everyone he sang 'I Can See a New Day', waved, Benson thought, straight at Benson . . . and disappeared.

Benson clapped on but Pete did not return. The audience gave up hope and quietly began to leave. Benson made his way on to Central Park West. He loked at his Timex. It was 10.15.

There weren't many people around. A few people from the audience had opted for the same walk, but most had made their way to the subway stations along Fifth Avenue. He passed men sitting alone on the benches by the wall. He wondered if they were homos. Yes, he thought, they probably were. Why else would they sit alone on a bench? A man was walking towards him. As he got nearer Benson could see that he was carrying a shoulder-bag and was walking in a mincing sort of way, a bit in the way Benson in his worst imaginings walked. As he passed Benson he worked his lips and raised his eyebrows. Benson could not resist looking back at the apparition. The man was also looking back at him. Benson quickened his pace. Gosh, he thought. The man probably thinks I'm attracted to him. And I'm not. I hope he doesn't follow me and ask me to leap over the wall with him. If he does I'll have to tell him I'm already spoken for. Which I am. Pablo would not like it if I played about with somebody while I'm going out with him. Why, he might even take a knife to me like Harry Belafonte did to Dorothy Dandridge at the end of *Carmen Jones*. And, of course, if he did I wouldn't have a leg to stand on. One minute I would have been serenaded by Pete Seeger – the very pinnacle of my life – and the next knifed down by a fiery, Filipino lover. No. I must be true to the person I am going out with. One at a time please.

In *To Sir With Love,* Sidney Poitier had told Lulu and Judy Geeson, *NOBODY LIKES A SLUT FOR LONG! ONLY THE WORST TYPE WILL MARRY ONE!* Benson had felt that Sidney could have been addressing him as he sat next to Jung-Ja sucking Jujyfruits at the matinée performance earlier in the day at the Jackson cinema. Life was definitely mirroring art.

So, chastened both by the idea of Pablo exacting revenge for his two-timing him and by Sidney's weighty words, Benson did not deign to look sideways at the lonely looking men sitting on the benches. No, he thought. That way lies total excess. It's bloody hard to find *anything*. But once you've found it you should try to stick with it, unless it is as miserable as Howell of course.

Benson thought about Howell, the Welsh farmer who had used him most roughly. Walking along a Manhattan street and thinking of a rough Welsh farmer struck him as surreal. It took a big leap in imagination for him to even contemplate the windy fields of Wales occupying the same continuous world that Manhattan sat on. With the great skyscrapers all round, the flashing WALK/DONT WALK signs, the honking streams of cars, the people everywhere, it was hard to consider the possibility of the cold Welsh landscape, the dingy room where Howell had done him, the pictures tacked to the wall. Ophelia was right: *O, woe is me t' have seen what I have seen, see what I see!*

Now where was I, he thought. I am thinking, that's true. But I am not thinking coherently. This is my worst fault and is definitely standing between me and my goal of being an intellectual. When Joan Bakewell interviews me and I wander off at a tangent, she's going to be bound to notice. She might be quite sharp with me. Even if she were not sharp she would definitely not have me on *Late Night Line Up* ever again. And why would she have me on the first time? Well, she might want to know about my ideas about being a homo. Yes, that would be good. I could tell her my theories. *Late Night Line Up* is on late enough that Dad and Alice will have gone to bed. 'Well I'm glad you asked me that question, Joan. Basically, I think that one should have one relationship at a time. I know it isn't a fashionable notion but it does not seem right to me to treat people as means to ends. Rather they are ends in themselves. I am also – and I hope you don't mind me mentioning the word on television – rather against masturbation. It is – I tend to think – the ultimate in laziness.' Bakewell tarts were nice. I doubt I could get a Bakewell tart in New York for love nor money. Concentrate! 'Also, Joan, when one thinks how homos are forced to meet and when you . . . and when one thinks about the difficulty in finding a private place to go, it really is not surprising if homos take every opportunity offered to have sex. The trouble is that sex is only a *part of the person.* The Body, the Living Clay. And once that has been discovered then the Soul – which takes great effort to get to know – is thought to be rather thin beer.' Joan nodded like mad.

He was passing The New York Society for Ethical Culture and the sight surprised him because he had not thought his walk across the park had made him wander so far uptown. He gave the bench on which he had interrogated Pablo an affectionate nod and was suddenly excited by the memory of what had occurred the previous night in the very centre of the Heckscher Playground. A car horn sounded. He gave the taxi a severe look. It moved on and he caught sight of a lit sign down West 63rd Street. YMCA. Yes, Lee-Chun said that it was cheap to stay at the YMCA. Was he trying to tell me something? Maybe I should think about it.

Benson stopped on the pavement. I should go back and check now. I mustn't keep putting things off. That's the Old World way. He crossed the street and walked towards the sound, not quite sure what to expect.

Ten minutes later Benson was back walking down Central Park West to Columbus Circle. The YMCA had smiled on him. They had offered him a choice of rooms, sharing for $18 a week or a single for $24. No, there would be no problem if he stayed until September. The only hitch was that there were no rooms available until the following Thursday. If he wanted to reserve one, a small deposit would be required. He had wondered if he should think about it. Then he thought the room might go if he thought about it. But could he afford a single? He would have to have a single. He couldn't imagine sharing. Knowing his luck he might end up with someone like Rod. There and then, in most uncharacteristic fashion, Benson laid

179

down a $5 deposit and told the cheerful Christian at reception that he would be back on Thursday evening if that was all right.

From then on, his walk back to Times Square became different. Benson was walking through his neighbourhood. Central Park would be only a few footsteps away. Could he afford it? Well, it was going to mean that his $60 a week would be almost halved. Still as long as he went on earning $60 a week, as long as he was careful with the money that remained, he would be able to manage. And Lee-Chun would be pleased.

Benson reached around for his subway token. He put it into the slot and went round the turnstile at the same time as a Negro and his white girl friend. He smiled at them approvingly. As the train emerged from the tunnel he said goodbye to Manhattan until Thursday. The following day Lee-Chun was taking them all to Jones Beach again. Sunday night he needed to go to bed early so that he would be ready to give his all at the Woodside Industrial Coathanger Factory. Monday night he would have to stay in too so that he could be near the phone when his new Filipino Dearest Him rang.

* * *

After a day's labour with the aluminium and steel rods at work, Benson wanted to get on his knees and apologize to Earl. The work was not satisfying at all. It was difficult to sort out the rods into different lengths and thickness, to distinguish between the different bore widths. Also, the rods were unwieldy to carry and insisted on slipping *en masse* down the wall where he placed them while attempting to bring order to the bundles. He was also working in a confined space that prevented him from making as many piles as he would have liked. Every time he moved them the noise they made set his teeth on edge.

He had waited to tell Lee-Chun about his room at the YMCA until they were splashing around between the lifeguards' flags at Jones Beach on Sunday. *By God, you shall not go down! hang your whole weight upon me.* Jung-Ja and Sung-Il had gone for a walk so Benson and Lee-Chun were spending most of their time in the water, keeping a careful eye on their things.

Lee-Chun's reaction, however, had not been what Benson had expected.

'Aren't you happy with us?'

'Yes, of course. But you're so busy. I must get in your way.'

'No. We like you being with us. Jung-Ja will be very sad.'

'But I thought . . . I mean, I was supposed to spend most of the summer at Camp Manley. It just seemed right and proper that I should go off on my own.'

'Well, if your mind's made up.'

Lee-Chun had given him a long lecture about keeping in close touch, about locking his room against thieves and faggots. *And do not call the tortoise unworthy because she is not something else.* He had even told him a story about a faggot he had encountered at the Minneapolis Y on a visit there with representatives of the Korean branch of the Asian Peoples' Anti-Communist League some years before. Benson looked suitably shocked, while filing the information away. He said he would take great care of his virtue.

On Monday at work, buoyed up by the thought of an interesting change in his circumstances, the tasks had been just about tolerable. He also consoled himself with the thought that Pablo would call him in the evening and offer to whisk him away to a job at the

Unitarian Medical Center. But Pablo did not call, though Benson had stayed by the phone all night, while engaging Jung-Ja in polite English conversation, waiting up long after the others had gone to bed, in the hope that it would ring. He watched the phone, willing it to ring. But at last he had gone to bed feeling greatly let down.

Tuesday he had found really difficult. He did not feel that he had anything at all to look forward to. The tubes still refused to come right. He felt that he was making a bigger mess of them than ever. Occasionally he thought that they were coming into some sort of shape, that he could see how they would all look eventually, but this vision faded as suddenly as it had appeared. He kept telling himself that really things were no different than they had been on Friday. On Friday he had had no Pablo in his life, no prospect of a different job, or a single room at the YMCA. The only thing that had changed was that, instead of components to be weighed and sorted, he was dealing with thousands of steel rods. And the rods were less satisfying than the more easily manipulated components, so any hope of being able to find satisfaction in an outwardly tedious set of tasks had died.

But on Tuesday night Pablo called him. He said that his sister was going away on Friday and that Benson could stay with him in Brooklyn for the weekend. They could also, if Benson wanted to, visit the hospital.

Life was looking up again.

Benson worked like a beaver for the next three days in anticipation of the idyll he would have with Pablo at the weekend. A way of sorting out the rods occurred to him and seemed to work. Their noise no longer bothered him. He even found himself quite taken up with his labour, found it, if not the challenge of the first week, at least tolerable.

After work on Thursday, Benson collected his red
Antler suitcase from the apartment and carried it to the
subway, promising a downcast Jung-Ja that he would
drop in on her soon. The case seemed to have grown
heavier since the day he had trundled it past Harrods –
pulling tongues at the stuck-up manikins in the windows – why couldn't they smile? – and, via the sweet
shop, into the Aer Lingus air terminal. Why it should
seem heavier he could not imagine. Perhaps youthful
vim and vigour were fading. Dad had told him to
guard the case with his life. But Benson had developed
a strong antipathy towards it. The grip pushed the
flesh on his palms half way up his fingers. It weighed a
ton even when empty. And it was bourgeois into the
bargain.

A different man greeted Benson at reception and
gave him his room-key after Benson had paid him for a
week's stay. He was excited to see that his room was
going to be on the ninth floor and had visions of a
wonderful view over skyscrapers. But when he opened
the door of his room, he found that it was facing a
blank wall and only by pressing his cheek against the
gloss-painted wall and squinting through the window
could he catch sight of life proceeding on West 63rd
Street. The room was not very nicely decorated either.
There was a single bed, a list of rules on the wall, a
built-in wardrobe, a little table and a chair. This he sat
in, looking around, twinges of regret pushing through
him. No basin! That means I'm going to have to rush
off down the corridor for a wee! He stood up, took his
key and left the room, locking it carefully behind him.
He might as well find out where the facilities were.

Happily the bathrooms were not too far away. He
went in. A bank of basins stood against one wall with a
continuous mirror above them. Behind these were half
a dozen shower stalls. Round the corner from these

were another half dozen toilet cubicles. Benson's mouth fell open. Both the showers and the toilets were exactly like Camp Manley. Not a door on any of them!

Benson was aiming deep frowns at the YMCA's barbaric ninth-floor bathroom when a man came in. Benson turned and the man nodded to him. He was wearing only a towel. This he discarded and stepped into the shower. Benson, thinking he had to do something to justify his presence, went over to the washbasins and washed his hands. He noted that the mirror gave him a splendid view of the man, his back turned to Benson, adjusting the temperature of the shower prior to getting in.

Benson washed and washed, then gave his face a good scrub. He then returned to his hands and scoured under every nail. The man was now showering and Benson took sideways glances at him. But he had already been washing longer than was respectable. Also, didn't he already have a friend? He left the bathroom, consoling himself that the man had not been *that* wonderful anyway.

By Friday, the rods had all been harvested, stacked up in neat piles and tied with string. He spent the afternoon happily enough, taking it easy, sweeping up the area and labelling all the rods. At four he went to see Mr Trabulsi to conduct him to his rod store and see what a good job had been done.

'Fine work, Martin,' said Mr Trabulsi. 'Now what are we going to do with you? I've been talking to the boss here. He says that we would like you to stay on the payroll but we don't want to go on paying the agency. If you'll come on the payroll direct, we'll up your pay to two dollars an hour.'

'That's nice, Mr Trabulsi. What would I be doing?'

'There are many odd jobs we could put you to. We

often get a rush unloading materials, loading consign-
ments. What do you say?'

'Could I tell you on Monday, Mr Trabulsi?'

'Sure. If you come in at the usual time then we'll set
you to work straight away. If you don't want the job,
just call me.'

Benson promised that he would. He was glad that he
hadn't said no to the prospect of staying at the job.
Who knows, the weekend with Pablo might not work
out at all. He was learning, he felt. He really was
becoming wise in the ways of the world.

He waited until he got to Times Square before
telephoning Pablo. Pablo gave him instructions on
how to get to the R train from Times Square to 45th
Street and Fourth Avenue, Brooklyn. It would take
about half an hour from Times Square. Pablo said he
would meet him at the station, and Benson, having
lashed out on a *New York Times*, read it on a hard seat
for two at the end of the carriage, the one which was
becoming his favourite.

There wasn't much in the way of news from
England. Well, he had almost given up looking for any.
The *New York Times* seemed to subscribe to Dr
Griffiths' view of places out of sight. Still, there was
quite a bit to keep him interested. A waiter in Robert
McNamara's dining room at the Pentagon had been
declared a leper. Benson thought they had definitely
diagnosed the wrong man. Still, it was a telling
metaphor. He turned over. Stella Stevens – whoever
she was – was asserting that Coppertone gave her a
better tan. Big deal. He pursed his lips at an advert
for *My Hustler*. *The Arrangement* by Elia Kazan was
still top of the best sellers. It had been at the top ever
since he'd arrived. However *A Modern Priest Looks
at his Outdated Church* had crept up from No. 10 to
No. 5. Also, 'Bitter Lemon has Schwepped the country.

Without a shot being fired.' That was good news. It was nice to see an English drink doing well. Maybe it would wipe out Root Beer. You could buy a four foot high statue of Michelangelo's David for $33.95, reduced from $185. There were only a limited number available. They had very slight damage. Fig leaf optional. But if he wanted one he would have to get to 1666 Route 46, Fort Lee, New Jersey. He might bump into Rod. Sterile gypsy moths had been loosed in Brooklyn in a bid to stop them breeding. Listerine could be had for $1.29 a quart. Detroit lay in ruins. 'Tareyton smokers would rather fight than switch.' Judy Garland was going to open at the Palace next Monday. A clam opener with a rock maple base and a stainless steel blade would cost him $4. 'It's not how long you make it – it's how you make it long!' Winston Super Kings. Yes, that was worth thinking about. Mennen Speed Stick didn't just protect him . . . it actually built up a resistance to odor . . . But Walt had said, *The scent of these armpits aroma finer than prayer.* Well, he thought, the compromised copywriters of Madison Avenue had turned their noses away from the prayers of America's finest poet. Let them! His truth would go marching on.

'You been waiting long? Sorry Martin.'

'No, I've just arrived, actually,' lied Benson. 'You came at just the right time.'

'And you can stay the whole weekend?'

'Yes, if you want me.'

'Yeah, course I do! We mustn't waste the weekend. It's not often that Theresa goes away and leaves me alone.'

'Where's she gone?'

'She went on a retreat to a convent in Bensonhurst.'

'Bensonhurst? My last name's Benson.'

'Yeah. It's an Italian neighbourhood. My sisters are

pretty religious. They've seen *The Sound of Music* ten times. In fact when they were in their *Sound of Music* phase it really helped me because they'd go out all the time and leave me by myself. I'd say goodbye to Theresa and then pick up someone and bring him home. I knew I'd be in the clear for at least three hours.'

'But weren't you scared taking someone home? They might have stolen things or something like that.'

Pablo shrugged. 'It was worth the risk. I get so horny all the time! All this week I've been really hot for you! When Theresa told me she was going on this retreat my cock just stood up to attention.'

'That's nice,' said Benson, rising to the occasion. 'By the way, I've moved to the YMCA. It's just across the street from the bench we sat on last week.'

'You horny bastard! Let's go home.'

Benson smiled to himself.

'I've made dinner. Do you like hot food?'

'Yes, I like anything. I don't think there's a single thing in the world that I don't like eating.'

'Yeah, I remember.'

They arrived at Pablo's house. It was part of a tall terrace and had a fire-escape snaking down its front wall. Pablo opened the door. A bank of letter-boxes that you opened with a key was set in the wall. Leaflets and newspapers were strewn around. Pablo opened another door with his key and they were in a dark hall. Then up two flights of stairs and Pablo started the lengthy procedure of unlocking the apartment door. He used four keys, the last one causing a clanking sound from inside the apartment. *Unscrew the locks from the doors! Unscrew the doors themselves from their jambs!* Pablo opened the door and Benson saw an iron bar sliding back – no doubt the cause of the clank. They went inside and closed the door. The bar clanked back into place, wedged against the door. Pablo put his key into the locking mechanism.

'That's a new sort of lock. I've never seen one of those before.'

'Theresa was burglarized. This one stops the door from being broken in.'

Benson looked around. It was a very bright room. Everything was patterned, each wall painted in different primary colours. On all the walls were religious pictures, *The Sacred Heart, The Immaculate Heart of Mary, St Thérèse of Lisieux.* A large crucifix hung behind the table, which was set for two.

'It's really lovely,' Benson said.

'Dinner will be ready in half an hour,' said Pablo and he started taking off Benson's clothes.

'Is this your room?' Benson asked Pablo, looking around the room into which Pablo had led him, guiding him by holding his erection.

'Yeah, the bed's a little narrow. Theresa has a big bed but I don't dare use it.'

'It's very nice too,' said Benson, though he was looking at Pablo's slim body. He was so slight that his penis came as a surprise, like that on a statue of Priapos pictured on an ashtray Ianto had thoughtfully brought him from Greece, and which he had to keep in a drawer.

'Lay down on the bed and let me look at you,' said Pablo.

Benson lay back while Pablo knelt on the end of the bed, staring down at him.

'You've got a nice body,' said Pablo.

'You too. Much nicer than mine. It's a nice, soft bed, isn't it?' He was happy to be surveyed in the horizontal. He had often taken a shaving mirror and inspected himself in that position. He had always appeared far more satisfactory to himself when lying down. Every-

188

thing seemed better-proportioned somehow. Odd that.

Pablo straddled Benson's body, sitting on his chest facing him. Benson looked hard at Pablo's phallus nudging itself towards his lips. He took it in and sucked on it, then looked up at Pablo who was looking down intently at what was happening below him. Benson set to work, his eyes open, staring straight into Pablo's eyes.

Then suddenly Pablo swivelled around and took Benson into his mouth. They worked on one another, Benson receiving the not particular edifying sight of Pablo's scrotum landing on the bridge of his nose. His mind was full of the two intense things happening to him. Why had he never thought of it before? This was wonderful. Complete. And it was so bloody obvious! This was how homos were meant to go about things. It was equal. He was doing what was being done to him. It was almost too much to take in. By varying his movements on Pablo he could show Pablo what he wanted for himself and vice versa. So why had it not occurred to him before? You'd think I'd have tumbled to it, what with all the thought I've given to sex over the years. God, I really am thick.

Long after they were both satisfied, Benson kept Pablo in his mouth, enjoying the sensation of the penis slowly settling down, becoming soft and friendly again as its time as weaponry passed. Then they came back to one another's mouths and kissed. At last, panting, they rocked. He let his eyelashes flutter against Pablo's cheek.

'I've never done that before,' Benson said.

'What? Sixty-nine?'

'Is that what it's called? That's a funny name for it. It's really lovely, though.'

Dinner consisted of lots of pieces of meat on skewers. Pablo showed Benson how to dip the meat in a sweet sauce that tasted of peanuts. Then he held a skewer out for Benson to try. It was delicious.

'I think this is nicer than Korean food,' said Benson. 'I really love the sauce.'

'I don't like Koreans,' said Pablo. Here we go again, thought Benson

'Why not?'

'They are very cruel. In Vietnam they are the soldiers that the Vietnamese most fear.'

'Well, yes. But there are good and bad everywhere. I suppose I feel a bit angry about the Japanese. They were very cruel to a lot of our soldiers during the war. It's funny how they all seem so polite and yet they can be so cruel. People are really odd.'

'My father was killed by the Japanese.

'Oh, dear, was he? I'm sorry. Er . . . a friend of my dad was in a Japanese prisoner-of-war camp. Dad says he's not been the same since. Have you read *The Naked Island* by Russell Bradon?'

'Our president was a great war hero in the Philippines.'

'President Marcos? He's just married a beauty queen, hasn't he?'

'Yes. Imelda. She is very beautiful.'

'President Marcos is really very attractive too. You look like him, a bit. You're much younger of course.'

Pablo seemed pleased. 'After dinner,' he said, 'we're going to have a really great time. I've got something for us that I've been saving up.'

'What?'

'It's a surprise. It makes sex really great.'

'Oh, you mean pot?' asked Benson in his studied man of the world voice.

'No, not pot. Better than that.'

'Well, I think sex was really great just now. Was it nice for you too?'

Pablo nodded.

'Have you ever slept with a woman?' Benson asked.

'Sure. Lots of times.'

'Have you?'

'Yes. Haven't you?'

'No, I haven't.'

'Why not?'

'I've never wanted to.'

'I'll probably get married eventually. Our families expect it.'

'I suppose ours do too. But I'll never get married. It wouldn't be fair on the woman.'

'Why not? Women want a home and a family. I can do that and still have a good time.'

Benson thought of himself married to Meryl. He couldn't imagine Meryl being at all pleased if he went out and did things with other men and then came back to her as she dusted and ironed and changed Hugo. 'I think our women are different. They expect you to devote all your time to them.'

Pablo nodded. 'It's the same in America. The women are very demanding. Our women are brought up to see the man as king. They would not question what he does outside the house. As long as he provides food and shelter, they are quite happy.'

'I suppose it all depends what you expect from marriage. We are taught that it is ... well sort of everything. Couples pair off and just shut the door on the outside world. They form the nuclear family. I think what you have must be the extended family. Yours is a much better idea, I think.'

Pablo yawned. 'Do you want to come to the Unitarian Medical Center tomorrow? Mrs Muñoz will be there and I mentioned you to her. She really needs new people.'

'Does she?'

Pablo stood up. 'Let's go back to bed. I'll get the surprise.'

'Oughtn't we to wash up?'

'We can do that later. I don't want to waste any time.'

Benson climbed out of his clothes again while Pablo went to find the surprise. He was lying on the bed when Pablo came in. Benson could see no evidence of the surprise. Pablo took off his clothes and lay down next to Benson. They kissed for a while, then Pablo held out a small cylinder of cotton wool. 'This is the surprise.'

It didn't look like much of a surprise to Benson, though he tried to appear enthusiastic.

'It's a popper from the hospital. It's medicine for people with angina. That's a heart condition. Inside the cotton there's a little glass bottle. You break it and sniff.'

'Why?' asked Benson.

'You'll find out.'

'But isn't it dangerous to inhale medicine intended for someone who's sick? I mean, shouldn't we have a prescription?'

'It won't hurt you. I've done it before.'

Benson was not at all sure. 'But why do we need it? Weren't we managing very well before? I really enjoyed myself.'

'This makes you into a real wild animal in bed,' said Pablo.

'Does it?'

'Once won't hurt you,' said Pablo.

Benson wasn't so sure about that. People were always saying that. Meryl had probably told herself that when she fell under the sway of Enoch Moham-med. It *had* hurt.

'To tell you the truth, I'm a bit scared of drugs. I hate

being sick. Even three beers makes me feel sick.'

'Don't you trust me?' asked Pablo, seizing hold of Benson's erection and squeezing it hard, then hugging him until Benson exhaled and could hardly breathe in again so strong was the embrace. He let Benson go and looked at him hard, with unblinking eyes.

Benson said that he did, of course, as the chemicals of closeness coarsed through him.

'What we do is this. While we are kissing, I crack open the ampule. Then we inhale it and you'll see. It doesn't last long. I've got four. If you don't like it the first time I promise I won't use any more.'

Benson nodded. They kissed and Benson heard a crack and then smelled something odd. He breathed in as instructed and was about to say that it hadn't made any difference when a rush of energy came into his body. He felt his erection pounding and had a desire which he could not resist to take Pablo into his mouth. He inverted himself and found his nose nestling against Pablo's pubic hair, his phallus down his throat. And the bulk of it did not make him want to gag. He pushed farther down on it, felt Pablo working on him and set to work himself. Pablo reached down and placed the ampule next to Benson's nose. Benson inhaled greedily and the same ineffable appetite returned. Nothing in the world existed except Pablo's penis. Then that obsession opened out to all the other penises he had seen, touched, dreamed about in his lifetime. Howell the farmer was back at his rudest and Benson replied in kind. Had his mouth not been full he would have used his tongue to tell Pablo all the disgraceful things he had ever thought. Then the feeling began to fade and the ampule was back under his nose. He inhaled, and concentrated on bringing Pablo to his climax.

'Well, how was it?'

'Gosh, that was wonderful, Pablo! I've never felt like that before.'

'And you don't feel ill, do you?'

'Not in the least.'

'I told you.'

'But you say it's for people who are sick?'

'Yeah, people with angina. That's a heart condition.'

'Do you think they feel like that when they take it?'

'No, they're too busy trying to feel better. They take it when they feel their blood pressure going down.'

'I suppose it's just as well really. I mean it wouldn't do for heart patients to start doing the sort of things we were doing, would it?'

'No. It definitely made you different, Martin. You were real sexy. You really opened up.'

'But wasn't I good the first time? I mean, I thought the first time was good too.' He felt it was important that Pablo said he had been fine the first time. The first time he had been himself. The second he had been inhaling a substance to help the heart along. Though it had been strange and wonderful it had not really been him.

'Sure, you were OK. It was nothing great, though. Just about average.'

'Yes but . . .'

'But with the stuff you were great! Some people need a little to bring out what's inside. I'm going to take a shower.'

Benson was left to wonder about that. It was a bit much to hear another homo imply that his technique wasn't any good. He had always felt that, were he with a woman, that is what would be said. Women were notoriously difficult to satisfy. You had to find this little thing called the clitoris and play about with it for ages and ages. Then, once you were inside, you had to go ever so slowly and put off the inevitable because women took for ever. He could see why he might not pass muster there. But now Pablo was implying that he was only *really* good when he was under the influence of heart medicine. He thought of Dexter.

Pablo came out of the shower still wet. He told Benson that there was a towel for him to use. Benson took a shower, noting all the feminine talcums and creams and potions. They must have cost Theresa a fortune. Poor Theresa! But then Theresa was only using these things to doll herself up and make herself more attractive to men. That was fair enough. But would Theresa pop some ampules of heart medicine into her bag before leaving for a night on the tiles? No, she would probably say that if the man didn't like her as she was – albeit at her best turned out – then he could just take a running jump at himself.

Benson came out of the shower determined to tackle Pablo about the problem. A friendship must be based on truth. I must try to show Pablo what is going on in my own head. After all, he was not slow to tell me about my fluttering eyelashes.

'Pablo, what you said before about my being only average the first time. Did you mean it?'

'Nah, I was joking. But it's much better with the stuff, isn't it?'

'Well, it was different. I've never felt like that before. It's just that it worried me. I wasn't myself. I was more like some of the men I've been with in the past who were really rough and unfeeling.'

'Hey, give me their addresses!' said Pablo.

There was no answer to that. Pablo wanted to go out for a drink. Benson got dressed and followed him out of the apartment. Pablo locked up while Benson stood next to him, wondering how Pablo could pluck up the energy to go through that complicated ritual of

195

locking every time he left. Sorting out aluminium rods had to be less boring.

In Smoky Mary's that night Pablo had seemed on very friendly terms with lots of people. At one point he had left Benson alone to go and meet somebody that a friend of his said was there but on the other side of the crowd. Benson in the meantime tried to bob his head around to the beat of the music and smile at anyone who caught his eye. But no-one he smiled at smiled back. He had never in his life before been under the same roof as so many homos . . . gay boys, as Pablo called them. It was wonderful in a way but he wondered why no-one came up to say hello and ask him how life had been for him. They had surely so many stories to share; so many guilts and strange experiences in common. But instead of talking to him they seemed to be studiously turning their back. God, imagine if I am not attractive to men! That would be the last straw. Maybe Pablo needs stuff in order to be able to go with me. Maybe he thinks I'm really plain. Maybe I've got *Dull Sex* written all over me. Or could it be that I'm not dressed properly? No-one else is wearing sandals like mine, that's true. But Crimplene trousers are up to the minute. I've got on Mennen deodorant so it can't be that. But maybe the Mennen is gluing my natural scent – *finer than prayer* – in! But it must be something. People were much more friendly in O'Toole's Tavern than they are being here. Stop it! You're being dithery. That is just not sexy. You must attempt to appear to be suave and in charge even if you don't feel it.

Imitating a look similar to the one that Cheyenne Brody might have worn had he found himself in Smoky Mary's in Brooklyn on a Friday night, Benson once again looked around, trying to connect. It worked no better than his dithering had done. He lapsed back to his usual self, placing one hand on his hip while he licked the rim of his beer glass with his tongue. After all, why am I trying to be other than I am? Everyone everywhere is pushing me to play act all the time. I have to play act being spectacularly proficient at sex when I'd far rather cuddle and have a good play around. In everyday life I have to give firm handshakes and keep my wrist straight and my voice deep and my walk manly. Then, when I finally find myself in a place where there are other homos, they just ignore me. It ought not to be allowed!

Thankfully, Pablo returned before too much time had passed and given Benson a chance to return to the existential gloom he had discarded in favour of Walt Whitman. They stood opposite one another for a while. Benson slipped his hand into Pablo's. Pablo squeezed it but soon let it go. Then he found another friend to talk to.

Returning home with Pablo, Benson had been quiet while Pablo talked at length about his friends in the bar and how much fun they were. Pablo made it sound as if returning home with Benson for the night was robbing him of a night of fun and laughter.

Once home, the three ampules on the bedside table next to a tube of vaseline, Pablo had been frank about what he wanted Benson to do. Benson had got on with it with the aid of the fumes. Seeing Pablo passive beneath him he felt a certain contempt for him writhing there below him, opening his mouth wide, running his tongue around his lips, saying things which made Benson feel like Howell the farmer. But there was excitement in the contempt. There was excitement down the most unexpected back alley-ways.

* * *

'Maybe we should go and see Nurse Muñoz on another day,' said Benson.

'No. I told her I'd come and see her this morning. She loves to meet her old students. I work in a part of the hospital she never visits.'

Benson bowed to the inevitable. Well, he thought, maybe I do have shadows under my eyes but Nurse Muñoz will be looking for other qualities. She won't be interested in how sexy I am, just whether I can look after patients.

On the door was written 'Nurse Instructor D. Muñoz' and beneath a stick-on label, 'NO SMOKING THANK YOU'. Well, he thought, maybe Nurse Instructor Muñoz was allergic, like Rod.

Inside, there was no sign of Nurse Instructor Muñoz. The large room looked like a hospital ward. There were three beds, all neatly made up. On one bed lay a mansize pink dummy. The dummy was nude and anatomically correct right down to a perfect (circumcised) penis and testicles. Benson gave the dummy's anatomy the once over, deciding that he and the dummy were about equally well equipped. It had a bandage round the head and the left arm was in a sling. Next to the male dummy was a female and she seemed in a very bad way indeed, bandaged all over so that hardly an inch of skin was showing. Next to her in the same bed lay a dummy of a child of about three years old. He or she had a nappy on. The third bed was empty.

Pablo became very animated when he saw the dummies. 'You're all still here!' he told them. 'And still so sick! Poor things!' He approached the man dummy and kissed him on the cheek. 'Martin, this is Arthur. Arthur, Martin.'

Benson looked at Pablo, then at Arthur.

'Well aren't you going to say hello to Arthur? First impressions are important.'

'Hello er . . . Arthur,' said Benson, thinking about a shoe sitting on top of his sandals.

'Martin will be taking care of you, Arthur. You'll be just fine with him. Tell you the truth, he's a bit of a dummy himself sometimes.' Pablo turned to the woman dummy. 'And this is Anita.'

'Hello Anita,' said Benson without prompting.

'Poor Anita, baby! I've never seen you in such a bad way! What have they been doing to you, honey?' And Pablo stroked one of the few bare sections of Anita's arm. 'What did you say, Anita?' he asked and bent towards her bandaged face. 'Yeah, he sure is. But he'll open up.'

'What did Anita say about me?' Benson asked.

'She said you seem pretty cold.'

'Well, we've only just met.'

A strange high-pitched voice responded to Benson's statement. At first Benson wondered if it were Pablo mimicking Anita. Benson said 'Sorry?' and the statement was repeated by a small woman of about fifty standing by a door that Benson had not noticed in all the activity over introductions.

'Why shame on you! Only just met indeed! Love 'em from the word go!'

Benson looked at the nurse blankly.

Pablo turned and opened his arms wide: 'Mrs Muñoz! You look wonderful! Great to see you again!' He ran to her and they hugged. Then Nurse Muñoz disengaged herself from Pablo, looking past him. 'This is your friend, I guess,' she said. 'Well, we still haven't taught him his first lesson, have we?'

'No, we haven't,' said Pablo.

'And what is that first lesson?'

'T! L! C!' shouted Pablo, like a crowd.

199

Benson placed his left sandal on top of his right and folded his arms.

And Nurse Muñoz was standing in front of Benson, looking at him hard. 'Your friend's not saying anything. He's sure a slow learner, ain't he?'

Pablo nodded slowly, finding time to give Benson a knowing look. 'He sure as hell is, Mrs Muñoz.'

'I guess he needs some TLC himself. Don't you think so, Pablo? Have you been giving him enough?'

'I sure have, Mrs Muñoz,' said Pablo.

Benson looked from one to the other.

She gestured for Benson to sit down in one of the student chairs. He had to lift the little writing desk attached to it, in order to have enough room to sit down. 'Not all our patients are in bed,' said Nurse Muñoz. Then she added, 'Who said that, Pablo?'

Pablo shook his head. Nurse Muñoz tutted and raised her eyebrows as she seated herself up on the teacher's stool in front of her blackboard, on which was written,

'To fight and to HEED the wound!'

Benson was still devoting his full attention to a consideration of Nurse Muñoz's body. He had been trying to think what it reminded him of. He had come up with a possible parallel, drawn from an object at home. She looked a bit like the crocheted lady who sat on top of the spare toilet roll on the window-ledge in the toilet. Its top half was petite too, but the toilet roll made her huge below. Of course, lots of women had huge hips. He had quite big hips himself. But in Nurse Muñoz this tendency had really been allowed to take over. The hips had bloomed out of control. Would the same thing happen to him if he did not control his appetite?

200

Self-discipline, that's the key, he thought. What starts as a bore becomes a basic recipe for survival. Mind you, it probably goes on being a bore as well.

'How could you forget? "Not all our patients are in bed" was told to me by my teacher in this very room. And my teacher's name was . . .' Nurse Muñoz pointed to Pablo, then moved the pointing arm in time to his reply.

'Miss Olive Dvorak, Mrs Muñoz.'

'Right! Now, Martin, what do you think that means?'

'Er . . . I suppose it must mean that there are people who need help whom we might not think are sick,' said Benson.

'Right! You must always be on the look-out for the walking wounded in this world. And especially at the Unitarian Medical Center. The loved ones of our patients often need as much TLC as the patients themselves. Neglect them and you neglect your duties.' Nurse Muñoz rotated her left hand across her tummy in a clockwise direction, wearing a look that betokened a tummyache. 'And, if you don't do your duty to the best of your ability, if you don't give everyone you come into contact with one hundred and one per cent of your love and effort, how will you feel at the end of the day? Pablo?'

'An empty feeling that no food can fill, Mrs Muñoz!' said Pablo.

Benson had to hand it to Pablo. He had certainly learnt his lessons well. He wondered why he was prepared to sit through his Saturday off and listen to Nurse Muñoz treating them both like schoolboys. It was odd, but it revealed a nice side to Pablo's character, a side he had not seen before. It made him hopeful.

Benson put his hand up. 'Please, Mrs Muñoz, what's TLC?'

'Pablo, tell him.'

'TLC means Tender Loving Care,' said Pablo.

The words stirred Nurse Muñoz to action. She bounded down from her stool with great energy, placed her hand on the side of her bubbly brown hairdo in the vicinity of her invisible left ear, and shouted, 'I can't hear you!'

'Tender Loving Care,' said Benson.

'Speak up! I still can't hear you!'

Benson making a face, looked down at his desk. He felt suddenly that he belonged at the Woodside Industrial Coathanger Factory, chewing on submarine sandwiches, telling lies to his workmates, counting rods, sitting on the subway back to the Y, like Tom Joad, glorying in his dirty jeans. He looked up at Nurse Muñoz. She was looking back at him with a look of great intensity. I'll show her, he thought. 'TENDER LOVING CARE!' he bellowed at the top of his voice.

'That's RIGHT!' said Nurse Muñoz, and she started applauding Benson, encouraging Pablo to join in. Pablo did so. Benson looked about him.

Then suddenly Nurse Muñoz was serious again, addressing Pablo, asking him about his sisters, and people whom Benson had never heard of. Benson was left to think to himself how peculiar America was. It was the more peculiar because you didn't quite expect it to be peculiar at all. It didn't approach you at once and sock you in the teeth with the intensity of its peculiarity. You had to be around for a while. He could not have imagined going for a similar job with the National Health Service and being made to shout out like that. Years of devoted viewing of *Emergency Ward Ten* had in no way prepared him for what he was going through. Stop it, he told himself. You're judging again.

Then he heard Nurse Muñoz ask Pablo, 'And where did you meet Martin?'

202

'At the movies,' said Pablo.

'You like the movies, Martin?'

'Oh, yes I do,' replied Benson. 'Of course, there's a lot of rubbish around, but there's nothing nicer than a really good picture.'

'Have you seen *The Sound of Music*?'

'Yes, several times.'

'It's my favourite,' said Nurse Muñoz. 'You talk like Julie Andrews.'

Benson sincerely hoped he didn't. 'Er . . . she's English too,' he said. 'She was originally in the London production of *My Fair Lady* but they didn't give her the part in the film. I'll never for the life of me know why. I'll probably go to my grave wondering why she didn't get the part. I mean, Audrey Hepburn was all right but she didn't even sing her own songs! She mimed the whole time. That's no good, is it? Of course, there's been a lot of that – miming – too much if you want my opinion. Deborah Kerr mimed in the *King And I*. So did Dorothy Dandridge in *Carmen Jones*. Hollywood seems to think that looks are everything. And they never give any attention to the poor woman who actually *did* do the singing. I just don't think it's fair myself.'

'I never knew Deborah Kerr was miming,' said Nurse Muñoz.

'Well, I'm sorry to have to be the one who disillusions you, but it's true, I'm afraid.'

Nurse Muñoz seemed stunned for a moment. 'My,' she said. 'It just goes to show.'

Benson nodded his agreement. Something very close to his core felt extremely pleased to be able to disillusion Nurse Muñoz. 'Your name's interesting. Is it Spanish?'

'Yes. My husband's called Pedro. He's from Puerto Rico. But I'm not Spanish myself, Martin. My family's from Ireland originally. My maiden name's O'Hanlon.'

'Oh, yes?' He wondered for a moment whether his whole life was fated to be spent sitting in classrooms with Irish teachers.

'So you want to be a nurses' aide?' asked Nurse Muñoz.

'Well . . . er . . . I'd like to have a go,' said Benson.

Nurse Muñoz frowned at him. He knew exactly why she was frowning. It was not a frown that intimidated him. It merely explained.

'Yes, I would like to be a nurses' aide,' he said.

'Good.' She turned to Pablo. 'Pablo, why don't you go to the cafeteria and get yourself a cup of coffee? You might meet some old friends there.'

'Sure, Mrs Muñoz.'

Nurse Muñoz crinkled her nose at Pablo and smiled. Then, when he had closed the door behind him, she stood up and gestured Benson to follow her. Benson did so with alacrity. She opened a door which led into a small office with a window directly opposite the door. Through the slats of the blinds Benson could make out the end of a blank brick wall and a view south to the Verrazano-Narrows Bridge. She walked to the left of the window, lifted a kettle, testing it for water. Satisfied, she turned and smiled at Benson and said, 'Goodie.' Then she turned on the hotplate and asked Benson whether he preferred coffee or tea.

'Coffee, please, Mrs Muñoz.'

'Milk and sugar?'

'Neither, thanks.'

Nurse Muñoz got the cups ready. As she did this, she kept looking at him hard, appraising him. He knew that and had to stop his eyes from fluttering. The smile was still there but she could have been on her second trip to the dress shop, casting an eye over a dress she was mindful to buy but wasn't yet one hundred per cent sure about. Benson filled in his embarrassment by saying that in England most people had electric kettles and that he had been surprised to find that in America – where everything seemed so up-to-the-minute in most ways – they still put their kettles on the stove.

She nodded, but did not say anything. Benson found himself looking her straight in the eye. He wondered why she hadn't responded. Usually women liked talking about gadgets. She kept on looking at him. He wanted to look away, but he didn't. Instead he concentrated on thinking how very blue her eyes were, how probably Mr Muñoz had discovered her through those eyes and been captivated, hypnotized, and had just not noticed how strangely put together the rest of her was.

The kettle whistled. She turned to take care of it and Benson looked out of the window and started panting. He had not realized that he had been holding his breath throughout their silent exchange of looks. I wonder if there's a business in importing electric kettles from England? It would definitely be providing a much-needed service. I might be able to get Russell-Hobbs to rub out their name and put mine on instead. I could call it the Benson Kettle. It might make a mint and save me from having a boring job. But then he thought about how the voltage was different in America and what a lot of work would be involved in changing the plugs. He saw himself hunched over a bench changing plugs from dawn to dusk. Yes, knowing my luck I'd probably spend my whole life putting American plugs on English kettles. And then they wouldn't sell and I'd be stuck with them. Yes, that's how it would be.

'Thank you,' Benson said as his black coffee was placed in front of him on the desk.

'You're welcome,' replied Nurse Muñoz. She sat down opposite him.

'Nice coffee,' said Benson.

'You're not an American citizen, are you?'

Benson was at once on his guard. If he were going to be honest he should tell Nurse Muñoz here and now that, far from being an American citizen, he was merely a tourist. Instead he said, 'No, but I've got a social security number.'

'Well, that's something. Almost everybody you meet here is illegal anyway. But what I want to know is whether you'll be staying with us. Before we train you we'd like to be sure you'll be around for a while. Are you prepared to stay?'

He was not sure what to say. He tried to remember what Pablo had told him, but was unable to. Had Pablo told him anything? He looked steadily into Nurse Muñoz's blue eyes. A yes would be simplest. She might believe him. But then again, she might not. He felt his face reddening. It prickled with guilt pressure. Nurse Muñoz would be bound to notice. Those blue eyes noticed everything. 'Er . . . I'm not sure. You see, I'm not certain whether I'd make a good nurses' aide. It's hard to give you an honest answer.' That was true.

'Do you want to be a good nurses' aide?'

'Yes, I'd like to try.'

Nurse Muñoz frowned. 'I'd prefer you to like to BE rather than like to TRY. There is a difference you know.'

'Is there?' He couldn't think of the difference. Was Nurse Muñoz going to turn out to be a transatlantic Dr Griffiths?

'Think positively, Mr Benson!'

He nodded, though he was more inclined to shake his head and tell Nurse Muñoz about the Manleys. 'Yes, I'll try,' he said.

'Yes, I WILL,' corrected Nurse Muñoz.

'Yes, I will.' I see, he thought. Yes, now I understand what she's saying. I think. But to be positive is to tempt fate rather. Sparky was as positive as anything about his ability to play his piano and that led to his abject humiliation on the stage of the Carnegie Hall. Positive thinking has an edge of pride to it and you know what pride leads to. Icarus and melting wax, feathers all over the place and a big splash. Still, the immigrants were trying to eliminate the negative . . . You do that? YOU can't do that!!' Negative thoughts were banished or turned into positive ones by a tiresome sea voyage, an act of will and the first sighting of Liberty. Look at Walt. *Clap the skull on top of the ribs, and clap a crown on top of the skull.* He was endlessly positive. And Walt had been a wound-dresser during the Civil War. Not that it HAD been civil . . .

'What will happen – if you decide to join us here at UMC – is that I'll be teaching you in the morning and then you'll do practical work on the wards in the afternoon. What you learn here each morning by practising procedures on our little family of model patients over there are things which every health professional needs to know; how to give a dignified and pleasurable blanket bath, make beds beautifully, change dressings while you reduce the ouch factor to zero. You'll learn how to do a lot of things down here with me and then have a chance to practise what you've learnt in the wards. Also, most importantly, I'll be developing in you what you hopefully already possess. Now, what's the main thing we need to bring out in you?' Nurse Muñoz raised her eyebrows and cocked her head sideways.

Benson knew that one. He smiled at Nurse Muñoz, 'TLC,' he said.

'You're a fast learner.'

'No, not at all. You're a good teacher. I don't think I'll ever forget what TLC means.'

She smiled at him and he felt himself softening like butter placed next to a sunny window. I like you, he told her silently. And, as he often had before, he saw himself on his death bed about to depart this life. He was in a hospital bed surrounded by several nurses' aides. They wept copiously because they were about to be deprived of the man who had lifted the profession of nurses' aide to heights deemed impossible back in the dark days of the nineteen sixties. What have you to tell us, O President? they asked him. Benson smiled and tousled the hair of the young positive-thinking nurses' aide near his pillow. 'First and last and in between,' he croaked, 'and in every fibre of your nurses'-aide-being is TLC. My only request, apart from that you live TLC, is that you venerate the memory of dear Mrs Muñoz and my long-term companion and helpmate, Pablo Suarez.' Benson's grieving apostles said they would. Benson turned his head towards the healing ward in the sky and departed, wearing his special knowing, positive smile.

Nurse Muñoz went on to ask him questions about his education. She seemed impressed as he rattled on about his O and A levels. Nurse Muñoz said that he would easily be accepted at Nursing School at Brooklyn College, despite his lack of a science. 'When can you start?' she asked him at last.

'Tuesday?'

'Monday would be better. I've got three others starting then. It would be great if you could all be there together from the very first day. It makes things real easy that way.'

'I'll have to tell my present employer, but I think I can.'

'*Think?*'

'I can . . . er . . . I will,' he said, mentally kicking himself for the elementary mistakes he kept making in the American language.

'She's very nice, isn't she?' Benson told Pablo as they walked home half an hour later.

'More than nice, man! If it wasn't for Mrs Muñoz I don't know where I'd be now.'

'How do you mean?'

'Well, same as I got you to see Nurse Muñoz just now, my sisters took me to see her three years back. They'd just about given up on me, you know. When I came to join them from the Philippines I just went crazy. I wouldn't settle down to anything. New York City was just one big candy store. If you think I'm wild now you should have seen me then! I fucked my way up and down the five boroughs. Took job after job, then left when they balled me out about something. My sisters told Nurse Muñoz about me and she said she'd see me. I went there and I thought what a fuckin' yo-yo she was.'

'How do you mean, a yo-yo?'

'A weirdo. I mean, that's what everyone thinks of her at first. She runs off at the mouth so damned much.'

'I didn't think she was really . . .'

'No, well you're a yo-yo too. You two should get on just great.' To his credit Pablo saw Benson's hurt expression and decided that some TLC was called for. It was lucky for him that he did because Benson had had it in mind to litanize some of the ways in which he thought Pablo was a yo-yo too. His list would have gone up and down many times.

'Thanks for taking me to see her.'

Pablo held Benson back from crossing an intersection against the light. Two Austin Eleven Hundreds passed one after the other. 'They're both British cars,' Benson told Pablo proudly.

'They're Austin Americas. Crap. Real crap.'

'No, they're not. They're very good. Economical and dependable. My dad's friend has got one and he swears by it.'

'You can't get spare parts for them. What's the use of having a car if there ain't no spare parts for them?'

Benson wondered whether he should write to Harold Wilson to tell him about the problem. But didn't he have diplomats employed in Washington to deal with that sort of thing? Still, it was well known that diplomats were all Tories and public school to a man. They would probably be trying to sabotage Britain overseas so that some horrible Tory government could get back in and make the poor pay sixty dollars a day plus all dressings and procedures for a hospital bed, which was what Pablo said it cost to be in UMC. Yes, that was how it was. He knew he was being cynical, but still. That's how things were in the Old World. 'What are we going to do now?'

'What do you want to do?'

'What's that bridge at the end of Fourth Avenue? Shall we go and see it? I like bridges.'

'That's the Verrazano-Narrows Bridge. It's new. But you'll have time for that. Let's go home and enjoy ourselves. I have to work tomorrow afternoon anyway. I hate to waste an empty apartment. It doesn't happen too often that I have a place. Hey, maybe we can get together in your room at the Y.'

'That'd be really lovely,' said Benson.

They returned to Pablo's apartment. Benson thought of the ampules that remained on Pablo's bedside table. He was quite looking forward to having another go with them. Yes, there was such a lot to look forward to, so much to be positive about. Pablo had proved his friendship by sacrificing his day off. He looked across at Pablo's face. A sudden wind of emotion, sweeping hot down a gloomy canyon of phallic skyscrapers, hit him suddenly. It engorged him and caused his heart to beat wildly.

'I love you,' Benson told Pablo.

'Yo-yo, fuckin' yo-yo!' replied Pablo amiably.

4

TENDER LOVING CARE

To turn, turn will be our delight
'Til by turning, turning we come round right.

Shaker song

Benson pushed an elaborate letter of resignation into the mailbox at the Woodside Industrial Coathanger Factory and smiled at the shuttered gate. I have other experiences to take in, he told it. I must crush the bunch of grapes that is the New World against my face and let the juice run down. You were good. I shall miss you all, O Workers of the New World! I shall miss you, O Sons of Pioneers! And you, O Makers of Sandwiches as big and generous as America! But now Voyagers, I must depart! I embrace my friends, leave all in order! I depart to tend the sick of Brooklyn! Farewell, my Fancies!

Would he make a good nurses' aide? Well, he might. No, that's not the way I'm supposed to think. I WILL be an excellent nurses' aide. That is how it WILL be. No two ways about it.

He found that he was automatically walking in the direction that would bring him to O'Toole's Tavern. He looked at his Timex. It was only one o'clock. Still, people drank in the afternoon, especially on Sunday. Of course, he might be becoming a bit fond of Guinness. Alice had once come in while Benson was quaffing sherry. 'You don't *like* it, do you?' she had asked, all worried. Benson assured her that he didn't. It was purely medicinal. That was true in a way.

O'Toole's Tavern was much more crowded than it had been on any of Benson's previous visits. It took him a moment to adjust to the gloom after the daylight. Groups of men were seated at the bar talking, and the place went momentarily quiet as Benson stood on the threshold, then let the swinging doors close with a whoosh and a bang that made him jump. This silence happened in English pubs too but here in America the ambience at once brought westerns to mind. When Bronco Lane entered a saloon something terrible was bound to happen. Bronco asked for trouble by requesting a glass of milk. This inevitably caused some particularly disreputable customer to cast doubt on Bronco's manhood. If it had happened to Bronco, God knows what might happen to him.

Benson scouted about for an empty bar stool, at last finding one at the far end under the pictures of Irish hurling teams and a St Bridget's cross made out of straw. Benson ordered a Guinness. While he waited for the drink, he looked at the St Bridget's cross, wondering how anybody could have come up with such a complicated design. Who first made one? Poor, dear, Anon.

The barman put his Guinness on the bar. It wasn't Mr O'Toole. He was probably keeping the sabbath holy. Benson took a long draft from the drink and waited for it to calm him down.

From tomorrow his mind would be full of TLC and procedures and learning the names of patients, trying to please them and Nurse Muñoz. He hoped it would also be full of Pablo. He thought of Pablo and got an erection on the spot. Gosh, I won't forget that lovemaking with Pablo in a hurry. The stuff definitely brought out the animal in me. But is that good? Maybe I won't be able to enjoy sex without it in future. You've got to watch everything like mad. He looked at his empty glass of Guinness. Where had it gone?

He ordered another Guinness. When he had come in he had thought just to drink one. But it did not happen like that. The first calmed him down and made him forget his objections to having a second. The group of men nearby were talking about either baseball or American football. It was not immediately clear to

Benson which was which in conversation. It could even have been the netball that tall Negroes seemed so good at. Anyway, he hoped he would never be able to sort out all the games. A priori they were uninteresting though, as a phenomenon, beguiling. To venture thousands of miles across the ocean and find men talking about competitive sports. That was typical of so-called real men.

He thought of Pablo again. Then he thought of sixty-nine. That had been wonderful. It worked so well. It made such a lot of sense. Of course, sixty-nine was not one hundred per cent satisfactory because you weren't able to kiss while doing it. Still, he had to accept the fact that this was not an ideal world. Sixty-nine was about as good as things could get on this side of the grave. Funny name, though.

'What's on your mind?'

'Sorry?' Benson asked, hoping that what was on his mind wasn't showing.

'You seemed a long ways away,' said the man. Benson had not even noticed that someone had seated himself down next to him. Gosh, he thought. Maybe I was so far away that he could have pickpocketed my wallet and taken my social security card. Benson felt his chest, but everything seemed to be in order. He turned the checking feel into a scratch so that the man would not think he was checking.

'No, I was just thinking.'

'Are you foreign?'

'Yes, I'm British.'

'Oh, you are? And you're in an Irish bar. Isn't that like walking into the lion's den?'

'How do you mean?'

'Well, from what I pick up there's a lot of bad blood between the English and the Irish.'

'Ireland's independent now.'

'Not all of it, though.'

'Northern Ireland. That belongs to England.'

'I wouldn't say that too loud in here if I were you.'

'Why not?'

'Because they wouldn't agree with you.'

'I'm against nationalism,' said Benson. 'It causes wars. Like religion. Anyway, I'm part Irish myself.'

'Catholic?'

'Sort of. I'm lapsed. Are you Catholic?'

The man smiled assent. He was quite heavily built, about thirty, Benson thought. He had the makings of a double chin but to counteract this his hairline was very low, coming down to his forehead thick and black. Benson wished he had a low hairline like that. You could afford to lose so much more before being declared bald. The man was in no danger of that happening to him.

'The name's Martin,' said Benson. What do you mean, *the*?

'Patrick. Pleased to meet you, Martin. How about another Guinness?'

'Thank you very much. I'm not sure I should. This is my second.'

The man did not take any notice of Benson's doubts. He signalled the barman to bring them refills. 'So what brings you to the United States?'

Benson told him.

'It's a great country.'

'Yes, it is. It isn't what I expected, though. It's much more foreign than I'd thought it would be.'

'Well, you've got so many different kinds of people here. They all contribute a little of themselves to the stew.'

'Yes, that's what I like about it.'

'Are you going to be travelling around at all?'

'I don't know. Most of the other students who came

218

over on the flight with me had those three month tickets on the buses. I thought I would be working at Camp Manley in the Catskill mountains and then travelling a bit, but things haven't worked out like that.'

Patrick nodded. He reached across Benson for an ashtray and Benson found that Patrick's leg was up against his. When he moved back, the leg stayed where it was.

Patrick started talking about union corruption in New York and Benson listened, though most of his attention was focused on the feeling of Patrick's leg against his. He held himself still. To move at all would mean giving a signal, and Benson was not ready for signalling. If he moved away Patrick might be insulted. He might have been looking for someone like Benson all his life and would see Benson pulling away as a sign that he had no chance, that the ideal he had sought for so long had not reciprocated. Benson sat very still.

'So Mayor Lindsey said to the mafia bosses, "Now look it here. Just get those Italian kids off the streets and see if we can bring the temperature down."'

'Er . . . and did it?'

'Sure it did. But then the voters of Bensonhurst turned on him and accused him of caving in, making the mafia respectable. Well, he was but this city works in that way. Take away the graft and corruption and the whole shooting match would fall apart. I tell you, Martin, the Borgias had nothing on New York City. It ain't pure but it works most of the time.'

'I don't think we have problems like that in England . . . Britain,' said Benson.

'Oh, you don't huh! Pull the other one, Martin. It's just that you don't *know* about it, that's all. Those rich bastards with their kids in swanky private schools and fancy universities. Do you really think they don't give

219

the jobs to their own kids and the boys of their buddies? You got one big private club back there which says to everybody else, Keep Out! Haven't you figured that out yet?'

'No,' lied Benson. 'I'm the son of a policeman but I'm at university. Not Oxford and Cambridge, true. But then I didn't get good enough results to go there. A friend of mine did, though.' And he thought, and look what happened to him! Damn you, Laurence! 'Anyway, we've got a Labour government now.'

If anything the leg was pushing against his much harder than before. And jiggling up and down too. O insupportable! Benson felt his own leg – rooted to the spot in an attempt to be uncommunicative – going to sleep.

'A Labour government isn't going to solve your problem. It's all underground, Martin. The fact that you don't know about it is because the British are so damned subtle. Believe me, every state on God's earth is as corrupt as hell. It's just that the style of their corruption mirrors the national soul.'

Benson would have been greatly enjoying this discussion – Patrick was much better at argument than Ianto, Benson's Welsh Nationalist friend and sparring-partner at Aberystwyth – had it not been for his fidgety leg against his. He tried not to think about it. 'It's greed that causes corruption and greed is deeply ingrained in the systems we live under. Change the system and you banish corruption. Take the Catholic Church, for instance. The Catholic Church has wandered so far away from the original intentions of Christ that it's pathetic. All the churches and cathedrals, all the treasures. And have you noticed that the houses the priests live in are always much bigger than necessary? Now I've nothing against beautiful buildings and art objects but they don't fit in with the unworldly, crazy vision of Christ. If you want to know what I think, I think that Christians should appear to be clowns in this world. They should give away what they own. But what do they do? They do what the rest of the world does. They fit in. The world fits organized religion like a glove.'

'Are you a practising Catholic, Martin?'

'No, I'm not,' he said, shaking his head vehemently as he lifted his Guinness to his lips.

Patrick was trying to attract the barman's attention. 'My turn,' said Benson. Patrick shrugged and Benson ordered another round.

'So how are you going to change it if you're not part of it?'

How was he? He took a slug from his Guinness to gain some time. 'Er ... do I have to become a prostitute to reform prostitutes?'

'Maybe you do,' said Patrick. 'Only a prostitute knows what needs reformation.'

'Yes, but ...' The drinks arrived and Benson paid. Then he said he had to go to the bathroom. It was a relief to remove his leg from Patrick's. At the door he read BUCKOS and COLLEENS, made a face and went through Buckos as there did not seem to be an alternative that exactly fitted Benson.

He was standing by the urinal when someone else came in and stood next to him.

'You set me off.' It was Patrick's voice.

Benson felt himself stiffen. He fought it. For more than a year he had managed to stay away from toilets. He had not once gone into one with a nefarious purpose in mind. Partly this was because he felt he was never going to meet Dearest Him in one, partly because he had almost got caught in one when a police car stopped outside. But it took only one small thing for the erotic geography to cock him once again. He tried

221

to think of cold things to get him back to normal . . . iceberg, Mivvi, Orange Maid, Brother Hooper, mountain stream, Anglo Saxon . . . but he continued to rear up. His flow was abruptly cut off. He sought to cover himself, to bend forward so that nothing would show. But he was not sure he was doing a very good job because there was no barrier between the urinals. If Patrick were looking he would know where Benson stood. He would probably put Benson's lack of response back at the bar to English reticence and hypocrisy. He could hear the flow from Patrick splashing into the bowl. It was a healthy, manly sound, much deeper than his even at the best of times.

Patrick had gone silent in the way that most men did in urinals. Benson stood on uselessly. What he ought to do, he felt, was just leave. There really was no point in hanging on. He looked over tentatively at Patrick. He looked away. Then he pushed himself back into his trousers.

Patrick followed shortly after. They washed in the basin. Patrick saw that Benson was looking at him in the mirror. He winked at him.

I wonder if Pablo would mind, Benson thought. I know it isn't ideal to have two friends at the same time but it would be nice to have a go with Patrick. Funny that he didn't make a move in the toilet. Still, he probably didn't want to cheapen the experience. Quite right too.

They were seated again. Benson felt his leg was in the same position as before and within easy reach of Patrick but he had made no attempt to place his next to Benson's. He had started talking about New York neighbourhoods again.

Benson had to excuse himself again a few minutes later. When he got back, Patrick had stood up from his bar stool and was chatting with the barman. Benson drank the remaining Guinness in his glass. He had decided that Patrick had probably seen him in the toilet and reckoned that he did not come up to his exacting expectations. He felt a bit let down by this turn of events. He had just been won round to the idea of a good time with Patrick and now here he was about to be frustrated. He tried to pick up the pieces of his shattered morals.

Just as Benson was busy both giving up hope and thinking how he would now be able to be faithful to Pablo, Patrick turned to him and said, 'Well, Martin. I'm off home now to grab a bite to eat. I wonder if I could persuade you to join me. I have some cold roast beef at home. Lots of other good things too. And I may even be able to find an old bottle of Guinness some-where. How about it? You like the sound of that?'

'Er . . . are you sure? That's very kind. I am a bit hungry. But are you sure it's not too much trouble?'

'No trouble at all. It'll be nice to have company.'

I'm sorry, Pablo, Benson thought. Still Walt would approve: *The dear love of man for his comrade, the attraction of friend to friend.* Yes, that's it! I must shake off these Old World strictures. Here I will love comrades! I will hang on neck after neck! I will make the earth warmer with the strength of my youthful embraces. Patrick? Pablo? You are not enough to satisfy my great beating heart, my pounding lungs, my healthful bowels! Come all!

'Do you know Whitman's poetry?' Benson asked Patrick as they walked along Roosevelt. Coming out of the bar felt like leaving a cinema after a matinée. The light hurt their eyes. There was something obscene about it. Still, it was obvious that Patrick was lusting after him like mad.

'We read him at school. "O Captain, my Captain," that sort of thing.'

'I don't like that one. But I love Whitman. He's my favourite.'

'Well, maybe I should have another try. I often find I like things I had to do at school, though I didn't like them much when I was doing them.'

Benson deftly flicked his erection upwards. He wasn't going to break any promises to Pablo, was he? There is such a thing as Wild Oats and it really is about time to sow a few. I'm like a man who has grown up in a severe famine. Now I'm in the midst of plenty. I mean, I can count on the fingers of one hand – well two – the number of people I've played about with. It really is time to experience. Then he wondered if it was the Guinness talking.

'Do you have any brothers and sisters?' Patrick asked him.

'No, I'm an only child,' Benson replied. He did not much like confessing to being an only child because the prevailing wisdom had it that only children were spoilt and selfish. 'Of course, my mum and dad wanted more, but they couldn't.'

'Glad to hear it,' said Patrick. Well, what did that mean? Was he glad to hear that Mum and Dad had tried or that they couldn't manage any more? 'I'm one of twelve. But I was the only boy. Imagine that!'

Benson said he couldn't. 'I expect the girls all made a great fuss of you.'

'Yeah, they sure did. You're not getting tired are you? My place is just a few feet around the next corner.'

'No, not at all. I could go on like this for ages. I like walking.'

They turned left at a church. '"Our Lady of Perpetual Help",' read Benson. 'In England we call her Our Lady of Perpetual Succour.'

'I live just here.'

224

'You're very handy for the church, aren't you?'

'Yeah, I guess I am.'

Patrick turned two keys in the locks of the front door, and stepped aside, holding it open for Benson to go in ahead of him. Benson found himself confronting, across a wide hall, an only slightly less than life-size crucifix. From the parquet floor rose the aroma of wax polish.

'Hold on, Martin. I'll go and say hi to the canon.'

Benson watched Patrick disappearing through a panelled door to the right. Canon: the larger the gun the greater the bore. Then he looked back at the crucifix, frowning. Just my luck, he thought. Patrick's staying with a priest. He then aimed a scowl at St Thérèse of Lisieux, had been about to stick out his tongue at the smiling saint when a door he had not noticed just to the right of the crucifix opened and in came a large, grey-haired woman wearing over a flowery frock a blue oilcloth pinafore with 'Atlantic City' printed on the front in red.

'Er . . . Hello,' Benson said.

'Hello yourself.' She seemed nonplussed to see him there, just as he was nonplussed to see her there. Hope was fading along with his erection. Of course, Patrick might have an apartment of his own in this big house. Then he remembered what he had said about priests' houses. 'I'm with Patrick,' he said.

'You'll be wanting lunch, so. Were there many at O'Toole's?'

'Quite a few. Yes. You've got an Irish accent, haven't you?'

'I must have. I've only lived here thirty years. It just doesn't rub off, I guess.

'I wouldn't worry about it.'

'I don't. What's your name?'

'Martin.'

'Would that be after Martin de Porres?'

'No, worse luck. St Martin of Tours,' said Benson.

'Well, he was a good old stick. Didn't he cut his cloak in half to give it to a beggar and didn't the beggar turn out to be Jesus?'

'Yes, but he was also a shocking persecutor of pagans,' said Benson. 'He went around destroying pagan temples.'

'What's wrong with that?'

'Well,' said Benson. 'It seems to me that to a pagan his beliefs are as valid as those of a Catholic. An awful lot of the harm in this world is caused by people who are certain of their rectitude.'

'Well, I suppose you're right. I'm just a silly old woman, I guess.'

'No you're not!' asserted Benson.

'You're sure?'

'Absolutely positive!'

'Sure, I thought it wasn't a good thing to be too sure, according to your way of thinking.'

Benson opened his mouth, shut it again. Then he smiled. 'It's a complicated world, isn't it?'

'Isn't that the truth?'

'Is it?'

Benson laughed. He had never imagined, even on the wilder shores of his fantasies, that he would ever again enter a presbytery, let alone laugh in one.

'Is that accent English?' she asked.

'Yes, I'm afraid so,' said Benson.

'What are you afraid of? I can't see anything to be afraid of. Half my family are in England. Liverpool. They were too scared to get on the boat again after that shocking trip from Dublin. I couldn't get enough of the sea. I came on. Whenever I can I take the Staten Island ferry and feed the birds. It's a great bargain that ferry. Have you been on it?'

'No, not yet.'

'You've got a treat in store, so.'

'I'm from near Liverpool.'

'Well fancy that. Isn't it a small world? Still I expect you don't need me to tell you that. My elder brother, Jack, lives in Liverpool.'

'What's his surname?'

'Same as mine.'

'What's yours?'

'O'Neill.'

'I know some O'Neills,' said Benson, 'but they live in Wallasey. That's just across the river from Liverpool. My dad gives Mr and Mrs O'Neill a lift home from church most Sundays.'

'No, that can't be Jack. Jack isn't married, though he keeps threatening to. He won't though. Jack wasn't made for marriage. Same as me. But we've got some cousins, and Jack's mentioned taking a ferry-boat to see them. I remembered that because I'm partial to ferry-boats, like I said.'

'Well it could be them, I suppose.'

'It certainly could.'

The door opened and Patrick came in. 'So you've met Miss O'Neill,' Patrick said to Benson.

'We certainly have, Father Patrick. And do you know that your young visitor may know my cousins in England. Isn't it a small world, Father?'

Father Patrick nodded, while Benson nodded too, but to himself. So small was the world that in his mind he was back at Devil's Bridge in the company of Dr Leptos, thinking how nothing was as simple as it at first appeared. 'Is there any lunch left for two drunken sinners?'

'I think there might be a bite or two,' said Miss O'Neill with a smile. Benson and Patrick followed her through into the dining room where a table groaned with cold cuts and steaming potatoes and vegetables. Benson forgot his turmoil. It was all too complicated anyway and would have to be sorted out at a future date when he was sober and not the guest of a priest in a presbytery. He felt like burying himself in Miss O'Neill's ample bust. He sat down opposite Patrick and she served them. He smiled up at her and she smiled down at him. There was a brief pause in the proceedings while Patrick bowed his head to say Grace.

'Right. Nosebags on,' said Miss O'Neill. She left the room.

'Er . . . I didn't know you were a priest. I wouldn't have said what I said in the pub if I'd known,' said Benson, accepting a pile of beef and ham.

'Honesty is the best policy,' replied Patrick. 'I have to take a lot worse than that from some of the heathens at O'Toole's I can tell you. A part of me agreed with you. But you've heard of *felix culpa*, haven't you?'

'Yes, it means "Happy Fault".'

'We don't mention it but once in the liturgy. It's a way of saying that we are happy with the way things have turned out. If there'd been no original sin there'd have been no redemption. And if it weren't for the Redemption there'd have been no Bach or Beethoven or Dean Swift.'

'But what about every sin twisting a dagger in Mary's heart, recrucifying Jesus; that isn't happy, is it?'

'It's just a metaphor, Martin. So much is a metaphor. Hell is one too.'

Benson smiled at his unexpected lunch.

'What are you smiling about?'

'I don't know whether I should say.'

'Go ahead.'

'It's just that the goal posts are being shifted. When I was growing up everything seemed so hard and fast. I took everything I was told literally because that was how I was told to take it. Nobody mentioned metaphors then. I felt damned on and off for years. Now all I keep hearing is how I shouldn't have felt damned at all. There was nothing so very terrible about what I was doing. And that shocks me. Well no, that's not quite right. I'm past being shocked by it. I just can't take it seriously. My indoctrination won't allow me to pick and choose. I have to take all or nothing. And I can't take it all.'

'So you take nothing?'

'More or less, yes.'

'Sure, you're a young man yet. That'll pass.'

'Maybe.'

'Eventually, you'll be able to meet the Lord half way. That's about as far as any of us can get.'

'Yes, I might be able to if there wasn't such a terrific amount of obligation that He puts on His friendship.'

'When you get to my age . . .' But Benson was looking at Patrick and he stopped. Then he started again. 'What I mean is that you mustn't let yourself swallow a load of contrary dogmatisms. You could get caught in them just as you got caught the first time.'

'I don't think there's much danger of that.'

'Oh, you don't?' said Father Patrick. 'Pass the mustard, would you?'

Benson did so. 'No. Catholicism was such a wonderful, all-embracing set of dogmas. Nothing really compares. Of course, I can't believe it now. I think I'll always drift.'

'What's your Achilles' heel, Martin?' Father Patrick asked.

Benson's mouth was full. He gestured to it, trying to think of what to reply. 'I've got lots of them,' he said at last.

'Nothing that stands out?'

'Yes, but I don't like to say.'

'I think I know.'

Benson said nothing.

'I know because it's mine too.'

'Is it?' Benson asked. 'It must be hard for you. Do you sublimate?'

'Not all the time. I'm flesh and blood, you know.'

'Yes, but what about your vows?'

Patrick smiled. 'After dinner I'll show you round the church. There are all sorts of interesting nooks and crannies. Would you like that?'

Benson's mouth was dry. 'I don't know . . . er . . . you see I start a new job tomorrow.'

'So you think it's wrong, do you? You still believe the whole thing. You're a cradle Catholic, I can see that. Deep down you're still rocked by Mother Church. You were quite happy to bump my knee at O'Toole's but now you know I'm a priest you're scared to death.'

Benson hung his head. Then he raised it. 'You're wrong, Patrick,' he said. Then, mentally apologizing to Pablo, he added, 'Yes, I'd like to see the church. It's neo-Gothic, isn't it? If you'll forgive me for saying so, it seems a trifle overdone.'

Half an hour later Benson followed Patrick down the nave of Our Lady of Perpetual Help. Patrick barely paused to inform Benson about the flying buttresses or the ornately carved pulpit. He genuflected in front of the altar – Benson bent his knee an inch to be polite – and then made for a door next to the Lady Chapel where two electric candles burnt in front of the icon of Our Lady of Perpetual Succour. The Christ-child's shoe had come off. He was looking at the instruments of crucifixion. Mary looked out morosely.

Benson gazed morosely back at Mary. He was excited, but the excitement was haloed by a memory of the old guilt. The empty air above his head was once again populated by spirits he had denied. Patrick's right. I am still in the cradle. The world distracts me like a child's rattle but soon anxiety returns and I start wailing for Mum. Maybe this'll be good for me.

They climbed a metal spiral staircase that jangled and shuddered under their weight. At the top they were in a small room whose ceiling was the top of the church tower. Nativity statues were arranged down one side, a paschal candle holder, a chipped statue of St Joseph.

Patrick placed two chairs side by side and motioned Benson to sit down. Then he sat down beside him. 'Here we are,' he said and unzipped his fly.

Benson's eyes were darting between the statuary and Patrick's hair-backed hand delving in his pants. 'Er . . . shouldn't you have dust-covers on the statues?' One of the three kings was looking straight at him and a shepherd playing a set of bagpipes also had a bird's-eye view of the proceedings.

'You're a hopeless case, Martin. They're idols, that's all.' And Patrick took out his penis and started pumping it up.

Benson forgot the plaster watchers as soon as his Achilles' heel hove into view. He reached across and held it, noting with his expert eye that it was thicker and longer than his own. Patrick told him to show him his. Benson did so, wanting very much to get down on his knees in front of Patrick and suck on him. After a few moments of playing about, he did so. But Patrick held his hand over himself and said he didn't do anything like that. Benson continued to nuzzle up towards what he wanted, thinking of himself with Andy in the cemetery. Then he had been the one who fought Andy's longing to take him in. He felt certain now that he would be able to break down Patrick's defences.

He was wrong, however. Patrick put his hand

against Benson's forehead, pushing it back, away from him. 'No, I don't like that. Just jerk me off.'

Benson said nothing. Feeling hugely embarrassed he stood up and then sat back on the chair. They crossed arms and masturbated one another, though Benson was greatly disappointed, had never seen the point in having someone else do what he could do with much more acumen. Still, he seemed to be pleasing Patrick, who leant back in the chair, his legs extended, only making a desultory attempt to excite Benson.

'I'm coming!' he said. At last, Benson thought, thinking his hand would drop off if he had to keep up the boring motion much longer. He consoled himself by taking pleasure in watching Patrick's penis further harden then spurt its load across the floor in a rainbow arc.

Patrick lay like a ragged doll on the chair, sighing. Then, as Benson watched, the sighs turned to moans and his face fell in on itself and tears flowed down his cheeks. 'God God God God God!' he said.

'Er . . . Patrick, are you all right?' Benson asked.

'It's the drink. Christ, if I hadn't drunk so much I'd never have . . .'

'How do you mean?'

Patrick looked at Benson as if he were a stranger who had surprised him. He sat bolt upright and put his penis away. Benson quickly followed suit. He touched Patrick on the shoulder but Patrick shrugged him away. The tears were still flowing as he stood up and, taking a handkerchief from the pocket of his trousers, got down on his hands and knees, and started to wipe up the liquid from the floor.

'Can I do anything for you? You seem upset,' said Benson.

Patrick had his back to Benson. He knelt back on his haunches facing towards the statuary.

'I think you should go. You can find your own way out.'

'But you're upset. I feel responsible. I understand how you're feeling.'

'Just go, OK?'

'Patrick, I'm sorry. I . . .'

There was no reaction from the kneeling man. Benson stood dithering on the spot for a moment. Then he turned away sad, clattering back down the spiral stairs.

As he crossed the church, coming level with the tabernacle, he automatically started to genuflect. He stopped himself, then faced the altar and addressed the Godhead or the bread within: Did *You* see that? That's the sort of thing that makes my blood boil! That's what your Son's gentle message had led to! The Church is so fucking fucked up! Why don't you DO something, instead of just sitting there being flattered. Get up off Your arse and do some worthwhile *work* for a change! You're supposed to be a Father. Well, let me tell You that Your kids haven't grown up yet. They still need Your Help. Get on with it! And you can start with Patrick. Amen.

And Benson stomped out of the church. He felt he understood Patrick perfectly. He could be me, he thought. In some ways he *is* me.

*   *   *

At the Unitarian Medical Center the following morning, Benson took his place beside three other trainees. Lester and Laverne were black and brothers. Veratunge came from Ceylon, but lived in the Lower East Side with his brothers, who owned a restaurant.

Nurse Muñoz gave them a tour of the hospital and explained the routine. Every morning they would have class with her. Each afternoon they would go to various wards to put what they had learnt into practice. On this, their first day, however, they would stay with her all day.

By lunchtime Benson was dressed in a white cotton suit. He was wearing a pair of white pumps like Nurse Muñoz's and sported a plastic badge with a flattering photograph of himself imprisoned inside, along with his designation: Trainee Nurses' Aide Martin Benson.

Benson stood with his tray and cutlery in the cafeteria food line. A salad, a hamburger and a strawberry Jello cost him seventy-five cents. That wasn't bad. Twenty minutes in the earning.

Space was limited but Benson found himself a place at a large round table, said hello to the other diners and started tucking into his meal. As he chewed he cast surreptitious glances at the ID badges of his companions. On his left was an intern doctor. On the right a gynaecologist. He was impressed to be in such exalted company. In England that would never happen. They'd put porters, nurses' aides, nurses, in one dining room and the doctors, almoners, and suchlike in another.

Here at the Unitarian Medical Center, on the other hand, he was sitting with the high and the low, with those who held lives in their hands and those who held bed-pans under comrades. Here was democracy in action! Walt would have been proud.

Not that anybody spoke to him as he made his way methodically through his lunch. Still, just being around the workers at UMC was enough. Lester, Laverne and Veratunge had found a table for themselves. The other person there was standing up to leave. Benson got himself a cup of coffee and went to sit with them.

'What do you think of it all so far?' he asked them.

'Not bad,' said Lester. He said it with a rising intonation, nodding.

'You look great in your uniforms.'

'They're going to be hard to keep clean. Do you think we have to do our own laundry?' asked Veratunge.

'No way,' said Laverne. 'I've worked in a hospital before. You can get as many changes of uniform as you need. I should know. Last place I worked I was washing the motherfuckers all day.'

'Well, it should be much better than that as a nurses' aide. I'm really looking forward to it,' said Benson.

'Mrs Muñoz is weird. Why can't she stay still?' said Laverne.

'I think she's lovely,' said Benson.

'The money ain't much,' said Lester.

Benson thought it politic to say nothing.

'Now, class,' said Nurse Muñoz, 'we haven't quite finished making our introductions. Follow me, please.'

They followed her away from the classroom area to the beds on which lay the three dummies.

'Now, we are going to meet Arthur first. As you approach the bed I want you to wear a smile. Always a smile. Never a frown. And never, never, a blank look. A smile is the first thing you have to offer your patient. Also, as we approach I want you to do so gradually. Now, what do I mean by that? Well, it could be that your patient is napping or thinking quietly to himself. We don't want to shock him, do we?'

They shook their heads.

'Do we?'

'No, Nurse Muñoz.'

'Right. Watch me approach the bed graaaadu-allyyyyy.' And Nurse Muñoz, her hands out at chest level, fingers uppermost, did what Benson felt could be best described as sidling up on Arthur. He felt that if someone approached him like that he would be, if not shocked, at least apprehensive.

Nurse Muñoz had reached the bed. She coughed in a way which indicated that she had absolutely no need to cough. 'Mr Zeigen! Mr Zeigen!' she said. Then she turned to her students and said in a noisy stage-whisper, 'We call our patient models the Zeigen family in honour of a grateful patient who provided us with the funds to purchase them. We put him back together after a horrible automobile accident. Note, class, that I use the formal address, MR Zeigen. There may come a time in your relationship with some patients – some, I do not say all – when you may revert to given names. It is a matter of sensitivity as to when or even if this will happen.'

She turned back to Arthur Zeigen. 'Mr Zeigen, I've brought four nice young men to see you!'

Benson had been watching Mr Zeigen's penis, trying to work out why the opening at the end was so large. If he had an opening as large as that he'd be able to make a really manly baritone gush.

'Mr Benson, pay attention,' whispered Nurse Muñoz. 'You're not looking where you're supposed to be looking. And where may I ask is your smile?'

Benson looked round at his companions, who were all wearing fixed grins.

'Now, each of you greet Mr Zeigen one by one. Ask how he is. Let's see which of you can be the most caring.'

Lester stepped forward, aiming a look at Laverne as he did so. Then he cleared his throat and pushed his neck forward for a moment, jiving his shoulders. He said: 'Howyadoin' Mr Zeigen?'

Nurse Muñoz looked pained. 'Lester, you are not at a Sunday night parish social and Mr Zeigen is not your contemporary. He is a sick man. He is also a client of UMC and deserves respect. You try, Veratunge.'

Veratunge stepped briskly up to the bed and gave Mr Zeigen a little bow. 'Good afternoon, Mr Zeigen. How do you do?' Then he looked towards Nurse Muñoz expectantly.

'Better than Lester, Veratunge. But I'm not sure about that bow. Perhaps it was a little formal. What I'm looking for is something in between yours and Lester's.'

Laverne and Benson had a go. Laverne just did what Veratunge had done without the bow. Benson felt that a certain amount of creativity was the order of the day. He approached the bed smiling, placed his hand on top of Mr Zeigen's, aimed a sympathetic smile at the patient and said, 'Hello, Mr Zeigen. Can I do anything to make you more comfortable?'

'Well, Martin,' said Nurse Muñoz. 'If Mr Zeigen was uncomfortable when you arrived, he'd be in downright agony by the time you finished. No, Martin, I'm sorry. Your body language was exaggerated too. You gushed. You did not come over as sincere.'

Benson stepped back to his place, mortally wounded. Still, he had to admit that Nurse Muñoz was right. He had only been thinking of impressing the bystanders. Mr Zeigen hardly figured at all. He would have to stop that.

'Now,' said Nurse Muñoz, 'our model patient's given name is Arthur. We'll assume that Mr Zeigen has given you permission to call him Arthur. Step back a little, class. I want you to look at Arthur and tell me what is wrong with him. Imagine that you have come into the room and you see Arthur as you see him now. What's the first thing you'd do?'

The group bit their collective lip.

'Martin, I noticed that you were absorbed in looking at Arthur's genitals just now. Can you tell us?'

'I er . . . wasn't!'

'Let's not be so uptight,' said Nurse Muñoz. 'Some healthy curiosity never hurt anyone, did it? But what I think is that Arthur might – can anyone finish the sentence?'

'Arthur might not like people looking at his pecker,' said Laverne.

'That's right. There he is all uncovered. Arthur is a modest patient. Trouble is he's not able to cover himself. That's where you come in. Now, what I want you to do is greet Arthur – call him Arthur this time – and then, without Arthur or your left hand knowing what your right hand is doing, cover him up. It's a small thing but TLC is a succession of small things which together add up to a rather large thing. Martin, you first.'

Benson approached the bed smiling. He greeted Arthur, asked him how he was and while doing this flicked a blanket over the patient's loins.

'Fine,' said Nurse Muñoz. 'But you seemed anxious. Don't on any account show the patient that you are embarrassed. Nothing embarrasses you. You're a Health Care Professional. Now, tell me, Martin. Does *anything* embarrass you?'

'No,' said Benson, still embarrassed about being exposed as a peeper at Arthur's penis.

'Does *anything* embarrass you?'

'Nothing embarrasses me!'

Nurse Muñoz shelled her ear.

'Nothing embarrasses me!'

'Right! *Now* I believe you!' exclaimed Nurse Muñoz. 'Let's give Martin a big hand, class.'

The class applauded Benson. Benson managed an embarrassed little smile.

Everyone had a go covering Arthur tactfully.

Nurse Muñoz turned back to Arthur. She waved to

him and said. 'We're going to leave you now, Arthur. But you've got your buzzer at your elbow. Don't hesitate to call if you need anything.' She tip-toed away from the bed and back to the classroom area, motioning them to follow her. They sat at their desks, while she ascended her stool. There she sat. Silent.

At last she spoke. 'Now, class, I want you to close your eyes for a moment and breathe deeply.' The class did as instructed. 'Fill up those powerful young lungs of yours. There are little attics that never get a change of air. Fill to the brim every little attic. Hold it. Now exhale slowly to the count of ten. One . . . two . . . three . . .'

Benson's lungs were empty by seven and he had to push like mad to last until Nurse Muñoz reached her leisurely ten.

'Did you empty out all that stinky old air from the cellars? No? Again, in to the count of ten . . . hold . . . breathe out . . . one . . . two . . . three . . .'

The class repeated the exercise several times, then Nurse Muñoz told them to listen to her words as they continued to breathe deeply. On no account were any of them to open their eyes. Benson at once did so, only to be confronted by her blue eyes. He closed his eyes again.

'You are feeling happy and relaxed. You have just met your first patient and it has been a valuable experience. You have given of yourself. Tender Loving Care has flowed out of you and into the body and mind of your patient. And have you noticed something as you were performing the action? A ray of satisfaction came back to you. When we are good to others we feel good ourselves. Each evening when you leave UMC I hope that you will be surrounded by an aura of sweet satisfaction. That is what I wish for you.' She told them to think about that for ten breaths.

When the breaths had been breathed they opened their eyes but there was no sign of Nurse Muñoz. They looked round and saw her standing by the empty bed at the far end of the room.

'Now, class,' she said, 'I want you to come over here. Walk gently. You have to pass three model patients on your way. Don't startle them. Spread sunshiny TLC as you go. Then come and stand by this bed. Two of you on each side.'

Benson followed Lester and Laverne over to the bed, while Veratunge came up the rear. He looked at Lester. Lester seemed to be swaggering. He was sure Lester would get into trouble. Benson was beaming a broad grin at the three dummies. He waved with his fingers at the little girl dummy.

When they were standing by the bed, Nurse Muñoz castigated Benson for his informality and Veratunge for his formality. Lester and Laverne got away scot-free. Laverne was sent back to show them how it was done. When he came back he hit hands with Lester, thumbs up.

There followed a lesson on bed-making. Benson was rather proud of his bed-making, but had been unable to manage the neat little tuck Nurse Muñoz insisted on. Everyone else had done it straight off.

Nurse Muñoz left her trainees to practise, disappearing into her office. Then she came back and invited them into her office for coffee. There they sat while she bent down over the fridge. Her bottom stuck out like the women on English postcards. Benson looked at Lester, who was licking his lips at Laverne, mock-lascivious. He stopped when he saw Benson looking at him. Benson wondered why he had stopped.

She produced a huge pie, paper plates and plastic forks. 'Banana cream pie. I always bake one for the first day of training. It's my way of welcoming you to

UMC. It's about four now. We'll eat the pie. Then we'll practise one more bed-making before class is dismissed. Tomorrow at nine sharp there'll be class, and in the afternoon you'll be sent to different wards in the hospital to DO! To FIGHT! and to HEED the wound!'

'Yaaay!' shouted Lester enthusiastically.

'Waaa!' agreed Laverne.

Benson and Veratunge nodded and smiled.

Nurse Muñoz gazed at them mistily. 'Tender Loving Care!' she said. Then she started tenderly cutting the pie with a scalpel.

*   *   *

Benson took the subway back to Manhattan accompanied by Veratunge. He gamely tried dredging up facts about Ceylon to use as fuel for a conversation. How long did it take to get from South India to Ceylon by ferry? Did the tea-pickers manage better than those under thrall to Brooke Bond? He had little success in conversation, however. Veratunge seemed preoccupied and got off at Canal Street station without giving Benson much information about his homeland. He had confided that Ceylon produced rubies, but that was hardly a jewel to spark a glittering dialogue in Benson's book. Benson sat on.

At Times Square he came up out of the subway, passed by the smoking manhole without a thought, and started walking towards the YMCA. But at 45th Street, he doubled back, threading his way south-west.

He drank a cup of coffee at the café on the corner of 42nd Street, where he had first met Virginia. As he drank he read his nurses' aide handbook, holding the cover so that its title could edify the other customers, looking around him from time to time in hope of catching sight of Virginia.

He considered 'In-Bed Washing'. The little cartoon illustrations in the book reminded him of those he had seen in copies of the *Catholic Digest of America*, that had somehow found their way into the Benson household. They were line drawings, but a wash of red made the background more cheerful. You could tell they were American because everyone in the drawings was handsome and tended to smile. In those *Catholic Digest* articles he had perused, like 'Pop, where do babies come from?', not only were father and son quite at ease as they talked frankly together about the Catholic views on the facts of life, they were also pretty ideal. The father tall and handsome with all his features in the right place, nothing sticking up or sticking out; the son with a careful parting, long trousers long before Benson had been allowed to climb into long trousers and luxuriate in the myriad protections they afforded. The son had always looked ready and willing to accept whatever his upright father told him. He was not the sort who would go out and seek out sins crying to heaven for vengeance in a neighbour's garage, or gorge on scones. He had always seemed like someone for whom Holy Purity would come as easy as getting a ball into a basket. Benson, fat and scruffy and short-panted, would look hard and long into those line drawings and realize what a gulf lay between him and his American Catholic brothers. Then he thought of Patrick. Was there really such a gulf?

Benson had finished his second coffee. He looked around the café, then outside to 8th Avenue. There was no sign of Virginia. He wondered whether he ought not just return to the YMCA and look for her another day. But then he saw himself in his little room, cursing himself for not telephoning his only friend in Manhattan. He took out his address book and left the café, looking for a pay-phone.

He dialled Virginia's number. No-one answered for a long time but he held on. Then the telephone at the other end was picked up and a male voice asked him what he wanted, without saying hello first.

'Er . . . have I got the right number? Is Virginia there, please?'

'Who wants her?'

'It's Martin. I'm a friend of Virginia's.'

He heard the telephone put down noisily on some hard surface. A silence, then distant knocking and the same voice shouting 'Telephone!'

Then more silence. Who was that? A friend of Virginia's? You'd think Virginia would make sure her telephone was answered courteously. This rudeness is bound to put customers off. First impressions and all that.

He hung on, kicking his left leg with his right sandal to expiate his last thought. Then, worried that he might get cut off, he inserted another nickel and heard the bell ring. It was a nice bell, much nicer than those horrible pips you got in England. They ought to send people over from England to study American telephones. He heard the telephone receiver being picked up after a hand had chased it, then grabbed it hard saying *goddam* as it did so.

'Yeah?'

'Virginia, is that you? It's me, Martin. I just rang to ask you how you were doing.'

'Oh, hi Martin. I was sleeping. I feel just awful. Where are you?'

'I'm at the café where we met. Can you come for a coffee or something?'

'Sure I can. Christ, it's good to hear from you. But let's meet closer to my place. There's a coffee shop on 34th Street and 8th. I'll let you buy me a hamburger if you like.'

'Yes, that would be nice.'

He rang off and started walking downtown, past the Port Authority bus station and the cheap shops, wondering who had answered Virginia's phone. He must ask Virginia. It would be the first thing he'd ask her over coffee before launching into his news. At Mum's coffee mornings Mum had always asked the other women questions. Gall bladders, new hats, births, marriages and deaths, had all been politely enquired about before Mum got down to what was really on her mind: how Benson was getting great praise for his essays and could learn poetry at an incredible rate of knots.

Distracted, Benson bumped into a man, and said sorry. He thought that the man said 'You are!' in an odd tone of a voice, but at once forgot that too when he noticed a Negro at a shoe-shine stand look down at his sandals. Benson smiled, but the man had already looked away. I'll have shoe-shine men at my coffee mornings. Walt Whitman of course. William Shakespeare. Brother O'Toole . . .

He looked about him. In this neighbourhood the people were very different from those you found in other parts of the city. There were young white people like him, many carrying big duffel bags and wearing colourful hippie clothes. A few women who looked like secretaries. But on the whole the people were black and brown. He felt much more comfortable here than he did on Madison or Park Avenue where everyone was white and well-heeled. There he had seen a woman walking a poodle with a tartan tam o'shanter on its woolly head. This sight had merited a postcard to Meryl right off. The men there were tanned and wore expensive suits. He could not get over the way old women looked in the rich neighbourhoods. They were heavily made up and wore clothes that were much too young for them. Their unsmiling faces seemed stretched. They didn't seem to think it a good idea to grow old gracefully. He thought of Auntie Muriel. She could be said to be growing old gracefully. Not that it looked graceful exactly. But inside she was graceful, whereas the women on Madison Avenue were probably a mess inside. Benson caught himself. Listen to me, judging again. Still Auntie Muriel would have said that there were more important things in life than looks. Her chin hung down and she was very wrinkled. He felt his own. No, it was as firm as anything. I suppose I'll hate to get all wrinkled and saggy but I'll just have to accept it as part of life's rich pattern. He adjusted his quiff so that it covered the bit that he fancied was receding rather.

The café seemed suitable. It had a notice which said: '100% Pure Beef Hamburgers 2 for 25 cents/2 Frankfurters for 25 cents'. That was reasonable. He went inside and ordered a small 7-Up, telling the man he would have something more substantial when his friend arrived. The man did not seem very concerned.

He had long finished his drink and felt he knew all that he would ever want to know about irrigating stomas, when Virginia came in. He did not recognize her at first. Her hair was all bubbly, surrounding her head like a halo. She was wearing a dress that looked like an oversized T-shirt. Her breasts stuck out and Benson, on the look out for tell-tale signs of masculinity, thought how ridiculous Pablo had been to think that Virginia could be other than a woman.

Virginia sat down opposite him. Benson got her a Coke. When he returned he asked her what she would like to eat. She said she'd have whatever he was having, so Benson ordered two hamburgers and two frankfurters.

'What's that?' he asked her, looking at a big box Virginia had brought in with her.

'A tape machine.'

He nodded, thinking it a strange thing for her to be carrying. 'How's your mum?' he asked her.

'Same as ever. She don't change too much, my mom. She about OK, long as she's got her stuff and the television. She hardly eats nothing 'cept Twinkies and French fries.'

'It must be very difficult for you, Virginia.'

'No, it ain't. You get kind of used to it, you know? Usually it just seem normal.'

Benson nodded. 'You can get used to anything, I suppose.'

'That's about it, Martin. Hey, I'm suddenly feeling like doing something real crazy. I ain't goin' home just yet a while. You're free, ain't you, Martin?'

'I suppose so,' Benson said. 'But tell me, Virginia, why are you carrying that tape recorder around? Isn't it terribly heavy?'

Virginia looked down at the tape recorder. 'It's on account of Mom. I take it wherever I go. She tend to pawn things. An' she got a man stayin' with her. I don't want to lose this.'

'Was that the man I spoke to on the telephone?'

'That's him. He's no good, Martin. But you can't tell Mom that.'

'Can't you?'

'You know what I think we oughta do?'

'No. What?'

'Let's earn us some money. Then we can buy some juice for this here machine and dance.'

'How do you mean?'

'Dance mean dance, honey. What can I tell yuh?'

'I've got money, Virginia. Well, enough for some batteries anyway.'

'Hell, Martin, I don't want no more free rides from you. You was real good to me once before, remember?'

Benson did remember but did not feel inclined to admit it.

'I know where we can each earn us ten bucks in half an hour!'

Benson looked doubtful.

'It's all legal! Honest!'

'How?'

'Ain't you never seen those blood banks on forty-second? Half an hour they can pump enough outa us to earn ten bucks apiece.'

Benson had seen the blood banks, had, indeed, shaken his head as he passed. It seemed so very different from the ladies who took his blood in Aberystwyth and then gave him a cake and a cup of sweet tea, sending him away feeling virtuous. 'We don't pay for blood in England. We give it for nothing.'

'It ain't like that here, Martin. Come on! If you don't come I have to go straight back home and turn tricks. Come on, Martin!'

Benson did not want to sell his blood, not even for ten dollars. But he let himself be persuaded and was soon following Virginia out of the café, back up 8th Avenue, carrying her heavy tape recorder.

The blood shop was quite full. Virginia seemed to know the man at the counter. They filled in a form, ticked boxes about their state of health and sat down to wait their turn. Benson thought of Broderick Crawford who, at the end of *Highway Patrol*, gave a little sermon about one's duty. 'Leave your blood at the Red Cross, not on the highway,' he said and gave Benson a stern look. Mum had always said she thought he looked like a potato.

A woman in a uniform, not dissimilar to his own at UMC, called him and Virginia to a curtained-off section at the back of the blood bank. She did not respond to Benson's attempt at banter, just told him to roll up his sleeve. Looking at Benson and Virginia's forms, she called him Mr Benson, and Virginia Miss Brown. They were told to lie down on cots little wider than stretchers. He heard Virginia give a little cry as the needle went in. He was scared suddenly. When the nurse came towards him with the needle and blood bag he turned away so that he would not see the procedure, but when it happened it didn't really hurt and then it was over and he was squeezing the rubber ball as instructed, was able to pluck up the courage to look at his arm and watch the blood leaving him, flowing into the bottle.

The procedure over, they were not given a cup of tea. Instead they signed another form at the desk and took their blood money.

'Was that easy or was that a cinch?' asked Virginia.

He admitted that it had been both, though he was suddenly feeling a bit faint. He stopped on the sidewalk.

'You feeling weird, Martin? Yeah, that always happen. What we need is a chocolate bar.' Virginia went into a shop with Flora de Oro Cigars on the front. She came out a minute later unpeeling a large chocolate bar. 'I got me some batteries too.'

Munching the chocolate, feeling much better at once, Benson asked, 'How often do you give blood, Virginia? You get almost as much for it as I earn in a day!'

'I know some folks gives two or three times a week, but that's risky, you know. It makes them weak. Me, I only give it when I really have to.'

Benson nodded. 'So what are we going to do now?'

'Let's go to the park. That's the best place.'

When they came to Columbus Circle, Virginia crossed

over to the island where the statue of Christopher Columbus stood. She stopped the traffic with her arm out while Benson, still holding the monster tape recorder, jittered on the sidewalk watching her.

'Why did you do that? You might have got yourself killed!'

''Cause I wanna see Mr Columbus.' And Virginia looked up at the statue of Christopher Columbus. Then, as Benson watched, she bowed her head, held her hands up prayerfully under her chin and started moving her lips.

Surely, he thought, she can't be praying to Christopher Columbus, can she? Doesn't she know that he was little better than a brigand? He waited for Virginia to finish, taking time to count the English cars that were passing. There were some Minis and Austin Americas and a few MGs. But on the whole there seemed rather more Volkswagens, which seemed a bit thick seeing that the Germans had lost the war.

'Now let's go into the park!' said Virginia. And she ran back again into the traffic with as much bravado as Columbus leaving Spain to travel west to India. Benson, carrying the huge tape recorder, still wondering how such a machine could be moved to action by a few batteries, followed on at a safe distance.

'Why were you praying to Christopher Columbus?'

'I want to is why.'

'He isn't a saint, you know.'

'How you know he ain't no saint? You been to heaven or *what*?'

'Well, no. But he hasn't been canonized. Why don't you try Saint Martin de Porres?'

'Who's he?'

'A black saint. He was a close friend of St Rose of Lima.'

Virginia did not seem particularly impressed by St

Martin's pedigree. They walked along pathways through trees for a while, passed people walking, sitting on benches, playing guitars. One man sat alone on a rocky outcrop playing a flute. He was wearing an embroidered waistcoat.

'There's one of them there hippies,' said Virginia. 'One of them give me a flower yesterday.' Then she stopped and grabbed hold of Benson's arm, pulling him to the base of the outcrop. 'Hey, look at them little shiny pieces in the rock. They just like silver.' She shook her head to make the rock glitter. 'You think it's precious?'

'Shouldn't think so,' said Benson. 'If it were it wouldn't be here. People would have hacked it up and carted it away. They'd make statues out of it. It's just mica in the rock. You know, Virginia, the reason that they can build so high in New York is because of this rock. It's really hard and provides a good foundation.'

'You don't say?' She seemed cast down by this. He was sorry that he had not gone along with Virginia and agreed that the sparkling rock was precious. Anyway, what was precious? It was a matter of consensus. Why shouldn't some people find things precious that others did not value? The hippie playing a meandering tune above them probably thought his tune valuable. It might not be a bad idea if people started seeking cheap things and investing them with value. Ianto treasured a piece of a dinosaur's fossilized dropping. Thieves would never break in and rob him of that. Dinosaur's droppings were a minority interest. Benson was quite partial to pebbles. Might it not be a good thing if he decided to collect pebbles and forget gold and all those other things which the majority thought precious? 'It's beautiful, Virginia,' he said, running his hand over the black, glittering rock.

Ahead of him Benson could see water through the

trees. They came to a bridge, crossed it and he followed Virginia along some meandering paths between trees. At last Virginia chose a bench and they sat down. Benson was greatly relieved to be able to give his carrying arm a rest.

'What are you going to play on the tape recorder?' Benson asked.

'That's a surprise, Martin.'

It was still light. When Benson looked up he could see the sun speckling the leaves, hear music on the breeze. It came and went. It disappeared completely as he wondered how he was going to start telling Virginia all his news. 'Virginia? What do you think is going to happen in the future? Do you think you'll stay with your mum?'

'Hell, I don't know, Martin. She need me. Christ, do she need me! Still, I guess I need her too, you know.'

Benson nodded, though he could not imagine what Virginia would miss in that rude, untidy woman. Then he told himself that he was thick. 'But I've got news, Virginia. I've moved into the YMCA. It's just off Central Park West.' He pointed over the lake. 'And I started my new job today. They really need nurses' aides. Why don't you think about becoming one?' He was about to pursue the topic when Virginia put her hand on his shoulder, signalling him to be quiet. They listened.

'Goddam!' she exclaimed. 'How could I be so dumb? That's a carousel, Martin! Come on!'

He started to make a complaint about having to pick up the tape recorder and Virginia made to take it herself. He told her it was all right then and followed her back across the bridge. She skipped away ahead of him, only turning now and then to encourage him to catch up. Well, he wouldn't. He had already put in a full day's work learning how to dispense TLC, had had a pint of blood drained out of him. He was not going to run now, carousel or no carousel.

Arriving at the carousel, Virginia seized the tape recorder from him and gave it to the woman at the cash-desk to mind, at the same time buying enough tickets for three rides each. At this rate, he thought, she'd be back at that blood shop in no time. Where was her moderation? Why couldn't she find pleasure in sitting on a bench, with him telling her about his day?

She jumped up and down, waiting for the ride in progress to finish. When the people had come out they jumped on to the carousel. Benson followed Virginia round, watching her as she stroked a painted horse, went on to a lion, trying to decide which she would ride. At last she chose a white horse. Benson got on a hen.

When the ride started, Benson realized that he had been wrong about the carousel. It was glorious to swing round and round, the green park and the skyscrapers and the setting sun reflected in a million windows. He felt disembodied and elated. Virginia kept looking back at him, shouting whoops and messages that he could not catch. Maybe it would be a good idea for him to go to a fun-fair on a regular basis. Wild rides might do the job which, thus far, only sex and hard work seemed able to manage. Maybe he should learn to drive.

The ride ended, but Virginia just stayed put and handed two more of her tickets to the woman who came round. The carousel started again. Even the music seemed just about ideal. He had always thought the organ a bit overblown, but this organ went with the movement and the smooth weightlessness of the experience. It was chirpy. It made him chirpy. It would be wonderful if the laws of science would permit him to disengage himself and his hen from the ride and cheerily set out on a quest for Dearest Him across a green undulating landscape in which bunnies waved, brown people in bright shirts beckoned him down and fed and watered him and his hen for the night . . . No, I've got Pablo. He gripped the metal rod. Hmm, two inch diameter. In all likelihood a one inch bore. Heavy-duty.

But by the time the third ride was finished, he stumbled off the carousel feeling ill. He wondered for a moment if he were going to be sick. Sitting on a bench, he took little notice of Virginia trundling the tape recorder over. He was rather short with her when she suggested buying another couple of tickets. 'Enough is as good as a feast, Virginia!' he told her.

She stopped, placing both hands on her hips. 'No it ain't. Who tell you that?'

'Lots of people. It's common knowledge.' That was a strange expression. Common knowledge.

'You OK?'

'I'll be all right in a while.'

Night was beginning to fall. They bought two frankfurters each from a stand. Benson had recovered enough to notice that the man charged exactly twice what they had paid at the café. Then they returned to the place by the lake.

'What happens when it gets dark?' Benson asked.

'When it get dark I'm gonna dance, Martin!'

They moved on until they found an open place. Benson could see the Metropolitan Museum through the trees. He silently greeted the Negro on his mastless sail-boat waiting either for a ship or a shark to pluck him off. He hoped he would make it through another night.

In the centre of the field Virginia told him to set down the tape recorder. Then she knelt down beside it, took the lid off and switched on. Nothing happened.

'Damn! I must've put the batteries in wrong.' She took them out, then tortuously loaded them in again. The tape started to turn.

Benson had been expecting something full of soul, but instead found himself listening to orchestral music that was familiar to him.

'Isn't that Miklos Rosza? I've got an LP of *More Music from Ben Hur*. I like him. He's much better than Wagner. Lots of good tunes.'

She did not reply. Instead she danced around the tape recorder to the music, danced in the same way that he had often danced when alone in the lounge, or in his room at Aberystwyth. She jumped and whirled and ran around while Benson sat watching. She did not ask him to join in but at last, having made sure that the coast was clear, he did so.

They did not dance together, though at one point he danced her way and confided further insights about Miklos Rosza. Then they went their separate ways, Benson thinking how much they had in common. He ran about watching the skyline of Central Park South, the huge neon sign for the Essex Hotel. He made everything blur by whirling about, raised up the skyline, then pushed it down, hid it from his gaze with an artistically held hand. Then he ran and realized that he could make his own carousel ride if he wanted to. Yes, he should do this more often. Truly when he danced he was at the still point of a wildly turning world. Why could he not ride the carousel all day and every day, wearing a chirpy smile, feeling an inner elation? The thing was that if you could forget about people watching it did not matter a fig what you looked like. He looked up, trying to see stars. The sky was clear, a deep navy blue. The lights of the city had put the stars to flight. A pity that, but he would not have wished for even one of those city lights to be extinguished. There were enough places on the planet where the stars shone down thick and bright. He danced faster, could hear Virginia singing and crying and hooting. Trundling that damned big tape recorder around is most inconvenient. You'd think the park people would broadcast music. Then he thought, maybe I should ask Virginia again if she'd like to be a nurses' aide.

Benson gave up at last and lay back on the grass long before the tape had wound to its end. Virginia just went on dancing, oblivious to him.

Benson watched Virginia. She'd definitely be just right for *Top of the Pops*, he thought. Better than all those camera-hogging trendies. Virginia didn't dance just to be seen. She danced because she needed to dance. Then, quite suddenly, she stopped dancing, looked around and yanked up the front of her dress. Benson sat up ramrod straight as he caught sight of Virginia holding her long black penis, intently and methodically spraying the grass in front of her.

He looked round to see if anyone else could see what he was seeing. Then he looked back at Virginia. She had seen Benson watching her and shouted over the din of 'In the Valley of the Lepers', 'Christ, Martin, I been dying for a leak!'

He nodded and even managed a smile, not for one moment letting his attention wander from the sight in front of him. Pablo was right, he thought. And Virginia's got a whopper too! Where does she keep it? Gosh, if I had one like that I'd . . .

Virginia, her legs apart, shook her penis. Benson looked round again, now more concerned that people would see him peeping or, worse, see what he was thinking. Then she was walking over to him. Virginia again. She lay down next to him. He looked into her face. She was sweating.

'Wow, that was jus' great! You like it Martin?'

Virginia turned on her back, her arms supporting her, looking up at the sky and panting.

'Yes, very much, thank you. Er . . . it's nice to get a bit of exercise. It blows away the cobwebs, doesn't it? Er . . .'

'Yeah?'

'Er . . . nothing. I was thinking . . .'

'What were you thinking?'

'Er . . . nothing.'

'Cat got yer tongue?'

'No. Nothing. I mean . . . er . . . how much does a tape cost?'

'Three or four bucks. 'Course one tape fits a whole lot of music. My good sister Levancia records for me. She's got a real great record library. She in bed with hay fever. She sneezes right through the summer. Spoils things for her, you know.'

Benson nodded. Virginia lay down full-length on the grass and closed her eyes, giving him an opportunity to collect his thoughts. Yes, Pablo had been right. But why hadn't he noticed before the obvious hit him in the balls? In his mind's eye he could still see Virginia waggling her penis about. The thought engorged him. But Virginia had not made any attempt to hide herself. She could easily have gone off into the bushes. She must think that he knew all the time. He thought about that.

'Virginia?'

'What now?'

'Er . . . I couldn't help noticing just now . . . er . . .'

Virginia sat up. 'Martin, what your problem? You acting real weird.'

'Yes, I know. I'm sorry. It's just that just now you had a wee and . . .'

'Yeah? So you want to phone the *New York Times*, or what?'

'No, but you've got a er . . . dick.'

'Sure I got a dick. I got to piss, don't I?'

'Yes, of course, but . . .'

Virginia opened her mouth and let out a little scream. 'Hey, you mean you didn't *know*?'

'No. Pablo – that's the chap I was with last time I saw you – he thought you weren't a woman. I told him not to be so stupid.'

'Hey, I thought you was just being po-lite.'

'How do you mean?'

Virginia frowned at Benson. 'No, you wasn't being po-lite, was you? You really took me for a woman!'

'Yes, of course. And today I looked at you very carefully because of what Pablo said and I still thought so.'

Virginia lay back down on the ground and kicked her legs about, whooping and jiving her head. Benson watched her helplessly. Then she was on top of him, kissing his face. 'Thanks, Martin.'

'Why?'

Virginia shrugged. Then she got up and started fiddling with the tape recorder. After a couple of false starts she found what she was looking for.

'That's "Stand by Me", isn't it?'

'Gi' dat man a dollar, Charmaine! Let's you and I dance a little, Martin.'

Benson was not sure, but she reached down to him and he let himself be pulled to his feet, pushed his shirt-tails back under his belt while Virginia enfolded him.

They swayed together to the music, Virginia singing along to the words.

'You sing very nicely, Virginia.'

'I know't,' said Virginia, and she started bumping up against Benson while Benson, mortified, wondered if she could make out his erection. Dreading that she might. Dreading that she might not.

'You're real sexy, you know that?'

'No, I'm not. I have my moments of course but usually . . .'

'How'd you like to sleep with Virginia?'

'Er . . .'

'No money or shit like that. Friends get to fuck for free.'

'That's nice. Thank you very much. But you see I'm homosexual.'

'What difference that make? Don't you like me?'

'Yes, of course I do. You're really lovely . . .'

But Benson did not proceed with his sentence for at that moment Virginia took his hand and placed it against the front of her dress.

'You like it, Martin?'

'Yes . . . but . . .'

'Good,' she said. 'Let's you and I go home and party!'

Virginia kissed him and bent down to turn off the music. Only then did Benson hear the cheering and applause. Two swaying men were standing nearby, both wearing white ponchos and Benson-preferred sandals.

'Peace! Love! Black and White Together!' they shouted.

Virginia put the top on the tape recorder and bowed, while Benson searched around for his flight-bag in a panic. He found it, innocently sitting on the grass where he had left it. The shamrock made him think of the Trinity. St Patrick had bent down and picked up a shamrock and said: 'God the Father, God the Son and God the Holy Ghost. All one but all separate.' Well, he thought. The heathens must have been impressed. Look at Ireland. But at that moment the Trinity seemed a simple thing indeed compared with the mystery of Virginia and sexual attraction. He picked up the flight-bag, threaded the plastic strap over his body like a sash and let the bag conceal his excitement from the gaze of the supporters on the sidelines.

Arm in arm they walked back the way they had come what seemed to Benson an age ago. A part of him was embarrassed about the prejudiced looks he imagined he and Virginia were prey to as they passed people. But most of him felt comfortable. After all, if Harry the sandwich man could see me now he'd think what a rake I am. He'd probably tell everyone.

At Columbus Circle Virginia insisted on stopping again, crossing over, dragging Benson along with her through the hooting traffic, to the base of the statue. 'Say a prayer, Martin. I bet you know some fantastic prayers.'

'I've forgotten them,' he lied.

'No you ain't.'

He pursed his lips, shifted his flight-bag and had a sudden inspiration. '"Hail Glorious St Columbus, dear saint of our isle. On us, thy poor children, bestow a sweet smile. For now thou art high in thy mansions above. On Manhattan island look down in thy love. Amen."'

'Amen,' added Virginia. 'That was real pretty, Martin. Now let us go on home.'

'Er . . . but won't your mum and her friend be there?'

'Sure they will, but they'll be more upset if I go home *alone*.'

Benson thought of breasts, but then his mind descended to other things. 'Right-ho. I know, I'll give you my blood bank money as if I'm a customer. But I mustn't stay too long. I've got work in the morning, Virginia.'

'Honey, you got work *tonight*!'

'Have I?'

It was past one in the morning when Benson left Virginia's apartment building, staggering down the street in a merry daze. The lights on several of the floors of the Empire State Building had waited up for him, and he saluted the structure as he turned on to 8th Avenue, heading back to the YMCA.

Virginia's professional embraces had rubbed him raw. When he looked at himself in her bathroom he wondered whether his sorely tried penis would ever be fit for anything again. After washing, he rubbed some of someone else's Oil of Ulay on it in the hope that it would hasten the healing process. Still, he'd thought as he gazed at his manly self in the mirror, even if it drops off tomorrow at least I've experienced a perfect moment with it. Three, in fact.

He whistled his way uptown. At 49th Street a taxi nudged into the back of a stationary Volkswagen. The drivers got out, shouting and gesticulating. Why can't we all live happily together? he asked the red traffic light. We share the same bucking carousel, but manage to make it as flat as a bus ride to Birkenhead. He thought of Dexter. Of Patrick. Then he thought of Virginia, of Virginia's breasts cupped in his hand, breasts that had grown by taking tablets. I bet Boots would have a fit if I asked them for some. Typical! . . . Then of Virginia's penis that he had been able to play with to his heart's content while he made strenuous love to her. And then he thought of Pablo. Lummy, what will Pablo say? I told him I loved him forty-eight hours ago! Am I becoming shallow? What *am* I becoming? Something that is probably not particularly becoming. Benson dithered for a moment, wondering if he should stay around, like an impersonation of a good citizen, to act as a witness to the accident. But reasoning that little harm had been done, he shrugged, climbed back on to his hen, imagined Virginia nude on her white horse beside him, and trotted off chirpy and painfully tumescent into the navy-blue night.

Butte, Montana
10 August 1967

Dear Martin,

Thank you for your letter. I'm glad you have a social security number and a satisfying job.

Here in the middle of the wilderness the truth of how difficult it is to appreciate the present moment keeps returning. I look around me at the mountains and the wildlife and I laugh at myself that I had managed to idealize it last summer. For some reason that I cannot fathom, I am unable to capture the peace and beauty this time. I'm as jumpy as a cricket and cannot settle down to reading. Instead of all the worthy works I had thought to wade through happily I have only been able to read trash. Why this should be I do not know. Perhaps it is because I have started idealizing my time at Camp Manley. I miss everyone: you, the kids, Becky and Debbie, even – though I hate to admit it – the dreadful Rod.

Regarding the Manleys, I have had no word as to whether or not the police have caught up with them. It does seem impossible that they could make it across state lines without being noticed. However, it has not escaped my attention, even in my fastness here, that there seem to be a great number of strangely painted campers wending their way out west. A *Time* magazine came to my attention which burbled on about San Frncisco as THE place to be this summer. I can only assume that if *Time* has got hold of the story it is probably already over. You are better off staying a continent away. Whatever interesting little plants may have sprung from the soil of the Far West will not long survive the full glare of media attention.

261

As for me, there is nothing to be done. I will just have to sit it out here, hoping that my mood will change for the better. Surely Thoreau must have had times like this at Walden! I am flattered that you took my 'good advice' to heart. What did I say exactly? I can remember riding a rather high-flown hobby-horse about pure relationships et al. Please, Martin, don't look to me for wisdom. I was thinking out loud. If you want to know the truth, I've been 'tossing off' every night since getting here. You, on the other hand, seem to have been using your time to better effect. I applaud you.

Please, though I have feet of depressingly soft clay, do not stop writing. Your letter cheered me greatly.

Always,
Dexter

The letter, sent on to him by Lee-Chun, had been considerably slipped under his door, awaiting his arrival back from Virginia's. Benson felt a little let down by it at first but, unwilling to think badly about his friend, got down straight away to writing him a cheering letter back about life on the carousel.

Before dropping off he wondered whether Virginia might be Dearest Him. Imagine taking Virginia home to Dad and Alice! He saw himself opening the front door of home, with Virginia nervous behind him. His hand shook as he turned his key in the lock and confronted the hall and the ticking grandfather clock.

'It's only me, Dad! I've brought a friend of mine to meet you!' He shuddered as he got into bed and worried about getting up in time for work. Of course, Dad might be quite relieved to see I've come home with a girl. He wouldn't mind that she was black. He was always putting money in the black baby box. No, he'd be more worried about her being Catholic. But maybe he'd realize she wasn't a girl. He must bump into some things at work that he never talks about. Maybe it's only me who's *that* thick. Then Alice might take her upstairs for some woman's talk and . . . He decided not to think about that. Still, I could take her round to see Mr and Mrs Clitherow. They'd break out the sherry and chat to Virginia for hours. But . . . but mercifully sleep engulfed him.

The following morning Nurse Muñoz announced that Veratunge had decided that he did not want to be a nurses' aide. After making the announcement she looked out sadly at those remaining. Benson tried a grin, but she gave him a mournful look back. Then she shook herself, 'In-bed washing, class,' she said. 'Let's go and greet the Zeigen family!'

She taught the three remaining trainee nurses' aides how to wash a patient in bed. Art was stripped – with great sensitivity – and then gently draped in towels. Each of the trainees in turn then had to wash his whole body bit by bit using soapy water and a type of cloth Benson had never seen before. It was blue and felt like material, but you could tear it like paper. Another American miracle, he thought. He'd definitely take some home and swank, like Walter Raleigh must have done with tobacco. He told Lester that they did not have them in England. Lester looked at him oddly, saying it was a J-Cloth.

While the others were taking their turns at bathing Art, Benson thought about J-Cloths. A sure-fire winner! He should definitely import them into England and make a fortune. Damp dish cloths would be given the heave-ho. Good riddance. They invited germs. He would be doing a service for humanity as well as feathering his own nest. The best of all possible worlds.

Lester went right ahead and started washing Art without first asking the patient's permission. Nurse Muñoz gave Lester a little slap on the arm, then shook her finger at him. 'Why is that a no-no, Lester?'

Lester was stumped.

'Because maybe Art would prefer to do it himself, Nurse Muñoz,' said Benson after a decent interval. 'I mean, he may not be able to, but he should at least be given the opportunity to have a go.'

'That's exactly correct, Martin!' said Nurse Muñoz. At last! he thought. I've actually managed to get something right. My night with Virginia must have released blocked brain cells. Yes, I'm definitely firing on all cylinders today.

Nurse Muñoz nodded to him. Benson began blanket-bathing Art.

There was a knock at the door.

'Come in.' It opened to reveal a tall Negro in a nurse's uniform. Nurse Muñoz said, 'Hi, Carlton!' and gave him a hug. Carlton was smiling, looking directly at Benson. Benson looked back but, meeting the frank gaze, fluttered and looked at his pumps.

Gosh, he thought. He's nice. I don't suppose he is one, but imagine it if he was! J-Cloths whizzed off the carousel of his mind to be replaced by the vision of loveliness standing a mere two yards away.

'Martin, you're dreaming! Arthur will catch a chill.'

'Sorry? Yes?'

'I was just saying that one of you will be under Carlton this afternoon for his first ward practice. Still, I'm sure Carlton doesn't want you, Martin. You're such a dreamer. He'd rather have someone with his eye on the ball.'

Benson looked at Carlton, who was smiling at him. 'I

264

don't know about that, Nurse Muñoz. I think I can keep Martin alert. Sure, I'll take him. I'll report back to you on how he shapes up.'

'Well, if you're sure. You wouldn't like one of the others who manage to stay alert?'

But Benson felt extremely gratified by the exchange. It felt as if he were a purchase at a slave auction. Also, there was something camp about Carlton. He played with the gold chain round his neck. His voice was soft. Hope reared up.

Carlton left, while Benson appraised his walk. Hard to tell.

Lester had not the least doubt, however. 'If I was you,' he whispered to Benson, 'I sure as hell wouldn't turn my back on that mother.'

'How do you mean?' Benson asked.

Nurse Muñoz assigned Lester to Emergency, and Laverne to Geriatrics. 'We'll meet here at one o'clock sharp and I'll take you to your assigned stations. Now before we take a break I think we should review bed-making...'

'Now you stay close to me,' said Carlton. He had grasped Benson by both upper arms, one in each hand, and was looking down at him from the heights. 'You're a rookie. You don't know *shit*. Where I go, you go. I don't want you to do nothing, nothing at all without my say-so. You hear what I'm telling you?'

Benson nodded. Yes, I will meekly follow. The sick will call out to the gentle black giant and his devoted swab-bearer and Walt Whitman, like old God, will look down and speak: *Over the carnage rose prophetic a voice, Be not dishearten'd, affection shall solve the problems of freedom yet.*

'I will do as you say,' said Benson.

Carlton looked at him. 'You OK?'

'Me? Yes.'

'Good.' And he gave Benson's arm a squeeze. Benson flexed his biceps, thinking *He must be*! but was just too late. Not that his biceps were anything to write home about, but he could have presented a more solid arm if he had thought about it.

The ward was not like any that Benson had seen in England. It consisted of an open area full of potted plants, where the lift and the reception desk were, then a long corridor with doors leading off. Some of the doors had windows with venetian blinds next to them. These were the patients' rooms. Each one had its own toilet, washbasin and shower. There were other rooms off the corridor, two sluice rooms, a small kitchen, a room with easy chairs.

'This is much nicer than in England. There it's just lots of beds in a row.' Benson told Carlton. 'I suppose we don't have wards like this because people might like to come into hospital too much. As it is everyone dreads the prospect. My Auntie Muriel kept putting off her gall bladder op, even though she was in considerable pain, because she was worried she would have to be next to a stranger, and possibly a rather common stranger.'

'This is how the sterilizer works,' said Carlton. He put an empty steel bed-pan into the machine and closed a door on it, then turned a lever. Next, he pressed a button and there came a sound of churning water. After ten seconds or so, he turned the lever again and out popped the steaming-hot bed-pan.

'I've never seen one of those. That makes everything much easier. I don't think we have that in England either. They're probably too expensive and the government is too mean. They don't mind spending money on warplanes and Polaris and things like that, but ask for a bit extra for the health service and they become suddenly poor. It's a disgrace.'

'Now I'll take you to meet some of our patients. We have a lot of post-op care in this section. And, Martin, try not to talk too much. Some patients find it hard to take.'

However, before Benson could get into his stride behind Carlton, a buzzer sounded and a light went on over the door of one of the rooms.

Carlton at once set off at speed with Benson following purposefully behind him, adjusting a disgraceful erection. *Make room there! I'm a nurses' aide. This is an emergency!* Benson told the potted plants. He also had time to notice how Carlton's bottom stuck out through the back vent in his jacket in a fashion he considered wondrous. Then he tried to concentrate.

Carlton opened the door. Inside a naked man of about sixty was standing in the middle of the floor, one arm out holding on to a structure from which a drip was suspended. He was talking loudly to some invisible person, saying that he had a three o'clock appointment downtown. It was imperative that he clinch the deal today. The whole of the man's mid-section was bandaged up. He had a huge stomach. What was so alarming about the sight was that a tube led from the man's urethra and ended up in a bag three-quarters full of urine. And the bag was half lifted from the floor by his standing up.

'Mr Wagner, baby, what have you been UP to?' said Carlton.

'A damned important meeting at three,' said Mr Wagner.

'Martin, pick up that bag. He's going to drag the catheter out.' Benson picked up the bag, the urine inside the colour of dead autumn leaves. He held it up, close to Mr Wagner as Carlton lifted and encouraged the patient back to bed. 'There you are, Mr Wagner, honey. That's good. There ain't no meeting, Mr Wagner! What you got to do is rest up! When you're good and rested and out of here, then you can go to all the meetings you want!'

They manoeuvred Mr Wagner back to bed. Benson, while making sure that the urine tube did not go taut, also had to pull the drip-feed stand to a position next to the bed. The drip led to a plaster on the back of Mr Wagner's hand. Finally, he replaced the urine bottle in its container.

'Martin,' said Carlton, 'I want you to stay and TLC Mr Wagner while I go and get him his medication. I won't be no more than a minute.'

'Fine,' said Benson. It was too. He knew exactly where all the tubes started and finished, that none of them was pulling. He also saw where the buzzer was. He sat on the bed next to Mr Wagner. 'Don't worry. Everything is all right,' he told himself and his patient.

Mr Wagner continued to ramble. He was no longer talking about the meeting. He looked at Benson and said, 'For Christ's sake, don't sell the house!' Benson assured Mr Wagner that he wouldn't. 'If you sold it what would you live on after I'm gone? The rental units are trouble but they're all we've got.'

'I promise I won't sell it. Now just relax and try to sleep.'

'And don't let Heidi have the car. She'll only crash it or sell it. You can get your licence renewed. I'm not having you walking the streets with all them hoodlums.'

'I won't sell the car,' said Benson.

Mr Wagner came to himself. 'Who the fuck are you?' he asked. 'Did she sell you the house? She doesn't have to sell it. They can't force her. I've seen to that. They can whistle for the damned money! Yes they can!' Mr

Wagner gave a little laugh, then closed his eyes and sighed. The exhalation brought an oscillating string of snot out of his nose. Benson reached for a tissue. 'Give a good blow!' he commanded.

Mr Wagner didn't, so Benson pinched the base of Mr Wagner's nostrils, removed the tissue and saw that he had pinched up all the snot. He smiled a smile of satisfaction, crumpled the tissue and dropped it into the wastebin by the bed. It landed dead-centre.

Carlton returned with a kidney-bowl on which was a cloth and a syringe. He rubbed Mr Wagner's hairy upper arm with a swab and deftly sank the needle in. Benson watched steadily. When the needle went in he pressed his lips together, pushed his tongue against the roof of his mouth hard in sympathy, but Mr Wagner had not seemed to notice what was happening.

'That's a sedative. In a minute Mr Wagner will fall asleep. You seem to be managing OK, Martin. I'll take away the syringe. I'll show you where they go another time. You stay with Mr Wagner. Hold his hand. He likes that.'

Benson held Mr Wagner's large right hand. It was much bigger than his own. He ran his thumb back and forth along the back of the hand as the man started speaking unintelligibly, as though in sleep, then began snoring mightily.

Sweat broke out on Mr Wagner's brow and Benson, carefully disengaging his hand from his patient's, tip-toed over to the washbasin where there was a neat stack of J-Cloths. He took one, wet it under the tap and went back to the bed, where he laid the cold cloth against the forehead of the sleeping man. The cloth soon became warm. He wet it again and laid it back down.

His patient was now sound asleep. Benson just sat, on watch. Later when he tried to recall the scene he realized he had been perfectly at peace.

'He OK?' asked Carlton.

'Yes, fine I think.'

'We got to keep an eye on him, but right now I think we can let him sleep.'

'What's the matter with Mr Wagner, Carlton?'

'Later, Martin. Follow me.'

Obediently, Benson did so.

In a room exactly similar to Mr Wagner's, Carlton greeted an elderly man lying in bed. His head seemed very small against the huge pillow. He had a full head of white hair, but his cheeks were sunken, their bones high sea-cliffs emerging from a tide at full ebb. His body under the grey counterpane hardly swelled its contours. He was wearing a striped pyjama top, his arms lying on the coverlet. The hands were long, slim and brown, covered with liver spots. Mum had had those. She had tried to fade them away, but the expensive cream hadn't worked and Boots wouldn't take it back. Thieves!

'How are you doing, Mr Fucci?'

'Not so bad, Carlton. Just weak the whole time. Like a baby, you know.'

Carlton nodded and fondled Mr Fucci's hand . . . 'I'd like you to meet a new member of our team. This is Martin, Mr Fucci. Today's his first day.'

'Happy to make your acquaintance,' said Mr Fucci.

Benson beamed and said the feeling was mutual.

'We won't be letting him off the reins just yet, though,' said Carlton. 'He don't know shit.'

Benson was rather shocked that Carlton should use such a crude term in front of a patient, but Mr Fucci seemed to enjoy it because he started to laugh reedily. 'You mean he sticks suppositories down your throat and capsules up your ass?' he asked, slipping Benson a wink.

'Like that. Anyway he's under me and I'm going to be on his back the whole time.'

'Rather you than me, son,' said Mr Fucci. 'This 'ere Carlton can be one hell of a mean son of a bitch!'

'Now you know you wouldn't have me any other way, Mr Fucci!' said Carlton, checking the flow of Mr Fucci's drip.

'You stick with Carlton. You'll learn a lot from him. 'Course maybe what you'll learn are things you shouldn't be learning.'

Benson nodded, as-if-knowingly.

'You gossiping about me and distracting the help?' Carlton asked. He had lifted Mr Fucci's hand, looking at his watch. His big chin was stuck out, his big bottom lip covered the upper one. Benson gazed at him admiringly.

Mr Fucci looked up at Carlton too. A happy expression came to his face, which suddenly turned to a sad one. He seemed on the verge of tears.

'Such health! Will you look at that man! My God, I'd give everything I own for a year of that guy's life!'

Carlton looked at Mr Fucci. For the briefest of moments the gaze he gave his patient was made up of great sadness and pity, but in a flash the look was gone and Carlton had put his hand on his hip, twisted his body in a way Benson judged to be camp and said, 'Mr Fucci Honey, if you could SEE my life for ONE MINUTE I think you'd settle for what you GOT!'

Mr Fucci shook his head. He did not believe Carlton. Neither did Benson. Mr Fucci looked at Benson and Benson nodded back knowingly.

Towards the end of the afternoon they stopped for coffee. By that time Benson had assisted in presenting the commode both to Mr Fucci, and a young accident victim called Emerson who shared a room with a man

271

called Elias who did not seem to have anything wrong with him. Emerson had farted a lot. Benson could hear him through the curtain and tried to cough loudly and in time with the farts, while engaging Elias in polite conversation.

'Keep up that farting, Emerson, and you may learn to shit one day!' Elias shouted.

'Go fuck yourself!' Emerson shouted back amiably.

Benson had surprised himself. There had not been the least feeling of revulsion, even when the fumes had reached his nostrils. Only the desire to be efficient and not to embarrass Emerson. Emerson, in fact, had not seemed in the least embarrassed. Still he was American, had probably attended summer camps and YMCAs where there were no doors on the toilets. He also wanted to show Carlton that, though he might only be a rookie, he could be as efficient as someone with lots of experience. And then, beyond all that, an ineffable feeling that he was of use. Something akin to love was coursing through him. It was a sweet sensation that took him back to himself when young, dropping pennies into the poor box in the back of a deserted church. His mite might do a modicum of good. The feeling of his pocket money slipping away like tiny components into a bin, joining all the other offerings, more than made up the lack of sweets. The feeling had the surge of sugar. Much too good to be good.

'What's the matter with Mr Fucci?' Benson asked Carlton, back at the Nurses' Station.

'What isn't the matter? He's got uncontrolled diabetes. That leads to all kinds of other problems. The doctors are deciding what's the best thing to do. He has a bad problem with his feet. He may have to have an amputation.'

'Poor man.'

'Yeah. Mr Wagner was admitted for an operation for stomach ulcers but between you and me the doctors found more than that. He's been in severe pain and we've had trouble stabilizing the medication. He's been having delusions. Needs careful watching.' Then, Carlton added, 'Like you.'

'Me?'

'Yes. Still, I think you'll be good. You're not good yet, but one day you may be. What are you doing Friday night?'

'How do you mean?'

'Pablo and me's good friends. Maybe we can go out as a threesome. You like dancing?'

'Dancing?'

'Yeah, dancing.'

'Have you got a record player?' asked Benson, for something to say. Then he started worrying about Pablo and Virginia.

'Sure, but Pablo and me go to a dancing bar. We can dance together there.'

'Can we?' It sounded beyond the realms of possibility.

'Sure we can. Just as long as we don't touch.'

Benson nodded. 'But nobody minds? The police don't come?'

'Who can tell? Lilly Law will come if she wants. It all depends on whether she's been paid off. The bar Pablo and I go to has never had no trouble far as I know. What do you say?'

'Yes, I'd love to. But Pablo . . . er . . . and . . . ?'

'Pablo suggested it,' said Carlton. He came up close to Benson's face and Benson worried about his breath. He stopped breathing. 'You know what I'd like? I'd like to whisk you back to my place right now. Problem is I'm on duty till nine. Our schedules don't jive until Friday.'

'Don't they?' asked Benson, trying not to release too much air with his question.

'Don't they? Listen to you! Wow, you're a camp.' Then he said, 'Come on, back to work!'

Benson followed after Carlton, relieved in a way to be able to breathe freely again. I love you, he told Carlton's rear. Then he remembered that he had said that to Pablo the previous Saturday and over and over again to Virginia the night before. Yes, I am becoming shallow. *They think it's love but it's only lust.* Will everyone become beached on the shoals of my fickle, shifting, estuary? He thought of Parkgate on the Dee Estuary. Once Parkgate had been a great port, allowing ships from all over the place to come in and dock. The water had been deep then. But slowly it had silted up. Grass had grown on the silt. Cattle had grazed on the grass. Mary the shepherdess had minded the cattle. John Masefield had written a poem about her calling the cattle home. And we know what happened to her! But no longer did big ships come into Parkgate. Trippers came to watch Wales and buy ice-cream. As Parkgate declined Liverpool had grown fat because the Mersey was a bottle-shaped estuary, deep enough to accept ocean-going ships. Benson could see himself becoming as silted up as the Dee Estuary. Ships with their cargo of affection would avoid him. He had promised a safe haven to them once too often. They would go elsewhere and he would miss out. Nobody told me it would be like this. No, they were all so busy telling me how wrong it was. But they could not see clearly that, even according to their own benighted standards, some ways were wronger than others. Total condemnations snuff out any chance of light. What's to stop me having every gay boy in New York? It's no worse, according to *them* than cleaving to one through thick and thin.

That satisfied him for a while, but then he wondered what he thought himself. Where do I stand on this issue? *They* don't have to live my life. *I* have to live it. He pulled a face. That was the problem really. Most people had help – little red books, moral A to Zs. All he could do was plot out a route from hearsay, then mount his hen and, borrowing inspiration from Walt as he went, hope that he would arrive somewhere worth the journey and not just go endlessly round and round.

On the other hand, Walt would have been able to have three comrades at a time and still write pages and pages. Clearly for me famine has turned to feast. And not before time. *Lovers, continual lovers, only repay me.*

Armed by Walt and mad chemicals, Benson started to look forward to Friday. Then, at Times Square, he telephoned Virginia to ask if they could meet that night.

5

SHINE

If you have in your Psalter,
Father of Love, one note
That may reach his ear,
Then wake up his heart!
Open his clouded eyes
To the thousand oases
That well up for the thirsty
In the desert.

Goethe
(from Brahms' 'Alto Rhapsody')

'It's just one of them things, Martin. It's my third time this year. Ain't no problem. I'll give you the address of the clap-clinic. Ask for Adrienne and mention my name.'

Benson looked at Virginia. It was Thursday evening and until a few moments before he had been thinking of another spectacular evening with her. He had been going to ask her to come to his room at the YMCA, had even reconnoitred a route up to his room by means of a back staircase. Not to mention having bought peanuts and a big bottle of Coke to fortify them. 'But didn't you know before, Virginia?'

'No, Martin. If I had I sure as hell would have done something. You don't think Virginia would give the clap to a frien'?'

'No, of course not. It's just so er . . . inconvenient.'

Virginia went off to the ladies. Inconvenient! That's not the word. It's a fucking catastrophe! Just as I was starting to have a really good sex life too! It's so bloody typical. God's at the back of it. He just can't stand to see me having a good time. And all those Virgins and Martyrs must be as pleased as punch to see me in a mess. Not to mention Patrick. Perhaps it was what I said to the Blessed Sacrament. Jesus, Mary and Joseph! And what about Friday?

The whole of heaven, he felt, was in a state of mirth and finger-pointing. A thunder-clap of *told-you-so! Serve-you-right — lecturing-the-tabernacle-like-that!* had knocked him off his hen on the Road to Damascus. Humbled, he would have to stagger into the clinic and confess. Sin did not usually show. It spotted the hidden garden of the soul, and the neighbours behaved as if everything in the garden was lovely. But not this one. He'd go into the clinic and everyone would know. Bloody, fucking typical!

Virginia returned. 'Martin, don't look so down. You may not have it. Still, you'd best check it out, you know.'

'I know.' Then a thought struck him. 'You don't think you could have got it from me, do you?'

'Hell, no, Martin. It take way longer than that to come out.'

Well, that was a relief. He wrote down the address of the clinic.

'You want me to come with you? They all know Virginia there.'

'No!' Benson said, the screen of his brain suddenly filling with an image of Virginia leading him through the clinic without shame. It would be like taking Andy into confession with him. He tried again. 'No, thank you. I'd better just go by myself.'

On his way to the clinic in Greenwich Village Benson thought about tactics. I'll roll in all nonchalant like a sailor off a tramp steamer and confess to dubious nights in Hamburg. In England there's bubble-gum that has tattoo transfers inside. If I had some now I could put one on the back of my hand to prove I'm a sailor. No, I mustn't be proud. That won't cut any ice. I'll ask for Adrienne and mention Virginia's name.

By the time he arrived at the door of the clinic he had decided that humility was the best tactic. Yes, that is what he'd do. He'd abjectly throw himself on the mercy of the New York City Public Health Department.

He approached the reception desk, eyes downcast, unwilling to look to his left at the rows of men and women leafing through magazines. A middle-aged woman in a nurses' uniform like his wished him good evening and asked how she could be of assistance. Benson looked at her. She seemed so dispiritingly wholesome.

'Er . . . I think I might have a problem. I'm not sure but I might have. I thought I'd better come and make sure.'

'OK. The doctor will see you shortly. Take a seat.'

The woman smiled at Benson and gave him a number on a card. 'Thank you,' he said.

'You're welcome.'

Benson turned away, then turned back to the nurse. 'This is my first time,' he said.

She smiled again. 'Sure. Take a seat, sir. The doctor won't be long.'

Benson's eyes darted over the sinners on the seats. He found himself a place at the end of the back row, fidgeted, then dug out his nurses' aide handbook from his flight-bag.

It took ages for the numbers to creep up to his. Fear returned and he thought again how similar this was to shuffling up the long line in the confession queue when he had something really huge to confess. Saliva turned to gum in his mouth. His penis, so perky all week, had retreated into him like a puppy – caught in the act of slipper-chewing – under a sofa.

Say the doctor makes me take off my pants! He'll have to search around to find anything! He recited a litany of eroticism to coax his troublesome appendage out of its shell of shame. Thoughts of Virginia worked too well. He'll think I'm a sex maniac! If I am, I'm a sex maniac in hell at the precise moment.

'Sixty-nine!'

Somebody giggled.

Jesus, Mary and Joseph, assist me in my last agony! screamed Benson inwardly. He walked towards the

281

open door of the consulting room, feeling his penis pushing itself back inside him. You're bloody useless, that's what you are. You can't do anything right! he told it.

'Good evening,' Benson said to the elderly doctor.

The doctor nodded and held the door open for Benson to pass through.

'What can I do for you?'

Benson told the doctor his worst fears. 'I came straight round to see you. Of course it may be nothing but I thought I ought to be on the safe side. It wouldn't do to spread the infection. Not that I'm sure I have er . . . it. Still, I might have.'

The doctor nodded and asked Benson about his sex life in a matter-of-fact manner. Then he told him to remove his trousers and lie down. 'I'm just going to take some swabs.'

'Ah, yes. Swabs. Er . . . I'm a trainee nurses' aide. But this is my first time here.'

The doctor nodded and pulled down Benson's underpants.

'I only started on Monday. I'm at the Unitarian Medical Center in Brooklyn. Of course er . . . it's early days but at the moment I'm really enjoying the work.'

The doctor did not say anything. Still, he hasn't said how small I am. That's something. He's probably thinking it, though.

'Turn over, please.'

'Er . . . right ho.'

He felt his bottom exposed. Now he's seen every-thing, he thought. Fat bottom. This is definitely hell. They don't need red hot pokers. This is quite sufficient, thank you very much.

'Try to relax.'

'Yes, of course.'

An intrusive stab of discomfort while Benson

thought how he would never ever have sex again. From now on it's chastity for me. I'll just have to live on my memories. I'll sublimate my sexiness in good works for the greater good of mankind. I'll get a job with the UN, disappear into a Lima slum and die in the odour of sanctity. Yes, that is how it's going to be. I've rediscovered the Real Me. Take away sex and it's as easy as anything to be virtuous. This could be the best thing that has ever happened. The healing of my Achilles' heel. He saw himself on his hen – on which was emblazoned the UN flag – flying down to South America. Chaste Benson the only hope for our wormy world . . .

'OK. You can put your trousers on now.'

Benson did so with alacrity while the doctor washed his hands. Then he sat down at his desk and motioned Benson to take the seat opposite.

'Do you know all your contacts?' the doctor asked.

'Yes. If there is a problem I'm pretty sure where I've caught it.'

Another nod. 'Right. We'll be sending these swabs for analysis. The nurse will draw some blood. Call next Monday for the results. And in the meantime you should avoid further sexual contact.' And the doctor yawned.

'Yes, of course. Er . . . should I call round or call on the telephone?'

The doctor looked at him oddly. 'A phone call will be just fine.' He stood up.

'Thank you very much doctor. Good evening, doctor.'

The doctor nodded, stifling another yawn.

Benson gave blood unflinchingly and left the clinic. As the swing-door of the clinic closed behind him the relief was heavenly. He at once started looking for a pay-phone to call Virginia.

'Did you ask for Adrienne?' she asked him.

'I forgot.'

'Oh, *Martin*! Adrienne's real sweet. She's the old guy. He'd have treated you real good if you'd mentioned my name.'

'Is Adrienne a man?'

'Kinda, I guess.'

'And a doctor?'

'That's her. She look so buttoned down and all but it's just an act. You should see her do Mae West. Better than New Year's.'

'Who's Mae West?'

Virginia screamed down the line sufficient to cause Benson to remove the receiver from his ear and stare at it. He put it back to his ear in time to hear her telling him how naive he was.

'Well that's as may be. But your Adrienne was a bit cold with me.'

'Serve you right for not mentioning Virginia.'

Benson was silent.

'You there? Anyways, I'm on the wagon for a week or so, Martin. I guess you won't want to see me for a while.'

'That's not true,' he said.

'How's about tomorrow?'

'Er . . . I'm going out with a couple of nurses from UMC tomorrow. I'll ring you next week when I've got my results.' Then he thought of Carlton. What was he going to say to Carlton?

'Promise?'

'I promise.'

'And you're not sore at me?'

He thought about that. 'No, but it's given me a bit of a turn.'

It had too. He said good night to Virginia and walked back uptown, worrying about Friday.

*   *   *

'See that guy over there? The one in the T-shirt? I've been after that guy for weeks. He keeps giving me the eye but when I go over I get the open fridge door. Tonight it's happening all over again. He's looked at me like he's hot to trot. The guy he's with can see what's happening because whenever he dances around so's he's looking at me I get one of them mom-you-forgot-the-fuckin'-sugar looks.'

'If I was him, Pablocito, I'd come right over here and scratch your narrow little eyes right out!' said Carlton.

Pablo made a face at Carlton and wandered off back towards his quarry, feeling up total strangers as he insinuated through the crowd.

Benson was trying to sort everything out. Either Pablo is telling me that he no longer wants me, or he is not bothering to tell me and just behaving in a loutish manner. Anyway, it's over. It was just not meant to be. I'll have to get wedded to my work. But what am I going to do if Carlton asks me home? O insupportable!

The music stopped and a voice came out of the loud-speakers. 'No touching, people! If there's any more touching I'll just have to pull the socket out of the juke-box and that will be *it*! Play by the rules, OK?'

Benson reckoned that Pablo was the cause of the outburst. He had absolutely no shame. Play by the rules! What rules? If rules there be, I think we should be told!

Carlton called out, 'Hey, Martin, you want another drink?'

'Right-ho, it's my turn.'

'Mine's whisky sour.'

'Right-ho.'

Benson ordered a whisky sour for himself too. The beer he had chosen for his first drink had done nothing for him.

285

They sipped their drinks, watching Pablo dancing alone near the man he wanted so badly.

'Do you think he'll get him?' Benson asked.

'Pablo usually gets his man.'

'It doesn't seem fair to try to pinch that chap from his friend.'

'Pablo ain't known for being fair.'

'No. Did he tell you where we met?'

'He sure did. I would never have had you down as a SLUT!'

'Me? He started it. I was just watching the film.'

'But Central Park? That really is tacky. And in the Heckscher Playground of all places!'

'Pablo said a dark open space is safer than undergrowth. It was rather nice, though.'

'Are you coming home with me tonight?' Carlton asked him, suddenly serious.

Benson was not ready. 'Well, I . . . er . . . really would love to but I'm not sure I can.'

'Martin, you're not still carrying a torch for Pablo, are you? Look at him! Who do you think told me that there was a fresh young gay boy at UMC? Pablo and I go way back.'

'I don't think I ought. I mean . . .'

'Martin, you weren't ever going to be able to tame Pablo. Anyway not for a year or two. He's deep into the candy store and he ain't able to leave it. But me? Well, I'm thirty-six. I'm ready for something more.'

I'm twenty-one and I'm ready for something more . . . but not until I'm cured. 'Are you? You don't look it . . . er . . . I mean you don't look thirty-six.'

'Thanks. But you haven't answered my question.'

'Sorry?'

'You coming home with me?'

'Carlton, I'd love to er . . . but not tonight. Er . . .'

'OK. Suit yourself,' said Carlton, looking out over his

286

glass at a group of wallflowers, their eyes everywhere.

What does that mean? 'Er . . . I'm sorry . . . er . . . I'm going to have to be working on another ward from Monday.'

'Yes. Mr Fucci will miss you. I guess I will too. Say, why don't you call in on him? He'd appreciate it. All he's got by way of visitors is a sister and she has to come in from New Haven. Tonight he was very down. The amputation's going ahead.'

'Poor Mr Fucci. Yes, I'd love to visit him. You too. Carlton . . . I . . .'

But Carlton stepped on Benson's attempt at putting his best foot forward. 'Come Monday, you're going to be the only trainee nurses' aide, Martin. I met Mrs Muñoz in the cafeteria. She said the two black guys have decided they want out.'

'Lester and Laverne?'

'I guess. Hey, Martin, come home with me!'

'I can't.'

'Has Pablo been talking about me?'

'How do you mean? I haven't seen him all this week. No. It's just that I've made a mess of things and I've got to sort them out.'

'But all week you seemed hot to trot.'

Hot to trot summed it up rather well. Benson said nothing.

'Mrs Muñoz thinks you'll go too. I'll tell you something about her, Martin. Between you and me, OK? Mrs Muñoz used to be the head of nursing at UMC. Then she started getting bouts of depression. She was off work for long periods, had ECT and all kinds of therapy. Since she took on the job of trainer she's been much better. But I didn't like how she looked on Friday. She said she felt she was losing her touch.'

'But she's a wonderful teacher, Carlton!' replied

Benson vehemently. 'She can't help it if her trainees give up. I think Laverne and Lester thought the money was too low.'

'Yes. But she needs TLCing too. You get me?'

Benson nodded.

Carlton drained his drink. 'So that's it, then?' he asked. 'I think I'll go on home.'

Benson did not say anything. Carlton waved as he walked away, head and shoulders above the crowd, towards the exit.

* * *

'Let's you and I do something in the city tomorrow night,' Pablo said to Benson in the UMC cafeteria the following Monday. 'I'd kind of like to see your place at the Y.'

'I suppose we could. Do you want to ask Carlton, too?'

'Carlton isn't talking to me,' said Pablo.

'Why not?'

'He says I've been bad-mouthing him to you.'

'You haven't, though.'

'That's what I said to him. He was real pissed you wouldn't go home with him Friday. He'd set his heart on you.'

'I couldn't.'

Pablo shrugged. 'Carlton reckoned I'd told you about his little problem.'

'Well, you didn't,' said Benson. But it looks like you're going to, he thought.

'He's never able to hold on to a man. Sad in a way, seeing as all he wants is a lover. He ain't like me in that. I guess gays all think he's got a massive piece of meat. Christ, when we were together I was really pissed off. You need a pair of tweezers.'

288

'How do you mean?'

Pablo shrugged.

'Is that it?' Benson asked Pablo.

Pablo placed his hand in front of his mouth. 'Oops!' he said. 'Me and my big mouth!'

'Pablo, I should *slap* you in your big mouth for that. You're a bitch, a ruddy bitch! From this moment you had better consider our so-called friendship at an end. If you want the truth, the reason I didn't go with Carlton last Friday is because I may have caught something. I'm waiting for the results from the VD clinic. When I'm clear I'm going after Carlton and I don't give a fuck how he's built. Do you really suppose that a big cock is the meaning of life? Doesn't goodness have anything to do with it?'

'Christ! You haven't given it to me, have you?'

But Benson had been distracted, thinking about what he had said to Pablo. 'What?'

'Clap.'

Benson saw an opportunity to get his own back on Pablo. He rather relished the thought of him having to go through the hell of the clinic. But he relented. 'No. You were my first in New York. The first for more than a year, if you want the truth. If I've got it, it happened after.'

'Phew!'

'Quite,' said Benson. 'But you can forget about seeing me at the YMCA, Pablo. At this moment I don't ever want to see you again.'

'It's your funeral,' said Pablo archly. He stood up and whispered in Benson's ear. 'You were a lousy lay anyhow. You and Carlton are made for each other.' And he walked out of the cafeteria, extravagantly greeting friends as he went.

* * *

That evening Benson went straight back to the YMCA. He had urgent calls to make. The lady at the clinic told him that he was in the clear. Full of joy he rang Virginia's number, but there was no answer.

Benson sat on his bed, cradling his flight-bag on his lap. He noted that the bag was becoming rather grimy. He would have to take a J-Cloth to it. The strap was beginning to fray, a bit of cotton hung off. He pulled on it and instead of breaking off it popped thread after thread. He stopped pulling, got out his Imco and broke the thread with the flame. No, the bag wasn't going to last long. At this rate it wasn't going to be fit to be seen by the time he got back to Aberystwyth. That would be a pity. Half the fun of travel was being able to show off about it when one returned. Still, maybe people wouldn't be that impressed by an Aer Lingus bag. They might think he'd just been to Dublin. Lots of people had flown to Dublin. How would he be able to convey the fact to the passers-by that he had been much farther? He could buy one of the Statue of Liberty statues to impress people who came to his room but that did not solve the problem of what to wear about his person on the street. Maybe he could buy a Pan Am bag. But that would be extravagant. He already had one. Yes, but he could give the Aer Lingus bag away as a present and keep the Pan Am one. But it's a bit worn to give away. People will think I'm tight. Of course, I could give the Aer Lingus bag to Ianto and say it was old-looking because it had seen so much. If Ianto did not appreciate a much-travelled bag would I think the worse of him? What would that say about him? Well, it would probably say that he doesn't have much imagination. Is that it? I wish I had Dexter here to explain it. He bit his lip. But what do I think? Ought I to be spreading myself around like this? It was lovely with Virginia, but what about Patrick? And what do I think of Carlton? I think he is good and beautiful. So why am I worried? If Pablo's right – the bitch! – does that mean I no longer am attracted to him? Is that all I want? I might as well bow down and worship a Dutch cucumber and a couple of spuds in a bag. *Those who suffer from this disability* – A lack of ability, that means. Roy Jenkins was probably referring to my lack of ability to form a relationship with a woman. Well, I don't accept that. I'm not going to start worrying about that again. But maybe I do have a disability. It's possible. I am looking for an ideal man. Carlton seems pretty ideal. Am I going to let that stop me from loving him, assuming Pablo's right, that is? But do I even know what love is?

Benson dithered on before turning his attention to what he should do that night. He decided to touch base by going to Jackson Heights.

* * *

7 Revere Street
Butte
Montana
19 August 1967

Dear Mr Benson,

You don't know me. I am Dexter Bulkington's mother. I found your address in Dexter's address book.

I am sorry to tell you that Dexter was killed by a bear last week while working at the Lewis and Clark Cavern State Park. My only consolation is that he died while trying to help two hikers who were being attacked by the grizzly, and managed to allow one of them to escape.

But there is really nothing that can console me at this time. I am writing letters now on the kitchen table in order to stop myself from going crazy. I don't know whether you know it or not, but Dexter was our only surviving child. His elder brother died tragically in an automobile accident when Dexter was in his sophomore year at high school. We had such hopes for him. He was a wonderful person. But, if you knew him well, you know that well too.

Please pray for us.
Yours sincerely,
Marvel Bulkington

Benson had collected the letter from Jackson Heights, along with others from Dad and Alice, and Meryl. He read it on Jackson Heights station. A train stopped and the doors opened. He let them close again, watched as it left, picking up screaming speed. Then he walked towards the exit.

He was outside the presbytery of Our Lady of Perpetual Help without knowing how he had got there. He rang the doorbell and Miss O'Neill answered it almost at once.

'It's Martin, isn't it?'

'Yes.'

'Consider yourself lucky, young man. I was polishing the doorknob. Normally it takes me a good while longer to answer the door. Now what can I do for you?'

'Is Father Patrick in, please?'

'You know, he isn't. He's just gone to hear confessions.'

'Can I leave him a message? It's just that I want a mass said. A friend of mine has been killed. I don't know how much they are and I haven't got a mass card.'

'Come on in, Martin,' she said.

'But aren't you busy?'

'Never too busy for a lad from Liverpool.'

'Well, it's not really Liverpool. It's just near.'

He went in. 'The doorknob's really shiny,' he said. Then, once the heavy door had closed behind him, he started to bawl like a baby.

She took him to her kitchen and held his hand until he had recovered. Then she made him a cup of tea.

'You know, this is the first proper teapot I've seen since I came here.'

She nodded. 'Milk, Martin?'

'Yes, please. Thank you. In England we put it in before the tea. You put it in after.'

'That's right. You do it the Protestant way. As a girl I worked for a Protestant family near Sligo. They'd always insist on the milk going in first.'

Benson tasted his tea. It took him straight home. 'It's lovely,' he said. 'Just right.'

'There. You've learnt something. You can do it the Catholic way from now on.'

'Yes. You mentioned Sligo just now. Dexter – that's the friend who was killed – he talked about a battle there. It was about a book. St Columba copied a manuscript and St Finbar said he stole it. Thousands were killed.'

'The War of the Book. I've been to Inishmurray. We'd take a picnic out there. I'd look out at the Atlantic. The bucko I was stepping out with used to swear he could see America.'

'What happened to him?'

'He came here.'

'Did you ever meet him?'

'I did. He'd married. But I'll tell you a coincidence, Martin. Father Patrick is his son.'

'Is he?'

'Yes. And I didn't meet his dad until he knocked at the presbytery door like you.'

'That must have been a shock.'

'I was past shock. It was just a nice surprise. Life's full of them, you know. And Death is too.'

Benson looked into Miss O'Neill's eyes. 'Do you think so? Nice surprises?'

'I think so. As long as you do your best down here.'

'I think Dexter did his best. I only knew him for a while but I won't forget him.'

Miss O'Neill nodded. 'Why don't you go and talk to Father Patrick, Martin?'

'But he's in confession.'

'So? When did you last go?'

'Er . . .'

'Forgive me, Father, for I have sinned. It's been about three years since my last confession, Father.

'Father, it's hard for me to confess because I am not even sure I believe. I am homosexual and I don't think it's a sin. But I have the feeling that I'm becoming shallow and rudderless. Last week I had sex with a man and caused him a lot of sorrow. I am sorry that I caused that man to be unhappy, Father. I am also a prig. I judge others all the time. I am lazy and too easily influenced by people. My motives are mixed. I worry about what people think of me all the time . . . and I don't know if I can love . . .

'Er . . . for these and all my other sins which I cannot now remember I humbly ask pardon from God. Penance and absolution from you, my Ghostly Father.'

There was silence from the other side of the grille. Then a long sigh. 'It's Martin, isn't it?' said Father Patrick.

'Yes, Father. Miss O'Neill sent me. I came here to ask

you to say a mass for a friend of mine who has died. His name is Dexter Bulkington. I wrote it down for Miss O'Neill. I've left the money with her. Er . . . I . . .'

'Of course, I'm very sorry to hear about your friend. I'll say the mass, Martin. And Martin, I'm sorry for what I did to you. I think you understand how it is. I've got a lot of things to sort out.'

Benson did understand. He understood all too well.

'You'd better be off, Martin. People will be thinking you're a mass-murderer.'

'That doesn't matter. What about my penance, Father?'

'Come and have a Guinness with me some time soon.'

'Right-ho,' said Benson. He bowed his head as the priest absolved him of his sins.

'Martin?' said Patrick.

'Yes, Father?'

'Patrick. Don't be too hard on yourself, OK? It doesn't do any good. You should have learnt that by now. Go and find yourself a friend.'

'Yes, Fath . . . Patrick.'

On leaving the confessional and heading back out into the night street, Benson was amazed by how – in spite of everything – he felt light and happy. Did you see that? he told the opaque sky above Jackson Heights. A bit of decent advice for a change. You know, Dexter, I think that's what I've been waiting to hear. You told me that too, of course. But hearing it from Patrick in confession! Well!

His hen drew up and bowed down for its master to ascend.

'Take me to Manhattan, my trusty steed!' he commanded.

* * *

The following day, after running around after Nurse Gonzalez in Emergency, Benson went to visit Mr Fucci.

Carlton was on duty. 'How are you?' he asked Carlton.

'Just fine. Yourself?'

'I'm OK. And Mr Fucci?'

'Not too good, Martin. He's having the operation in the morning.'

'Poor Mr Fucci! Does his sister know?'

'No. He doesn't want to upset her.'

'Carlton, I want to talk about . . .'

A buzzer sounded. Carlton strode away. Benson watched him go and opened the door of Mr Fucci's room.

'Hello, Mr Fucci. Sorry I'm late.'

'Martin! Where have you been? I've had bad news. You heard from Carlton?'

'Yes, Mr Fucci. I'm sorry.'

Mr Fucci was shaking his head. 'I like that man.'

'Me too.'

'You do? He's been talking to me about you. He likes you.'

'Does he?'

'Sure he does. 'Course I know about Carlton. He came straight out with it when I asked him about wife and kids. In the tailoring business you meet a lot of them. I should have known. He says you are too.'

'Er . . . yes.'

'You know it was that damned sewing machine that got me the sore on the foot? Hell, I thought it would be OK but I kept catching the foot under the treadle.'

'The treadle?'

'The thing that powers the machine. Didn't seem no more than a blister. It sure as hell is now but back then – before I came in – it weren't no more than a blister.

Seems like it's going to make me lose the whole damned leg. I should've gone electric, but I was used to the treadle.'

'I'm sorry, Mr Fucci.'

'Like I said, there are worse things than losing a leg.'

Benson nodded. He could not think of a worse thing. Then he thought of one.

'Hey, I nearly forgot. I got something for you.' Mr Fucci reached over to his bedside table and passed a brown paper bag across the bed to Benson. 'Some friends in the neighbourhood gave it to me when I got my citizenship. I can't say as I've read it much. I want you to have it.'

'Me? Why?'

''Cause I think you'd use it. Look on it as a bribe, if you like. I want you to keep coming to visit.'

'There's no need, I er . . .'

'Go on, open it!'

Benson opened the bag, reached in and brought out a hardback book. It had no dust cover and at once reminded Benson of school. There was a picture of grass growing on a grave. A bearded man was crouching at its foot. One of the man's hands was held out to a hand coming out from the grass. The man's other hand pointed towards the sunset – or was it the sunrise – and between the cemetery scene and the sunset was the kingdom of the living: men arm in arm, mothers wheeling baby-carriages, Negroes with manacles being broken off their arms, strong men laying down railroads, building skyscrapers. Above the scene in green lettering was written:

Leaves of Grass
Walt Whitman

He opened the fly-leaf. It cracked. Inside was written,

12 May 1946 to Mario Fucci on the occasion of his receiving citizenship of the United States of America, and below this inscription about twenty people had signed their names.

'This is beautiful, Mr Fucci. But you can't give it to me.'

'Why not? My sister won't know what to do with it if I go.'

'Go? You're not going to go anywhere. You're not going to let us down!' said Benson.

Mr Fucci smiled. 'Maybe not.'

Benson returned to accepting his gift with fitting reluctance. 'Well, I mean, you shouldn't give . . .'

'You're right. You should pay me something for it. I'll tell you what. Read to me from it and it's yours.'

'But . . .'

'Read, goddammit! What the fuck's *wrong* with you? Are you going to go through life making excuses all the time?'

'How do you mean?'

'Martin, you've got to have the courage of your convictions. You gotta. It's one thing this country has taught me. Sure, there's a lot wrong with it. Helluva lot. But there's one helluva lot right with it too. Take the damned book! When you read it, think of me. OK?'

'OK.' Benson ran his hand across the cover.

'So read!'

Benson opened the book again. 'I'll read "Out of the Cradle Endlessly Rocking". It's a bit long, though.'

'I've got time.'

Benson found the page. 'It's about the poet seeing two mockingbirds in Paumanok – that's the Indian name for Long Island. That's all you need to know really, except that the mockingbirds are a metaphor.'

Mr Fucci nodded. 'Yeah, yeah. Read!' Benson began reciting. He had not recited to an audience since those

298

long dead days at school. He thought of Brother O'Toole who had encouraged him. Then he thought of Dexter. But thinking of Dexter made his eyes cloud over and he tried then to think of nothing but the poem.

> Shine! Shine! Shine!
> Pour down your warmth, great sun!
> While we bask, we two together.
> Two together!
> Winds blow south, or winds blow north,
> Day come white, or night come black,
> Home, or rivers and mountains from home,
> Singing all time, minding no time,
> While we two keep together.

Benson had thought he knew the poem well. He had thought that its meaning was clear. But now, with Mr Fucci there in the bed, Dexter dead far to the west, he was reading it as if for the very first time.

> The boy ecstatic, with his bare feet the waves, with his hair the atmosphere dallying,
> The love of the heart long pent, now loose, now at last tumultuously bursting
> The aria's meaning, the ears, the soul, swiftly depositing,
> The strange tears down the cheeks coursing.

He glanced over at Mr Fucci. His friend had fallen asleep. But Benson kept on to the end, hoping that Dexter could hear, and, hearing, understand how wonderful Walt was:

> Death, death, death, death, death.
> Which I do not forget,

299

But fuse the song of my dusky demon and brother,
That he sang to me in the moonlight on Pauma-
  nok's gray beach,
With the thousand responsive songs at random,
My own songs awaked from that hour,
And with them the key, the word up from the
  waves,
The word of the sweetest song and all songs,
That strong and delicious word which, creeping
  to my feet,
(Or like some old crone rocking the cradle,
  swathed in sweet garments, bending aside),
The sea whisper'd me.

Then he closed the book. He listened for a moment
to Mr Fucci's snores, choosing to regard them as
tumultuous applause. He bowed to his sleeping patient
and, placing the book in his flight-bag as carefully as a
mother laying down her sleeping baby in its cradle,
tip-toed from the room. On his way down the back
stairs he stopped, leant his head against the banister
and began to howl.

*   *   *

Nurse Muñoz smiled at her lone student. Benson
caught the smile and lobbed it back extravagantly.
'Thank God you're still here, Martin. Every morning I
wake up with the thought that I'd come in and find you
gone and only the Zeigen family for company. You
won't go, will you? Pablo's sure you're going. He says
you're determined.'
  The bitch! The fucking bloody bitch! 'No,' he said,
and he blushed.
  'Miss Fern in Admin has been placing ads for
Nurses' Aides in all the papers, but we haven't had one

reply. You know what I did last night? I was on the way home. I'd bought Pedro – that's Mr Muñoz – some cold cuts for his dinner. It's been so hot. There were some kids sitting on a stoop playing a radio real loud. I don't know if seeing them made me angry because they were so damned lazy looking or because the music was too loud. Anyway, I went right up and told them that they ought to come and join us at UMC. They could do such a lot of good TLCing the patients here.'

'That's the spirit!' said Benson. 'What did they say?'

'They just looked at me like I was a crazy lady. They may be right.'

'No, they aren't right, Mrs Muñoz,' said Benson. 'You are a wonderful teacher. Every day I learn something that I know I'll never forget.'

Nurse Muñoz went coy. She played with her halo of hair. 'You're just *saying* that! My, you English have a way with words!'

'Don't be so hard on yourself! I'm only telling you the truth.'

'Are you?' She was serious again. He knew exactly what she meant.

'Yes,' he said.

Nurse Muñoz, her old self again, resumed tendering exclusive love and care on Benson. From time to time he would look at the dynamo teacher in front of him, wondering how he could possibly extricate himself from her, from the whole web of interest and responsibility, caring and possibility, in order to return to Aberystwyth to finish his American literature course. He saw himself opening the first text of the new academic year in his seat at the library overlooking the sea, the sea that went, past Ireland and Inishmurray, to the New World. His eyes would cloud over with tears of regret and recrimination. Hadn't he had enough of all that? But . . .

301

*   *   *

Mr Fucci had his operation that day. Benson called in on the ward both to ask about him and to see Carlton.

'Mr Fucci's fine, Martin. He's sleeping still.'

'So I should be able to see him tomorrow, maybe.' Carlton nodded.

'Carlton? I'm sorry I was peculiar last Friday. Er . . . I thought I had VD. I was waiting for my results.'

'Why didn't you tell me?'

'I was ashamed.'

'You'll have to get over that.'

'Yes, I suppose so. Er . . . I was wondering, though. Is the offer still open?'

'I'll have to consult my diary,' Carlton replied. He mimed turning the pages of a book. 'There's been an unexpected cancellation this evening. Will that be suitable?'

'Give me a mo. and I'll check.' And Benson delved into his flight-bag.

Back at Carlton's apartment, Benson asked if he could use the telephone and dialled Virginia's number. He let the phone ring and ring, but there was no answer. He put down the receiver, thinking that he would have to go round and check.

'Who were you calling?' Carlton asked. He had taken off his uniform and stood in the middle of the living room wrapped in a white towel. Benson admired his monumental torso.

'Er . . . Virginia. She's a friend. Actually she's the one who thought she'd given me VD.'

'You've been playing the whole scene, haven't you?' Carlton said.

'Yes, I have a bit. But Virginia's really a man. Well, a bit of both.'

302

'A drag queen?'

'She's more than that. I'm very fond of her.'

Carlton nodded, then sat down on the sofa, motioning Benson to sit down next to him.

Benson did so, suddenly apprehensive. 'I thought I ought to tell you about all my playing about. Do you mind that? I'd quite understand if you did.'

'How you do go on,' said Carlton amiably. He reached over and ruffled Benson's hair, pulled him towards him. Benson saw the dark lips approaching his. He thought of a nasty joke. Then their lips were touching and he forgot the guilt that had followed the thought. Carlton's lips fitted around his. Then Carlton began to move his lips to left and right, grazing Benson's, tickling them. Benson boldly ventured to explore the contours of Carlton's lips with his tongue. Carlton drew back then and looked at him hard. Benson looked straight back and lifted his hand, running it lightly over Carlton's hair. It feels lovely, he thought. 'It feels lovely,' he said. Then he buried his fingers in the hair.

Carlton started to undress him on the sofa. His shirt came off and Benson sucked in his tummy and held himself straight so that no spare tyre would show. Then he forced himself to relax.

Soon Benson was lying naked on the sofa while Carlton appraised him. 'I'm a bit soft. Rather second-rate, I'm afraid.'

'Just relax, OK?'

'Right-ho.' But he was shaking.

Carlton rubbed the back of Benson's neck. 'You're still tense. All knotted. Stay right there.' And, still wearing his towel Carlton stood up and walked off, returning with a bottle and bath sheet which he spread on the floor. 'Lie down on your stomach. I'll TLC you for a while.'

Benson did as instructed and Carlton knelt down beside him and poured scented oil from the bottle on to his palm. Then he started running his hands over Benson's body. 'Christ, you're tense, Martin. Just relax, OK? You're perfectly safe.'

'Yes.'

Carlton straddled him, sitting heavily down on Benson's bottom. Benson tensed but was told quietly to relax and did his best to do so. He felt Carlton's hands on his back, smelled the perfume of the oil, the sudden cold of a stream of oil poured on to his back. 'This is nice,' he said.

'Haven't you ever had a massage before?'

'No.'

'Where have you been! Still, you're getting your first from an expert. You may learn something. Your patients like a massage. It's the greatest thing for relaxation.' And Carlton pushed and prised away at the knotted muscles in Benson's neck.

Benson breathed into the towel. The only thing in his experience akin to this was the artificial respiration practice he had been subjected to while doing the Bronze Medallion life-saving practices on the edge of his local swimming pool. But that was a million miles away. A smile completely unselfconscious in origin had appeared on his features, a smile that did not fade when Carlton's fingers pummelled his bottom, insinuating around his arsehole and the back of his scrotum. He felt as if his body was sinking into the floor of the room.

'Turn over on your back, Martin.'

Carlton knelt behind his head, anointing the oil into his shoulders and arms, lifting his rag-doll arms one at a time and bending the hands and fingers this way and that. Then Carlton was sitting on Benson's stomach, laying his hands on his torso and sides, tracing a course across the vertebrae of his rib-cage, pushing beneath, up against his liver and pancreas. Benson sighed and suddenly let out a loud fart.

He opened his eyes. 'God, I'm sorry about that. I don't know what came over me! I . . .'

Carlton was no longer wearing his towel. Benson looked up at the smiling face and then down at Carlton's erection. *Pablo, you bitch! You lying bitch!*

'You're all tense again, Martin. What's a fart between friends? It showed me you're relaxed. Come on, back to dreamland.'

Benson closed his eyes but was unable to massage his mind back to reverie. What had made Pablo say that about Carlton? Such a damned lie. A part of him felt cheated. Now he would not be able to prove to Carlton and to himself that it did not matter. Still, maybe it didn't matter, but it was nice that it wasn't true.

Carlton moved off Benson's stomach, a perch made uncomfortable by Benson's erection, and started massaging his legs. Soon there remained only one section of Benson unanointed.

'Let's go to bed,' Carlton said.

'I'm not sure I can get up.'

'Do you want me to carry you?'

'I'm much too heavy.'

'I'm strong. You will be too if you stay around UMC. I get all the weight-training I need shifting people like Mr Wagner in bed.'

'How is he?'

'Hanging in. Just. He still can't stop talking about the house and his daughter Heidi.'

'He wants to make sure everything's done right, I suppose.'

Carlton told Benson to put his arms around his neck. Benson, after protesting, did so. He felt arms push under him, lifting him from the towel. He was carried like a baby into the bedroom.

There, on Carlton's white sheets everything occurred that had occurred to Benson before. The parts and acts of that night were like some red-hot braille in Benson's brain. A book of touch and sensation whose every erect character repeated the lessons of his life thus far. Brother Michael was there. Clitherow. Andy. The man below him at the orgy. Dr Leptos. Enoch Mohammed. Howell the Farmer. As he gagged happily and unselfconsciously on Carlton's bulk, Pablo was there too. As he thrust and sucked, licked and opened himself up farther than he judged to be either wise or possible, Patrick appeared, down on his hands and knees with his handkerchief, mopping his soul. And Gareth weeping into his chip-fryer. As he came he thanked them all, offered prayers for them all.

Carlton got up to fetch them a drink. Benson lay on the bed, his limbs spread out, as though laying claim to every inch of its territory.

Only then did he think of Dexter.

He told Carlton everything that had happened. Carlton listened attentively, stroking his hand as he had stroked Mr Fucci's hand.

Then he remembered his manners. 'Tell me about yourself, Carlton. I want to know everything,' he said, sipping on an ice-cold beer.

'OK. But are you staying?'

'How do you mean?'

'Staying the night.'

'Sure. I can stay but I don't want to get in your way. I mean, if you've got things to do.'

'Will you STOP it? Are all you English like this?'

'How do you mean?'

'So fuckin' po-lite all the time. It's a wonder you ever

306

get anything done. Still I hear you all imitate the Queen.'

'No, we don't!' replied Benson. 'If I had my way we wouldn't have a royal family at all. They're really useless. Also, they stand at the head of an outmoded class system that is strangling us. You're right in a way, though. Many people do aspire to being like the Queen and the aristocracy. It's supposed to be a democracy but there are so many divisions. People are either looking up or looking down. They never seem to manage a good straight man-to-man look.'

'What brought that on?'

'I'm not sure really.'

Carlton was suddenly serious. 'Pablo says you're not staying. Is that true?'

'Where?'

'In America.'

Benson gazed down at the dark hand, noticing how it made the white sheet seem luminous.

He thought of himself and Carlton in bed. He looked out at the city of possibilities in the distance. 'I don't know. I've not really thought about it. You see, I'm only a tourist.'

'Martin, half the folks at UMC are *only tourists*. Without illegal immigrants this country would grind to a halt.'

'But isn't that worrying? Doesn't it make you anxious all the time?' He felt that it would make life rather similar to being at Sissy's Saloon. At any minute the police would come in and arrest you. 'Er . . .' He changed the subject. 'What's the matter with Pablo?' he asked.

'Did he say something to you about me?' Carlton asked.

'Yes. He's been saying things to Mrs Muñoz . . . to you too. About me leaving.'

'What did he say about me?'

'I don't like to say.'

'I guess I know the sort of thing. He tries to frighten people away from me. You see, Pablo and I were lovers for a while. He lived with me here. We were getting on real fine except that he couldn't stay faithful. I couldn't take that. I threw him out. He's never been able to forgive me. Tell you the truth, he's never been able to *understand* it. Still, I thought he'd stopped bad-mouthing me.'

Benson nodded.

'Think about staying, will you? I know it's early days and I don't want to crowd you but I think we'd get on just fine. One thing though, you are tired of the candy store, aren't you?'

'Er . . . it's all there is . . . was . . .'

'No, there's more.'

Benson nodded. 'And that reminds me,' he said, thinking of Joan Bakewell. 'When did you first decide you wanted to be a nurse?'

*　　*　　*

Mr Fucci was recovering well from his operation. One evening he told Benson that Carlton wanted him to stay on in America. Benson already knew that.

'I wish I could stay, but how can I, Mr Fucci? I'm two years on with my degree. I don't know what my dad would say. And all my friends are there.'

'Not all your friends. What about us? Do you have anyone to worry about back there?'

Benson thought about that. 'No, I don't think so. I worry about my Auntie Muriel sometimes. She lives alone in a neighbourhood which is becoming quite rough.'

'How about here? Do you worry about people here?'

He thought about that. 'Yes,' he said.

'There you are then.'

'How do you mean?'

'Back in Italy we had a saying, "Home is where your worries are." Think about it, Martin. We all need someone to worry about.'

'I was worried about *you*.'

'That's a start. And you like the US, don't you?'

'Yes, I like it a lot. I'm very happy in my job. In a way I think nursing may suit me more than whatever I'm going to be fit for after the degree. I don't think I want to teach much and I can't think of anything else. I've been racking my brains like mad.'

'But doesn't your family want you to be happy?'

He thought about that. That was a hard one. Probably they would prefer him to be good. But what did that mean? 'I suppose they do. Not that they'd ever put it that way.'

'How would they put it?'

'Well, I don't know. It never seems to come up. We don't talk about things like that.'

'God, you're a tight-assed crew, you Limeys.'

'We embarrass easily, I suppose.'

'That's what I'm saying, tight-assed.'

Benson did not comment. Instead he started reading some of Whitman's 'Calamus' poems to Mr Fucci.

* * *

Having still been unable to get any reply from Virginia, Benson took the subway into Manhattan that evening to see what had happened to her. It seemed odd that no-one was picking up the phone. After all, Virginia had told him that her mother seldom went out.

He noted the couples walking arm in arm along

Manhattan's streets. A COUPLE. He played with the word, rolling it around his mouth like a boiled sweet. Of course, it was too early for him to consider Carlton and himself a couple. When would that happen? Would it happen? Were it to happen? ... he saw himself walking through the streets of Manhattan with Carlton. People looked at them. Did they suspect? Benson rather hoped they did. If they did become a couple he did not think he would like to have to keep it to himself. No, he would like to be able to tell the world – or at least that part of the world that would not bash him up. Anyway, they would be a wonderful example to the populace. Truly it is right and fitting for brothers to dwell together in harmony. *Harmony*, another word to suck on and savour. Carlton had said – more or less – that he wanted him as Dearest Him. This was his chance. There might not be another. Then again, there might be. Would he run away back to England, worried about petit-bourgeois things like degrees and work and stability, or would he take life into his hands and jump into the dark? At one moment he thought he would stay. He badly wanted to see how his story would turn out if whoever was writing the book flicked him over an ocean and away from the Old World where, he felt, his sad ending had already been sketched out.

Then, just as he had grown happy with that, faces and places of home made him gulp, and not going home seemed like sin.

Benson arrived at Virginia's building. He rang the bell, but there was no answer. Then an old lady approached the door, opening it with her key. Benson held the door open for her and she looked at him oddly. He was too anxious to bother trying to explain and started up the stairs, two at a time.

The door was just as he remembered. The 9 still

310

upside down. He banged the door, called out Virginia's name. But there was no answer.

'They moved out,' said the old woman.

'Did they? You don't know where they went, do you?'

'Away, thank God,' she replied. 'They was trash.'

Benson saw that the old woman was carrying what seemed like a heavy bag. A part of him wanted to ask if he could carry it for her. Then he thought better of it. 'They're my friends,' he said.

*   *   *

A week later Benson had still not heard any word from Virginia. Neither had he reached a decision about his future. He spent much of his time kicking himself for his indecision, jittering about, setting himself tests. If the light changes by the time I count to five, I'll stay . . . but when the light co-operated Benson would just frown and look round for another test. He threw J-Cloths at distant sluices, held his breath between subway stations, opened *Leaves of Grass* at random . . . but nothing could decide him. Then he sat down and compiled a for and against column, but for every pro he found a con.

He had more or less moved in with Carlton and day by day more and more of his belongings disappeared from his room at the YMCA to become a pile at the bottom of Carlton's closet. He kept asking Carlton to make the decision for him, but Carlton just shook his head. 'You know what I want, Martin. But it's up to you.'

One morning Benson arrived at work to find Nurse Muñoz sitting on her teaching stool deep in conversation with a man in jeans and a T-shirt.

'Martin, I'd like you to meet Virgil Brown. Virgil has

311

been saying how much he admires you.' Benson held out his hand and dumbly shook Virgil's hand. He looked into the face and thought he saw Virginia there. Then he saw Virginia there. His mouth fell open.

Virgil and Benson stood looking at one another dumbly for a long moment. Nurse Muñoz said, 'For two friends you don't have very much to say to one another. Now, Martin, we want Virgil to stay with us. I don't want to lose any more! I've been giving Mr Muñoz a bad time about it. Make Virgil feel at home. I'll go and fix coffee.' She made off for the kitchen, then pointed over her shoulder. 'Introduce him to the Zeigen family.'

Benson stepped over to the dummies. 'This is Arthur Zeigen. He's the man. And this is Anita Zeigen. She's the woman . . .' Virgil was nodding, giving Benson the quiet Virginia smile he knew well.

Virgil spoke for the first time, sounding like Virginia with a cold. 'Don't you know me, Martin? I tried to get you at the YMCA to tell you, but they couldn't find you. I needed your help, tell you the truth. I just couldn't decide whether to turn up for duty as Virginia or Virgil. Fin'lly I just flicked a coin. It landed tails.'

'But where did you go, Virginia . . . Virgil? I called you up every day and then I went to your place but there was no sign of you.'

'Is Martin TLCing you OK, Virgil?' Nurse Muñoz called.

'Yes, Mrs Muñoz . . .'

Benson turned to Virgil. 'And this is baby Zeigen. We practise procedures on the family and then we go to the wards and work on real patients . . . Er . . .' He could not think of anything else to say, and shrugged.

'Mom decided to move. The landlord was threatening. I just went with her to her boy friend's place. But I couldn't take it, Martin.'

'So where are you living now?'

'I'm with Levancia. She still sneezing. That hay fever's a real killer. Hey, this job sure don't pay much, do it?'

'So why have you decided to take it up? You didn't seem that interested when I mentioned it to you in the park.'

Virgil was stroking the legs of Anita with his long right hand. He was about to reply when Nurse Muñoz called them in for coffee and banana cream pie.

'I hope you stay!' Benson told Virgil on the subway to Manhattan that evening.

'I want to. You know, I really liked it. Nurse Muñoz is sweet, ain't she?'

'Yes, she is. And it's a job with prospects.'

'But you're going back to England, Martin. So it can't suit you.'

'I'm supposed to go on September the eleventh. That's when my ticket is for. I'm going to try and change it, though. There still seems such a lot to do. I hope they'll let me change it.'

'I guess you gonna go eventually,' said Virginia sadly. Benson was reminded of her pessimism about the future of the Negro in the painting.

'Virginia . . . Virgil, it suits me down to the ground. And I think I may have found myself a friend.'

'Virginia. So stick with it, then. What's Mrs Muñoz going to say if you go? She really likes you, you know. Says you'll make a great nurse. You're a good fuck too.'

'Am I?'

'Christ, Martin, I can't wait to get back into my real clothes. It's a real drag wearing pants.'

Benson nodded. 'How have you made your bust go flat?'

313

'Length of fabric. Either way, something had to get tied down.'

'But what decided you to come to UMC?'

'Just tired of the hassles, I guess. Remember the painting of that big nigger on the ship?'

Benson frowned.

'Well, I don' wan' no sharks to get me. And there's lots o' sharks out there. Anyways I called up the hospital and they took me. Nurse Muñoz must've been desperate if she took me!'

'That's not true!' said Benson, thinking of his difficult interview, unwilling to allow his vocation to be devalued, or for Virginia to devalue herself. 'She must have thought you'd be good! You mustn't keep putting yourself down. At UMC you'll have friends who will worry about you.'

They went their separate ways at Times Square, as Benson wanted to go to the Aer Lingus office on Fifth Avenue to delay his departure. He was feeling scared about this, sure that the Aer Lingus people would say no.

Worrying like mad as he walked past the 42nd Street Public Library, Benson felt an excruciating pain in his arm, as if some terrible beast were trying to yank it off his trunk. Then he was staggering backwards out of control and hit the sidewalk, landing squarely on his bottom. The pain in his arm diminished and he sat, dazed, watching a man running down Fifth Avenue carrying a flight-bag in his hand. I've got one just like that, he thought. Then he came to himself and realized that it was *his* Aer Lingus bag in the man's hand. And in that bag were his ticket home, his nearly new address book, some J-Cloths for Meryl and Mr Fucci's copy of *Leaves of Grass.*

He jumped to his feet and ran off at speed after the man. For block after block he ran, ignoring the DONT

WALK signs until his left sandal flew off and he could run no more.

He stood, panting, wanting to cry at the thought of the precious flight-bag and its contents in the hands of a thief. He retrieved his sandal, ignoring the strange looks of the populace. Still, there was nothing to be done and he had better accept the fact that he had been robbed. He turned round, walking back the way he had come, stumbling into his sandal. The buckle had come off. The last straw, he thought. The fucking last straw! He sat down on the steps of the Public Library and pulled tongues at the grand lions above him.

Limping into Times Square subway *en route* to his date with Carlton, he passed the shoe-shine stand. The Negro looked at Benson's sandals, looked away, then looked back at them.

'The buckle's come off,' Benson informed the man.

'I can fix that.'

'Can you?' He was shown to the throne. The man gave him a slipper to put on and took out a thick needle. He broke off some cotton and threaded it through the needle at the first attempt. Benson congratulated him on his eyesight, worrying whether he would have congratulated a white man in a similar situation. Yes, I would have. I'm well brought up. The man hummed a tune as he worked at the buckle. Benson surveyed the distracted rush-hour people. He felt odd sitting there at a still point in the turning subway station. But it was nice too. His heart was slowing down and thoughts processed through his mind in an orderly line. 'I've just been robbed,' Benson told the man matter-of-factly. 'The buckle broke while I was running after the thief.'

'Sorry to hear that,' said the man. 'Say, you a visitor?'

Benson thought of his ticket and his book . . . of

Dexter's mass card; of Mr Fucci still to TLC; of Carlton to make Dearest Him by an act of will of a Dexterish sort he had never before tried; of Virginia; of Nurse Muñoz and Patrick . . . He had so many obligations, so many people to worry about. 'No,' he said. 'I think I'm er . . . sort of an immigrant.'

'That a fact!' He handed the sandal back to Benson.

'How much do I owe you?'

'No charge,' said the man. 'But, I'd appreciate your business when you come back some day wearing shoes.'

Benson thanked the man and, feeling that even being mugged had its positive side, set off to catch the exciting subway home.

At the second stop a man got off, vacating Benson's favourite subway seat. Benson darted into the breach, beating a couple of New Yorkers easily. Safely ensconced on his bit of the rock, he settled himself down to read the ads and conjure up his future in the dubious dark of the tunnel zooming past the window. Then, tiring of that, he surrendered his seat to an elderly passenger, rested his whole weight on a swinging hand-grip, and turned his attention to other matters.

THE END

Sucking Sherbet Lemons
by Michael Carson

'A splendidly articulate and witty first novel'
Simon Brett, *Punch*

Benson is fat, fourteen and inspired with Catholic fervour.
He dreams of heaven as a place where Mars Bars grow on
trees . . .

Benson is also a founder member of the Rude Club, at
whose meetings 'irregular motions of the flesh' set off
attacks of guilt that send him scurrying to confession.
After one such attack he finds himself pledging his
unclean soul to the service of God.

But at St Finbar's seminary the temptations put before the
novices are as great as those of the outside world;
especially from Brother Michael, who entices boys to the
rubbish dump on cross country runs. Expelled from St
Finbar's, and back at school, Benson befriends the sixth
form's star pupil. Together they attend Benson's first orgy.
It is both the culmination of his sexual insecurity and the
beginning of self-acceptance . . .

'Funny about two notoriously difficult subjects,
Catholicism and homosexuality. He is the real thing, a
writer to make any reader, of whatever sexual or religious
orientation, laugh'
Joseph O'Neill, *Literary Review*

'Graphic but not pornographic, humorous but never
sniggering, this is a marvellous first novel'
Fanny Blake, *Options*

'A funny, gay, Roman Catholic *bildungsroman*'
Philip Howard, *The Times*

0 552 99348 4

BLACK SWAN

Stripping Penguins Bare
by Michael Carson

'As gay, Catholic, comic writers go, Carson is difficult to
beat. In *Stripping Penguins Bare* he fires a resounding
answer to Lodge's *How Far Can You Go*?'
Bernard O'Keeffe, *Literary Review*

Martin Benson, the 'fat homo' hero of Michael Carson's
widely praised *Sucking Sherbet Lemons*, is now at
university, devouring the lyrics of Dylan and paying
homage to Plato, his catechism and prayers to St Maria
Goretti forgotten. But Benson is easily influenced by those
around him and soon he is beset by the same worries and
anxieties he thought he'd left behind at St Finbar's
seminary.

Ruminating on life's imponderables, Benson is swept up
by his role as Vice-President of the Overseas Students'
Society, and he battles through social injustices, hot on the
heels of the prejudiced landladies of Aberystwyth. But as
he strives to carve out a philosophy for himself, Catholic
doctrines return to pester him, and dark fantasies of
seduction by the world in general and Enoch Mohammed
in particular serve to thicken the cloud of unknowing that
surrounds him.

'Martin Benson, an anti-hero in the tradition of Kingsley
Amis . . . *Stripping Penguins Bare* has moments in which
the ridiculous successfully ambushes you'
Sabine Durrant, *The Times*

'Michael Carson is wonderful on wince-making
undergraduate habits . . . I find myself looking forward
very much to the third Benson novel'
Jennifer Selway, *The Observer*

0 552 99465 0

BLACK SWAN

Coming Up Roses
by Michael Carson

'Irresistibly funny'
Peter Parker, *The Listener*

King Fadl stares at the bejewelled map of his kingdom on
the wall of the royal rumpus room. Part of neighbouring
Zibda intrudes into his territory and he wants it. He
telephones impoverished Sultan Nabil of Zibda to make
him an offer he can't refuse. GCHQ is listening in. Top
Secret files are consulted. Charlie Hammond, a disgraced
MI42 operative with a weakness for shopping, is sent to
gather information. He meets Armitage, an
English teacher, seduced into a job in the Arab world after
seeing *Lawrence of Arabia* 25 years after everyone else.

When the Ministry for the Suppression of Vice and the
Encouragement of Virtue orders the circumcision of all
expatriates, Hammond and Armitage's troubles are just
beginning. Caught *in flagrante* by Abdul Wahhab
Higgins, Jesuit turned Muslim zealot, can they escape the
Anderton Lash'em?

Michael Carson's sparkling new novel confirms him as
'one of the freshest comic voices on the current scene'
(*The Literary Review*). His *Sucking Sherbet Lemons* and
Friends and Infidels are also available in Black Swan
paperback.

'A splendid novel . . . in the tradition of Waugh's *Scoop*
and Updike's *The Coup* . . . Very funny indeed'
Richard Murphy, *The Literary Review*

'A warm, imaginative and funny book'
Books

0 552 99421 9

BLACK SWAN

A SELECTION OF FINE NOVELS AVAILABLE FROM BLACK SWAN

THE PRICES SHOWN BELOW WERE CORRECT AT THE TIME OF GOING TO PRESS. HOWEVER TRANSWORLD PUBLISHERS RESERVE THE RIGHT TO SHOW NEW RETAIL PRICES ON COVERS WHICH MAY DIFFER FROM THOSE PREVIOUSLY ADVERTISED IN THE TEXT OR ELSEWHERE.

All Corgi/Bantam Books are available at your bookshop or newsagent, or can be ordered from the following address:

Corgi/Bantam Books,
Cash Sales Department
P.O. Box 11, Falmouth, Cornwall TR10 9EN

UK and B.F.P.O. customers please send a cheque or postal order (no currency) and allow £1.00 for postage and packing for the first book plus 50p for the second book and 30p for each additional book to a maximum charge of £3.00 (7 books plus).

Overseas customers, including Eire, please allow £2.00 for postage and packing for the first book plus £1.00 for the second book and 50p for each subsequent title ordered.

NAME (Block Letters) ....

ADDRESS ....

....